Praise for *Th*

'Full of dark intrigues, wonderfully layered characters, and a dazzling plot that twists and turns in satisfying ways, this book is masterfully written and just bloody fantastic to read.' **Sebastien de Castell, award-winning author of The Greatcoats and Spellslinger series**

'A cartful of courtly intrigue, a menagerie of plots within schemes, and a massive dose of debauchery. All tied up in J. L. Worrad's effortless way of making a world feel real and lived in.' **Rob J. Hayes, award-winning author of The Mortal Techniques and The War Eternal series**

'A gloriously gory Jacobean romp with a festive setting and twists that keep coming right to the end.' **Dr. Fiona Moore, author of *Management Lessons from Game of Thrones: Organization Theory and Strategy in Westeros***

Praise for *Pennyblade*

'*Pennyblade* doesn't so much reinvent well-worn fantasy tropes as stab them to death in a dark alley. Kyra Cal'Adra is a lethally alluring protagonist weaving an intricate tale rich in ferocious action and multifaceted intrigue, all topped off by a deliciously vicious twist.' **Anthony Ryan, author of *Blood Song* and *The Wolf's Call***

'A violent, and wildly imaginative, riot of a book.' **R. J. Barker, author of *Age of Assassins* and *The Bone Ships***

'The changeling offspring of Jorg Ancrath and Phèdre nó Delaunay. Filthy, furious, wonderful.' **Anna Smith Spark, author of *The Court of Broken Knives***

'Provocative and decadent, crude and funny, and an altogether entertaining fantasy adventure.' **Edward Cox, author of The Relic Guild series**

Also by J. L. Worrad and Available from Titan Books

Pennyblade

THE KEEP WITHIN

J.L. WORRAD

TITAN BOOKS

The Keep Within
Print edition ISBN: 9781803362977
E-book edition ISBN: 9781803362991

Published by Titan Books
A division of Titan Publishing Group Ltd.
144 Southwark Street, London SE1 0UP
www.titanbooks.com

First Titan edition: March 2023

10 9 8 7 6 5 4 3 2 1

A CIP catalogue record for this title is available from the British Library.

Printed and bound by CPI Group (UK) Ltd, Croydon, CR0 4YY.

For Max, George, Michael, and Sarah.

Patience beyond saints.

SEVEN NIGHTS TILL YULENIGHT EVE

1

Mother Fwych

'Never seen such a beautiful hall,' the lad said.

'It's a roadside inn,' Mother Fwych replied. 'Uglier by daylight, inns.'

'All things are,' the lad Gethwen said, the fool, and his breath curled up into the night.

Miserable place. But Aifen-the-Tom had lost all lust for the mountains of his forebears and Mother Fwych refused to walk the miserable tracks of a flatland city. A roadside inn were the best place either might stoop to meet each other.

She looked at the flicker of the inn's windows in the lad's frost-blue eyes. *The lad thinks this pile pretty.*

The path to the inn were churned mud hardened by frost, cracking beneath heel and toe. Night sky naked above, her black skin twinkling. *Yulenight soon,* Mother Fwych thought. So little time left. So little.

Something flickered, a movement along the inn's white wall.

She stopped. She squinted at where the movement had been. The roof hung lowest there, and the wall's white paint mottled into moss. A shadowed place. Her eyes, and the powers Father

Mountain had blessed her with, insisted upon it. A shadowed spot. There was nothing there that breathed or moved.

'Mother Fwych,' the lad whispered.

She ignored him, straining to see into the shadows, to see a flicker there as she had seen it before. She touched the hilt of her shortclaw.

No. Nothing. But her hackles were up. Something were wrong.

'It's naught, lad.' She grinned at him. 'Mother Fwych is getting old, she is.' Sixty now. And the rest. How had that happened?

The lad were older too. Mountain's love, but 'lad' were a dead word for him. Twenty summers? A man now, Gethwen, girlish-handsome, with the lip and brow rings of a man. But to Mother Fwych he were still that cursed boy they'd brought her.

'Be warm inside,' Gethwen said.

'I'll go first,' she told him.

She turned the iron ring and opened the door inward. Hearth warmth greeted her, the sort that makes men tellers of tales. Yeast and pottage filled her nose, so too the sweat of flatlanders hemmed in like the pigs they kept. She'd no love for these places. None.

The chatter did not stop when she entered. Mother Fwych had never known that to happen. Inns fell silent when mountain folk entered, at least in Mother Fwych's experience. Silence, then muttering, and then the words. One time they had even tried to scalp Mother Fwych, back when her hair were still red and mountain folks' red hair fetched a price. She'd taken a scalp or two herself that night. Cask of cider too.

Ten men stood or sat around the room, a young woman behind the bar, and though every one of them glanced a moment, their talk never broke step.

'Good evenin',' the young woman said, approaching. She wore a big daft dress that made her body look too big for her head. Or maybe her body had grown to that, years spent by hearth and spit.

'My lady,' said Gethwen, putting on flatland airs. Plainly it weren't just an inn the boy had hoped to see. Devious boy.

'Sir.' The young woman curtsied. 'I believe you've a friend who awaits you. No offence, but might I ask for your blades while you dally here? It is the custom, knives and ale being what they are.'

'The other guests keep their knives,' Mother Fwych said.

'Knives for eating,' the young woman replied.

'Three have swords. Must be a stretch to their plate.'

'Those are regulars,' the woman said. 'Please, my lady. I cannot let you—'

'Fine,' Mother Fwych said, pulling her bronze shortclaw from her belt. 'If it keep you at ease.'

She passed the blade to the woman and Gethwen gave his own.

The inn-woman smiled. 'I'd not seen scythe-swords until this night.'

'Keep 'em safe,' Mother Fwych told her. She had another shortclaw tied to her back under her coat, a smaller one in her boot. A mountain mother always kept at least one claw hidden.

'Your friend is in the snug over yonder,' the woman said, nodding toward a nook in the far corner. 'I'll bring you both some ale, eh?' With that she grinned and left them, stopping only to let a ginger cat pass.

Aifen-the-Tom were sat in the snug like the woman said, sat on the right-side bench with arms stretched wide across the cracked wooden table, a cup of ale between them.

'Mountain's grace, Mother Fwych,' he greeted her, his voice as cracked as the table and his grin sharper than a shortclaw. Aifen-the-Tom was scarcely younger than Mother Fwych and scant larger. His red beard and hair were wild as a valley forest but his pate was peak-bare. It would have gleamed in the lamplight if not for the black tattoo of a wildcat's face upon it. 'Sit, sit.'

'Mountain?' Mother Fwych said. 'When last did you stand within a mountain's shadow?' She let Gethwen sit first, upon the bench facing the tattooed man. She sat down beside him and budged him up.

'Within a mountain's shadow?' Aifen-the-Tom said. 'Must have been younger than this one.' He tapped Gethwen's chin with his thumb then reached into his own shirt. He pulled out a necklace. An oval of grey stone hung upon it. 'But we of the wandering sort all carry a piece of the Spines upon our hearts.'

'I like that,' Gethwen said, smiling.

'We shan't be staying long,' Mother Fwych announced.

'Have an ale at least,' Aifen-the-Tom said.

Mother Fwych tutted and looked about. This snug offered some protection with its wooden sides, but it also hemmed them in. The wall to their left had no window, no escape. She squinted at the ceiling. A wooden square up there, directly above her. A closed hatch. Now that she did not like. She did not like floors above heads at the best of times. Doorways from floors above to heads below were outright treacherous.

'Relax, woman,' Aifen-the-Tom said.

'Mother,' she corrected him. She weren't taken by this way he had, of delighting in others' discomfort. Not a man in the Spine Mountains would dare as much, not with a mother.

He gave her a pitiful look. 'You're in no danger—' He raised his eyebrows. '—*Mother.*'

'Let's be having it,' Mother Fwych commanded him. 'Then we'll be gone.'

Aifen-the-Tom chuckled and reached to one side. He pulled up a small hessian bag and dropped it on the table with a clank.

'Glad to be rid,' he said.

'A most shadowed thing,' she agreed.

'A pain in the arse, more like,' he said. 'Fleawater's full of screaming and nonsense cuz of it. Our own "mother", the dark woman, she's been churning folks to madness. Was she who had word sent.'

'So why are you here and not her?' Mother Fwych asked. 'And why come here so bloody alone?'

'I'm headman at Fleawater, not her,' he answered, waving to the inn-woman to bring more ale. 'Folk gotta know I'm tough and keen, tougher than, like as not, the next ten men who follow.' He looked at Gethwen. 'That's how it is being a man, boy.'

'Fool,' Mother Fwych snapped. 'With a fool's vanity.' She snatched the bag and stood up. Her arm got a queer, numb feeling, like when you bang an elbow. It vanished soon enough. *Full of shadow,* she thought of the dull weight inside. She passed it to Gethwen.

The inn-woman came toward them, a kind smile on her face and three beers on a tray. Her smile vanished.

'Now!' she screeched and she threw the tray at the snug.

Cups smashed against the wall. The tray clattered on the table and Mother Fwych were showered with ale. Gethwen screamed. Her eyes met Aifen-the-Tom's: he looked as stunned as she felt.

A spear's tip drove down from above, flashed silver before Aifen's face and punched into his belly. He stared silent at the pole before him. The spear twisted and pulled out.

Damned hatchway!

Mother Fwych seized the bloodied spear as it lunged for her throat. A face leered down from the open hatchway: a young man, grinning with the strain.

'*Fall!*' Mother Fwych said, using the tongue.

The man dropped the spear and threw himself out of the hatch and on to the table face-first, sending up a puddle of ale. Mother Fwych lifted the spear and rammed it into the man's spine with all her might.

Her shoulder burst with pain. She yelled and looked. A feathered bolt had torn her furs, sliced her flesh and lodged into the snug.

Mountain's luck it had not hit square on.

She saw the inn-woman reloading a crossbow.

Mother Fwych pulled her smallclaw from her shoe. Four inch o' bronze. She aimed for the inn-woman.

A man were charging at the snug. One of those 'regulars', sword up high, bearing down on Mother Fwych.

'Hold!' Mother Fwych tongued and the man froze and stumbled, his mouth wide with confusion, a look she knew well.

The smallclaw found his eye. He dropped upon the tiles and shrieked.

Folks were bolting for the door.

'Table up,' she told Gethwen.

They hauled at the table. The spearman's body slid forward on to the floor beyond the snug. The pain in her shoulder wasn't so bad now her blood was up. Be a beast soon after, though, she knew that much.

They got the table on its end, blocking off the snug.

'Ban-hag!' the man on the floor was screeching. 'Cunt's a ban-hag!'

'You never mentioned a witch, Selly!' another man yelled at the inn-woman.

'Shut up!' the inn-woman, Selly, barked. 'Just keep mindful her words can take you. That way she'll have no power.'

The lamps had gone out above and it was dark in the snug now, the only light coming from the space between the table's edge and the ceiling. Everything stank of ale. Gethwen still had the bag. He were close to weeping.

'Let me think,' Mother Fwych told him.

Selly had looked bulky in her dress, Mother Fwych realised, because she'd chainmail beneath. Then there were the men with their swords. *Regulars, my arse*. Damned pennyblades, that's what they were. Scum of all flatlands. Scalped mountain folk for coin. Child-killers and rapists and pissers-on-shrines.

She reached out and felt the room. Selly's mind was too hard and focused to tongue-puppet. She must have tangled with mothers before.

Mother Fwych felt three men: one-eye on the floor and two others across the barroom. One-eye was too pained and anguished to listen, the other two had hardened their minds but lacked Selly's flint. They'd lose focus soon enough and then Mother Fwych would have her way right enough. But the tongue worked best if they saw her eyes.

'Lad,' she said to Gethwen. 'Tie that bag to your belt. On my say, climb for the hatch above.' She slapped the table legs; he could use them to climb. Nimble, Gethwen. Quick wits too, though she'd never told him so.

'Ban-hag,' Selly the pennyblade called, 'I'm an artist, ban-hag. I paint pretty pictures with my crossy here.' With all Selly's speechifying Fwych tried to feel out her mind but, Mountain's balls, Selly kept focused. 'You're thinking of that hatch above, ain't yer? Well there's a yard's space between the table edge and the ceiling and that's plenty. I'll stick you both like honeyed fucking pigs.'

'Shut up!' Mother Fwych yelled. 'Or Mother'll pounce and gut you!'

'And we'll all thank you for trying,' Selly said. 'Savage.'

'You only scratched me just now, Selly. You missed.'

'I was just playing,' Selly said. 'I like to bleed a bitch.'

Mother Fwych nodded for Gethwen to get back against the wall. She stepped over to Aifen-the-Tom's corpse and slipped her arms under his armpits. He stank of sweat and ale and his forehead smacked her collar.

She looked over her shoulder at Gethwen.

'Make for the hatch when I say.' She thought a moment. 'Run for the city, lad. The city. They won't think o' that. Seek out our folk.'

'Ban-hag!' Selly shouted beyond the table's wall. 'We just want the crown.'

'The what?' Fwych said, acting unaware. She looked at Gethwen again. 'I'll be right behind you.'

The lad nodded. He said nothing. She had expected him to plead, say he would never leave her to die, but no. Gethwen was eager to take the only chance he had. It stung Mother Fwych, that. But he was what he was. A tricky-man.

You've raised a survivor, she told herself. *You've done that, at least.*

'We know you have it,' Selly called. 'Be happier for everyone if you came out. Hand it over and be on your way.'

'If that were true you'd have robbed our man when he entered.' Mother Fwych took a breath – wound be damned – and braced to lift Aifen-the-Tom, his beard scratching at the valley of her teats. 'You're getting coin to shut lips.'

'Stop being daft,' Selly said. She laughed. 'I'll even give you your swords back.'

'I've plenty enough, thank you.' She lifted Aifen-the-Tom's body, ignored the pang in her shoulder. She leaned Aifen against the table and his head fell back, his eyes still shocked. A thought came. 'Hey, Pennyblade!'

'Yes, witch?'

'Who's it paying you?'

A pause. Then Selly said, 'Interesting fucking story, that. But I ain't—'

Mother Fwych heaved Aifen-the-Tom up.

'Now,' she barked.

A cracking sound and Aifen headbutted Mother Fwych, dark blood pouring from his mouth on to her hair and nose. Selly's bolt had hit the back of his skull.

Behind her Gethwen clambered up, his boots pushing on the table's legs and he was gone like a ferret out a burrow, long before Selly might reload.

Mother Fwych dropped Aifen-the-Tom. She reached into her

furs and round to her back. Drew out her longest claw, a curved bronze length long as a hand and forearm.

The road brings me here. She had to keep their attention, stop them from chasing Gethwen down. Now she either died or became a living hearth-tale.

Selly's crossbow would be loaded by now. The fear came to Fwych then. Of the pain. Of Father Mountain's embrace. Mother Fwych placed her free palm against the upright table. She would scream and push it over. In that confusion she would tongue Selly's mind and slay her, then the two men.

Well, this were it, then.

'*Ah-lee-lee-lee,*' a new voice said, neither man nor woman. '*'Tis Red Marie!*'

A silence followed in which only the one-eyed pennyblade moaned.

'The fuck?' one of the men said. Then he screeched, high as a hawk.

'*You know me, little Selly!*' the voice said. '*Up from the river I come-come-come, a very wonder of the world!*'

'Please,' Selly begged.

'*What? You think me a folk tale?*'

The table flew sideways like a door on hinges. Mother Fwych was there for all to see but no one cared. One of the men leaned against the bar, clutching the red patch of his trousers where his bollocks had been and staring at where they now were: draped upon Selly's still unloosed crossbow. Torn and matted and red.

Selly saw Mother Fwych and jolted. For a second Fwych thought she'd get a pair of bollocks in her ribcage. But Selly never loosed her bolt.

Mother Fwych nodded to Selly for truce. Selly ignored her, eyeing every shadow in the room. It only dawned on Mother Fwych then that the table had moved all by itself.

The shelf behind the bar collapsed, cups and tankards rattling. No hand had touched it.

'Fuck this,' the other man said, and he ran for the door.

Something flew through the air and hit the back of the man's skull. His face mashed into the studded oak door. He dropped, leaving a blood flower upon wood and iron.

'Don't you want to playyy?' the voice said, everywhere and nowhere, tinkling like a stream. *'I put nails in babes' mouths and sew them shut! I'm Red Marie! I make carnations of spines! Oh, I'm Red Marie!'*

The thing that had flown at the man lay on the floor: a severed head. The head of the man whose eye Mother Fwych had taken.

Selly saw it too. She was shaking.

Shaking at that name, Mother Fwych thought.

'Strength,' Mother Fwych told Selly. Then to the room: 'Show yourself, beast!'

The bollock-less man dropped to his knees and collapsed, empty of blood.

Footsteps padded across the room. Tittering.

Mountain protect me, Mother Fwych thought. 'Show yourself!'

More tittering. Everywhere. It were the thing Mother Fwych had sensed outside earlier, she were sure. Impossible to see when still, too swift to be seen when moving.

'Selly,' the voice said, *'remember the time I danced in your dreams?'* Red Marie giggled. *'You were so little, Selly.'*

Selly was sobbing, clutching her crossbow like a doll.

'Show yourself!' Mother Fwych roared with the tongue. *'Show!'* But her power was spread too thin. She had nothing to look at. She swung her claw at nothing. Again and again.

'Hello, Mother,' the voice whispered in her ear.

Her jaw wrenched. It cracked. The softness inside quivered and tore. The world flashed white and tittered.

SIX NIGHTS TILL YULENIGHT EVE

2

Larksdale

Sir Harry Larksdale had a drunk and weeping playwright to deal with. Drunken playwrights were common as sparrows, of course, and weepers hardly unknown, but a drunk *and* weeping playwright sitting high up on a stage rafter? It was really too-too much. Absolutely and utterly utter.

Well, Larksdale thought, alone upon the varnished stage of the open-air theatre, *I do so like a challenge.* Which was true, albeit long after it had ceased being a challenge and had become mere story.

'Tichborne?' Larksdale called up, his breath steaming in the December air. 'You'll find no inspiration up there. In fact, I'm told there's but a pigeon's nest.' Larksdale stroked his beard with a gloved and many-ringed hand. He noted the birchwood ladder lying nearby upon the stage. He gestured at it. 'Now that's not clever is it, Tich-o, me-lad? You've gone and marooned yourself.'

A clay bottle smashed upon the boards. Quite empty, of course.

'Piss your breeches, Larksdale,' Tichborne barked. 'You're just the money! Grubby fingers in a silk purse!'

'You wound me, sir,' Larksdale said. 'As only a mortal angel capable of golden verse can.'

'Up your arse.'

He hasn't finished our play for Yulenight Eve, Larksdale surmised. *Worse, likely not even started.* The symptoms were familiar enough: the vulgarity and nihilism, the disregard for flasks.

'I'll pass you the ladder,' Larksdale said.

'Don't bother,' Tichborne replied. 'I'm soon to throw myself off.'

'And what?' Larksdale chuckled, stroked back a stray lock of black hair. 'Break your ankles?'

'Not if I dive head first.'

Then you'd likely bounce, fathead, thought Larksdale, but it was an uncharitable notion. The dear fellow was suffering, after all. Larksdale wasn't eager to scale a rickety ladder, but he wasn't eager to waste an hour shouting up at an inebriated quill-jockey either. Larksdale had an engagement – a royal engagement at Grand Gardens, no less – to attend at noon. It seemed the time had come for ol' Harry Larksdale to become a man of action and valour, despite that being the very sort of man he crossed streets to avoid.

'Tichborne,' he called up, 'I'm going to climb up beside you. Please don't push the ladder away and send me to my death. I'd never say a nice word about you again.'

The playwright ignored him, staring at his own hanging feet.

'Right,' Larksdale muttered. He gazed at the ladder upon the floor as if it were a chore he'd been avoiding, which increasingly it was. 'Right, then.'

The scuffle of boots upon wooden stairs came from stage left and Boathook Marla emerged. For such a slight woman she had an uncanny talent for stomping.

'Boss,' she said to Larksdale, 'it's all going to shit out there.' She thumbed behind her, toward the backstage chambers.

'Wonderful,' Larksdale said. A thought struck him. 'Wonderful that you're *here,* I mean. Come, sweet Marla, and be my foundations, my rampart, my very rock.'

'Y'what?'

'Hold this ladder up.'

She gestured behind her again, toward the wings. 'But, boss—'

'To each matter its *time*, Marla.'

She shrugged and went to pick up the ladder. Like many things in Tetchford borough, 'Boathook' Marla Dueng was a wonderful mass of contradictions: a woman who dressed like a dockhand; possessor of a nickname all spoke but none knew the provenance of; her features and complexion that of her Chombod father topped off with her mother's far more local blonde hair, the ends of which curled and bristled out from beneath her red woollen hat. Exactly the sort of person who'd never be permitted in Becken Keep, of course. Which was precisely why Sir Harry Larksdale enjoyed her company, along with everybody else's at the Wreath Theatre.

'Your rump-part and rock's ready,' Marla said, her shoulder against the now raised ladder. She had been careful to place its end to one side of Tichborne up on his rafter. 'Y'alright, me duck?' she called up to him. Boathook Marla hailed from Hoxham city, which meant she referred to people as ducks from time to time. To each their own.

Tichborne made no reply.

'He's in the pit of self-recrimination,' Larksdale explained to Marla. He began to climb.

The breeze got stronger as he ascended; sea winds from Becken Bay scraping over the theatre's circular roofs and pulling at his long coat. If anyone but Boathook Marla were holding this ladder he might well have made his excuses. He soon reached the top and, if he hadn't the courage to sit on the rafter and meet Tichborne eye-to-eye, he could certainly curl his left arm over its varnished oak and meet Tichborne eye-to-thigh.

'Listen well, playwright,' Larksdale said, 'for I will mutter discreetly.' He sighed. 'I wish to spare you humiliation.'

Tichborne looked at him, his button nose wrinkling.

'You're not drunk,' Larksdale said. He gave the young playwright a stare he normally saved for enemies and lovers. 'So drop the damned act.'

Tichborne shuddered. 'How'd you guess?'

'It took me some time,' Larksdale said. 'I suspected a ruse by the third step on my climb and was adamant by the eighth. Your performance is too-too laboured, my boy. Furthermore, you've a love of history I'd overlooked till now.'

'What?'

'Kit Kimble pulled this very ruse twenty years past, bless his memory. I was nine years old then but even I heard tale of it. Yes, word reached even Becken Keep.' He brushed hair out of his eyes. This breeze was a menace, really it was. 'Kimble's *very* public cataclysm atop a rafter earned him extra coin and extra time, both of which he spent down the Carnation inn with hearty aplomb.'

Tichborne gave a coy sort of look that almost rustled Larksdale's heart. 'A little of both would not go amiss,' he said.

'I've neither.'

'You have money, Harry,' Tichborne protested.

'It's all tied up in mustard right now,' Larksdale admitted. 'Figuratively, I mean. A merchant ship at sea. So best we clamber down and act like nothing happened, eh? If we're seen up here we'll both be forced to act the drunkard.'

'*Foul buggerers!*' A man's voice boomed from somewhere in the corridors behind the stage.

'Boss,' Boathook Marla called up from below. 'That other matter...'

'Noted,' Larksdale said. He looked up at Tichborne. 'Come on, me Tich-o.'

'I'm tired, Harry!' Tichborne shouted.

The force of it made Larksdale clutch harder to the rafter. It seemed real pain hid behind the fakery of anguish. It shone in Tichborne's eyes.

'I cannot write another folk-play,' he muttered, eyeing below to see if Marla might hear. 'I cannot repeat the same bloody scenes, the same gang of saints and miracles, the same victories of Neyes the Child and japes of Dickie o' the Green and villainies of Red Marie.' He growled. 'And if I have to write *another* scene where a sinner is jabbed in the arse with a poker—'

'Oh, but the crowd simply *roars* at that,' Larksdale said. He remembered to shut up. 'Pray continue.'

'And every line I write some miserable eye judges – some priest or Perfecti, some ghoul of the Church – and scratches out the slightest word that grasps for the sublime.'

Risky talk, this. Larksdale was happier for the fact they conversed alone and at altitude.

'Tichborne, I'm aware a folk-play has its limitations, but you are a true talent. Try not to see the medium as a pair of manacles but more as a chessboard, having hard rules that—'

'I haven't written your next folk-play,' Tichborne said. 'I have written a keep-play.' He laughed. Shook his head. 'Isn't that pathetic?'

'Pathetic?' Larksdale smiled sadly. *Poor, sweet fellow.* 'Well… not in the sense you mean.'

Keep-plays were a world away from folk-plays and obscured by ramparts and walls. They were performed within Becken Keep, of course, and in nobles' halls throughout the Brintland and beyond. Keep-plays were cut from the same material as ancient Mancanese drama, full of richly drawn characters and ethical dilemma, hubris and wrecked kings. They were not, convention held, for the common man's consumption. Not slightly.

'So you see,' Tichborne said, 'I really *should* throw myself off head first.'

'No, no...'

Well, here was a moment. Larksdale was at a crossroads, faced with the sort of decision he'd hoped to make a year or more hence. He had not even mentally listed the allies he would need for that next vital step in his great plan, his life's work, let alone marshalled them. *Perhaps,* Larksdale reasoned, *God or providence pricks me on.* 'Listen to me, Jon Tichborne. You know of Sir Tibald Slyke, yes?'

'He's Master of Arts and Revels,' Tichborne said, squinting, 'up at the keep.' Hope lit his features. 'You are on good terms, you and he?'

'Pilgrim's mercy no,' Larksdale replied, 'he thinks me a dangerous fool.' As Tichborne's hope sank Larksdale pressed on. 'And the only good thing I have to say for him is he shall retire soon. So rumour has it.'

Tichborne met Larksdale's gaze. 'Leaving you to...' He gestured at Larksdale.

Larksdale gestured at himself. 'Leaving me. A man with not a single clue as to how to write a keep-play.'

Tichborne chuckled gleefully. Below, Marla muttered in a way that was as much a performance as anything seen upon that stage.

'It's certain?' Tichborne asked. 'You have our king's blessing?'

'Am I not his brother?' Larksdale said, avoiding the question.

'One of a hundred bastards.'

'The old king was prolific, granted,' Larksdale said.

'And his work of variable quality.'

Larksdale grinned. 'I should push you off of here, Tichborne, really I should.'

The two men laughed. *An ally is a fine thing,* Larksdale told himself. It was as if a weight had been removed. He wanted to spill more, speak of his greater plan, the audacity of it. But he could tell none.

'One more folk-play, eh, Jon?' Larksdale said. 'One more hot poker to a sinner's rear. That's all I beg.'

'For you, Sir Harry,' Tichborne declared, 'I'll sear every buttock in hell.'

Footfall and shouting burst on to the stage below. Larksdale's boots slipped off the ladder's rung and he fell. He gripped the ladder's sides, slowing his descent, and was shocked to find his feet had landed safely upon the floor.

The hullabaloo had cut silent and everyone – some fifteen people or more, mostly the Wreath's staff – were staring at him. Larksdale realised they all thought he'd purposefully meant to descend so rapidly. He didn't disillusion them.

'What ribald hell is this?' he demanded of the crowd. 'I'll permit no drama here.'

Boathook Marla muttered to him, 'Said it had all gone to shit, didn't I?'

A burly, whiskered and well-dressed man glared at Larksdale. Two large men – identical twins with curly blonde hair – stood behind him, long-knives at their belts.

'Well, well,' the man spat, waving his walking cane at Larksdale. 'Who is *this* hawk-nosed popinjay?'

'Aquiline,' Larksdale corrected him, pulling a splinter from his gloved palm. 'The term is "aquiline", or so Mother assures me. And who, *sir*, are you?'

'A gentleman retrieving his property,' the man said. 'The name's Cabbot. I assume you command this chamberpot of face paint and buggery?'

'I've a controlling interest,' Larksdale said.

'Thief!' Cabbot lifted his cane in the air, a fine thing of black lacquer topped with a brass figure. He pointed it at the gaggle of theatre hands. 'That woman is my wife!'

A screech went up from the mob and the seamstresses of the

costume department surrounded one of their number, a frail and sunken-eyed woman whom Cabbot glared at. Larksdale had never seen her before.

'Seize her,' Cabbot told his two lackeys.

The large twins looked at one another uncertainly.

'Lazy sops,' Cabbot told them. He raised his brass-topped cane. 'I'll bloody do it.'

Larksdale strode over and seized the cane from Cabbot.

'Do not break the king's peace, Cabbot,' he told him. 'For I am his brother.'

One could usually rely on that to quench a common man's resolve. Not so Cabbot.

'A bastard,' he said. 'I'm no peasant, sir. I'm landlord to half of Fleawater. I've friends up at your brother's keep. I regularly play a few rounds of archery with Sir Tibald Slyke. We are to go into business. That name familiar?' He looked Larksdale up and down with pointed disdain. 'I respect a royal bastard but I'll not be cowed. You've no land, no livery.'

'But I've your cane.' Larksdale wiggled the thing. 'I note you're not so forthright without it.'

Cabbot eyes were coals of rage. He was a big man, certainly wouldn't need his guards to beat Larksdale to a pulp. But Cabbot didn't know that. Most royal bastards were reared to be knightly killers, after all.

'I *want* justice,' Cabbot hissed as if releasing steam.

'Then *adhere* to justice,' Larksdale replied, 'and don't threaten folk.' He broke from Cabbot's stare and looked to the man's wife. She looked frailer and more frightened than ever. 'She's right to a divorce, should she wish it.' The woman nodded. Larksdale looked back at Cabbot. 'Should you accept payment.'

'From you?'

Larksdale nodded. *Please no,* he thought. *Please. It's all on* The

Flagrant Bess *with its hold of mustard powder*. But he held his expression, trusted he had laid his trap. That he knew Cabbot's type.

'I'll adhere to justice,' Cabbot whispered with a grin. 'Happily. Trial by combat.' He looked over at his woman. 'Husband and wife.' He looked at Larksdale again. 'You can't buy me, bastard.'

Larksdale feigned slightest shock.

'It's the law, is it not?' Cabbot said and then he laughed, whiskers shaking on his ruddy cheeks. 'You were all for justice a moment ago.'

Larksdale shook his head. 'So be it.'

'I'll break her and take her back home. As a husband should.'

'And I'll preside this trial and tourney,' Larksdale said, 'as is a royal bastard's right.' He looked for Boathook Marla so as to gesture to her to talk to Cabbot's wife, whatever her name was, and was pleased to see Marla was already about the business.

'Fine,' Cabbot replied. 'Pick your day, sir.'

'How about now?' Larksdale said. 'How about here?'

'Trial by combat occurs within a courtyard or field,' Cabbot replied.

'This stage has played those parts many times.'

'What of witnesses?'

'Good point,' Larksdale said. He called out to Norton, the Wreath's fool. 'Go outside and tell 'em there's a show, free to all.'

Norton slipped on his boar mask and, running over to the Wreath's double doors and kicking them open, proceeded to cartwheel and declaim in the square outside.

'Listen, you,' Cabbot said, 'I'll be no mummer for the public's folly.'

'Fine,' Larksdale said, 'then I'll pay for the divorce. A man like me can buy a man like you as he wishes.'

'How dare you,' Cabbot raged. He pulled off his coat and slung it at one of his identical bodyguards. 'I've a house as big as this shithole! I've a permit to wear finery! I'm officially recognised as a gentleman!'

'But you are not one,' Larksdale said, shrugging. 'Else why mention it?'

'Give me my weapon, mollyboy!' Cabbot demanded. 'Let's raise the deal too: I beat her and win, then I fight you. What say you to that?'

'Whatever tickles your fancy.' Larksdale turned to Cabbot's two bodyguards. 'Today's show is free to enter but I'd be grateful if you could stand by the exit and request a farthing's donation from all leaving. No threats; mere looming will suffice. Keep one in ten farthings for yourselves.'

The twins beamed. Clearly Cabbot didn't pay them enough. 'Thank you,' the right one said in a falsetto voice.

'Welcome to show business,' Larksdale told them both. 'Any questions?'

'Why's that man up in the rafters?' the left one asked.

'He's writing a play.'

The twins nodded and headed for the doors. The Wreath was getting a modest crowd now, some twenty or more. Mainly housewives and children, a few varsity students.

'Welcome all!' Larksdale announced, his arms wide. He found Cabbot's lacquered cane to be a wonderful gesturing tool. 'Today a husband and wife do battle, one for cruel dominion, the other for freedom. Who will God on high judge worthy?'

Someone hooted in the crowd.

'You'll all have seen your share of divorce duels,' Larksdale continued, 'and so you'll know the husband receives a club to defend himself and his wife a stone inside a pair of tights.'

The weapons were handed to the two opponents. Cabbot's wife could barely hold her tights and stone. She could barely stand, such was her shaking. A crowd-winning performance that, though no performance at all. Cabbot himself had no interest in the growing crowd which only made him more brutish. *A most wondrous matinee this,* Larksdale thought, *just too-too utter, all of it.*

'Right,' he said to Cabbot, 'get in the pit, there's a love.'

'What?'

'A question of fairness, sir,' Larksdale replied. Loudly, so the crowd might hear. 'The husband stands knee-deep in a pit so as to negate his strength and virility.' The stage's left trapdoor – the shallow one – opened on cue.

'You're making this up,' Cabbot protested.

'No he's not!' a woman yelled in the crowd. 'Get in the pit, you shit!'

'*Get in the pit, you shit!*' the crowd chanted. Their number and enthusiasm were still on the rise. The Wreath would have to make this a regular thing in future.

One figure in the crowd, down near the very front, did not partake of the chant. He seemed startled by the Wreath, his eyes darting left and right.

A young man. Red of hair, dark of eye. He was beautiful, made all the more so by his aura of helplessness. Larksdale had that familiar and powerful urge to help him. He'd been prey to the pleading eyes of lost men and lost women many times. It never ended well.

He shook the feeling off and smiled at the crowd.

'As a royal bastard,' he announced, 'and descendant of St Neyes himself – albeit the lowest sort – it is not in my blood to stand idly by as a woman finds herself in peril. My lady...' He turned to look at Cabbot's wife who was calmer now, likely having been advised of matters by Marla, who still stood beside her. Larksdale took a silver coin from his long coat and flicked it over to Marla, who passed it to the wife. 'Hopefully,' Larksdale said to the crowd, 'that should be enough for a champion to fight in her stead.'

The crowd cheered approval.

'A what?' Cabbot demanded.

Larksdale turned and looked down to see Cabbot already knee-deep in the trap.

'A wife can pay for another woman to fight for her,' Larksdale explained. He nodded and Marla plucked the coin from the wife's fingers.

'A champion!' Larksdale announced to the crowd. 'Boathook Marla of this borough!'

A few who knew of her reputation clapped.

'We wanted the wife to fight,' a man in the crowd shouted.

'Tough,' Marla replied, and got a laugh. She took the tights with the stone inside and tested its weight.

Cabbot looked less nervous now; his wife's champion was confident, yes, but still a girl. A slight one at that.

'Better get him a helmet,' Larksdale told Norton the Fool. 'So that he may yet live.'

Norton was quick about it, fixing a theatrical helm with rabbit ears to Cabbot's head while the man was startled by Larksdale's words. The crowd hooted.

'Let God and his Holy Pilgrim judge!' Larksdale announced, and a trumpeter signalled the duel.

Cabbot turned in his pit as Marla circled him.

'Come at me, waif!' he yelled above the crowd's jeers.

The waif did. She ran, leaping right over his arcing club and over Cabbot himself. Before he could turn, Marla unleashed her tights. The stone therein cracked against Cabbot's shoulder. He yelped. He spun, only to receive the stone in his crotch, Marla using the tights' elasticity to sling and retract. He jack-knifed forward and she booted him in the face. Only then did she signal for the crowd's applause. She got it.

Boathook Marla kept a lot of occupations around Tetchford,

paid champion for women lured into combat trials being one of them.

Marla hopped into the pit with Cabbot and wrapped the tights around the stunned man's throat. His head went back and blood rolled from his cracked nose, filling his mouth.

'*Yield! Yield!*' the crowd chanted.

The trumpeter played a merry jig and Norton the Fool, dancing across stage in his boar mask, rubbed his voluminous buttocks in Cabbot's face for the crowd's delight. Hardly standard legal procedure, admittedly, yet it sped the trial to its conclusion.

'I yield!' Cabbot managed to yell out between arse rubbings. 'Yield!'

The crowd, some sixty or more now, hollered and cheered. It took three men to pull Cabbot out of the pit and he did not thank them for it. He slapped them away and, clutching his bloody face, made a run for stage right, and in all likelihood out of the Wreath and Tetchford altogether.

'We haven't heard the last of this,' Marla muttered later as the audience began to leave and several signed affidavits actualising the divorce had been taken.

'Doubtless,' Larksdale replied, studying his newly acquired lacquer cane. 'Cabbot's soon to be the talk of the town.' The cane's brass head was of some bird, perhaps even a lark. How utterly perfect.

Some altercation was occurring across the half-empty theatre. Whatever its manner, it was blocking people from leaving. Larksdale hopped down from the stage and made his way over, slipping through the crowd that was waiting to leave.

Cabbot's twin bodyguards – if Cabbot's they still were – were manhandling the redheaded youth. The young man was a flurry of scratching and hissing and curses of unknown dialect.

'We just wanted to look in his bag there,' the left twin said.

'Wouldn't give us a farthing,' said the right.

'You're too-too eager, me lads,' Larksdale said. 'In future merely *look* like you'll manhandle folk.'

The twins squirmed at the rebuke, then just as swiftly realised they had new jobs.

'Who is this fellow?' Larksdale said.

The twins let go and the young man ceased caterwauling. The youth was a spineman, though quite unlike those who lived in the city by Fleawater's riverside. He'd tattoos up his arms like many a fleawet, the bronze rings in his nose and ears too, but his clothes were of some rough woollen material. Of the Spine Mountains, perhaps. A true spineman. He clutched at a hessian shoulder bag.

'Poor heart,' Larksdale muttered.

The lad lunged at Larksdale, embracing him, his head buried in Larksdale's chest. His scent was earthy yet sweeter for all that.

'Protect me, lord,' he said. 'I beg sanctuary in your mighty hall.'

'Er...'

A crash came from the stage. A scream.

'It's Tichborne!' Marla shouted. 'He's broke his ankle!'

3

Fwych

Mother Fwych awoke on tiles wet and warm, fingers slipping through blood.

A worm lay before her, red and still.

Her tongue.

Mother no more. Oh, Mountain. Mother no more…

She winced and her jaw throbbed.

She pushed herself on to one side. Still at the roadside inn.

Selly stood nearby, looking down upon Mother Fwych, breathing heavy. Two wide eyes above a ruddy hole. Shorn of lips and nose, Selly, palms pierced together by a crossbow bolt. Blood, dark and lumpen, splattered between her feet like some tragic birth.

Fwych tried to comfort Selly with her eyes. For she'd tongue no more. No more.

Gently, Selly turned widdershins and Fwych realised she did not stand. Selly hung, her boots brushing the floor. A meathook were buried between her shoulder blades, its rope tied to the beam above.

From the shadows, Red Marie spoke.

Fwych felt cold breeze on her face. She were awake. She opened her eyes and the sky blazed white and blue.

She tried moving but only heaved and choked. Something filled her mouth. It were like some round bag of sand or seeds and it stank of flowers.

Fwych were on her back on hard floor. The inn's floor? Then why did the winter sky beat at her twitching eyes? Why did her stopped-up mouth burn?

My tongue, she remembered again, *my tongue*. There were no room for it in the stuffed cave of her mouth. She winced. *Oh Mountain, Father Mountain…*

A twinge in her shoulder where Selly's bolt had torn flesh. She remembered that. The floor beneath trembled and creaked. She were moving. Fwych lay on a cart's flat bed.

'Master Smones!' A far voice, a man's, growing louder. 'Wait, Master Smones! I beg of you!'

A throat grumbled close by, like a slumbering hearth-dog bothered by a child.

'Squints, Goitre,' the grumble said. 'Hold up.'

The creaking ceased and the sky came to a standstill.

Her chance to run. Gethwen in peril, she recalled, the world itself. But she could barely raise her head. Something tight around her wrists too: hemp, dirty and rough.

'Look at this facker run.' Foul that voice, rusted and sweet and evil, oozing its way into Fwych's ears. 'Too much rich food in that there Abbey.'

'They'd gobble him up in the city, boss,' a squeak of a voice said.

A hiss-and-rattle of laughter. 'Indeed they would, Squints. Indeed they surely would.'

Fwych's head lay on a sticky cushion. She dipped her chin and the sky gave way to her feet and a man running toward them down a tree-lined path. Robed and half-staggering, he came to a stop an arm's length from Fwych's boots and immediately bent at the hips, clutching his knees and panting. His scalp was shaved and he wore a big brown sack.

'In yer own time, Father,' the evil voice oozed.

This 'father' lifted a hand and, heaving, said, 'She cannot travel in her state.'

'And yet she does,' the voice said. 'Tough, these ban-hags.' A hawking of phlegm, soon spat out.

Father looked in the direction of the voice, barely hiding his disgust. 'Could you at least *hide* her, Master Smones. Many saw her carried out from that inn, she is the lone witness to—'

'Do not permit a ban-hag to live free,' Smones growled and Father seemed to shrivel. 'That's a Church rule, ain't it, Squints?'

'*Life of the Pilgrim*,' the squeaking voice said. 'Book thirty, verse nine.'

'It were ban-hags hung him up, wasn't it, Father?' Smones continued. 'The Pilgrim hisself. Hook through his feet and hung from a tree, like in all them paintings. No doubt watched his piss an' shit roll down his body for days, they did. Filthy fackers.'

Father made a gesture with one hand against his chest and mouthed something. 'Do not speak so.'

The Pilgrim. Fwych knew that name. The name flatlanders gave the-man-who-bled-the-mountain. They gave prayer to the Pilgrim, the flatlanders, as if a man could be a rock or tree.

'That what you think, Father?' Smones said, his words a mocking grease. 'That Smones'll get stopped on the road and asked who gave him a facking ban-hag? Think he'll tattle-tale on you and yer abbey?'

Father shook his head.

A clawed hand flew into Fwych's sight. No, not clawed. Fingernails clipped to points and painted black. Fingers like a famine, stretched flesh over bone, black with ingrained dirt. A tattered sleeve once patterned so fine.

'Allow me to instruct you, Father,' Smones said, 'how the world works outside your holy house. No one gives a shit. Not a single rancid facking turd. Not for some cunt in a cart.'

Father looked at Fwych a moment and Fwych closed her eyes before he might notice.

'I wish you did not talk so,' Father said. 'These vulgarities…'

'Apologies, Father. I'd give you my confession.' He chuckled. 'But I really don't think you'd want that.'

Fwych opened her eyes to see Father wince.

That laugh came again, the hiss and rattle. 'Father, Father…'

Smones came into view. Tall and thin, he were, unnatural so, like those stick-and-grass men flatlanders use to scare birds. He'd a tall and crooked hat. He reached up and cradled Father's cheek.

'Let's part on good terms,' he said, and reached into his jacket with his other hand. He pulled out five gold coins, which he sprinkled atop Father's shaved head. 'There'll be more, Father.' He grinned. 'I'll be back here. You watch me.'

Father looked forlorn at that, as if he often dreamed of never seeing Smones again.

'I must not pry but…' he tried. 'Where she is going, she will remain unseen, yes?'

'Oh, she'll be seen,' Smones said. 'Seen by the highest people. People who answer to man or God's laws only when it suits 'em.'

'Becken Keep?' Father said, startled.

'Indeed. That menagerie-maze they 'ave there. I mean, a banhag in all her pierced and tattooed glory but with no tongue to ensorcel folk? Why, there's a conversation piece for the finest cloth in our land.'

'They'd keep a woman in some cage?' Father said, frowning. 'Among animals?'

'There are men of this earth,' Smones said, 'so savage they're worth gawping at through bars. Like our girl there. Entertaining *and* educational, see? Fetch heckuva price. Trust me.' And then he tapped Father's cheek. 'Now back to yer abbey, there's a boy.'

Father's cheek had three black fingermarks upon it. He took one last look at the cart and then squatted to pick up the fallen gold.

'Move it,' Smones told whoever were drawing the cart. He looked back down the path. 'Oi, Father!'

Father stopped picking up coins but did not look up.

'Next time I come,' Smones shouted, 'I'll bring you another sweetmeat from the Hook. Blonde and silent, father. I know your type.'

Father trotted on down the path, never looking back.

Smones hiss-laughed and followed the cart. His eyes met Fwych's and he grinned, and Fwych reckoned he'd known her awake all this time. He'd eyeshadow, Smones, and his teeth were brown and black.

His face tore a memory from Fwych. The inn. Another face there, leering from out the gloom. Her sockets black and empty. She'd had nails for teeth.

Red Marie.

You're nothing now, she had said. *Nothing.* She had sliced up Mother Fwych's tongue to mush and tittered as she did so.

And now Mother Fwych was Fwych, and Fwych was nothing. She shuddered and her sight watered and Knucklebones Smones whistled and hawked up more of his strange black spit.

4

Larksdale

Every royal occasion was a chance to show off one's crestmen. Larksdale, a royal bastard, was permitted but one, another of Boathook Marla's occasional occupations.

She strode ahead of her master, her feathered hat, tunic and hose all sage green and fern: the livery of Larksdale's house, and so far no one had questioned his presumption in having one. Marla held the royal stave aloft in both hands and every comer proved wise enough to step aside. The crest of Becken and its royal family – a bat with wings outstretched – perched atop the stave. The bat was bronze, an alloy symbolic of bastards.

The young man from the mountains – Gethwen, he called himself – drew closer to Larksdale's side.

'You have to keep behind me,' Larksdale reminded him, gesturing with his newly acquired cane. 'A step behind and to my left.'

'Too many here,' Gethwen said, eyeing the crowds. 'It's never safe when there's too many.' He tried putting his arm through Larksdale's.

'This is too respectable a street for anyone to get stabbed,' Larksdale said, removing his arm from Gethwen's. It was too respectable a street to be seen with a pretty lad hanging upon your elbow too. Strange, how holding another man's hand might not bat an eyelid in a Tetchford alley nor the gilded hallways of the keep, yet in a street of clerks and merchants' wives it was cause for alarum. 'You're quite safe.' He smiled at him. 'Absurdly so.'

'You will take me to my people tomorrow?' Gethwen asked. 'I do so hate to ask, sir.'

'In time,' Larksdale said with comforting smile. Personally he was in no rush to walk the muddy alleys of Fleawater.

Gethwen smiled back. 'You are good to me, sir.'

By the Pilgrim, the lad was comely, like a statue of St Mattias made flesh. Giving him the role of page with all the finery and tights had made for a regrettable distraction, but one Larksdale could not help but relish.

Men could be heard at tourney within the giant tent. Even at a distance of a quarter-mile the clamour of violence travelled. No cheering though, despite all the spectators who would be inside. Excitement was the provenance of the more public tourneys, where the common man might watch his betters spar with elan. Brintland nobles watched to learn, and the ladies accompanied the men.

Still, a few ladies were wandering the gardens, dutifully pursued by their maids. A tourney at Grand Gardens was one of the few times one could reasonably expect to be free from husband or family. Larksdale had made pleasant – if foolhardy – use of that phenomenon in the past. Today, however, was rather too cold. Not that that stopped him drinking in the ladies in their ermine-lined winter dresses. One or two of them, Larksdale was sure, drank him in too.

'What's the fundamental rule, Gethwen?' Larksdale said.

'Keep silent,' Gethwen answered behind him. 'And I have been, sir. Really I have. I—'

'Gethwen.'

Larksdale met the collective warmth of bodies and braziers as he approached the tent's entrance. He nodded at the four guards in royal livery and passed into the gloom of the tent's innards. Gethwen tried to hold his arm again, but was dissuaded with a look.

Six men duelled in couples like dancers at springtime. They wore chainmail and crested helms, wielded painted shields and swords of yew. Cowled adjudicates stepped in occasionally, breaking up duellists who had grappled into rough embraces. It reminded Larksdale of his childhood in Becken Keep's training yards, bruised and sweaty memories he dreaded to recall. It had taken the weapon-masters, grown adults, a year and a half to realise what the eight-year-old Harrance Larksdale could have told them that first morning: that his soul was not tempered for the conventional duties of a king's bastard. The descent of St Neyes' blood was not always so straightforward.

Beyond the front line of spectators Larksdale could make out the spired tops of two wooden thrones. His Majesty King Ean would be sitting there, of course, spectating with his newest wife, Third-Queen Emmabelle of Duxby County, who was heavy with Ean's child.

Larksdale needed to be seen. It was not good to be forgotten, not when the role of Master of Arts and Revels hung for the taking like a game pheasant. One had to keep on the periphery of Ean's awareness. Larksdale made his way to the front, slipping between the gaps, a genial eel. He hoped Gethwen had the sense to follow.

A space lay between two men and their pages, wide enough for Larksdale to glide into without seeming uncouth. Prime territory. The two men's silhouettes, caught in the gold light of a nearby brazier, became recognisable. Larksdale considered retreating. But no. A little awkwardness could not dissuade him.

Neither man noticed him standing there, intent as they were on the nearest duel. Resting both palms upon his new brass-tipped cane, Larksdale feigned spectating while he eyed his two peers. To his left, 'Sir' Willem Cutbill, captain general of the city guard, his knighthood and position gifted to him on account of no one knowing what to do with a common soldier whose swift rise through the ranks had culminated in him saving the kingdom. Decades past he had ambushed and routed the grand army of Hoxham. Now he hanged the city's pie thieves and got mocked in whispers at court. Cutbill was still an ox of a man, though fifty or more, with shaved scalp and jet-black beard.

To Larksdale's right, Sir Tibald Slyke, Master of Arts and Revels. As old as Cutbill but far thinner and exceptionally more acidic. His characteristic wide-brimmed hat he'd even more characteristically not removed, for he'd never cared one jot for anyone behind him. Slyke had a cane, too. Larksdale realised with self-recrimination that Slyke had had one for some months now. Slyke would think the cane Larksdale had acquired from the bully Cabbot was aesthetic theft or, worse, unthinking imitation. Larksdale almost panicked and turned about until he noticed Slyke wore brown leather gloves with one or two gold rings worn on the outside. Pilgrim's heart. Wearing rings over leather gloves was Larksdale's thing. Always had been, the only difference being he'd good taste enough for silver rings over black gloves. Damned Slyke. The fellow was just too-too utter. A shameless beast.

Larksdale felt Gethwen's chin upon his left shoulder. The young spineman was trying to watch the tourney. Larksdale reached behind and pressed a palm against the youth's belly. Gethwen stepped back. At least he was keeping silent.

The king's crown shone beneath the tent's mosaic of lights. Ean, young and vital, had a natural talent for being watched. With his curling blonde locks and triangular beard he seemed St Neyes returned, Neyes the wise, defender of the true Church and saviour of the land. Ean's new wife, Emmabelle, complemented him well.

The same blonde locks and a face for courtly ballad, wide-eyed and guileless.

Can you see me, Ean? Larksdale thought. *Your capable servant, your brother. Waiting upon your slightest word.*

'Sir Harrance.' The voice came from his left. Cutbill. The duels out on the floor had ended and the old warrior had become aware of his surroundings.

'Sir Willem,' Larksdale replied. 'You seem in good health.' They had nothing in common, he and Cutbill, neither in background nor character. Indeed, Larksdale would wager there were hunters in unknown jungles at the edges of the world with whom he might banter more comfortably. There was one matter they could discuss though, one wholly inappropriate for the time and setting. Trouble was, Sir Willem Cutbill hadn't the breeding or nuance to realise that. With luck, more duellists would soon take to the floor and hook Cutbill's attention once again.

'Your coin and luxuries arrived at Wessel Bridge,' Cutbill said.

Oh, and there it was.

'Obliged,' Larksdale replied.

'All accounted,' Cutbill said. 'You can trust the city guard not to help themselves.'

By God, Cutbill's talk was forever loud and practical. An intolerable combination.

Larksdale smiled and nodded. 'Who was your preferred man in the duels just now?' He gestured at the floor before them.

'Your two associates are living well indeed,' Cutbill continued, senseless to Larksdale's evasion. 'For the cells of Wessel Bridge, I mean.'

Larksdale could sense Tibald Slyke beside him. Doubtless drinking it all in.

'Gratifying,' Larksdale said to Cutbill. Awkward as this scene was, he was pleased to hear the news.

'Your colleagues from the playhouse?' came Slyke's nasal voice. 'The two in the clink? What you Tetchford folk get up to staggers me. One has to laugh.'

'Indeed,' Larksdale replied, 'my colleagues couldn't resist a chuckle themselves as the city guard clapped them in irons.' He turned to Slyke. 'Hullo Tibald.'

Slyke half-smiled and raised an eyebrow when he spied Larksdale also had a cane. His expression became more circumspect, however, when Larksdale eyed the rings over Slyke's leather gloves.

Stalemate, Slyke.

'What was their misdemeanour?' Slyke said. But he knew perfectly well.

This was grating. He'd promised himself he'd work on Slyke, bring the rivalry between them to some detente even if he could not bear to befriend the wretch. The man had the very job Larksdale wanted most in all the world and, though Slyke was in no position to give it him and Larksdale would never pander, it surely did not help to lock horns with the fellow.

Tolerate him, Larksdale thought, *be butt to his barbs*. Yet, Pilgrim's love, Slyke did *not* make it easy.

'They had a slip of memory,' Larksdale answered.

'Tax evasion,' Cutbill explained to Slyke.

Slyke chuckled while simultaneously frowning with distaste, a performance Larksdale wished dearly to throw rotten vegetables at. 'Ah,' he said, 'that crime of common folk cursed by ambition.'

'Better than crimes of no ambition at all,' Larksdale replied, looking at the next set of duellists taking the floor. 'Did you arrange today's entertainments?'

Slyke sighed. 'The king asked for tourneys.'

'Yes,' Larksdale said, trying his best to smile with genuine grace. 'Of course.' But it came out sarcastic. *Why can't I stop myself?* Forever meeting Slyke's acid with acid, knowing full well the folly.

Some people had that effect on Larksdale and always had. First-Queen Carmotta in particular.

Come to think on it, where *was* Carmotta? The first-queen was not on the stage with her husband and sister wife. Strange she should miss a tourney; Carmotta loved watching dim men fight, armed or otherwise. Her absence wouldn't go unnoticed by anybody in the great tent, least of all her husband.

'Count Osrin,' Cutbill said out of nowhere. He was watching the tourney's next entrants. Cutbill actually smiled. 'A killer, Osrin,' he said.

'I'm pleased you like my show,' Slyke answered him. He eyed Larksdale.

Osrin, newly count of Whitecliff and royal bastard of highest standing, was something, all right. He strode on to the floor in naught but hose and belt, his bare torso smooth in the brazier light and striped with shadowed muscle. A smallish man but, like many smallish men, his condition had honed his bearing. So too the scars upon his face: two diagonal lines that made a V, crossing just below his lips. His presence in the king's tent was as a blaze.

'The ladies flock to see him duel,' Slyke said. He looked Larksdale up and down. 'You're keen to watch him fight, I see.'

'I'm thinking he would make an excellent St Neyes for one of our performances,' Larksdale said, only half-ignoring Slyke's insinuations. 'You'll recall we are both of Neyes' blood, both sons of the old king.' He looked at Slyke. Damn being civilised. 'Or had you forgotten, old man?'

'Bastards,' Slyke replied.

'The honest kind,' Larksdale said.

Two wooden swords were passed to Osrin, the left shorter than the right.

'Doesn't he get a helmet or something?' Larksdale asked his companions.

'It would just get in his way,' Cutbill said.

Count Osrin lifted a sword in salute of the king.

'Your Majesty!' he proclaimed. 'My sacred brother, I salute you and congratulate your queen. With your permission?' The king nodded and every spectator clapped politely. Osrin turned to the crowd. 'What you are about to witness is a style of swordsmanship practised upon the commrach isle. Few humans are permitted there. Fewer return.' He spun the shorter sword around his index finger like it was a sail on a windmill. 'I spent a year in their gymnasia.' He gestured at the scars upon his face. 'They were not shy with their lessons.'

Two men in chainmail and helm, swords in hand, approached Osrin from either end of the floor.

'Two opponents,' Cutbill muttered beside Larksdale. He shook his head with a boyish wonder.

'Finally,' Larksdale said. 'Showmanship.'

Cutbill ignored him, appearing embarrassed by the statement. Larksdale eyed Slyke. The Master of Arts and Revels had clearly taken umbrage at Larksdale's idle comment.

Larksdale ignored them. Neither of these men were his kind of people, and each in their own painful and teeth-pulling way had now forced Larksdale to do the very thing he'd hoped to avoid when coming to this tourney: spectate.

Certainly, Osrin's promise of two assailants had been distracting, but now they actually fought it was the same old physical malarky. Could have been a hundred opponents and Larksdale wouldn't have understood the difference. Granted, there was something of a dance to Osrin's strange style, a fluid motion that made fool of his enemies' swings, but it just made Larksdale hungry to know about *actual* dancing styles over on the commrach isle. Whenever he'd a chance to press Osrin on such matters – the sculpture, the murals, hell, the great towers of wrought iron and pewter that were said to loom over that secretive and misty isle – Osrin merely looked at Larksdale like, well, Larksdale watching Osrin fight. Which was like a goat regarding a brick.

Oh, but the men. The men who watched, these gentlemen of arms and violence: they were enthralled. Cutbill and all the rest of them, drunk on Count Osrin and everything he evoked. Larksdale hadn't seen it before but the reality of it hit him like an arrow from a hedge: Osrin was like his father, the old king, the king of campaigns and red glory, not the king of quiet prosperity who watched others duel from his dais. It dawned on Larksdale with increasing discomfort that if he, a noted popinjay and featherwrist, could see it then for how long had every battle-scarred knight and ambitious wife here in this tent seen it? And had they ever dared talk to one another on the matter?

Gads, Larksdale thought, *this is the last time I take in a tourney.*

'Everyone knows you're after my job,' Slyke said. He stood closer now.

'I've never hidden the fact,' Larksdale replied, surprised at Slyke's candour. 'But I've never tried to undermine you for it.' Which was true enough, though he'd often fantasised.

'No doubt you know I'm to retire,' Slyke said. One of Osrin's opponents grunted and fell. 'It's a draining, thankless role and I'd happily wish it on you, Larksdale. You deserve to get what you want. But the Crown deserves better than you as Master of Arts and Revels.'

Larksdale thought to mention Slyke's financial dealings with that wife-beating slime Cabbot. Yet it was uncouth to talk of self-made nabobs at court events. Larksdale would be no better than Cutbill.

'All I can offer is my all,' Larksdale said at last. 'Body and soul.'

'Farce and disaster,' Slyke said.

This was becoming intolerable. 'Sir, why bear such ill will?'

'Because I love my country and my king. And those two qualities propel me to pray you waste your life away in that tatty theatre.' He shook his head and for a moment Larksdale was scared he might lay eyes on Gethwen. 'But it's no matter. You've no chance of appointment.'

Larksdale looked at Slyke. The clatter of wooden blades became more rapid between the two remaining swordsmen. 'You know something I'm not aware of, Slyke?'

'I know something simply *everyone* is aware of. That you're our king's procurer, arranger of discreet dalliances and pleasures. It's how he sees you. How we all see you. Always and for ever.'

Larksdale had no reply to such barbs, for they were mirror to his fears.

'Sir Harrance,' a voice said behind him. The two men turned to see a royal page. 'The first-queen would speak with you in the old ruins.'

'First-Queen Carmotta?' Larksdale said with comically feigned surprise. He placed a gloved palm upon his collarbone. 'With me?' Then he looked at Slyke and smiled. 'Must be off.'

Larksdale took the path that led to the ruins, Gethwen in tow.

The Mancan emperors had once ruled from the hill where Grand Gardens now stood and today it seemed Queen Carmotta intended to rule from there too, albeit briefly and with Larksdale her lone subject. Carmotta's people had never gotten over their fall from domination, that was their problem. Then again, the modern Mancanese were never short of a gargantuan ruin or sprawling canal system to remind them of it. Sad, really, and Larksdale might even have pitied them if only they hadn't given Carmotta Il'Lunadella to the world.

He stopped upon the path and turned to Gethwen. 'Actually, a few ground rules. Now, I do not mean to panic you on your first day as page but you've had little to no training and you're about to meet the queen, so—'

'I'm not really a page, though, am I?' Gethwen frowned. He clutched at his hessian bag. 'Please, I just want to meet my people in this city. I *need* to.'

Larksdale sighed. 'Gethwen, that's *not* the attitude of a page about to meet his queen. Listen, the fundamental rule is to hold silent, like I told you. With royalty, as with nobility, behave as if someone took your tongue.'

Gethwen opened his mouth to reply then closed it and nodded instead.

'Stand way behind me,' Larksdale said. 'Do not look Her Majesty in the eye. In fact, look no one in the eye.'

Gethwen looked down and grasped the strap of his satchel tighter.

'I mean it,' Larksdale said. 'It's not inconceivable she may address you directly so as to annoy me. Her bodyguard, Dulenci, is an arrogant cockswaggle who may address you directly so as to amuse her. In neither scenario should you reply.'

'That's rude, isn't it?' Gethwen said. 'Not replying?'

'On the contrary, it's expected. If it's any consolation, you can reply to her handmaids if they address you directly. But they won't. They'll be too scared of me addressing them directly for my own amusement. Any questions?'

'How do you people fucking live like this?' Gethwen said, confusion and fear quavering his voice. 'Sorry sir. I'm all a-panicked I am. Back home folk look in each other's eyes.'

Larksdale put a palm on Gethwen's shoulder. 'It is I who should apologise, Gethwen. I can be insufferable in trying moments. You are a wonderful man, a free and marvellous creature, and I have promised to protect you.' He recalled something and chuckled. 'You know, I once overheard a servant say to another, "When you are nervous before the nobility, imagine them all naked." It levels all ranks, apparently.'

Gethwen looked up. Then, slowly, he looked down again, taking in Larksdale's body from head to foot.

'Thank you,' he said. He met Larksdale's gaze once more and a grin – half lascivious, half coy – lit his smooth face. 'My panic fades.'

Larksdale was stunned. His stomach quivered in the most pleasurable way. He remembered where he was.

'Follow my lead,' he told his page, and made his way toward the ruins.

The queen sat upon a cracked marble pedestal, swirling a steaming bronze chalice with one hand. The usual pack of catchfarts surrounded her: her cousin Dulenci with his smirks and taffeta and blades, and three handmaidens each wearing a colour of House Il'Lunadella, topaz, cream and indigo. Indigo held a steaming silver jug, its handle wrapped in cloth.

'Your Majesty,' Dulenci declared once Larksdale was within earshot. 'A miscreant approaches. Perhaps I should pat his body down for weapons?'

'It's not your birthday, Dulenci,' Larksdale said with a dutiful smile. He turned to First-Queen Carmotta and bowed. 'Your Majesty.'

'Cousin Dulenci,' Carmotta said, 'you should know by now our dear friend carries no weapon save that which he keeps in his mouth.'

'And I only ever use it to disarm, Your Majesty,' Larksdale said, rising and never taking his gaze from the queen's own.

Her smile never slipped. Pilgrim's blood, but the bitch looked ravishing today. Her black hair was braided and wrapped with silver pins and lilac silk, her brown skin moisturised to a honeyed shine. Carmotta was fat, inarguably, but of that plumpness that glows and glides through this world, its buoyancy and vitality swallowing the wits of all men who gazed upon it.

Not this man.

'I am honoured you require my presence,' Larksdale said. 'But I'm at a loss as to why you'd wish me to bear witness to the lost zenith of your people.' He gestured at the ruins all around.

Even the handmaids looked askance at that. Dulenci rested his palm upon the hilt of his sword.

'Because a man of your country,' Carmotta replied, 'should see what an actual zenith looks like.' She nodded at her chalice. 'Mulled wine,' she explained. 'I found the very idea an affront when first I came here. That you Brintlanders should take wine and defile it with spice and heat.'

'An answer to the inferior wines that reach us,' Larksdale said. He glanced at Carmotta and Dulenci both. 'Manca does not always send its best.'

'But I've come to quite like it,' she said, ignoring him. 'It is a palliative for your interminable cold. Indeed, aside from my husband the king, mulled wine is the best thing in all Brintland.' She spoke to her second handmaid – Cream – in Mancanese and she came forth with another chalice. Indigo followed with her jug. 'And so I call you here, Sir Harrance, that you may partake of this splendid… once-wine.'

A strange game here, though far from her first.

'Your Majesty would never be so unimaginative as to poison me?' Larksdale said. He grinned.

'I lack the mercy.' Her expression was blank a second. She pouted her sensuous lips and patted a space beside her on the pedestal. 'Come.'

Larksdale took a deep breath of cold noon air. He noticed a carved skull in the pedestal, its eye sockets weeping moss. *Whatever she plans, it will be over soon enough.* He approached the pedestal.

Dulenci stepped in front of him and held out a palm. He eyed Larksdale's cane.

Larksdale gave it to him then sat by Carmotta. He was careful to keep a half-yard's distance between his own rear and hers – as distant as the pedestal might permit – but her perfumes and her presence raged beyond her physical borders, as always.

Cream offered him a chalice and he thanked her and took it. He could physically feel Carmotta's embarrassment for him, thanking a servant like that. *Damn it, Harry. Too long at the Wreath.* When Indigo poured the mulled wine he was careful not to even look at her. The whiff of cinnamon filled his nostrils.

'Now there's a pretty one,' Dulenci said. He was looking over at Gethwen. 'A youthful statue come to life I think.'

'He's from the country,' Larksdale said. 'His ways are simple, Dulenci.'

'I'll complicate them,' Dulenci said, 'gladly.'

Gethwen looked down and clutched his shoulder bag.

'Oh,' Dulenci said. 'But he is shy.' He made show of shuddering with vicious delight.

Carmotta laughed. 'Behave.'

'I try,' Dulenci said. 'I try.'

'Quite,' Larksdale muttered. Dulenci's showiness perennially sickened him. With his shaved face and bright clothing, his flamboyant gestures and graceless quips, Dulenci was every inch the cliché of a sodomite, specifically of the Mancanese variety. Thus he was permitted to be at his cousin the queen's side at all times, even in her chambers. Dulenci could kill manlier men in a heartbeat and thus manlier men were careful not to taunt him. But Larksdale did. A matter of principle.

To adore another male was a pure desire, and, Larksdale firmly believed, when doing so one should be as a spectator before a work of art, all hushed appreciation and considered words. Yet to Dulenci such desire was a joke, a gaudy performance all centred around himself and never his intended. There was a whiff of the travelling hawker to Dulenci's lusts, of the purveyor of false ointments and wrong measures. Dulenci sickened Larksdale. He embarrassed him.

'Drink,' Carmotta said.

'To Queen Emmabelle,' Larksdale said, and he raised his chalice.

'To the third-queen,' Carmotta said, and sipped.

The wine was good. Hot and spiced and charmingly free of hemlock.

'This is all very kind,' Larksdale said. 'I'm stuck for words.'

'How refreshing,' Carmotta said.

'Savour it,' Larksdale said, 'because it's already over. Why are you not beside your king, Your Majesty? I think that noteworthy. Others might think it an insult.'

Carmotta put a hand to her lips and made a scandalised expression that delighted her cousin no end. Then she looked at Larksdale like he was the worst bore.

'Is that what you're insinuating?' Carmotta said. 'That I'm, ooh, jealous of my sister wife because she is with child and I am not? That I wish all the court to know my pain?' She shook her head. 'Larksdale, you are no fun any more.'

How can you not be upset? Larksdale thought. *You should be scared, at the minimum.* But these were dark waters. Carmotta had lost a babe in the womb three years ago and to Larksdale that was a taboo isle. *There are rules to our cruelties, Carmotta.*

'No,' Carmotta said, taking another sip. 'I was late arriving because I had a previous engagement. Giving coin to the needy.'

'And which balcony did you toss these coins from?'

'I'm surprised you weren't down there,' she said, laughing. 'Dulenci tells me all your money is at sea. A ship's hold full of… what was it?'

'Mustard,' Dulenci replied.

Had she a spy at the Wreath? 'I'm saddened Her Majesty should take such interest in my personal business.'

'Even the loftiest play has its lowly fool,' she replied. 'But come, let us toast again. I invited you here so that you might share in Dulenci's recent good fortune.'

Here it came.

'I've acquired land,' Dulenci said, 'in, er, how is it said now?' He grinned. 'Tetchford Eve.'

Larksdale leaped to his feet. 'The Wreath?'

'Just so.'

'No,' Larksdale said. 'No, I own the Wreath.'

'But not the ground it stands upon,' Carmotta said. 'That's Dulenci's.'

Dulenci shrugged. 'What can I say? I like ground.'

This was intolerable, just too-too utter.

'And where does this fool's money come from, hmm?' Larksdale asked Carmotta. 'That's city land, there's rules about royal—'

'You *insult* me,' Carmotta said in that playful bloody way of hers, a hand upon her collarbone. 'Dulenci merely took a loan from my father the Duke, an ordinary deal between a man and his nephew. No royalty involved.'

'Your father,' Larksdale said. 'Of course.' He was furious, looking down upon Carmotta smiling into her mulled wine. He was also now keenly aware of her breasts, a phenomenon that happened whenever she made him mad. He looked at a nearby column instead, quite defeated. 'How, then, may I be of service?'

'You tell me.'

'You wish me to step away from the king,' Larksdale said. 'From arranging his little… diversions. His parties.' The king's approval was everything, Larksdale's path to being Master of Arts and Revels and the great plan that lay beyond.

'Ean would soon replace you.' Carmotta looked peeved at the mention of her husband. 'No, the way you can be of use to me is…'

She frowned, smiled. 'You know, I think my requirements can wait.' Carmotta held her empty chalice and the cream-dressed handmaiden dutifully took it away. 'But I'll let you know, Sir Harry. I will let you know.'

'I do so enjoy surprises,' Larksdale said tightly. 'But now, Your Majesty, I must away.'

'You've a theatre to run,' Dulenci said. 'A treacherous pursuit, I'm told.'

'All pursuits are,' Larksdale said. 'That's their attraction.' He held out a gloved hand for his cane.

Dulenci passed it to him, but not before acting out a few playful sword feints with it. Absolute arse of a man.

The nearest gate out of Grand Gardens was further down the Old Ruin's path. He gestured for Gethwen to follow.

Gethwen passed between Dulenci and the queen.

'Wait,' Carmotta said.

Gethwen stopped. He did not turn to face them.

'Look at his hair, Dulenci,' Carmotta said. 'So *red*. I've never seen the like.' She was genuinely in awe. Larksdale hadn't seen her make that face in years. For a second it warmed him like the wine.

'He hails from the Spine Mountains,' Larksdale explained. 'It is common enough there.' He nodded to Gethwen to keep walking.

'I've never been,' Carmotta said.

'You needn't travel so far to see ginger hair, Your Majesty,' Larksdale said. 'Merely walk through the city you rule over.'

Her nose wrinkled at the thought.

Dulenci was looking Gethwen up and down once more. He pouted lasciviously.

Larksdale stepped in front of Gethwen. 'Cheerio,' he said to Dulenci.

With that he strode off, growing more angry with every lawn and flower bed he passed.

'Sir,' Gethwen said behind him. 'Sir.'

'Do keep up.'

'Sir.' He grabbed Larksdale's shoulder and turned him around.

Larksdale stopped and stared at Gethwen dumbfounded, aghast. No one ever laid hands upon him like this. He was quick to look past Gethwen, to see whether the queen and her cronies had witnessed it. But no, they were already gone from the ruins.

'There's protocol, lad,' he told Gethwen.

'I don't even know what that means.'

'Codes of behaviour.'

'Who says?' Gethwen nodded back to where they had come from. 'Them? They're silly people, sir. Souls made of air. I wanted to shout at them, I did. I wanted us both to.'

Larksdale placed a gloved hand on Gethwen's shoulder. 'I am grateful you did not.'

'In the mountains you live by the strength of your fist and the truth of your words.'

'And you shiver in the night and hunger by day, I'll wager,' Larksdale replied. 'For a people to flourish, a little dignity must be sacrificed upon the altar of privilege.'

'Better to shiver. Better to starve.' Gethwen placed his own hand upon Larksdale's, which still sat upon Gethwen's shoulder. 'I'd take you from all this sickness. If I could, sir.'

It was laughable really, him saying that. It was the finest offer Larksdale had known.

'I shall ask you to behave yourself in future,' Larksdale said. He placed a thumb under Gethwen's chin. 'But not too much, eh?'

Gethwen smiled. 'Larksdale, sir, are you trying to complicate me?'

Larksdale had a powerful urge to lean toward those lips and kiss them. They would be willing, those lips, he knew.

Horns blared in the distance. Back in the great tent people were applauding the royal couple upon their dais.

Larksdale drew a deep breath and gazed at the cold ruins back down the path.

'Come,' he told Gethwen. 'Let's return to the theatre. The real one.'

FIVE NIGHTS TILL YULENIGHT EVE

5

Carmotta

Carmotta wished to visit the man behind the black door. In the hope that no soul would see them, she and Dulenci had taken a most obscure route around the keep. It had very nearly worked.

'Well met, Your Majesty,' Count Osrin, best of bastards, said. He bowed and arose, the light from the stained-glass windows that lined the corridor mottling his scarred face. 'I would not have expected to see you in so remote a part of the keep.'

'Nor I you, sir,' Carmotta replied. She nodded toward him and his three acquaintances – Sir Quendle, Sir Bergenhaim and Sir Pym, all true-born lords of the Brintland and seasoned war-hounds to boot. She steepled her hands and feigned serenity. Behind her, Dulenci drew a long breath.

A silence followed, one she would let them break. When a woman in a room of men keeps silent, one man will blurt something out soon enough. An advantage so few women knew they possessed.

'I was showing the lords these windows,' Osrin said. Interesting that he should break first. She would not have predicted that. 'They're modest, but very fine.'

'Neyes the Child,' Carmotta said, looking up at the series of images in green and purple glass. A blind peasant boy given sight by the Holy Pilgrim's blessing. The founding tale of the Brintland. 'I'd not have thought this stage of the Saint's life would draw you, Osrin. Surely you must prefer—'

'Neyes the Conqueror,' Osrin said, cutting her off. A most brazen act. 'You would be right, Your Majesty. But Neyes the Child...' his V-scarred face looked to the stained glass and took on green and lilac hues '...inspires me. That a blind bastard could be touched by heaven. That speaks to all bastards' souls.'

'Especially bastards of his blood,' Sir Lilas Pym said, pink-faced and hearty, two qualities in Brintland men she particularly despised. Pym slapped Osrin on the shoulder and the two men grinned.

'Chosen to rule,' Carmotta said. 'That is a destiny most men shall never be given.'

'Some simply take it,' Osrin said.

'Explain, sir,' Carmotta said.

Osrin smiled at Carmotta.

'I refer', he said, 'to the emperors of the Mancan empire. Ever the lesson in tyranny.'

'Of course,' Carmotta said. 'How slow of me. My husband the king...' she let the words hang in the air awhile '...holds court today. I trust I shall see you all there.'

They all smiled. They were like naughty boys, covered in scars instead of mud. A secret between them. That was why they loitered in this obscure corridor. *Yes, they plot, quite flagrantly.* Carmotta could tell now where she had only suspected before. They kept to the required politeness but the four men eyed Carmotta like a hanging carcass, sizing her up for cuts of beef. She was harmless, or so they believed, now that the king's third wife was with child, something Carmotta had failed in.

Dulenci stepped forward. 'My sweetest darlings,' he said to them, 'the queen must be on her way.'

'And so must Her Majesty,' Pym muttered. The men chuckled.

'Is that some slight, Pym?' Dulenci said. 'You slight our queen?'

Pym straightened. 'No. A joke.'

'You *joke* about our queen?' Dulenci stepped forward again. Carmotta could not see his face but knew from the back of his coiffured head his killer's stare was in play.

'No,' Pym insisted. 'I jested about you, sir.'

I should stop this, Carmotta thought. But it served as a diversion. Neither Osrin nor his gang would think to ask what she and Dulenci were doing in this dusty part of the keep. Or where the queen was going.

'About me?' Dulenci asked Pym. 'Explain this jest, Sir Lilas. Brintlander humour eludes me so.' He stepped closer still.

'Gentlemen,' Osrin said to them both. 'Let's have no ill will.' A performance, Carmotta could see. Magnanimous, regal. 'Bile leads to swords, swords to regret.'

'Swords?' Dulenci laughed. He unbuckled his belt of blades and tossed it away behind him. 'A man needs no swords to ask questions. What was this "joke" about me, Pym?'

'I called you a queen,' Pym said, his face reddening. More than usual.

'How so?' Dulenci stood a pace from Pym now.

'Like a lady,' Pym said, confident in himself now swords lay to one side. Pym was bigger than Dulenci, wider at the shoulder and waist. 'A fine, soft lady waiting for her knight.'

'I appreciate your candour,' Dulenci muttered.

Pym toppled backwards. Dulenci had put a foot behind Pym's ankle and pushed his chest. Dulenci dropped to one knee and grasped Pym like a fainting lover.

'My knight is here!' Dulenci declared. He kissed Pym on the

mouth, vigorously and long. Pym struggled but Dulenci had him in a wrestler's grip.

Compelling viewing, yet Carmotta kept her eyes on Osrin, the only man in court who could best Dulenci. Osrin flashed a look back at her. For that second the two most dangerous people in the corridor appraised one another.

'My one true love!' Dulenci yelled and got back to slobbering over the bearded and ruddy chin.

Pym's hand, held at the wrist, flailed like a dying spider, the pale hairy fingers trying for the hilt of the dagger on his belt.

Osrin drew it out instead. Carmotta froze, expecting Osrin to pass it to his troubled comrade, but instead he stepped back, keeping the blade from harm's way.

'Cease, Dulenci,' Carmotta said.

Dulenci shot up, letting Pym drop on his back to the floor. Picking up his belt Dulenci paced back toward his queen, glee etched upon his face.

'You've wronged me!' Pym bellowed, getting to his feet. 'You've made me—'

'Aroused?' Dulenci said, cutting him off.

'I demand satisfaction!'

'Pym, we've company,' Dulenci said with mocking softness.

Carmotta had business to attend to, amusing as this all was.

'Pym,' Carmotta said, 'we apologise. Call it another jest.'

'Indeed,' Osrin said. 'Humour is subjective, Your Majesty.' He passed Pym his dagger and nodded for his gang to leave. All but Pym bowed.

The hallway was empty now, save Carmotta and her cousin.

'They needed a lesson,' Dulenci said in answer to Carmotta's stare. 'I won't have these Brintland goatfuckers treat you so.'

'Pym is a martial powerbroker, you realise?' Carmotta said. 'He can call three thousand men to his banner.'

'Then I suppose I should be flattered.'

'Idiot.' She studied the space where the nobles had stood. She didn't believe their talk of looking at stained glass, not slightly. This hallway was high and remote within the vast keep, one of the places feet rarely trod through. They had come here to talk, plainly. 'It is of no matter, Dulenci.'

'How so?'

'Osrin has no use for us as allies, so better to be seen his enemies. We become a beacon to others who would stand in his way.'

'You confuse me when you talk like this,' Dulenci said.

'Osrin would wear the crown, Dulenci. I've suspected a long time but now I know. He has the friends, the charisma. Just not the right.'

'I had no right to ravish Pym just now,' Dulenci said. 'What does right matter?'

'In the Brintland? More than army and coin.' She gestured at the windows along the walls. 'The blood of Neyes, Dulenci. The blind child who grew to be the conqueror against the dark, who brought the light of the Pilgrim by sword and vow, who took this very keep with but twelve men because God showed him a way. Neyes is everything to these horrendous fucking people and his true descendant must sit the throne. Not some bastard.' Strange, then, that a bastard should even begin to fancy his chances. What did Osrin so confidently depend upon that she could not see? 'Come, coz, let us be on our way.'

They turned right into another, narrower corridor and were immediately greeted with the *clunk-clunk* sound of wood against wood and the creaking of chain. At the corridor's end were the twin thresholds of the paternoster. The two doorways flashed night black and velvet red as the chain of vertical passenger compartments passed by endlessly, rising on the left threshold and descending on the right.

Carmotta and Dulenci took the right. Her stomach lurched with the sudden drop, a sensation like being on the deck of a sea vessel. The moans of chains straining and shifting echoed within the shaft their compartment descended. Somewhere above them hundreds of Becken's criminals turned the wheel, their meaningless and squalid lives put toward something useful.

Pilgrim's love, but a dainty thought struck her. Larksdale loved his commoner's theatre; might the threat of its destruction be enough to persuade him to poison Osrin's wine? A simple flick of the wrist, after all. He was coward enough.

Dulenci took her hand.

'Look what you do to me,' he said, and he pressed her palm against the hardness in his tights. He leaned in and brushed his lips against her cheek.

'Not now,' she whispered. 'It's not safe.'

'Please,' he whispered, hot breath against her ear. 'Please, my love.'

Already she felt her body defy her mind. Dulenci's audacity was irresistible. Kissing a manly enemy, pressing himself against her when they might be seen: these things stirred Carmotta. She could feel the shape of his bulbous glans in her palm. She squeezed, stroked. He groaned, his face lost in her collarbone.

Oh, but Larksdale. To have him poison Osrin would be to make him a true confidant, an ally. *Not that bastard,* she thought, pumping Dulenci's cock. *Too much history there. Too much he has wronged me with.* In killing Osrin, Larksdale too would have to be—

'No,' she said, and pushed Dulenci away. 'Not here, fool.' She took deep breaths, reined herself in. 'Later, my love. I promise.'

'Cruellest monarch,' he murmured, and he leaned back against the compartment's velvet wall. 'I only love you the more.'

She would not meet his stare nor look down at her old friend in his tights. She might lose her wits again. She loved Dulenci so.

'When I've drained Larksdale of gold,' he said, 'we shall be free to run.'

'He's a pauper now,' she replied. 'Thanks to his lost cargo of mustard. No, we torture him for sport, not gold. Gold hasn't the same lustre.'

'To live and to love, my Carmotta,' Dulenci said, ignoring her talk of Harry Larksdale. 'To be free of every fool.'

She licked her lips and leered at him, like he was a sheep and she the lion. She had been drunk and furious the night Ean had bedded his new queen Emmabelle and she had loudly fantasised about running away. That fantasy had since become scripture to Dulenci. But it kept him happy. So happy. Dulenci was both fearless fighter and hopeless puppy, enamoured enough to follow Carmotta to Becken, brave enough to act the flamboyant man-lover before all the court.

Simply to be by her side.

6

Larksdale

The king's laugh was as kind as it was hearty.

'And so,' Larksdale continued from the other side of the table, 'he asked for a helm and we gave him one. With rabbit's ears.'

The king slapped the table. 'I trust the crowd enjoyed that.'

'Your Majesty, not as much as the thrashing the wife's champion gave him. She was upon the knave in but moments, swinging her stone in its tights right at his nutmegs. *Bullseye!* Then our fool rubbed his buttocks across the husband's jowls.'

The king clutched his chest and guffawed. Actually guffawed. His gold crown caught the purple light from the window above. He wiped a tear, his shoulders shaking.

The anecdote had worked. The trick was never to practice the thing beforehand. Let it flow like a stream, racing over the rocks and sandbars of the listener's individual taste.

Larksdale smiled and looked up at the square stained-glass ceiling some thirty feet above: Neyes the Child, his face impassive as the masses crowned him saint and king. They were sharing a joke beneath their ancestor. The pair of them were in one of the royal solus chambers, high-ceilinged yet cramped rooms with space enough for a table and chairs. These chambers were where every secret deal was made, every stratagem debated. Conspiracies were birthed here, at least all the ones that benefitted Crown and nation.

'Have no fear for the music, sire,' Larksdale said, returning to business. 'Three flautists late of the court of Ralstone. Not a lute in sight. I know you hate them so.'

'Appreciated,' Ean said. He was two years younger than Larksdale with golden hair that curled wonderfully at the ends. The very mirror of Neyes the Conqueror, Neyes the Merciful, Neyes the Wise. 'I do not thank you enough for your tales of the street and the common folk. You are my eyes to a secret world.'

'It does not have to be so,' Larksdale said. 'The Wreath is for ever at your disposal, sire.'

'This champion,' Ean said, 'in the trial. The one who vanquished the husband of the beautiful wife.'

'Marla,' Larksdale said and immediately cursed himself for so doing.

'A she-warrior. Fascinating.' The king's brow furrowed. 'What is she like?' He gestured at his own face and torso.

'Noseless,' Larksdale lied. 'A mishap with a—'

'You were at Grand Gardens the other day,' Ean said, already losing interest, thank God.

'You saw me?'

'No, Carmotta told me you spoke.'

Larksdale's hands felt greasy inside his gloves. 'Yes, Your Majesty.'

'I love her, with all heart,' Ean said. 'But the first-queen has never appreciated a great man's need for diversion. Men weighed by responsibility need to put that weight to one side once-a-while, eh, Harry?'

'Or life sours,' Larksdale said. He smiled.

'The first-queen perceives you as a bad influence, when all you've ever done is facilitate a long tradition.'

'Thank you, sire. I like to think it's in my blood. I was conceived at one such gathering.'

'Fascinating. Well, I just wished you to understand that I do not share our wife the queen's dim view of you.'

'The queen's reserve is understandable.' *If only you knew the half of it, sire,* Larksdale thought. *That best-forgotten summer.*

'You think?' He sighed and, removing his crown, placed it upon the table. 'She's a will on her. To despise our diversions is one thing, brother, but to despise a king of the Brintland taking wives is plain irrational.'

'Your Majesty...' Larksdale stumbled for the words. He couldn't believe Ean had called him brother. 'Her ways *are* foreign.'

'They give their women too much latitude over there,' Ean said, shaking his head. 'Practically equals, strutting around like those she-demons of the commrach. A queen should know not to insult her husband's friends, nor her sister wives. She trusts no one, Harry.'

Friend, Larksdale thought. *He calls me friend and brother.*

'I can see His Majesty is perturbed,' Larksdale said. He could wound Carmotta here, if he were brave enough to seize Ean's mood. 'Perhaps the people she brought from Manca could be sent home? They prevent her from engaging with life in the keep. Her cousin particularly...'

'Dulenci speaks against me?'

'No, no,' Larksdale said. 'Merely the impression I have is, er, one of cushioning Her Highness.' He had lost his chance. He had not the resolve of the false witness.

The king stared at his crown. 'Sending him back might be taken poorly. By the whole Mancan court, I mean. The alliance is vital.' He smiled. 'You said your theatre is at my disposal?'

'Naturally, sire.' What was this?

'And you are performing this yulenight?'

'A lowly folk-play, sire. As is custom.'

'Bring it here. To the keep. On Yulenight Eve.' He stared at Larksdale, clearly enjoying his bastard brother's astonishment. 'And, for the Pilgrim's sake, man, whenever we are in this room call me Ean.'

It was as if a giant had seized the solus chamber they sat within and turned it upside down.

'High time we saw a folk-play,' Ean said when Larksdale could say nothing. 'We nobility could learn much from the common man's entertainments. Carmotta especially.'

'But—' Larksdale almost said 'Ean'. '—Yulenight Eve is for keep-plays, sire. For high drama.' He pictured the court of Becken Keep watching actors searing one another's arses and wearing false bosoms. 'Folk-plays are very… *very*.'

'I'm *sick* of keep-plays,' Ean said. 'As I am of lutes. Everyone is, but no one admits as much. What the court needs is good earthy fun.'

'As Master of Arts and Revels, it is Sir Tibald Slyke's role to produce a play on Yulenight Eve.'

'Slyke is old,' Ean said. 'His plays older still.' With that, he looked deep into Larksdale's eyes. 'Never allow humility to hold you back, brother. Power, true power, never forgives that. Bring me a play. Should it please us, well, you'll have little use for humility thereafter.'

'I'm honoured,' Larksdale said. 'I shall give every effort. Ean.'

Pilgrim preserve! It was happening, actually happening. Master of Arts and Revels, there for the taking. The path of his great plan lay wide open. He wanted to squeal, to laugh like some cider-soaked mooncalf.

'Quite a trap we spring on the court, eh?' Ean said. 'You and I.'

'Imagine their faces.' It was all Larksdale could get out.

Ean leaned back in his chair. 'Best be about your work.'

Larksdale stood up and bowed. 'Your Majesty.'

'Oh, before you leave. Tomorrow night's diversion.'

'Yes?'

'I would lay our eyes upon the wife,' Ean said. 'Bring her to me.'

'Who?'

'The one in your tale. The one the noseless wench fought for.'

Cabbot's wife? Once-wife. With her new life at the Wreath.

'Sire, she is not worth your time.'

'Let me judge that, Larksdale,' the king replied. 'You called her ravishing, did you not?'

Larksdale nodded. He had improved the tale somewhat. 'In her fashion.'

'After all,' Ean said, 'her husband would fight to the death for her.'

'Your Majesty,' Larksdale tried, 'the woman I've already curated for you, Abercine, is that beautiful Antardes woman, yes? You liked her. The most exquisite companion in all Becken.'

'I've had her,' the king replied. He put his crown back on. 'I want the wife. What's her name?'

'I don't know. Your Majesty, I can bring you trained companions. I can bring you sweet Abercine and, and *two* others. The finest in all the Main.'

'Sounds like too much work,' the king muttered. 'Larksdale. What was it I just said of your humility?'

'That I should not allow it to hold me back.'

'Precisely. Perfume this mysterious lady and dress her fine.'

'Your Majesty.' Larksdale nodded. *Sacrifice,* he told himself, clutching at his cane. *All great plans require... they require sacrifice.*

7

Carmotta

Three figures strode toward them, half-silhouetted in the gloom of the carved stone tunnel.

Dulenci stopped Carmotta and stepped in front of her. He gripped the hilt at his belt. This was the subterranean hallways of Becken Keep, after all. Almost no one had reason to be down here amid the black stonework and inexplicable humidity.

The figures stopped too. 'Identify yourselves,' a man's voice called out. 'In the name of the queen!'

'The queen,' Dulenci replied. 'Now identify yourselves in her name.'

A brief silence followed.

'Greetings, sister,' a woman's voice called. Third-Queen Emmabelle.

Well this was inarguably fucking odd. Emmabelle and her two guards had clearly come from the direction of the black door, which was exactly where Carmotta was going. There were obvious questions that needed asking of Emmabelle, the exact same questions Carmotta had no wish to answer herself.

'Greetings,' Carmotta replied. She slipped past Dulenci and walked toward her sister wife. Emmabelle's face emerged in the lamplight. An archetypal 'rose of the south', the third-queen was all blonde hair and healthy round features, her belly the roundest of all. Young Emmabelle was perhaps a month from giving birth. Her white dress shone gold in the light of the bladder-skin lanterns, the silhouette of pig's veins stretching across her stomach.

Carmotta held out her hands and Emmabelle clasped them. They smiled at one another, neither acknowledging the underworld they stood within.

Dulenci came to Carmotta's side. 'Dear boys,' he said to the two bodyguards, back to his act, 'why all this "identify yourselves in the name of the queen" farce? Really, now.'

Neither man spoke. They both wore chainmail.

'It was like some line from a courtly play,' Dulenci told them. 'What dramatic queens you both are.'

'Point to someone in this corridor who isn't,' Carmotta said to him. She looked back at Emmabelle, hoping the candour of the joke might ignite something in her face, frame the awkwardness of this encounter with detachment and humanity. But no, Emmabelle only looked more polite and confused. The very model of a royal wife. Stupid bitch.

'Sister,' Emmabelle said. 'Might we speak one-to-one?' Her eyes seemed to beg.

'I should like that very much,' Carmotta replied. She eyed Dulenci and the two other guards. The men walked off, a little way down the corridor in the direction Carmotta had come.

'You should be resting,' Carmotta told Emmabelle. An observation she hoped might move things forward inoffensively.

'The babe,' Emmabelle said. 'I've had complications. Our own doctors could offer little. Then someone told me—'

'I quite understand,' Carmotta said. She took no joy in Emmabelle's admission.

'When God blesses you with a child you will do anything for it.' Emmabelle glanced at Carmotta. Even in this strange moment she was making the most out of her condition and her sister wives' lack. 'Anything.'

'And so you visit the man behind the door,' Carmotta said, meeting Emmabelle's superiority with sharp fact.

'The Explainer,' Emmabelle said. 'That's how he was described to me.' She squirmed. 'I'm a fool, aren't I? For going. A sinner.'

Carmotta placed a hand on her sister wife's shoulder. 'No sin to love your child.'

Emmabelle nodded. She made a show of innocent confusion. 'Why are you here, sister?'

'The month's curse,' Carmotta lied. She looked behind her, toward the men, and then back again. 'Its cruelty is such I cannot arise from my chamber for days.'

'I suppose that might be reason enough,' Emmabelle said, looking askance.

Carmotta fantasised about what a slap across that coy round face might do. 'I cannot abscond my duties, sister. I am first-queen, after all. Strength.' She realised something. 'Sister, how did you get past the doorkeeper?'

'Coin.' She sniffed.

'Of course.' For Carmotta it had been blackmail, the soundest recipe for both coercion and silence. She stepped back from Emmabelle and gestured to Dulenci. Turning back to Emmabelle she said, 'I think we are both wise enough to know this never happened.'

Emmabelle gave a sagacious expression unsuited to her seventeen-year-old face. 'Whatever do you mean?'

'Good girl.'

They kissed each other's cheeks and went their separate ways. Once she and Dulenci had gotten a little distance, Carmotta said, 'If that's Ean's babe inside her then I'm the Emperor of Chombod.'

'It only takes the one time,' Dulenci said.

'One time being the operative term,' Carmotta said. 'She'll have kindled Ean's ardour the once from novelty alone and it is that one time alone that saves her from beheading. Once novelty is dispensed with, our king's flaccid as a scarf. Trust me, that strumpet is safe harbour to another man's seed.' She half believed herself.

Dulenci shrugged. 'The season's fashion, it seems.'

Carmotta stopped and punched Dulenci's shoulder.

'Why is nothing ever serious to you?' She shook her head. 'Oh, Emmabelle's smarter than I thought, granted. Wily enough to risk the black door. But she's not my equal, despite what she might think.'

Dulenci rubbed his shoulder. 'Can I make an observation? Without fear of further pain?'

'You can try.'

'Emmabelle was bright enough to take two guards. Armoured guards. I may not have been able to beat them.'

Carmotta laughed. 'Emmabelle? Murder us? She would not dare.'

'Down here, who would ever know?' Dulenci's face was uncharacteristically stern. 'Carmotta, we men have to spend our whole lives thinking like this. And if you insist on being the queen that plays king, who rules behind her husband, so must you.'

Dulenci was right, of course.

'It's not fair,' Carmotta muttered. 'If I were permitted to carry a sword I'd be fine. Nothing would happen.'

Dulenci snorted. 'Believe me, if you carried a sword simply everything would happen.'

Old Jans the doorkeeper, before his small door of ebony, looked shamefaced. *And well he might,* Carmotta thought. Bent-backed, skin pale as porridge and with a moustache that hung down like wet tights, old Jans clutched his sack of keys.

'Maj'sty,' Jans mumbled.

'And how many times have you said that today, Jans?' Carmotta said.

Old Jans squeaked, the last defence of a broken man with a single duty. He was aged before his time and his mind was part gone.

'Jans,' Carmotta said, 'does everyone in this keep know your dirty little secret? Hmm? Give me the key, Jans.'

He did so.

'And the other key,' Carmotta said.

Jans hesitated, reached into his doublet and drew a far slenderer key, cast – if cast it were – from some manner of silver.

'Step aside.'

She opened the black door. A stone stairway beyond, descending into a blackness save for a thumbnail of silverish light below.

'Dulenci.' She held the silver key above her shoulder. 'Hold this for me.'

They descended. She could see the silver light below unnerved Dulenci, and Carmotta put her arm through his and encouraged him onward. The air became warmer, somehow thicker, as they reached the bottom of the stairs.

A glowing lunar haze lit the hollow's wide floor, a ghostly halo around a large object that, from Carmotta's view, seemed the silhouette of a rocky outcrop. This shadowed object was dwarfed by the hollow, the great vault it stood within. The hollow was no natural cavern, rather a square and stony wasteland surrounded by four granite walls that rose up into darkness to a ceiling unseen. A mighty fortress built inside out. A bulwark against the hollow's secret and ungodly contents.

Carmotta stepped daintily in her soft shoes. The hollow's floor was a collage of natural rock, cracked tiles and warped mosaic, as if the very ground shrugged off the ages' attempts to cover it. The mosaics had once depicted human faces and figures, perhaps even acting out scenes, but all were practically illegible now, worn away by time or obscured by black lichen. They passed several tripods from which hung clay discs that shone as the moon. Isle-magic, fashioned by that devil the Explainer, the man behind the door. The giant outcrop was no longer a silhouette.

The keep within the keep. There it stood. Known to almost everyone inside Becken Keep, yet unspoken of outside, naturally. Roughly barrel-like in shape, the keep-within was in truth rather modest in size, being some three storeys in height and little wider than the townhouse of a comfortable merchant. Yet it was like no other building on earth. Its construction was that of a dry-stone wall, one flat stone piled upon another, yet the stones, each black as night, were the shape of a cat's claw or a shark's tooth, smooth and curved and coming to a sharp point. The keep-within was like a barrel made of black wet thorns and to touch a single stone was death, so it was said, though no one could say the manner. Its pointed roof was a thatch of interwoven branches yet the branches seemed to have long turned to stone.

A small door, barely as high as a man's chest and made entirely of bronze, lay nestled at the keep-within's base. The door was featureless save for a fist-sized embossment at its centre for which no one knew the purpose. Above the door loomed a thin window, a hole into unguessable blackness. No face had ever been seen to peer out of it. The fear always remained that one might.

Dulenci squeaked and almost doubled over. He had blinked, of course. She really should have told him about what would happen when he did that.

She closed her own eyes. Her world turned black, as was to be expected, yet the keep-within remained, clear as if she had never closed her eyelids. As if the edifice refused her even the privacy of her own mind. The keep-within… had a way.

To speak of the keep-within *outside* of the greater keep and its grounds, to chatter of it in the streets of Becken or upon the canals of Manca – or even the very ends of the world, they said – was to guarantee your peculiar and agonising death at some point within nine nights' time. That last part may have been hearsay, however: the number nine had a malevolent reputation, for that was the number of days it had taken the Holy Pilgrim to perish upon his hook.

Yet the curse was far from tardy about its appointments. It was unavoidable and could manifest in any form. There were examples in living memory. Lady Cosmer had been bisected at the waist when a vegetable cart lost control and flew down a hillside street. Len Wolfingdon, esquire, had joked to a whore about it in Tetchford. Nine nights later a tile had been blown off a roof as he'd walked along the docks and embedded in his belly. No one found him for hours and by then he was a mewling wretch, his every extremity gnawed off by rats. As for the whore: a black leprosy was her due, of a kind hitherto unknown. Whomever she had told of the keep-within in order to receive such a death, by the seeming lack of further bizarre deaths, had sense to never speak of it. Within the vast walls of Becken Keep and its gardens, talk was safe enough. But outside it was a recipe for death, the ingredients for which were guaranteed beyond prediction.

'Visitors!' a male voice declaimed. 'Well now.'

'We're not your first today, Explainer,' Carmotta said, heading in the voice's direction. She pulled Dulenci along with her.

The Explainer – that was the name the order of natural philosophers to which he belonged called themselves – was sitting on a boulder some fifty feet from the keep-within. He was small, shorter than Carmotta by a half a head, his figure slight. He was no human. He was commrach.

The commrach lived upon an isle in the Wester Ocean, rarely visiting the Main. Tradition held that they were spawn of congress between demons and sinful women. The Explainer once told Carmotta mankind and commrach were distant relations, that all species shared ancestors, but he was full of such peculiar lies. One had to be careful with commrach.

His black hair was long, slick with grease and powdered with masonry dust. His skin – as olive as a Mancanese – was entirely smeared in some paste long dried into cracked white powder. Only he knew why. He wore nothing but a loincloth and a wide iron disc that circled his neck like a clown's ruff. His ears tapered into points and his eyes were gold-green.

'Idiot beast,' Carmotta said. 'I was a fool to trust you.'

The Explainer cocked his head like a cat. 'You've never trusted me.'

'I trusted your reputation.' She closed her eyes tightly and, to her left, the keep-within still loomed. She opened her eyes once again.

The Explainer slipped down from his boulder and stood before his visitors. Despite being shorter than them both his confidence only seemed to grow the more.

'I never wanted a "reputation",' he said. 'When you "noblewomen" of the keep come here begging for the basic medicines of civilisation, I provide them. I will see no animal suffer under absurd laws.' He half-smiled, revealing a row of dainty fangs. 'But mainly I wish to be rid of you people. Swiftly.' He gestured at the keep-within. 'If you hadn't noticed, I've the world's strangest object to observe.'

'I'm no animal,' Carmotta said. 'I am queen.'

'So I'm informed.'

'And your medicines are terrible shit. I am with child.'

'Oh.' He went to scratch his neck but the iron disc there got in the way. 'Your husband's?'

Carmotta scowled.

'Oh,' the Explainer said. He glanced in Dulenci's direction. 'I can see how that must be concerning for you both.'

She slapped his shoulder.

The commrach chuckled. 'I *told* you. I tell you all: slather is not one hundred per cent guaranteed for human women.' He waved a finger chidingly. 'That bit you girls all forget soon as you step out of here. You applied it properly, I trust?'

'Of course.'

'Deep as possible into the canal?'

She slapped his shoulder once more. 'Insolence.' She sighed. 'Yes.'

'Damned stuff,' Dulenci said to the Explainer. 'Turns my cock's end numb.'

Carmotta slapped Dulenci's shoulder.

'An axe waits above both our necks, cousin,' she told him in Mancanese.

His mirth vanished. He looked at the Explainer. 'I should run you through,' he told him.

The commrach shook his head. 'Concern for others truly is its own punishment, isn't it? Very well, come back here in two days' time and bathe beforehand. I'll remove the problem and you can never bother me again.'

'No,' Carmotta said. She stepped back and made the sign of the Pilgrim. 'No.' *Demon*, she thought, *animal.*

'It's a safe procedure,' the Explainer said. 'Though you'll need a day or so's rest.'

'I will not murder an innocent, devil-spawn.'

'You people.' The beast let out a long breath. 'Look, that thing inside you currently has no brain. It's as much a person as your kidney.'

'It has a *soul*.'

The Explainer looked at her like a cat watching a man jig. No morality these commrach. Beyond God's love.

'All right,' the Explainer said. 'How about just telling the king it's his.'

'He does not bed me.' Strange to say it out loud. Liberating. 'He has not done so for a year.'

The Explainer's eyes widened. A determined look overtook him. 'As I say, come here in two days' time and have a bath before—'

She shoved the creature and his back hit the boulder behind him. 'Devil! Child-killer!'

'All right,' the Explainer half-pleaded and half-barked. 'Run away, the pair of you. Live in an obscure village as common folk.' Carmotta saw Dulenci's face soften at the notion. 'I'm certain raising a child in that environment will be easy once you both pool your considerable life skills. What can you do? Baking? Hmm? Fletching? No?' He shook his head. 'And you say terminating the pregnancy is the immoral choice…'

'Help us, sir,' Dulenci tried.

'How about I do not?' the Explainer replied. 'How about you leave me to my work and never bother me again? And send Jans in on your way out. He's late.'

'You're as doomed as both of us, beast,' Carmotta told him. 'I'll tell the king of your medicines and false promises.'

'And every other noblewoman will deny it,' he said. 'The quality of their lives will drop immeasurably if my skills vanish. And I am suddenly struck with an instinct you are not popular with any of them already.'

He had the right of it, mostly. Time to play the last hand.

'Dulenci my dear.' She smiled at the Explainer and held her palm out flat.

Dulenci took the silver key from his jacket and placed it on her palm.

'You should not have that,' the Explainer said, his expression delightfully concerned. 'Jans has that.' He made to grab the key but Carmotta gripped it and placed it behind her back.

'How long do you have, I wonder?' Carmotta said. 'An hour? A half?'

'I'll tell the king,' he insisted.

'Like you have the time.'

The Explainer chewed his lip and stroked the iron disc about his neck.

The decapitator disc was proof to the Crown of the Explainer's good intentions and he had been wearing the device since he first sneaked into the keep. Every nine hours the clockwork required tightening or the blade therein would shear head from shoulders in a blink. The key for this task he happily offered to his dumbfounded hosts. He wished only to study the keep-within, he had told them, and, should he ever commit evil or run away, his life would be forfeit. For the disc could not be removed.

Ean's father had accepted his proposition, being more afraid of the keep-within than any commrach conspiracy. Their technology, after all, far surpassed that of the mainland. If any hope of mitigating the keep-within's curse existed in this world it lay with the commrach. How the Explainer had heard of the keep-within's existence in the first place was anyone's guess.

'Look,' the Explainer said. 'Let's start again, eh? How can I help?' He nodded. 'Your Majesty.'

'High time you addressed me correctly,' Carmotta said, beaming. 'These are the earliest days, there is still yet time. I need the king to lie with me. I want his desire. Do you understand?'

The Explainer squinted. 'You want me to… arouse him?'

'For a learned man,' Dulenci said, 'you're as thick as a post-banquet turd. She means your aphrodisiac. Your love drug.'

The Explainer let out a half-scared hoot. 'That doesn't exist. Please, Your Majesty, just give me the key.'

'Do not lie to me,' Carmotta said. 'The commrach lust-powder is infamous. We're not wholly ignorant of your demonic isle's ways, Explainer. Now bring your damned powder.'

'I…' the Explainer looked a fearful child, a scolded housecat. 'I honestly have no idea what the fuck you two are talking about.'

For a moment she could almost believe him. He played an excellent bluff. But she could play better.

'Very well,' she said. She turned around. 'Rest in peace, vile pixie.'

'Wait! Wait!' he said. 'I was lying!'

Carmotta stopped. The shadow of the keep-within lay at her feet. She turned to face the Explainer once more. 'Well?'

'Wait there,' he said. 'It's in my tent. Just, just wait there Your Majesty.' He belted off into the darkness. 'Wait there.'

'It's true about you queens,' Dulenci said. 'You're the most dangerous piece on the board.'

Carmotta smiled. 'Yet our survival depends upon the king.'

8

Fwych

It were late morning and every demon howled. A whole night she had been kept caged beneath a cloudless sky, naked but for a blanket. She shivered, though she had been colder in her life. The demons had kept silent at night. She lay beneath her blanket feeling the itch in her mouth, the humiliating ache of her stolen tongue. And with what powers remained, she could sense the hum beneath the ground, ancient and wrong. This was a land of evil within a land of evil, above and below. A cage-land where a hundred devils wept.

Fwych were opposite the hole for her wastings, her back to the limestone wall. She clutched the wool blanket over herself, yet kept wise enough to spare a little of it for her back and arse. The body betrayed heat into the ground it did.

Gethwen, he had never learned that. Had near died one winter when the two of them were about their curing wanders. What a joke that had been, ill folk seeing a mountain mother with a lad ill as they.

Demons hollered in their cages, screeched and tittered. Fwych had never known the like, she, a woman who had eaten the cap-of-the-way in a deep cave as a girl, who had consorted with the spirits of the air and felt the unseeable cavorting in the blackness. She had clambered from that cave half-broken, scratched and mewling as they had spoken dark, nasty things to her, the unseeable, told her her worst fears. But they had never howled like *this*.

I'm broken, she told herself. *I'm not beaten.*

She had found a sliver of pig bone in the slop her captors gave her. Sharp, it were. Would slide into a belly like a needle into tallow. Her captors' bellies were soft. Idle men these. Soon enough their idleness would give her an opportunity. Until then, she kept her little bone in a hollow in the limestone wall.

Her cage were five paces long, five paces wide. Beyond it were a path where the flatlanders passed, either her keepers with their prodding sticks or another bunch Fwych had come to call the gawkers. The women gawkers wore tents from their hips, wide and patterned, and scarves and hats that could never protect in a storm. The men gawkers wore stockings and tunics. Whenever the gawkers came Fwych's keepers would use their sticks to make her stand, make her drop her blanket. Fwych had made no sense of it at first. She had never been much to look at even in her flower, let alone now her flesh were sagging leather. But it were the mountain tattoos they wanted to see, that and the bronze rings in her face and dugs and quim. She let them see. No shame to a body. The shame were in gawking.

Were difference the gawkers wanted. She'd understood that after the first visit, when three keepers had entered the cage to her left and propped up the man in there so that a woman with piled hair might see. The man had skin black as wet bark and hair as wool. Fwych had afeared him at first. But he were dying, Fwych could tell even if the keepers could not, and Fwych felt only pity then. Left to his own, he merely shook, moaned some song of his people's hearth. This morning she had found him still as stone.

She had asked Father Mountain to light the man's way home. She had wept then. The first since she had lost her tongue.

Red Marie. Red Marie. Fwych could recall much of that night now.

'*You're nothing now,*' Red Marie had said as Fwych had stared at her own bloody tongue upon the ale-soaked floor. Red Marie's voice had changed once everyone else had died. Fwych hadn't noticed so much at the time but were sure of it now. The voice were no longer everywhere and nowhere. It had come from the bar.

'*You've relished your power over people, haven't you?*' Red Marie had said. '*Thought yourself the wise matriarch. But really you loved the thrill of controlling others. You're despicable.*'

Fwych had looked up from her tongue toward the voice. A slight figure leaning against the bar, head heavy with long braided hair. No; the hair was *rope,* scarlet and frayed. The figure wore a strange cloak covered with flatlander things: crushed tankards, snapped roof tiles, coins. Fwych could not see the face. Too much shadow, too much rope.

She could see a hand, though. Red Marie's hand were a hooked blade, a crescent of silvered iron. The monster was using the back of it to stroke a ginger cat that had climbed up on the bar.

'*Hello,*' Red Marie told that cat, loud enough so Fwych might hear. '*We're so so clever you and I, aren't we? Forever playing with our mice.*' She tittered. '*We are so very alike.*' She slammed the hook's point into the cat's head. '*I can't allow that.*

'*I let your boy escape, you know,*' Red Marie said. '*My lieges would rather have your black crown this very night but… well, fuck them.*' Red Marie tittered, like a child who had said something naughty. '*I want my fun. You told him to head for the city. Fool. That's my very hunting ground.*'

Fwych had trouble with the rest. She could not face the memory, not yet. But she had the facts, the meat. Whatever she were, the monster Marie had been arrogant enough to spill all that. She were after the boy. She were after the crown. Red Marie were a spirit, a servant of the wrongness in this land. Her 'lieges' must have been her name for that wrongness. And Selly, the pennyblade, she had been afeared at Red Marie's name, like a terrified child. Red Marie had preyed in this land for some time, it seemed. She were known.

Fwych tightened the blanket about herself. In the large cage on the other side of the path the little hairy man with a pink arse ran back and forth on all fours. He were mad or part demon and thought nothing o' slinging his shit about and milking his manhood openly. Fwych had no time for that scoundrel. She would escape soon.

A keeper were coming. The fat one with the shaking left leg. Another voice too, a man's. A lone gawker, perhaps. Maybe this were the moment.

She fingered the hollow in the wall and gripped the bone sliver. They would see it in her hand if they made her stand to be gawped at. Fwych popped the sliver into her mouth.

'She's a hardy one,' the fat keeper said. 'Lost her tongue and has a shoulder wound but still she keeps going.' A pause. 'Sorry, should I call you, er, sir? Lord?'

'You may call me Dulenci,' a man's voice said, 'but then I would have to beat you. So best call me lord, eh?'

'Yes, my lord.'

A young man, hair black and flesh tanned, his face beardless as a boy's. His clothes were bright as a valley of wildflowers and he'd a sword upon his belt.

'Has she been here long?' the young man said.

'One night,' the fat keeper replied. 'She's a genuine ban-hag, my lord. Captured in the Spine Mountains.'

Her keepers kept saying that to the visitors. As if these fools could capture anything in the creeks and crags o' home. She wondered if they had come up with the lie or if that dirty man in the crooked hat, Smones, had.

'Make her stand.'

She tossed her blanket to one side and stood up. The day wasn't as cold as all that.

The young man gazed at her naked body. 'Such artistry in their tattoos. Another set of circumstances, another life, the artist who daubed them might well have painted cathedrals.'

'I don't think so, my lord,' the fat keeper said. 'Spinefolk are natural savages.'

'We appear to have philosophical differences,' the young man said. He gawked at Fwych once more, then said, 'Fetch up some manacles. I shall take her.'

Fwych hid her smile. The bone sliver sat ready in the empty seat of her tongue. The young man were the danger – she could feel it when she reached her mind out, he were like a wildcat at rest – and so she'd drive the sliver into his neck. Then she'd take his blades and finish the keeper too.

'My lord,' the keeper said, 'she is not for sale.'

'Another philosophical difference,' the young man told him. 'You think I am paying. We're having quite the debate, my man.'

After she killed them? What then? A race through a land of cages, of howling hooting demons. But there would be no other opportunity.

'Lord, this savage is property of Becken Keep,' the fat man said.

'And who keeps the keep?'

The fat man thought about that. 'Our king?'

'And who keeps our king?' When the keeper had no reply the young man continued, 'Why, his wife the queen. The first-queen, no less. And she wishes to display this piece of royal property within her private chambers.'

'You'll need a cage,' the fat man said after a moment.

'We have one.' The tanned youth waved at the cage before him. 'Prettier than this.'

Fwych made no move when the fat man and his fellow keepers opened the cage. Why try anything here when a far better opportunity lay ahead? The soft chambers of a softer lady. A fine hostage, that.

She kept the sliver of bone in her mouth. Ready.

9

Carmotta

'Have yourself a drink,' Ean said, sipping the wine she had poured for him.

'I'm fine.' And she was. She had filled the decanter with the Explainer's aphrodisiac.

Her husband smiled. The strength of Ean lay in his repose. He could not help but look a king; men would have gathered around his presence had he been a serf. She loved him. She loved Dulenci too, for different reasons. And why not? It was the world's fault it could not value a woman with two hearts to give.

'Sit,' he said, and he nodded at the chair where the bastard Larksdale had sat. They had surprised each other, she on her way in to the solus chamber, Larksdale on his way out. They had both feigned cordiality before Ean.

Carmotta removed her crown, placed it upon the table and sat in his lap. He tensed in surprise, then relaxed. 'My love,' she whispered. She brushed fingers through his golden locks.

'Be present at court tonight,' he said, studying her lips. 'Osrin and Pym mean to bring a prisoner before me.'

Carmotta tensed. 'Who?'

'Some clipper,' he said.

'Those knaves who cut the edges of coin? That's beneath your attention.'

He drew a breath. 'I cannot conceive Osrin's reasoning.'

'Then *do* something, Ean,' she said. 'Take this prisoner from them before they bring him. We're the Crown.' *Dulenci would,* she thought. Carmotta would, and more besides.

'We cannot move too carelessly,' he said. 'The armies Osrin's faction possesses, I cannot lose that support. We must keep in their favour.'

'Ean.'

'You would not understand,' he said.

'So it is better not to move at all?' She hated that about him, his inertia, almost as much as she loved his self-assurance, though likely they had the same root. She had thought she would have reconciled the two in her mind by now. But no.

Carmotta sheathed her frustration. She was losing sight of her undertaking here.

'I apologise.' She took the cup from the table and placed it in his hand once more. 'You are right, of course.'

Ean downed the last of his wine, winced at its surprisingly bitter taste. 'You mean so much to me, Car. I do not say that enough.'

'Shh.' She kissed him. Once, once more, and then slid her tongue's point into his mouth. His lips parted to let her in. The taste of him, the scent of his skin. She had almost forgotten.

He pulled his head back from her. 'Not here.'

She giggled and stroked his jawline. 'Why not here? Why not, say, upon that very table.'

'It's not appropriate.'

'Looks sturdy enough to me.'

He smiled at that.

She stood up, drifted her index finger down his chest. A soft descent before him, a blown kiss as she came to her knees. His belt and hose were easy enough to remove: he lifted his haunches to aid the process.

Ean's member was limp, curled up against his thigh like some newborn pup.

So here is my work, she thought. Perhaps the powder in his belly had to be stirred to truly perform.

She grinned, lurched forward and, cradling the limpness between thumb and forefinger, kissed the tip of his cock. She had missed that taste also. She slid her lips over the soft crown, relishing the challenge. Her free hand caressed his inner thigh, then cradled the blonde nest of his balls. She moaned, a performance to let him know she was enjoying herself, that he was permitted too.

'Please,' he said and she moaned more, moaning to a hum. 'Please stop.' He extracted himself from her mouth and pulled up his hose.

Fuck. She clambered on to her feet and stropped around the table.

'Why?' It just came out. 'What's so wrong with me, Ean?'

'I'm weighed with matters.' He stared at her with those magnificent blue eyes. 'I love you, Carmotta.'

She slapped the table. 'Show, don't tell.' She had been a fool to trust the Explainer and his potions. A fool. 'Will these "matters" weigh so heavy tomorrow evening, I wonder? With your little party?' She could still taste him on her lips, the salt and musk. 'With whatever whore our dear Larksdale brings?'

He leapt to his feet and his hose dropped, the royal cock hanging there like a partridge on a chimney hook.

He froze. Then he laughed, a little bitterly. She had to laugh too.

Ean pulled his hose up, started to buckle himself. 'You will attend, won't you? Today, I mean, when the prisoner is brought before the Crown? Please.'

'I'm Queen Of The Brintland,' she said. 'Where else would I fucking be?'

She left the solus chamber before he might reply.

10

Larksdale

'I was frightened without you, sir,' Gethwen said as they traversed the eighth floor of the south-west tower of the keep – a wide tower. The eighth floor always smelled of soup and a little of dried faeces. The whole tower felt dried up.

'I'd have thought you more rugged this high up,' Larksdale said, 'my lad of the mountains.'

'In the mountains you can see a long way.' Gethwen slipped his arm through Larksdale's and Larksdale let him. 'They had me wait for you by a stone face. Ugly it were.'

'Your soul is too beautiful for this keep,' Larksdale said. 'One day I shall take you away somewhere full of beauty. Southern Manca, mayhap. The most beautiful realm come summer.'

Gethwen cradled his bag and leaned his head against Larksdale's shoulder. An action that made ol' Harry Larksdale feel a better, braver man. He had decided: he would tell the king that Cabbot's wife – whatever her name was – was sadly not available. Out of the city, yes. Or, better yet, dead. The king's appetite would drift soon enough; his loins were as the clouds. *She is a member of the Wreath Theatre,* he told himself. *And damn it, Harry, you have a duty of care.*

'I want you to take me to Fleawater, sir,' Gethwen said.

'That's, er, quite a comedown from Southern Manca, Gethwen.' Fleawater was two rivers along from Tetchford, a different neighbourhood where the Flume disgorged itself into Becken Bay. Larksdale knew only Becken Keep and his own Tetchford Eve. Fleawater was famously dreadful though, a slum, its residents terrorised by vile landlords like Cabbot.

'I need to meet my own kind there,' Gethwen said, squeezing Larksdale's arm with urgency. '*Really* need, sir. But I need a brave man, a wise and learned man like you, to accompany me.'

Larksdale stopped. He looked deep into Gethwen's anxious eyes. 'Why?'

Gethwen looked down. 'I'm sorry, sir. I suppose my worries can wait a night or so.'

He was hiding something. It only made him more delectable.

'Here we are,' Larksdale said, pointing at the thin cracked door to their left. He grinned at Gethwen. 'Best behaviour, if you please.'

Larksdale stepped over to the door. 'She has a special knock,' he explained. He knocked three times. Then once. Then three times once more.

Movement could be heard behind the door, as if someone were looking for something, then a dinging upon metal: once, thrice and four. Larksdale replied with a four and a two. A silence followed, then a single ding.

'We're good to go,' he told Gethwen. He twisted the iron ring and entered.

The room, L-shaped and dusty, was barely illuminated by two lamps set against bronze wall plates. Every object, from furniture to decoration, was covered with white blankets. Every object, that was, save Larksdale's mother and the chair she sat upon.

'Good afternoon, Mater.'

'Hello, Harry.' His mother smiled, the bronze gong and beater for her secret knocking codes in hand. She eyed Gethwen. 'Who's this? Can we trust him?'

'With our very souls, Mother.'

'Hello, Lady Larksdale,' Gethwen said. 'Your son's helping me find my way in the city.'

'Ooh, that's nice,' she said. She looked at Larksdale. 'I like this one. He's bound to our cause, yes?'

'If you like,' Larksdale said.

His mother shifted in her chair. 'Harrance Larksdale, there's no "if you like" about it. You lack gumption, that's your problem.' She looked at Gethwen once more, pointed at her son and said, 'No gumption.' She looked at Larksdale again. 'You're thirty now.'

'Twenty-nine, Mother.'

'Ooh…' She looked as disappointed as ever. 'I had my heart set on you being king by twenty-four.'

'I know,' Larksdale said.

'It's like you don't want to seize the throne.'

'I simply haven't the time, Mother. We've been over this.'

She sighed.

'Excuse me,' Gethwen said. 'Is this… is this plotting we're doing right now?'

'Chance would be a fine thing,' Larksdale's mother said, eyeing her son.

'Right,' Gethwen said. 'Maybe I should… close the door? Or something?'

'There is a draught,' Larksdale agreed.

Gethwen closed the door behind him.

'You're in the circle now,' she told him. She smiled and winked.

The greatest beauty in Lerchstoft, she had been. Had caught the old king's eye decades past. Now Larksdale's mother was as dusty as anything in this little room whose only notable feature was its adjacency to power. This room and Becken Keep entire had aged her well beyond her fifty years. *Perhaps,* Larksdale thought guiltily, *she should put a blanket over herself like everything else in here, keep herself fresh for whatever important visit it is she expects.*

'Still feel a draught.' He leaned down and kissed her cheek.

She patted his chin. 'You've royal blood, Harry. Can't say I didn't give you head start enough in life.'

He stood upright. 'I've a spare room at the houseboat, you know—'

She cut him off, as always. 'I've been busy.' She jutted a thumb behind her, toward a gloomy corner of the room obscured by a covered statue. 'Look over there.'

Larksdale stepped over. The draught was stronger there, likely due to the big hole halfway up the wall. The hole was square, a yard in height and width, and led off into untold darkness. Just below the hole, leaning against the wall, sat a framed painting of the Battle of Duxby. Larksdale recalled it hanging upon the wall on previous visits, exactly in the spot where the hole – or more accurately tunnel – now was.

'Took me ages to prise that painting off the wall,' his mother said.

'You're meant to just look at it, Mother,' Larksdale replied. He turned around only to find she was already approaching. 'This is too-too much. How am I to explain this to your servants?'

'My maid's loyal enough, son,' she said. 'Though sadly claustrophobic, it turns out.'

'She's not lodged in there, is she?' Larksdale asked.

'Focus, Harry.' She prodded his chest. 'This hole, do you see? It's going *inwards,* toward the centre of the keep.'

'Then it probably leads to...' Larksdale stopped himself. He mouthed *you know* to his mother and secretly thumbed toward Gethwen so as to make it clear he was ignorant of the keep-within-the-keep and its most unpleasant curse. 'Best covered over and forgotten about.'

'You daft pillock,' his mother said. She looked at Gethwen. 'My son's a pillock.'

'He's very brave,' Gethwen said.

'Is that what he told you?' She looked back at Larksdale again. 'We're too high up here for it to go—' She stopped herself. '—down below. The centre of the floor we're on is all grand stairs to the *royal chambers*. So this *has* to go up there.' She laughed. It was good to see her so happy.

'Have you ever considered taking up weaving?' Larksdale said. 'Painting, perhaps…'

'Grow a spine, dear,' she said. 'Look, this has always been a room for concubines and bastard-mothers; it would have been when this was built. Why make a tunnel between king's chambers and here? Hmm? A king can have a concubine sent up or he can visit her; either way it's the stairs. But a tunnel to the queen's chambers from here?' She laughed again. 'That's for some unspeakable passion.' She nodded. 'Or regicide.'

Time to dissuade her, if such were possible. 'What if it leads to Queen Violee?' Second-Queen Violee was confined to her chambers on account of believing herself a hedgehog. 'You could get fleas.'

'Look, Harry, there's three possibilities at the end of that tunnel. One: it leads to the second-queen's chambers and you turn around and give it up as a bad job. Two: it leads to the third-queen's chambers, you know, the one up the duff, then Ginger here—' She waved at Gethwen. '—can skulk in and pour a jug of baby-knacker in her mouth while she sleeps. I know a man. Well, I say "man"…'

'I see,' Larksdale said. 'And First-Queen Carmotta?'

'Well that's the *best* result,' his mother said. 'You get up there and seed her loam. She's always liked you, Harry.'

'She most certainly does not.'

'She will when you tell her you built an entire tunnel just to ravish her,' she said. 'She loves a man with gumption. Plus, she's Mancanese, they invented tunnels. She'll understand.'

'You mean sewers,' Larksdale said, dazzled by this onslaught of weird piffle. 'The Mancanese invented sewers.'

'Be sure to tell her that,' his mother said. 'It'll impress her. Strike tomorrow at noon. She goes to her chambers then and – listen now – her cousin, that flashy bum-boy with the sword, goes off to town until third hour or more. She'll be alone.'

Now this was something. 'Dulenci? Where is it he visits?' *The fool without his queen...*

'Who cares?' his mother said. 'You'll be too busy seducing the plump bitch. I'll have me a grandson on the throne and you can get back to your playhouse, job done.' She looked suddenly sad. 'I'd love a grandson.'

Larksdale sighed. He placed a palm on his mother's shoulder. 'This has gone far enough. I love you dearly, Mater, but tomorrow I'm going to have that spider-hole bricked up and you found new quarters.'

'You wouldn't dare.'

Larksdale did not reply. He nodded to Gethwen and the two of them, with some bother, lifted the painting and reaffixed it. The painting, it transpired, had a backing of solid wood that one had to lodge into the hole like a cork.

He turned and headed for the door. 'Good day, Mother. I'll have a man sent tomorrow.'

'You've the blood of Neyes in you, Harry. The Brintland could be *yours*.'

'Mother, I'm a bastard.'

'There's another bastard feels he's a right.'

Larksdale stopped. 'What bastard?'

'Osrin,' she said. She looked at Gethwen. 'Now there's a lad with gumption coming out his ears. Harry could learn a thing or three from Osrin, I tell you.'

'He's spoken to you?' Larksdale said.

'Of course not. I heard from his mother. I'm not the only one on this floor you know.'

'I know,' Larksdale replied. 'What did she say?'

'Ooh,' his mother said, pained. 'She was rubbing it in. Said he and his friends were going to visit the king and stab him while he held court. They'll hold the chamber and wait until the city guard surround Becken Keep. Him and his pals have paid 'em off, so she reckons.'

'What?'

'Don't fret, Harry,' she said. 'It'll fail. I told her as much and she did *not* like that.' She chuckled. 'I told her they'll be killed by the *palace* guard. Which they will. No brains, that Osrin lad. Not like you, sweet.'

'Mother, court's already being held! He's to meet the king!'

'Is it? No one tells me these things any more.'

The king in mortal danger. Carmotta too.

'Gethwen, we must run.'

11

Carmotta

Carmotta was sitting upon her ebony and velvet throne, one step lower than Ean's ivory and gold. There were seven thrones in all, set upon a wooden dais that rose like a ziggurat of the ancient Near West, the king's atop the summit.

Courtiers were funnelling in, their finery glinting beneath the hundred lamps that hung from the painted ceiling. Ean had been foolish to hold court in the secondary throne room. One of the lesser throne rooms would not have drawn such a crowd.

'They wear their best and latest,' she muttered to Ean.

'As well they should.' He said no more. He looked magnificent, commanding yet at ease. He wore his tallest crown, contrasting it with a simple tunic in the old style. Its silk caught each muscle in his torso. It was all Carmotta could do not to look.

The many courtiers parted to either side of the throne room. As if choosing her moment perfectly, Third-Queen Emmabelle entered the room, helped along by her equally blonde and vapid handmaids, all of whom made much of her condition. Carmotta was surprised. The bitch never came to these more dour, practical sorts of things.

Carmotta arose and extended her arms in sisterly greeting. She nodded to one of the stewards to help Emmabelle to her throne. Emmabelle, both arms supported, made her way up the dais. For the briefest moment she eyed the queen's throne on the same level as Carmotta, directly next to Ean. Poor mad Violee's throne. Emmabelle thought better of it, taking her actual throne, which was directly beside – and just below – Carmotta's.

'My love,' Ean said to Emmabelle, leaning a little past Carmotta to say it.

'My love,' Emmabelle repeated.

Carmotta refused to look at her dripping smile. Instead, she gazed at the line of stained-glass windows to her left, which were black as syrup against the winter night outside.

As the high steward reeled off the king's titles, Carmotta studied the nobles on all sides. What did these lords and ladies know of Osrin's intent? How many were as clueless as herself? She was glad for the presence of the palace guard in here, some twelve in all. Many of the male courtiers wore scabbards at their waist, as was their right in any throne room, but Carmotta had to wonder how many scabbards contained an actual blade and not just a false hilt? Old Tibald Slyke, Master of Arts and Revels, had both a jewelled sword and matching dagger, while big Willem Cutbill wore no weapon at all. As captain general of the city watch he must have felt usurped by Osrin and his fellow nobles seizing a prisoner. Or had he helped them? Was he their thing?

Paranoid, of course. But this winter was becoming a distrustful season. 'Permit them approach,' Ean told the high steward.

Carmotta snapped to her senses. Men were crossing through the throne room's gilt threshold, a hooded man in manacles at their centre.

Osrin led them, his beard clipped and oiled and a sword either side of his serpentine figure. Then came Lords Pym, Quendle and Bergenhaim, each armed and resplendent. The manacled man was just as much part of this theatre: someone had needlessly placed a hessian bag over his head. He was soon compelled to his knees before the dais.

'Your Majesty,' Osrin announced, bowing gently. 'Your Majesties.' He bowed to Carmotta and Emmabelle. His beard had been styled in such a way as to accentuate the V that ran from cheekbones to chin, his old duelling scars given to him upon that sorcerous isle. Carmotta liked it not. It was a beard to snare the gullible and dazzle the inane. 'I bring most terrible news. There exists a conspiracy against the Brintland entire and, by extension, against His Majesty himself.'

Muttering among the court. Ean raised a hand for silence then stroked his own beard in concentration. *My husband can put on a performance too, Osrin,* she thought. *One more practised.*

'Dear brother,' Ean said. 'Who is this man you bring before us?'

Osrin smiled and the scarred V warped.

Shouting came from beyond the throne room. Everyone turned to look.

Two palace guards raced in. Between them, urging them on with his new black cane, came Sir Harry Larksdale.

'Arrest those men!' he shouted. He pointed at Osrin and his gang. 'They would kill our king!'

The throne room burst into shouts. Emmabelle shrieked and Ean was up on his feet, gesturing to his guards. The guards surrounded Osrin's group and levelled their halberds. The group put their hands in the air. Their prisoner remained kneeling, the bag on his head wobbling as his head darted left and right.

'And Cutbill!' Larksdale barked, pointing a gloved finger. 'They've paid off the city guard! Our keep's surrounded!'

Emmabelle got up from her throne and trotted down the dais far faster than she'd ascended it. One of the ushers had opened a side door and was beckoning her on. The steward beckoned at Carmotta too but she ignored him.

A young guard had his halberd pointed at Cutbill's throat. The big bull was giving him a look that said, *Put that thing down before you hurt yourself.* Regardless, courtiers were stepping back from Cutbill as if he were suddenly a beggar.

'Silence!' Ean shouted. The throne room hushed. 'Sir Osrin, is this true?'

Osrin laughed bitterly. 'Your Majesty, Larksdale's lost his mind.'

'Take their weapons,' Ean ordered two of the guards.

The guards began doing so.

'You'll find them all fakes,' Osrin said.

One of the two guards held Osrin's scabbard upside down. He pulled on the hilt and got nowhere with it.

'Replicas,' Osrin said. 'As per throne room custom.'

'You're welcome to check mine,' Cutbill said, gesturing at his complete lack of weaponry.

Even at this distance Carmotta could see Larksdale gulp. He shook his cane at a man stood beside the hooded prisoner, some squire holding a heavy-looking sack. 'Check him, check the bag!'

Frightened, the squire opened the bag and poured. Coins fell, sparkling gold and silver beneath the lamplight, bouncing and rolling between courtiers' feet.

'Sire,' Osrin said, 'our prisoner is a clipper, arrested on Hollowlyve Road. These are the coins he has clipped and cheapened.'

Coins always made Carmotta shiver. Even when she gave to the poor she had someone else perform the act. She had held a bag of coins only once, back when she was seventeen and waiting at the port of Sant Ribot. That most dreadful of summer days.

'The other bag, then,' Larksdale said.

'The one on that man's head?' Carmotta asked. 'What's his weapon under there? Halitosis?' Someone laughed and the tension ebbed from the room.

'Please,' Larksdale implored Ean.

A guard reached for the bag and everyone drew breath. Once removed, everyone breathed out with disappointment. The prisoner was some bald, broken-nosed fellow no one had ever seen before. He blinked in the lamplight, his face a mass of contusions.

'Ah,' Larksdale said.

'Can I ask a question, Larksdale?' Cutbill said, eyeing the speartip before his belly. 'If my city guard are surrounding the keep shouldn't I be outside leading them?'

'Yes,' Larksdale said, deflated. 'That was occurring to me too. Thank you.' He looked at Ean. 'I beg your forgiveness, Your Majesty.'

Ean, still standing, nodded. 'You meant well, Larksdale. But, please, save these performances for your plays.'

Everyone broke into laughter. A shared relief.

Larksdale smiled and bowed. 'Sir Osrin, Pym, Quendle, Bergenhaim: my profound apologies. You are true sons of the Brintland. I was misinformed.' He looked around the room. 'Apologies to you all. I shall leave you.'

Carmotta had to hide her grin. This was delicious as a honeyed peach. Larksdale, his posture slouched, made his way for the exit. Who had set him up for this? Dulenci perhaps? But Dulenci was waiting just outside, preferring to hold on to his sword.

'Wait,' Tibald Slyke said. 'Who was it misinformed you?'

Larksdale kept walking.

Carmotta rose. 'Answer him.'

Larksdale stopped and straightened up. He turned to face the court.

'A poor source,' Larksdale said. 'Yet time was of the essence.'

Slyke rested his white-gloved hands upon his own cane. 'Who was it misinformed you?' He was relishing this. He famously disliked Larksdale. His lone redeeming feature, as far as Carmotta was concerned.

Larksdale stared at Slyke then looked up at the dais. Carmotta nodded. Ean nodded.

'My mother,' Larksdale admitted.

'Your mother?' Slyke said incredulously. 'The woman holed up in her cupboard all day?'

Even the king chuckled at that. Others fair hooted.

'Time was of the essence,' Larksdale told the room.

'Who was it informed her?' Osrin said. 'A cobweb?' More laughter.

'Your own mother, apparently,' Larksdale said. 'But I suppose mine must have misunderstood.'

'I'll bet,' Osrin replied. 'Mother's been dead these past eight years.'

Startled laughter followed. Harry Larksdale's jaw dropped. He turned and left.

How delightful.

'And I thought the streets were full of madmen,' Slyke said.

'Guards,' Ean said, 'return to your posts.' He looked down at Osrin. 'Apologies, Osrin. Perhaps a brief recess?'

'Unlike mummy's little angel,' Osrin said, 'we would not waste your precious time.'

Ean sat down. 'Proceed,' he said. 'Let us all pray there are no more distractions.'

'Thank you, Your Majesty.' Osrin bowed. 'As I said, this man was caught by my men in an inn upon Hollowlyve Road with his bag of clipped coins, that is to say, ladies and gentlemen, coins lightened at their edges by skilled yet malicious hands.'

'Osrin,' Ean said, 'we do not see how such lowly crime is worthy of this court's attention.'

'Your Majesty, not only was their clipped coin among this number.' Osrin waved a hand at the money upon the floor. 'The bag contains forged coinage of inferior substance. When put to the question, he told us of a false mint, one neither we nor the city's guard can bring to justice.'

'How so?' Ean said.

'The forgers are nowhere in the realm. They are past the border, over the Spine Mountains and in the lands of our old enemy. These false, lead-tainted coins were minted in Hoxham city, at their Crown's command.' Osrin knelt and picked up a single coin. He stood up once more and said to the room entire, 'This is a weapon, friends. It cuts our kingdom every time it is spent. Countless cuts, draining our blood. Our captive insists there are a hundred or more men just like him, taking forged and clipped coin from Hoxham into Becken and exchanging it for our own true coins. You see before you a callow but fiendish attempt to rot our economy. Make no mistake—' He held the bad coin aloft. '—I hold in my hand an act of war!'

Talk filled the throne room. The men, lords and knights, talking to one another, hard-jawed and cold of eye. The women looked to one another, to Carmotta, realising their place was no longer here.

Well, damn that.

'My husband,' Carmotta said. 'We cannot have war. Not for this.'

Ean was as a statue, grim and implacable, lower lip perching upon index finger, elbows resting upon the arms of his ivory throne. He seemed a general surveying a battle fought in a valley below, his emotions caged in the cellar of his skull. Appraising only the facts.

'Please,' Carmotta tried, but already she knew she had no power.

Big Willem Cutbill was trying to get Osrin's attention, but the smug bastard was too busy with his coin held high, pivoting on the spot so that all might see his pose, his kingly expression. A war-king, like Ean's father. Like his own father.

Cutbill stood between the dais and the group. He was saying something.

'A city guard matter. This man is ours.'

Osrin seemed not to hear. *War,* people were saying, the word repeating, rising. Pym, Osrin's second, his pate shining through his thin hair beneath the lamps, looked Cutbill in the eye.

'You were too slow,' Pym told him.

'You broke him, Pym,' Cutbill said, pointing at the prisoner. 'He'd confess anything. You'd wager your men's lives on that alone?' He shook his head. 'Course you would. Why ask?'

A bright one, Cutbill, despite his ill-breeding. A glover's son. He had a spy at Larksdale's theatre, Carmotta had learned, though the streets of the city were quite beneath her.

Carmotta turned to Ean again. 'My love,' she said, trying to be heard over the increasing clamour of voices, 'this prisoner needs to be questioned by you. Alone.' And Cutbill. The sanest man in this room, rough boor though he was.

Ean blinked. He had heard. He rose slowly.

'Silence!' he bellowed. Carmotta felt the word rumble through the arms of her throne. The court fell quiet. 'If this prisoner speaks true,' Ean said, 'then the Crown has no option but to deem this conspiracy an act of war.'

The throne room murmured.

'Winter is no time for battle,' he continued. 'We need not tell the old warriors in this hall that. Nor the young and eager.' He nodded to Osrin. This brought kindly laughter and Osrin seemed happy enough to receive it. 'We must never rush to raise the banner.'

The court nodded sagaciously, save for Cutbill, still close to the dais. He was squinting at Ean.

'We thank you, good sirs,' Ean said to Osrin's gang, 'for bringing this man to our attention. We shall take him into the keep's care and, with Sir Willem's aid, shall put him to the question.'

A change had come across the faces of those at the front of the crowd. They too were squinting like Cutbill. Carmotta saw one open-mouthed lady make the sign of the Pilgrim against her chest.

'But if Hoxham's treachery be true our realm shall not cower,' Ean said, lifting his arms as if to embrace all there. 'For we are the Brintland, seat of Neyes the Conqueror, home of a fearlessness tempered by nobility and old-fashioned fair play. For when the humble yeoman of old Mother Brint puts down his tools and raises his sword, let all the world beware!'

No one cheered. Everyone just stared at him. Ean kept his arms aloft, his face proud, but his eyes glanced hither and thither.

Carmotta leaned forward and turned her head to her king and husband. Two dark stains were upon his tunic, growing. Running down.

'The king!' someone shouted. 'The king is lactating!'

12

Larksdale

'Damn,' Larksdale muttered, striding through the gardens and colonnades in the cold starry night. 'Damn.'

'Slow, sir,' Gethwen said. 'Please, sir.'

'Keep up.'

Damned Carmotta. And Slyke, that snake in wide and ridiculous hat. Why did he have to wind Larksdale back in, ask for the cause of his false alarum? Things had been salvageable till then.

He was nearly at the outer walls, where the path became a wide square of granite laced with bronze lines and curves older than the keep, or so some claimed. It felt difficult to breathe, like he wouldn't be able to take a deep gulp until he was out past the outer walls.

But really it was his mother. He wasn't angry at the woman herself, rather at himself for not noticing her rot. He'd thought her merely obsessed, over-focused. She always had been so disposed. But now she was talking to dead women, having actual rivalries with them. She was losing her mind and he had not seen that, had done nothing but left her in her frigid chambers. He could cry. He…

'Sir, slow down.'

He stopped. Gethwen near-walked into him and Larksdale grabbed the lad's wrist and dragged him along at his prior pace.

'Come along,' Larksdale said.

'Sir.'

'A man should not have to drag his page around.'

'But I'm not—'

Larksdale was yanked off his feet, as if Gethwen's arm was the tail of a bolting bull. He hit the stones on his side, the air blown out of him.

Coming to, he looked for Gethwen. The young man lay yards away on his back. His hessian satchel lay yards away from him, as if it had yanked the lad as the lad had yanked Larksdale.

Larksdale darted over to Gethwen who, pleasingly, was sitting up. He appeared unharmed, though he was massaging his shoulder in pain.

Larksdale offered his hand.

Gethwen looked around. His mouth opened. A realisation seemed to take him. A terror. He leaped up, seized the bag and bolted toward the wooded shrine of the north eastern wall. He ignored all thoroughfares, leaping over a small hedge and cutting across a lawn, leaving two passing gentlemen aghast.

Larksdale set to chase him, then remembered he'd dropped his new cane. It was where he had fallen, where the ancient bronze patterning embedded in the granite reached its edge. He snatched it up. Gethwen was running into the many trees and hedges that comprised the wooded shrine. He would not get any further. He couldn't possibly climb the keep's fifty-foot outer wall.

Larksdale put on a confident stride, the very limit of acceptable velocity within the keep's grounds. He nodded at the two gentlemen who passed him along the path.

The spaces between the tree trunks ahead were tight and black as hell's halls. Gethwen had not re-emerged. Seeing no one nearby, Larksdale trotted the last distance into the trees.

'Gethwen?' Larksdale said aloud. To shout might bring servants or guards. 'Geth?'

The leafless branches and evergreen bushes became denser and Larksdale almost caught his hair in twigs, but he came out into an opening, to the edge of a black pond that showed the stars to themselves, that held a full moon cracked by winter-nude branches. At the pond's centre rose a man-high shrine, a rectangular pillar with a small statue at its pinnacle: a boy on his knees holding a lamb under one arm, a blindfold over his eyes. A hooded man with a crook had placed his palm upon the boy's forehead. Neyes the Child and the Visitation of the Holy Pilgrim. Larksdale had thought it beautiful before. Now, in this gloom, it seemed a gift from a better world.

Gethwen was standing at the edge of the pond, looking upon the dark water, at expanding circles upon its surface.

'I'm fine, sir,' he said.

'You're hurt,' Larksdale said. He walked around the pond to Gethwen's side.

'Just bruises,' Gethwen said.

'Why run from me?' Larksdale said, almost whispering.

'I'm sorry,' he replied. 'I got angry. And stupid.'

'Your strength. That is not natural.'

Gethwen looked annoyed, flummoxed. 'You're imagining. I just dragged you unawares.' He looked at Larksdale, his eyeballs twitching with too much thought. 'Can we not talk about this, sir?'

The anxiety. It was too-too much for Larksdale to bear. He squeezed Gethwen's shoulder.

'Of course. Tomorrow I'll take you to Fleawater, to your people. I promise. I cannot abide you sad, my Gethwen.'

Gethwen reached up and stroked Larksdale's fingers upon his shoulder. 'It's hard to be sad around you, sir. When you speak you light the world with a thousand lamps.' He frowned, almost cried. 'Sorry, that's a daft thing to say.'

'No.' Larksdale reached for his other shoulder and turned Gethwen to face him. 'Those are beautiful words.' Their faces were inches apart. 'Befitting of such... beautiful lips.'

Gethwen reached up and kissed him. Short and sharp and full of lightning.

'I'm dangerous,' Gethwen said. 'Danger follows me. I run from you to save you.'

'There's no saving me from you,' Larksdale said. He drew the young man to him, drew his mouth to his own. Gethwen let Larksdale's tongue slide between pouting lips. Gethwen's arms slid around Larksdale's torso, one rising to comb his hair, the other descending his spine, grasping his rear. Gethwen's manhood soon stiffened, full-hard against Larksdale's inner thigh. Larksdale let his own rage. It pressed against his lover's belly. The day's humiliations ebbed from his joints.

He gripped either side of Gethwen's head and ceased kissing. Gethwen's eyes opened in surprise.

'But you must promise to tell me all,' Larksdale said. 'Not tonight. But soon.'

Gethwen smiled. A blissful smile. 'I trust you, sir.'

'Harry.'

'Oh, Harry. I've trusted you from the first. We see, my kind. See the pattern of people. You have vision. It's wrapped all about you.'

Larksdale froze. How could he see it in him? Save for one old and bitter mistake, Larksdale had told no one of his great plan.

Gethwen stroked a thumb along Larksdale's eyebrow.

'I can see the way of people, Harry,' he said. 'That's all. I see your way and I feel safe in it. I love you, my Harry, and the day I tell you my secrets must be the day I learn your vision.'

Larksdale could only nod. He was lost in Gethwen, in his dark, wet eyes, like ponds beneath stars.

They kissed again, deep and long. A final kiss and Gethwen dropped to his knees. He began to unbuckle Larksdale and pull at his silken hose.

'Not here,' Larksdale said. It came out as a whisper, a sigh. 'This is a shrine.'

'In the mountains this is what shrines are for,' Gethwen replied.

Larksdale screwed up his eyes as the wet coolness engulfed him. Coolness turned to warmth, to tongue and moans and sucking. He ran his hand through Gethwen's plaited hair and suddenly realised Gethwen no longer carried his hessian satchel.

Ah, but the world was full of mysteries, and mysteries could wait. Certainly for the next five minutes.

13

Red Marie

Up in the rotten belfry she waited for her moment. This was, after all, a performance. Below, in the salt-soaked foundations of the rotting wooden church, her worshippers sang. The citizens of the Hook were devout, for each wished to avoid agonising death.

The Hook was a thin snake of land that coiled out into the sea, dividing Becken Bay from Royal Bay. Many was the time mankind had seen prospects in the Hook, had built warehouses and docks and brothels, and every time the dream corrupted, pissed away gold, and died. No one bothered any more. The broken ribs of their dreams lay all along roofless warehouses, sinking wharfs, brothels whose beds had collapsed to heaps of mould. Now, the Hook had but two uses: hosting a sewer pipe that carried all the waste from Becken Keep out into the sea, its brickwork length often leaking, and as refuge for Becken's most wretched. Those who had sunk to the bottom of humanity's pile and had been kicked out.

Red Marie loved the place. She loved to see humanity degraded.

'Children!' Knucklebones Smones was saying below, his twig-thin figure standing in a cracked pulpit, his arms stretched wide. 'Her red hour is upon us, let me facking tell you!'

The congregation cooed. Perhaps a hundred, perhaps less, they were an indistinct mass of rags and palsies. Red Marie was glad she could not smell them.

She could smell nothing. Not out here in the city. The skin he had given her, his great work, prevented that. She could not feel the sea breeze, nor taste its salt, nor the salt of her own tears, not that she had cried in a long time. But out here, in the open world, his skin kept her alive.

'Oh, Red Marie!' Smones shouted into the air. 'You beautiful, gore-soaked facker, please accept our most 'umble offering…'

The offering was screaming somewhere near the doorway of the old church. A lamp beyond, the cheap sort with the pig's veins in it, cast a light that held the stretched shadow of the sacrifice, their flailing limbs held by limbs more diseased.

Hurry up, Red Marie thought. *Morons.*

Frustrated, she looked out across Royal Bay, or batbay as the city's commoners preferred to call it. On the far side was a reef where stood the trade obelisk, a square black pillar some ten storeys high, its base wreathed in mist. An outpost of the commrach, the furthest one from their island. A greater species, the commrach, a finer civilisation. Red Marie often fantasised of flying about a-murder through the obelisk's halls, spraying its marble red with elfin blood.

The scum finally had the offering upon its knees.

Red Marie crawled down the wall of the wooden church tower. No one would see her just yet, not in her attire, her skin and cloak. They would hear the jangling first, the chatter of wood and shards of pottery. She dug her sickles into the tower's salt-caked skin, one then the other, again and again, a drizzle of splinters each time.

She landed on hoofed shoes upon the church floor. Everyone gasped. The offering – some young sow, some prostitute or weaver – stared in wide-eyed horror and Red Marie thrilled to see such wet eyes. She was smeared with green paint, a nod to Becken's oldest folk tale.

Red Marie would be a silhouette to the offering, a rising shadow, arms stretching wide to reveal glinting sickles for hands.

And the offering knew. Knew all those bloody murders were no mortal's work, knew the stories true. Red Marie, here, risen from the rivers of the city to claim another soul.

'*Priest,*' Red Marie hissed, and Knucklebones Smones ran toward her and fell to his knees. His head bowed, as if ready to be cleaved off. Which Red Marie could do whenever she pleased.

'Mistress,' Smones said. 'We are not worthy to lick your hooves.'

Then you are the wisest man in all Becken, she thought. Instead, she said, '*Why have you not brought the boy?*'

Smones paused, full of guilt and fear. 'I 'umbly beg your indulgences, oh queen of night. We've scoured the city, turned over every brick and wheelbarrow, but, fack me, that mountain boy's a right little stoat.' When Red Marie let silence reign Smones blurted, 'But we'll 'ave 'im soon enough. No one escapes Knucklebones Smones. I beseech you my goddess, three more nights. That's all I ask. And if I fail – which I most assuredly fackin' won't – I'll happily be dragged down to your tower in hell.' He shrugged. 'Can't say fairer than that.'

'*You've two nights.*'

'Four.' He gulped. 'I beg of you, sweet gutter of flesh.'

Four was more than that rascal had even begun with. She placed a sickle beneath his chin and lifted his face to meet her glassy eyes. He was perfectly, beautifully terrified. It was why she kept him alive.

'*Do not fail me.*'

'Not never,' Smones whispered. Black drool rolled from his lips.

Even at his most unctuous and oily there was something insulting in Smones's manner. An insolence as ingrained as the dirt in his fingernails. Red Marie had not expected the Spine Mountain boy to be here tonight, in truth. It was merely gratifying to see Smones scared.

She strutted toward the offering.

Too scared to even beg for her life, this one. A shaking vision in wet green. Wonderful.

Red Marie lowered herself so that her own face, painted and wooden, hung beside the one of trembling flesh.

'I'll permit you to run, sweetie,' Red Marie said. *'But you cannot escape me.'* A fire rose in her belly, in her loins. *'My lovely, I'm going to slice you from neck to sex.'* She couldn't help but titter. This world was hers and it screamed for her. *'I know all the insides.'* Red Marie felt her legs tremble with excitement. *'I'll show you your own… bladder, I think, make you chew on your own little piss-sack.'* She tittered. *'Or maybe your womb. Maybe neither. After all, there are those who call me deceiver.'* Yes, yes! The offering would run and be taken and, in the moment, Red Marie would find her relief. Her fire. *'You'd better run.'*

The offering wept.

'Run!'

The offering shuddered. She prayed through snot and tears.

Ah. She was going to be one of those.

Red Marie slit her wide and showed her the scarlet truth of the world. But Red Marie could not reach that place, that little moment where she vibrated with the universe.

Well then. The deceiver would have to roam a little more this night.

FOUR NIGHTS TILL YULENIGHT EVE

14

Larksdale

Red Marie jigged on to the stage.

'Avast, lost souls!' she told the Sinner and the Goodly Wife. ''Tis I, mother of blood, deceiver, devil's daughter! You shall be servants in my palace below!' Her prancing hooves hammered the boards. 'The reek of blood sings out to me! I must drink! Drink!'

With that, Red Marie jutted her tongue out of her rouged face. The jigging refused to cease.

Larksdale, standing before the stage in the near-empty groundlings, looked to Tichborne in his wheeled rowing boat beside him. The playwright, his broken and bandaged ankle up on the little boat's prow, a blanket covering him from the winter air, gave Larksdale the same look back. Gethwen, stood behind Tichborne's little boat in case it needed pushing, watched the stage with rapt curiosity.

'Darling,' Tichborne called up to Red Marie, 'quick question. What the godforsaken fuck are you playing at?' When Red Marie – played by Jack Poyter – ceased jigging, Tichborne continued. 'Red Marie is all the evil of men that sinks into the river ways of our dank city. That's her whole thing, that's her character. Red Marie *looms*. Red Marie *rises*. If occasion demands, she might even strut. What she *doesn't* do, Jack darling, is caper about like a sailor in a two-penny arse-house!'

'I'm trying to bring something new to the role,' Jack Poyter answered.

'Yes,' Tichborne said, 'and one time I thought I'd drop my cock on a church collection plate. Neither's a good idea, Jack. People look on in shock and no one gives a tuppence thereafter.' He sighed, slapped the parchments in his hand. 'Stick to the script, eh?'

'It's fine,' Larksdale said, patting Tichborne's shoulder guiltily. Tichborne was simply no director or, at least, a tyrannical one, which for Larksdale amounted to much the same thing. The trouble was both Hackett and Molm were recuperating after their sojourn at Cutbill's gaol, poor things, and Larksdale himself had too much fuss up at the keep to contend with, the king's banquet and all. Tichborne had seized the director's chair – or rowing boat, in this case – with grim enthusiasm. He was finding the game very different to ink and parchment.

'The cast,' Tichborne muttered. 'They're just shit. Just hopeless runny shit…'

'There, there,' Larksdale replied. He called to Jack Poyter, 'Jack, love. Might I just say you're a superb dancer? That is not the issue here. No one, not I nor Tichborne nor anyone else have the slightest bad word for your agility and glee.'

Poyter threw his Marie wig to the floor. 'Then why aren't I Dickie o' the Green?' He looked pointedly at Tichborne. 'Hmm?'

'Oh not this Dickie o' the Green shit,' Tichborne roared. 'You are Red Marie!'

'No one wants to be Red Marie!' Jack Poyter shouted. 'Dirk Scoggins can be Red Marie!'

'Dirk Scoggins is Dickie o' the Green!' Tichborne snapped. '*You're* Red Marie. Because *I* say so!'

'People, people,' Larksdale said. 'Let's not have another Dickie fight, eh? Not like last year.' He found he was loving this. The Wreath felt so refreshing after the keep's solemnity. 'Red Marie does not appear in the last act, right?'

'Tell me about it!' Jack Poyter moaned.

'Is there a rule against two Dickies?' Larksdale said, raising his gloved palms. His suggestion was met with confusion, which Larksdale had expected. 'In the final act Dickie gives his jig of spring, which I suspect, Poyter, is the bit you truly covet? Well then, how about this. Two dancers play one Dickie o' the Green. Scoggins jigs from stage right to left.' Larksdale gave a casual sketch of a jig, side-stepping and humming a tune. 'He exits stage left and you, Poyter, jig stage right. Both the same height, both wearing the same mask and costume; it will seem to our ever-dear audience that Dickie, being a magical fellow, disappears left and emerges right, faster than any human possibly could.' He looked to Tichborne. 'They'll love it.' He smiled. 'Boss.'

'Fine,' Tichborne said. 'Anything to stop this *incessant* bitching.'

Jack Poyter leaped, happy as Dickie.

'Excuse me,' came a woman's voice from stage left. Out stepped Cabbot's wife, a costume in one arm and a needle in the other. Larksdale still had not learned her name. It had reached that infamous point where it would be embarrassing to have to ask. 'I'm sorry, Sir, but might I speak?'

'Of course,' Larksdale said. He thought of the king, of his desire for this woman, or at least the idea of her. Of his command.

'I don't mind playing Red Marie,' she said. 'I'd love to.'

'No!' Jack Poyter said. 'That's my role!'

'Fuck's sake,' Tichborne shouted. 'You're Dickie now, you wanted to be Dickie!'

'I don't want to be second Dickie! Not to Scoggins! I'm Red Marie plus second Dickie!'

'Pilgrim's arse!' Tichborne yelled. He winced at his ankle.

'Arriet's a seamstress,' Poyter declared. 'She's no trained mummer!'

Larksdale gestured for quiet, relieved someone had said her name. He looked at her and said, 'Arriet. Arriet my blessed dear. Your wish is noted. The Wreath thrives on such enthusiasm.'

'It's why I left my husband,' Arriet said. And with presence. How strange. Before she had seemed a hopeless victim of events. Had she played that role to the fore? Larksdale had certainly believed it. *This Arriet is every inch the actress she desires to be.*

'Indeed?' Larksdale smiled as best he might. She had no idea of the king's desire for her. No idea. 'Then I promise you a role. Not this play but… soon enough.'

He smiled again and was sick of his smile. For practicality and his greater plan were whispering inside his skull. The situation had grown desperate regards the banquet tonight and the question of the king's paramour. Ean had said he was bored of sweet Abercine. Abercine was the best the city had, so much so Larksdale had not considered finding an understudy. Damale had been Larksdale's next option. Unskilled, they said, but fresh, wild and eager. Larksdale had made enquiries only to find Damale had married a merchant only last month, had left Becken. And Elisende, if only! Sweet Elisende, so pretty and graceful and full of wit! A perfect choice, save that beneath her gown she had a man's body. Ean was too conservative, he hadn't the nuance for Elisende, poor dear. *Out of options, Harry. Out of time.*

Arriet grinned. 'I'll finish this dress,' she said, full of joy. She ran off, stage left.

No, Larksdale, he thought, *no.*

Tichborne sat up in his boat. 'Let's have a break, eh?' he announced. Jack Poyter and the other actors sat down and were soon talking to one another.

'Tich-o, old boy,' Larksdale said, 'permission to board?' He nodded at the wheeled rowing boat Tichborne was sitting in. It had a forward thwart for someone to sit and face him.

'All right,' Tichborne said. 'But wary of my ankle, Harry.'

'Naturally.'

'Wait,' Gethwen said. 'I'll put the brakes on.' He leaned behind one of the wheels and did so. Pilgrim's love, he was beautiful.

'Ingenious,' Larksdale said and he clambered into the boat. 'You know, this is kind of fitting. A stage director is something of a ship's captain.'

'No similes, Harry,' Tichborne said, 'or I'll throw you overboard.'

'I'm merely saying a director has to be as reasoned and delicate as a ship's captain.'

'Captains give sailors the lash.'

'Oh. Bad analogy, then. Don't do that.'

'I hate being a director,' Tichborne admitted.

'Just this once, Tich-o.'

Tichborne groaned. 'You said that about writing this godawful play.'

Time to tell him. 'I've news, Jon. The king has spoken. He wants the Wreath to give his court a play. In the very keep. How d'you like that, eh?' He almost tapped his shipmate on the leg but remembered not to.

Tichborne was the very definition of agog.

'You did it, Harry,' he spluttered. 'You bloody well *did it,* sir.'

'Thank our king,' Larksdale replied. 'Which you will, come the night.'

The playwright near-squeaked. He controlled himself. 'How soon?'

'Yulenight Eve.'

'What? That's five days' time. I've my keep-play all written, of course, but—'

Oh.

'Sorry, misunderstanding,' Larksdale said. 'Not your keep-play. His Majesty desires a folk-play.'

'What?' Tichborne pointed at the stage. 'This turd?' The actors sitting about the stage looked at him.

'Morale, Tich-o, me lad,' Larksdale reminded him. 'You're the director.' He turned his head and shouted, 'False alarm, fellows. He meant some other turd.'

The actors returned to their chatter.

Tichborne leaned in and, subduing his anger, said, 'We can't put this old nonsense in front of the royal family. What's got into you?'

'His Majesty wants a folk-play.' Larksdale explained. 'He's never seen one.'

'There's a privilege he should hold on to dearly. Harry, we'll be a laughing stock. Actually, "laughing stock" would be the optimal result. The keep will be confused by a folk-play. Then bored into mass rage. I'll be put in the stocks.' He began to breathe quickly.

'Nonsense, dear heart,' Larksdale said. 'This is your way into the keep-play game. Your name will be known to every lord.'

Tichborne had turned creamy pale. 'It's over,' he muttered. He was on the verge of one of his moments.

Larksdale clambered out of the rowing boat and said to Gethwen, 'You had better sail him outside for a little air.'

'Yes sir,' Gethwen said. He blew Larksdale a kiss and trundled Tichborne toward the doors.

Boathook Marla passed them and made a straight line for Larksdale. She had a parchment in her hand.

'Boss. You have to see this.'

The paper was one of those scurrilous groat-sheets that multiplied all over Becken with every year. Any timid villain could build a press in his cellar these days.

He'd seen this title before: *The Wit*. Tantamount to fraud.

King Ean was the subject of the lone woodcut illustration. You could tell by the crown and the fact it read 'King Ean' above that crown. All similarity ended there, however, as the king's bare torso was now home to two large teats. Droplets fell in wild profusion from these kingly dugs on to a handful of courtiers half the size of Ean.

While at court our dear king did give milky issue as like a wet nurse. Many witnessed and were confounded. Devil's curse or heaven's punishment? Let our full-bosomed king pray not the latter!

'What baffling twaddle,' Larksdale said. 'You paid a groat for this?'

'Mercy, no,' Marla replied. 'They're lying around Tetchford. Everywhere.' She shrugged. 'Just thought you'd want to see.'

Larksdale nodded thanks. 'A strange slander.'

'It's a lie?' Marla asked.

'Of *course* it is. I was at court last night.' He recalled the whole farrago. 'Briefly. I'd have noticed milk-drenched nobles. Who's going to believe this nonsense?'

She shrugged. 'Stranger things have happened.'

He pointed at the woodcut. 'How strange can you blooming get?'

'King's titty-milk, apparently.'

'All right Marla, I'll be needing your skills in an hour or so if you don't mind.'

'Which sort?'

'The social kind,' Larksdale said.

'I'll dig out my clubs.'

'Gethwen wants to visit his people over in Fleawater.'

'I see.' Marla crossed her arms. 'That's gonna cost more than the usual, boss. Fleas don't mess about.'

'Doubtless.' Larksdale wasn't looking forward to it himself. 'Could you hold on till the end of the week? My shipment will come to port.'

'The mustard?' Her face flickered with doubt a moment. 'All right, me duck.'

'Ah, the bastard's theatre!' Dulenci's voice exclaimed. He was strutting through the open doors, all flouncy shirt and leather codpiece. 'How earthy!'

'Who's this prick?' Marla muttered to Larksdale.

'It's fine, Marla,' Larksdale said. He strapped on his best half-smile. 'Welcome, Dulenci. Where's your queen?'

'*Our* queen, Sir Harrance,' Dulenci replied. 'We are her subjects as much as *this*—' He stamped his foot. '—is my ground.'

'Yes,' Larksdale replied. 'Well, as you can see, it's not going anywhere.'

'Ah that famous Brintland humour,' Dulenci said. 'I should show my appreciation by raising the rent.' His smile vanished. 'Why should I not do that, eh?'

Larksdale took a long breath, in which he heard the theatre's carpenters hammering away. Going about their living. 'Apologies, Dulenci. As you can imagine, I'm a little overworked right now.'

'I can more than imagine. I can relate.'

Larksdale could not help but chuckle.

'It's true,' Dulenci insisted. 'Her Majesty takes a proactive stance with everything and I, being her bodyguard, must perforce do likewise. What spare time I have I use to come here and inspect my property.' He glanced at Marla dismissively. 'You stand here at my leisure, yellow flower.' He shouted to the actors, 'You all do!'

'Mancan prick,' Marla muttered.

'Dulenci,' Larksdale said quickly, 'perhaps you could shed some light on this…'

He showed him the groat-sheet.

'It is treason to read those things,' Dulenci said. 'I assume.'

'I'm minding the king's interests,' Larksdale replied. 'Just look.'

Dulenci did so. All smugness left him. 'The court are a pack of untrustworthy dogs. This should never have got out.'

'It's true? Ean produced milk?'

Dulenci nodded. He passed the sheet back as if it were a rat's cadaver.

Marla gave Larksdale a look that said *told you so*.

'Is the cause known?' Larksdale asked Dulenci.

'Do you think I have time for this, bastard?' Dulenci snapped. 'Ah, but I must away.'

He turned and stormed out the doors.

He knows something, Larksdale thought. But what? This matter was uncanny and deeply peculiar. And if Dulenci knew anything that would only be because Carmotta had let him.

'Marla,' Larksdale said. 'We've an hour or so before we approach Gethwen's people. Would you mind following Dulenci for me?'

'A pleasure,' she said. 'Anything I should be watching out for?'

'Mother says he visits Tetchford every few days. Discover why.'

'The Wreath may be his land,' Marla said, already leaving. 'But Tetchford is your manor, boss.'

High strangeness in the keep. His Majesty would be in a most unforgiving mood. He tended to simmer beneath the majesty, Ean. To lash out at the slightest mistake. Tonight's banquet could not fail. Life was a finer thing here, but change, real change, was only possible in the dour halls of the keep. Larksdale's life's plan was greater than his life and its pleasures. He had always to remember that.

'Sir Harry.' It was Arriet Cabbot, walking toward him. 'My apologies. For earlier.'

'No, no,' he said. 'Those who yearn to stride the boards must be audacious if they are ever to do so.'

She smiled. 'I knew you would understand, sir.' She did not look weak and hollow-eyed as she had the other day. Divorce was evidently suiting her. Indeed, she was comely now, almost the image of her that King Ean no doubt kept in his imagination.

Larksdale's gloved hand squeezed against the head of his cane. *No choices, no time.*

'Arriet, might we talk in my office?'

For the great plan, he told himself, *sacrifices must be made...*

15

Carmotta

'Explainer!' she yelled with no echo, her cry soon absorbed into the great hollow that held the keep-within. She walked a little further across the lumpen floor of untold antiquity. 'Come here!'

Something creaked behind her. She turned around. No one. Just the Explainer's tripods with their glowing clay discs. The keep-within, too, silent and looming. She blinked and the tower still stood in the blackness of her shut lids.

'What are you doing here?' the Explainer said behind her. He sounded almost furious.

At first he appeared as nothing but a pair of eyes above two rows of spiked teeth. He stepped closer and Carmotta saw his entire body was slathered in a dark grey paste. Likely the same stuff as the cracked and powdery substance he had worn last time, but fresh.

'You have to go,' he insisted.

'Silence!' she snapped. 'You poisoned the king with your powder!'

'He's dead?'

'No, he has teats, you savage!'

The beast's eyes widened. 'Fascinating. It was but a mood

enhancer. Hadn't been tested on humans though.' He shook his slick head. 'I haven't time.' He looked at the keep-within then back to her. 'Seriously, piss off. Now.'

She punched him, throwing her body into it like her father had taught her. The Explainer flew backward, his spine smacking flat against a mosaic of a woman, her face obscured by lichen. Carmotta rammed her foot atop the Explainer's chest, holding him in position. She had planned for this moment: commrach were supernaturally nimble creatures. Shock and force were the answers to their mischief.

Carmotta reached for one of the tripods nearby and lifted it. She readied to crush his skull.

'The last man who told me to "piss off",' she hissed, 'never fucking existed. You promised me lust-powder! Bring it to me, devil!'

The Explainer winced, too terrified to offer reply.

'Answer me,' Carmotta barked.

'The dust does not exist,' he said. He readied for his face to be staved in, eyes screwed up and lips trembling. 'I told you it doesn't. *Told* you. Why wouldn't you listen?'

'Why would you lie?' Carmotta demanded.

'Because you threatened to kill me!' he shouted. 'Is that good enough for you? It's some hogwash you humans must have come up with. I'm sorry. I'm *sorry*.' He took a hold of himself. 'You have to leave. It's not safe here.'

'Lies,' she said. 'You made my husband look a woman before his enemies.' Fury rose in her. She raised the tripod higher. 'You've endangered my husband and me and my babe. Now give me something! Use your witchcraft! He must think the babe his!'

'You cannot fool him into fucking you!'

The Explainer covered his face with his hands and braced himself.

Carmotta went still. Those words punched her, as she had punched him. It was so obvious. So true.

'Continue,' she said.

'You cannot force him into desire.' The Explainer, seeing Carmotta had lowered the tripod a little, grew surer. 'But, frankly Your Majesty, that's all I've seen of you: tricks and threats. But that's not enough. Not for a lover.' He gestured at her belly. 'Nor a mother.'

'Then what?'

'Talk,' the Explainer said. 'If he's not being intimate with you, ask him why. Talk. As equals.' He eyed the tripod's base. 'Preferably unarmed. You haven't even tried that have you?'

She shook her head. 'The last time I talked with an equal…' She could picture it. The dockside, Sant Ribot. No sign of him, every dream betrayed. She'd lied to her father later, when he interrogated her. Her first ruse, that. The first lie of necessity.

She placed the tripod where she had found it.

'Please,' the Explainer said. 'You must go.'

'Why?'

'This place.' He nodded at the keep-within. 'It releases energies at the turn of years, usually harmless. But this year's end…' His inhuman eyes studied the keep-within as if trying to comprehend why water drowns, why God plagues the innocent.

'What energies?' She took her foot off his chest.

'Nothing I can detect directly,' the Explainer replied, smearing the clay-stuff over the footprint her slipper had made on his chest. 'Only its effects.'

'Which are?'

'Profound.' He got to his feet. 'Come now.' He took her shoulder and tried to usher her toward the stairs.

She slapped his hand away. 'Fine. I'll go.'

She made her way toward the stairs. On her way she noticed one of the Explainer's tripod devices had a strip of pale leather hanging from it. She stopped in her tracks when she saw the strip had little black hairs. It was a strip of skin. Human skin.

The hairs on the skin-strip rose. A breeze came from the centre of the hollow. Dry stones creaked.

'Get down!' the Explainer yelled. 'Don't look at it! Don't—'

A blast of heat, like when a kiln is opened. She had felt a kiln once, on that happiest and truest day of her life. Funny how that memory came now. She covered her head and fell to her knees. The world creaked and cooked and blew. *My baby,* she thought, *God save my baby.*

16

Larksdale

It was a bracing walk, at least. Three bridges' worth, crossing the Tetch, the Brintchild and the Flume, all the while following Hollowlyve Road, Gethwen tight to his side and Marla striding just a little ahead. A journey that began pleasingly bawdy in Tetchford, rose to near-respectability in Longchapel before outright nosediving into misery in Fleawater. All of it littered with groat-sheets, copies of *The Wit*, this time with an illustration of Red Marie about her bloody business while the nobility cavorted inside the keep. Satire, apparently.

'What's a Red Marie?' Gethwen asked.

'Entirely fictional,' Larksdale replied.

'Been a lot of nasty murders,' Marla said, raising the back of her hand to yet another alley urchin who had spied Larksdale's cloak and doublet. The boy made a rude gesture and sped off down the muddy lane. 'Gruesome deaths all over.'

'Our fair city needs no help there,' Larksdale replied, looking about at the half-collapsed tenements and makeshift huts that lined the lane. 'Man's own awfulness is quite sufficient.'

Which brought Dulenci to mind. Marla had followed the crass tart earlier that day, only to find him giving two mollyboys golden pips from his purse and loudly asking for their company as if he were giving a soliloquy upon a stage. The three had then sashayed into the Carnation, a leaping-house of gaudiest repute. All very Dulenci.

And that was the problem. Unlike most noblemen, Dulenci had ventured into Tetchford not to live out some secret life but to be exactly who he already was. Why cross the city and herald the matter to all when the keep had its own coterie of discreet and obliging 'pages'? Dulenci was obtuse in his blatancy, dark in his sparkle.

Ah, Larksdale thought, *perhaps the man is just that dreadful.* Yet the matter gnawed.

The lane widened into waste ground, its mud and rock long turned over by hooves. The camp was visible here, the colourful roofs of wagons peered over the wall that blocked the road some hundred yards ahead. The wall was eight feet tall and made from all manner of discarded things, though mainly used timber and broken furniture. It had a locked gateway at its centre and before that stood two young fleawets brushing down a donkey.

'I'll do the talking,' Larksdale told Marla and Gethwen.

'Suits me,' Marla said. With that, she took a flask from her belt, uncorked it and took a swig.

Larksdale walked toward the young men, careful to step around a fresh and ambitiously large donkey dropping.

'Hoy there,' he said, raising his cane in the friendliest way possible. 'Well met, my fellows.'

He stopped some nine yards from the pair. Neither of them were giving off a friendly ambience. They merely looked at him. It was hard to make out their eyes. They had that hairstyle popular with young men of Fleawater, where the sides and back were short and the front long, obscuring the forehead and even the eyes.

'My name is Sir Harry Larksdale,' he tried. 'I'd be most obliged if I might speak to your…' He wasn't sure of the term. 'Chieftain?'

One lad chuckled and muttered to the other. That was something at least.

'Wait here,' the one who had chuckled told Larksdale.

The two of them turned and opened the gates. Before going through, the other lad told Larksdale and his company, 'Don't be touching our donkey, now.' The gates closed.

The ass looked at Larksdale almost accusingly. Which was fair; the fellow had lost out on a perfectly good brushing.

'Sorry, chap,' Larksdale told it.

The gates opened and five grown men stepped through, the two lads trailing after them. At front was an absolute monster, twice as wide from shoulder to shoulder as any man had any right to be, his bare torso a mass of tattoos and scars, his red hair in waist-length braids. He glowered on seeing Gethwen.

'Ye the tricky?' he shouted at Gethwen. 'Go now!'

No leader this, Larksdale realised, but the man who fills a situation with his own rage when his leader is not there to bridle him.

'Have we caught you at a bad time?' Larksdale asked.

'No,' the giant said. 'But you're all about to catch one.'

A woman stepped out of the gateway. She looked nothing like any woman he would have expected in Fleawater camp, her face darker than the earth they stood upon and decidedly comelier. No snow-skinned woman of the Spine Mountains, that was for sure. More surprisingly she wore the pale grey robes and habit of a Perfecti, those priestesses of the Church whom God has blessed with unworldly powers of speech. Larksdale could make no sense of it.

'There'll be no violence today,' she told the big fleawet, for which Larksdale was thankful.

'Are you leader here?' Larksdale asked.

'For lack of our old chief.' She looked at Larksdale. 'A knight of the keep,' she observed with soft distain. 'Did Sir Tibald Slyke send you?'

Larksdale was startled, nonplussed. 'Why would he, Sister? And how do you know of him?'

She did not reply. She grinned ruefully.

Strange, to hear a name from the keep on a mouth from the street. Larksdale wondered whether it had something to do with whatever business Slyke and that slime Cabbot were in cahoots over. It was all he could think of. But, oh, this was hardly what he'd come here for.

'My friend here—' He pointed at Gethwen with his cane. '—is from the mountains. He's lost. He wishes only to be among his folk in this city.' The woman and the fleawets stared at him. 'No offence but, er, I do not understand why his presence is so disagreeable.'

'Where's the mother?' the Perfecti demanded of Gethwen, ignoring Larksdale. 'Why's Aifen-the-Tom dead?'

'Tell her!' the giant yelled.

Larksdale looked to Gethwen. The lad stared at his own feet.

'The boy's a tricky-man,' said the Perfecti to Larksdale. 'Hasn't told you that, has he now? One in a thousand-thousand like him, they can play a man like a puppet, read his feelings. Takes a mother to counter his power. He's not permitted in here, not without her.'

'She bade me come,' Gethwen said.

'She was a fool too. Where is she?'

'Dead... most like.'

'Your mother's dead?' Larksdale asked Gethwen. Poor creature. Larksdale wanted to reach out to him.

'His mountain mother,' the Perfecti said. 'One is always bound to a tricky-man, to see they do no harm. You would call them ban-hag.'

Ban-hags. The witches of the spinefolk, who bound minds with their tongue, who consorted with screech-owls and ban-dogs.

'He didn't tell you that either, did he?' the Perfecti said. 'I'm Sister Ruradoola, minister here at the camp. You seem a good man in your way, sir, so listen. He carries the black crown. A thing of pure evil that no devil can touch that compels ignorant mortals to carry it to your keep. The crown was buried here in the camp for decades. For safety's sake. But mortal forces seek it now this particular yulenight approaches.'

'Why him?' Larksdale said, gesturing at Gethwen. He supposed he'd just have to endure all this superstition and balderdash.

'Only a mortal can hold the black crown,' Sister Ruradoola said. 'No demon nor spirit can touch it. But the devil played his card: only a tricky-man can hold the crown without pain. The least trustworthy of mortals. Thus…' She stopped. She eyed Gethwen up and down. 'Where the fuck is it?'

'Safe,' Gethwen replied.

Sister Ruradoola stared aghast. 'Safe where?'

The giant roared and barrelled toward Gethwen.

Marla swiped something against her leg and the top of her hand took alight. She put it to her lips and blew.

An orange flash. Warmth rolled over Larksdale and, squinting, he saw the big man aflame. He hit the floor, smart enough to fall in a puddle, and Marla whacked his shoulders with a club.

'Run,' she told Larksdale and Gethwen. She whacked the big man again. His face was immersed in water.

'*Sleep*,' Sister Ruradoola announced and Marla dropped on her side into the mud, narrowly avoiding the monster and his puddle. Larksdale scrambled over to Marla, shook her shoulder and found her unconscious.

Ruradoola strode forward. She came to a stop just before the monstrous man's head, bent down and turned his face so that his mouth was out of the water.

'I want you and the boy out of here,' she told Larksdale.

'My friend,' Larksdale said, pointing at Marla.

Sister Ruradoola stood up. 'You've a day to get the lad and the crown out of this city,' she said aloud so that everyone could hear. 'Get him to the mountains. For ever.'

She pointed at Marla and the two lads who had been brushing the donkey came over. They lifted the waif up and carried her off.

'Hey,' Larksdale said, standing back upright. 'That's my friend.'

'Insurance,' Ruradoola replied, nodding toward the camp. 'I promise as a Perfecti she will come to no harm.' She shrugged. 'If you do as you're told, "sir".'

'I won't leave her.'

'Leave.'

The word flooded through him, pulling upon his spine. He had to go. Now.

He turned, grabbed Gethwen's elbow and ran.

The urge to flee soon passed. But the value of getting out of there was not lost on him.

'Come,' he said.

'I should have told you,' Gethwen said.

'No matter.'

'So much I should have—'

'No matter.'

The lad had kept strange and vital secrets, though most of it superstitious dogma. This made him a liar and his lies had misplaced the only truth-teller in Harry Larksdale's existence.

'I'm so sorry,' Gethwen said.

Larksdale made no reply. He felt peculiar, like a puppet discarded. He had never experienced the holy command of a Perfecti before. *Perhaps,* he thought, *I should ask Willem Cutbill, call upon the city guard.* But for a mere servant? It wouldn't be enough. And even if it were, it was the manner of incident that started riot. It might even serve as pretext to burn the camp down entire.

Damn, he could only do as Ruradoola and her fleas demanded. This was too bloody utter by half. Time to be rid of Gethwen. *Give him up as a bad job, Harry. A bad job.*

People were watching. From windows, from the street. The urchins of course, but now men too. They seemed to be slowly closing in, as if the encounter just now had stripped Larksdale of standing, of invulnerability.

An alley through the hovels offered the riverbank and the promise of distance. Larksdale took it.

'How did Marla breathe fire?' Gethwen, behind him, asked.

'Her flask,' Larksdale explained and already it felt like talking of a long-lost friend. 'A flammable concoction.'

'She's…' Gethwen stopped.

Larksdale looked back and saw four men behind them at the alley's mouth. They seemed to be deliberating. Deciding.

Larksdale strode faster, praying for a ferryman ahead. He turned the corner out on to the riverside path.

''Ello, Sir Harrance.'

Knucklebones Smones stood on the path along with two of his usual cronies: the anaemic dwarf with priestly pretentions and the lumbering great thug with a baby's head half-grown from his neck.

'Master Smones,' Larksdale said. 'What are the chances of meeting you and your fine fellows here?'

'Miniscule indeed, sir,' Smones said. 'But most pleasing, sir, if I may opine like.' He grinned and looked at Gethwen like he was a honeyed cake. 'And you might be?'

'My page,' Larksdale said quickly.

A silence. Larksdale should have been thankful for Smones and his boys' sudden appearance, given the men at the top of the alley, but he could muster no relief. Knucklebones Smones, rake-thin, mouldy of garb and topped off with a tall and crooked hat, was gang boss of the Hook, that decaying promontory where all of Becken's hopeless washed up. He and his colleagues had what people called 'the Hooksie look': sunken eyes and pallid skin and even, as with Smones's case, black gums and blacker spit. Every entrepreneur in Tetchford knew Smones. He was simply too useful not to know. Only last Wednesday, Larksdale had sent a middleman to acquire a bushel of culoo – an invigorating white powder from the distant land Tlixulub – in a desperate bid to liven up tonight's banquet.

'Well, good day, Smones.' Larksdale smiled perfunctorily and moved to carry on down the river path.

Smones put a dirty hand against his better's chest.

'Sir, sir,' he said. 'I can see you and your lad here are in some consternation.' He nodded toward the men in the alley behind them who had increased in number. The street urchins had joined them, intent on watching the street performance. 'Me and my associates would be *most* gratified to offer you passage upon our rowing boat.' He grinned and a little black rivulet ran down from the corner of his mouth. 'Fleawater is an insalubrious district, sir. Most insalubrious.'

'A devil's den,' the dwarf added. 'Heaving with the blood of those who killed our Holy Pilgrim.'

It made sense in theory. But the idea of being squeezed into cramped conditions with this putrid trio made Larksdale queasy. He moved to leave again.

Smones's palm remained on Larksdale's chest. 'Come, Mr Larksdale, sir. You've no business being here.'

Smones seemed genuine in his fetid way, but the thug with a baby's head on his neck was no dissembler. He was staring at Gethwen, had stood to one side of him ready to grab. This was no chance encounter. They wanted Gethwen.

'Mr Smones,' Larksdale said, 'I'm afraid I must disagree.' He straightened, reached to his belt and unloosened his purse. 'I *do* have business here.'

'What business?' Smones asked.

'That business we call largesse!'

Larksdale scooped all the coins from his purse – some of his very last – and threw them high into the air.

Shocked yelps came from the alley behind him. Then the stamping of many boots.

Larksdale grabbed Gethwen's wrist and the pair of them started to run. Larksdale's arm jerked back and he almost toppled over. The midget – Squints – had grasped the end of his cane with both hands. Behind Squints tussled and rucked some fifteen men and boys, Smones's crooked hat poking out from the middle.

'Have it,' Larksdale told Squints. He let go the cane and the man fell on his arse. Larksdale belted along the riverside after Gethwen.

Larksdale hated running, for it was an admission of failure. He'd lost his cane, his coins, and his best servant and even better friend.

'You filthy facker!' Smones yelled from the scrum behind. 'I were tryin' to help, I was!'

Looking at Gethwen running just ahead, Larksdale could relate.

17

Carmotta

A copper flicker in the black-dust wind. She was drawn toward it, floating through hell's storm over a lifeless land, all rock and no soil. She was flying.

A steel sickle, blood running from its tip.

The light flickered in the black clouds of dust, its reddening glow only visible when the storms parted, exposed for a second before being swallowed up again.

A grey veil lifts halfway. A harelip behind, the mouth widens to a grin of sharp teeth, black gums.

Something steamed and glinted below her. She floated closer, over it. A curving path of molten bronze pressed into the rocky earth. It was the edge of a vast circle, she realised, with smaller lines and curves and patterns of molten bronze growing from its inner side. There was something about them she recognised.

The black door beneath the keep; no watchman stands before it. Something growls. The door shakes.

There were bodies upon the bronze, strewn all along the curve. Women with burnt hair, their blood and souls pooling into molten metal. Slender figures in strange armour stood over their corpses, silver blades in hand. She floated on, toward the scarlet light.

The harelip grin. The sickle.

The light was ever brighter. She was closing in on it. Below her a wall was under construction. Countless men moving rocks, placing them. Some choking, keeling over, their bodies dragged away by others. Some wore the armour of old empire, of her people long ago. She floated over the wall. Into the red light.

Fingers squeeze into a fist, a snake of blood across a bedsheet.

The keep-within. Its shark-tooth stones were in silhouette as ruddy light blasted out between them. She drifted down, down, her feet touching the frigid ground. The small bronze door of the keep-within was but ten strides away.

She looked down upon her body. She wore a simple black shift. No, the shift was slick with blackness, an oil of night. It dripped, dappled her toes, its touch warm and loving.

A man hangs upside down, his skin green as spring, his hair red.

The keep-within hummed. It wanted…

A weight upon her head. She had not noticed before. She reached for it, removed it from her crown. The thing was a circlet of dark metal, pure and blank and perfect but for a gap on one side. It tingled against her fingers. She raised the circlet up high in offering to the keep, to that which lay within, to the better world behind the door. From the window slit above something laughed.

A fire in her chest and she was pouring a black oil from her mouth.

'Hold her, Jans,' a voice said. 'She'll fall.'

A wooden bowl came into view, held by two dainty hands. The last of her vomit fell into it. It looked the normal sort.

'That's the lot,' the voice continued. The damned Explainer. 'Lay her back on the table.'

Greasy hands pulled her shoulders back and down. Sleep took her.

Carmotta awoke, her throat burning with bile. Her joints ached. The ceiling above was grey stone, a single lantern hanging from it. She was still in the underworld beneath the keep, then. But at least she was away from the keep's hollow heart.

She wanted away from here, for sunlight. The memory came unbidden of that summer afternoon when she was seventeen, the sheer serenity, like how she always imagined heaven. Sitting on a bench in Sant Ribot, that port town on her family's land, painting a freshly baked pot. Across the bench, he was potting, his hands wet and grey. There had been a moment hadn't there? Their eyes had met and they both knew. That here was life perfected.

Stupid girl. You should have known.

This present was preferable to that memory. She raised herself on to her haunches. She was sitting upon a low table in a room some ten feet by twenty, the walls carved rock and entirely bereft of decoration. Jans the worn-out doorman was there, his saggy eyelids like scrotums on a cold night. He seemed barely human to Carmotta, a thing thrown together by disinterested hands. Jans was looking at Carmotta, her body entire. Not lasciviously, but as if he did not know how to look a human in the eyes or where the eyes even were, which was somehow creepier. Had he been staring at her as she slept?

'You're quite safe.' The Explainer's voice. 'How are we feeling?'

She checked herself. Her limbs were fine, her dress un-torn if dirtied with black dust and the Explainer's grey paste.

She clutched her belly. 'My baby.'

'Have no fear,' the Explainer said somewhere behind her. He walked around the table, coming into view. The wet clay-like substance he had been covered in was entirely gone save for patches of it along his hairline. He wore some strange commrach garb, a long grey tunic with buttons down one side. 'I can find no blackness to your vomit. None of the oily taste either. So you've avoided contamination. At any rate, I've had far worse doses in my time. Never did me any harm.' His eyes crossed and his tongue stuck out to one side. Then he stopped. 'Apologies, Your Majesty. Bedside humour. Badly judged.'

He saved my life, she thought, *this devil. How unexpected.*

'How long did I pass out for?'

'Some two hours.'

'Shit,' she said in Mancan. Then, in Mainer, she said, 'I'll be missed.' Or perhaps not. She had told her handmaidens she would rest in her chambers and had then snuck out. Either way, she would be missed sooner or later.

'I saw things,' she muttered.

The Explainer stepped closer. 'Please, Your Majesty, tell me.'

She had never seen him so hooked. A strange creature, arrogant one moment, childlike the next. And… wait, did he say he'd *tasted* her vomit?

'You can tell me later,' he said, seeing the disgust on her face. 'It is never easy, I know.'

'It's fine, Explainer,' she said. 'I think it—' She waved in the direction she thought the keep-within might be. '—it showed me its interment, the greater keep being built around it. Men were dying laying those stones, men of the Mancan empire. And there were women, so many. Slaughtered by…'

'Commrach,' the Explainer said, filling her silence. 'I've been shown the same vision. Other things besides.'

'It happened,' Carmotta said. 'Those stones are visible in the hollow's walls.'

'And the bronze barrier your women died upon,' the Explainer added. 'You'll have noticed it in the grounds and gardens outside.'

'Yes,' Carmotta said. 'Yes, of course.'

'It's of commrach artifice, though impossible to construct at present.'

'It's in your people's histories?' she asked.

'Is the greater keep's foundations in yours?'

'No,' Carmotta said and was immediately struck by the utter strangeness of it. No one ever talked about who had built the greater keep, had not even created a folk tale or lie. Until this moment she had never thought to ask. No one did. Not once. 'I do not see how that's possible.'

'There's the troubling part.' He sat at the end of the table by her feet. 'My people built the great barrier that you and everyone else happily walk over daily. They built it, sacrificed telepheme blood over it—'

'Telepheme?' Carmotta asked.

'It's our term for the women you call ban-hags and Perfecti.'

'Ban-hags are witches,' Carmotta protested. 'Perfecti are blessed by God and his Pilgrim.'

The Explainer gazed at her like she was a child protesting bedtime. 'Regardless. It seems we commrach went to great lengths. Except we did not. It's as if we wiped away all our history of this colossal event. I cannot believe that. Neither can I believe your ancestors walled off the keep-within, losing thousands of lives, and then completely forgot about it.' He tapped her toe. 'The commrach in your vision wear armour from eight thousand years ago, while the "old" empire of Manca existed from one and a half thousand to a thousand years ago. Yet in the vision—'

'They happen simultaneously,' Carmotta said, interrupting the Explainer.

'Different peoples in different eras working together to bind and obscure a mind-poisoning edifice.' His lips tightened. 'I've been contaminated multiple times. More than anyone should.

I've… seen other people. A few. Strange folk, with strange artifices. They cannot be from our past.' He looked at Carmotta. He looked scared. 'I do not believe the obscuring of the keep-within happened once. I think it's *happening*. As if the very act has caused itself to… occlude from causality.'

'You're giving me a headache, Explainer.'

'A headache to you,' he replied, 'another Tuesday for me.' He hesitated, then said, 'A final question, if you please. Did you see the woman?'

'Woman?'

'In my visions I see her from afar, standing before the keep-within and lifting a small black crown from her head, about this big.' He curled his thumbs and index fingers in a rough approximation of the circlet that had been upon Carmotta's head. 'She offers it to the edifice. It's then I awake.'

'No,' Carmotta lied. 'All I see is the keep-within, lit from inside. A red light.'

He nodded. 'I would be in your debt if you speak to no one of any of this. It's beyond politics.'

The creature was right of course. But the implication they were now allies unnerved Carmotta.

'Who would believe it?' A thought struck her. 'If the greater keep was not there, if it collapsed, everyone would see the keep-within, would they not? They would all know the secret. And in speaking of it to anyone they would soon die?'

'And they would pass it on to others who would pass it on. A contagion of agony. Spreading over the globe.'

'I want to go back upstairs now,' Carmotta said, disturbed. 'Before I'm missed.'

'How do you feel?'

'Honestly?' Carmotta said. 'I want to fuck.'

The Explainer and Jans looked at one another uncomfortably.

'My *lover,*' she added. 'Or my husband, not that he'll have me. He's fucking some harlot at his damned banquet. Gentlemen, I've survived trauma. Thus I want to fuck. I love fucking and I'm tired of a world where I cannot say that.'

'I just meant, can you move your arms and legs and such,' the Explainer said.

'I'm tired of a world where I am bound to one man.' She could feel that old anger rising in her and, these two men being weird and below regard, she could express it. 'I'm greater than that but this world wants to keeps me small. I want my men and I want to rule, not rule through men. And I can tell you both this because I can break you, because you are both quite terrified of me.' Carmotta climbed off the table before either of them could offer help. 'I'll see myself out.'

'Wait,' the Explainer said. 'If you have any symptoms, no matter how small, come visit.'

'What symptoms?' Carmotta asked.

He shook his head, his wild hair flopping to one shoulder. 'Just being careful.'

'Safe than sorry,' Jans the doorkeeper croaked.

The pair of them! Life in this underworld had twisted them to parodies, husks of everything they might have been. They were quite beneath First-Queen Carmotta. Contemptible and weak. But they had listened. They had done that much.

She went to turn the door-ring, then stopped herself.

Weak…

'How did you bring me here?' she asked them.

'We carried you,' the Explainer replied. He smiled.

'You two? You two couldn't carry this.' She slapped her ample hips. She pointed at Jans. 'He's ancient and you, dear commrach, could not even carry a tune.'

The Explainer's eyebrows raised. 'Well, it was no easy task.

But Jans here has been carrying things his entire life; what he's lost in vitality he makes up for in knack. And it's a common misconception we commrach are weak.'

'Let's arm wrestle,' Carmotta said, and the commrach looked askance. 'I do not believe for a moment you two wilting daisies could carry my unconscious body.'

'And yet we did,' the Explainer said. 'Who else is down here?'

She supposed he was right, putting it like that. But still…

Ah, with luck Dulenci would be returning to her quarters by now. Mmm. She bit the side of her lip and twisted the door-ring.

18

Larksdale

'He is handsome, the king,' Arriet said.

'And a good man.' Larksdale nodded. 'A good man.'

Arriet turned to face the mirror of the ancient vanity. She had her own space behind a privacy screen over which could be heard the chatter of the other girls in this long and painted cellar that served as a dressing room. They were beneath Becken Keep, within its catacombs.

'I was surprised, that's all.' She laughed, short and sharp. 'That the actresses who perform the keep-plays take such a route.'

'I admit it's hardly a test of acting prowess,' he said.

'It is,' Arriet said. She lifted a goblet hidden somewhere between all the candles set upon the vanity and raised it to her own reflection.

'To His Majesty our king.'

She sipped, then shuddered. For a moment she seemed to choke. She put the goblet down then, with her other hand, brought a fist down on the table. She snorted then closed her eyes.

'Arriet?' Larksdale said. 'Are you well?'

'I'm trying not to cry, Harry,' she said to the vanity's surface.

She gestured at her face. 'I'll ruin this make-up.' She heaved and almost growled. 'Your helper took an hour to put it on.' She waved her hands about like a workman trying to wave away the pain in a hammered thumb. 'I'm *trying* not to cry.'

'Oh.' He wanted to say, *Then just leave, woman.* But the king. Everyone present tonight. His life's plan. 'He is a most gentle lover, Arriet. To be frank. Most gentle. Everyone says so. Everyone.'

'I'm happy to bed him, Harry,' she said.

He was relieved to hear she was eager enough, so *bloody* relieved. Then disgusted with himself for what he might have said if she had not been. 'So why do you cry?'

'I haven't cried.'

'And it's appreciated.'

'My love is the theatre, Harry,' she said. 'I sacrificed my safe life, my wealth and my admittedly dreadful marriage to be a part of it. Your Wreath seduced me. I…' Her face was dangerously close to leaking again.

'Woah, woah, have a care.' Larksdale waved his hands in front of her face as if that might stop her tears. He couldn't think of anything else. 'We'll get through this, Arriet.'

She sneered and snorted and grimaced and somehow prevented a single tear emerging.

'His Majesty is potent,' she said. 'As like his father and all his line. I've come too far, Harry, sir. I've risked too much to carry one of the king's bastards. I can't.' She looked up from the mirror to the wild hair of the ancient Red Marie mural upon the wall. 'This place. I could not live here with child, docile and kept. This place feels *wrong*, Harry.'

He had never heard someone outright say that. He had been raised here, so he had never been truly certain, but the streets of Becken had always felt lighter.

'This place is what it has to be,' he half-mumbled.

There were rumours of Ean's many bastards but Larksdale had never seen one. Somehow, legend of the king's fertility was unstoppable despite the facts. *Still,* he thought, *the chance always remains*. He looked around the privacy screen. Mistress McLach was still busy seeing to the cast of other girls. Larksdale dipped behind the screen once more and pulled open the bottom drawer of the vanity.

'What are you doing?' Arriet asked him.

He pulled out a clay pot, its cork stopper greasy with a grey substance. He placed it on the vanity before her.

'What's that?'

'Slather,' he replied. 'A commrach unguent.'

She squinted. 'Is it sorcerous?'

'Better. It's effective,' Larksdale replied. 'The keep's ladies use the stuff. I'm the only man who knows about it.'

'It's… a preventative?' Arriet asked, unsure.

'One that actually works. We haven't time for euphemism, so listen: take a pea-sized amount and insert deep into… the canal of love.'

Arriet's eyebrows raised. She shook her head and almost laughed.

'All right, maybe a little euphemism.'

'The ghastliest kind.' Her grin faded when the reality hit her, as it had Larksdale already. 'But that would be a sin, yes?'

'To deny the true seed of St Neyes,' Larksdale said. He would not varnish the matter.

'God's chosen.' She took a breath and pushed the pot away.

Larksdale pushed it back. He grabbed her shoulder and leaned in, his face inches from hers. 'I won't have it. You're too talented, Arriet. Too spirited and possessed of a wide and curious mind all your own. Your talent's worth a hundred holy bastards, do you hear?'

'But what of hell?' she whispered.

'Tell the devil it was my ploy,' he said. 'He likes an ideas man.'

She nodded. Her eyes were pools in the candlelight, green waters in some grotto.

He noticed her earrings. Two ruby sailing boats.

'You'd better swap those for another pair,' he said. 'Queen Carmotta wore them summers ago, at Moleford Waters.'

'His Majesty won't recall,' Arriet said.

'I do. So he will. Carmotta's hair was in a new high style. She dazzled all.'

Arriet gave a half-smile he could not decipher. She did not remove the earrings.

'I'll wait outside,' he said.

'I won't be long.' She gestured at the pot of slather. 'Thank you, Harry. You're a—'

'Bastard,' he answered, cutting her off.

19

Fwych

Fwych ignored the young tanned man on the huge bed, ignored the room the size of a hall that were used only for sleep. She rubbed her cheek and rolled the weapon therein, the sharp pig bone she had hid between inner cheek and row of teeth. She had had a night in her new silver cage to think. To reach out and feel.

Here were that fabled evil, the one the black crown had to be taken far away from so that the world would not die. The evil were a festering pit beneath this grandest of halls and the fester had long soaked into every stone. The wickedest of places. And yet—

A tap at her temple. The young man laughed.

He were still sat on the bed, now with a bowl in one hand. He had thrown her a nut. He threw another that hit her thigh and laughed.

'Eat,' he said.

If it'll shut him up. She picked up the nut. She had never seen the like, its shell covering the nut like a quim over a babe's breaching head. She broke the shell and popped the nut in her mouth. Soft and salty. She could still taste things, strong things, in her throat when she swallowed. She picked the other nut up and ate that too.

She would need the energy once she were out. To kill this man if nowt else.

And yet there were hope in this wickedest place. She had felt it last night right when they had thrown water over her and dragged her to her new cage.

A thousand screams had run through her. The cold, wet world sloughed away and she were drowned in power, a thousand mountain mothers' voices as one, half-mindless, pushing wickedness back, holding it here in this wicked place.

The thousand mothers. They were as a circle about this vast hall. She had not felt them when first entering, as if they let her in. For a blink she had been at one with them. She had remembered her power before. And somehow, she were certain, through their dream-like senses she had sensed Gethwen around here.

Had he the crown with him? If so he were a damned fool and she a greater fool still for telling him to run for the city. Back at the inn it had seemed a clever plan in its perversity.

Fwych would get out tonight. She would. Find a way out the cage and into the arms of the thousand mothers, whoever they were. She would speak with them the speech of souls and they would show her Gethwen and the evil crown. There were hope now. She should have known hope never left a soul for long.

A nut hit her forehead. Another bounced off a bar. He was aiming for her face. More laughter. *If the chance comes,* she promised herself, *I will choke him on his strange nuts.*

The double doors at the end of the hall flew open and four women strode through. Three, all terrible thin, tried to keep up with the fourth woman. She were beautiful, this woman, with a powerful body, the sort men of the mountains kill rivals for. She wore the finest dress of the flatlands, but her dress were dirty.

The young man leaped up from the bed and ran over to greet her halfway down the hall. He and the four women all had the same pale-brown skin, with the fourth woman, whom Fwych suspected their leader, darkest of all.

The thin women and the young man barked gibberish. The beautiful woman clapped and they all shut up.

'Must I forever remind you?' the beautiful woman said. 'In my husband's home we do not speak Mancanese. Ladies, your worry is needless yet appreciated. Now, please leave us. Your queen needs her rest.'

The three thin women did as she said.

'Have you been through a slurry pit?' the young man asked.

'The Explainer's nonsense,' she replied. 'It is no matter.'

'I'll kill him for you,' he said. 'The beast's no respect for your beautiful dress.'

'I shall ask you to have less,' she said. 'Tear it off me.'

He put a hand on her bare shoulder. 'Come, I've something to show you.'

He took her hand and drew her toward Fwych and her cage.

The Majesty came into the lantern light between the bed and the cage. She had dirt upon her chin and a powdering of clay all down her dress, yet her bare arms and shoulders almost gleamed in the light, her nut-brown skin impossibly smooth.

Evil was all over her. A cloud of it like flies, unseen to most but aglow to Fwych's mother-sense. The Highness were soft and young and comely and yet she had been dipped in that fester far beneath. Fwych scuttled back, her bare arse against the bars.

The Majesty stared at her, her eyes full of shock.

'Dulenci,' the Majesty said. 'What have you brought to my chamber?'

'A gift,' the man, Dulenci, said. 'A mountain woman. I saw it in the menagerie and thought of you.'

'This thing made you think of me?'

'You were taken with Larksdale's sweet catamite, yes? Back in Grand Gardens you were fascinated by the red hair. This one's is red. A delightful pet.'

Fwych had never seen a sweet-catamite. Some animal, by the sound of it.

The Majesty looked at Dulenci as if he'd claimed to wrestle elk. 'Have her removed.'

He kissed her hand. 'My love, you do not know the lengths I go to please you.'

'And you do not know the kind of fucking day I've had.' She drew her hand from his and the evil cloud around her swirled. 'I want her gone, Dulenci.'

Fwych readied herself. If the Majesty came close, opened the cage, Fwych would take the sharp bone and slide it into her eye. The rest would be chance.

'Wait.' Majesty took two steps closer. Her eyes were deep pools, enchanting. A fine target. 'She's tattoos. Their witches have tattoos!' The Majesty barked gibberish at Dulenci. She raised a palm to slap him.

'Hey, hey,' Dulenci said, amused. 'We are not to speak Mancanese, remember?' He seized her wrist and kissed it again. 'Carmotta, my love, do you think I would endanger you with witchcraft?'

The Majesty – Carmotta – frowned. 'I do not know what to think. It's impossible to guess such an idiot.'

'Relax, my sweet.' He let go of her hand and slid his body behind her. 'She is a ban-hag, yes.' He slipped his arms around her waist. 'But a useless one.' He rested his chin upon her shoulder. 'Where does a ban-hag's power lie?'

'In her voice,' the Carmotta said, studying Fwych.

'This one has no tongue,' he said. When Carmotta turned her head toward his, he kissed her cheek. 'Sliced off long ago by a good follower of the Church, so her keeper told me.'

'She cannot harm us?' Carmotta asked.

'And she can speak to no one. What was it you said once?' Dulenci asked her, sucking on her ear. 'That thing you said you've always dreamed of.'

Her lips shook an instant, then she replied, 'Someone to bear witness to our love.' She grinned, tilted her head so that the young man could place kiss after kiss upon her neck. 'Someone we could trust never to speak…'

He tugged down the top of her dress and her big firm dugs came free. He began to squeeze and roll them in his hands, curled his finger about a mud-brown nipple. She moaned, met Fwych's stare and grinned.

'She understands Mainer, yes?' Carmotta asked Dulenci.

'Comprehensively.'

Carmotta removed Dulenci's arms from her torso and took another step closer.

One more step, woman. One more…

'Listen, witch,' Carmotta said. 'Keep watching.' She pulled her dress down over her wide hips and she was naked save for her shoes. 'If you close your eyes I'll know.'

'We'll know,' Dulenci said, removing his shirt and pulling down his tights. His cock was startling large and as hungry as any Fwych had ever seen.

'Avert your gaze,' Carmotta told Fwych, 'and I will ensure you starve.'

The evil upon her throbbed at that, as if feeding upon the words. She strode away from Fwych and mounted her lover upon a bed fit for twenty more.

20

Larksdale

He led her down the corridor arm in arm, as if she were his noble wife and he not some contemptible pimp.

All for the good. For the plan.

Men were shouting and singing behind the door ahead. They sang 'On Duxby Field' – a call to arms and glory. Her elbow tightened against his own.

'Come now,' he whispered.

He pushed the door open and the smell of sweat and melting wax filled his nostrils. Five hundred candles illuminated the underground hall. Shadows cavorted against walls, figures stretching and shrinking across ancient murals of beasts that never were. Knights and lords revelled over a long table. His Majesty was sitting at the far end in a high-backed chair.

Larksdale felt a tension leave Arriet, her presence becoming lighter beside him, as she poured herself into the role.

'Gentlemen,' Larksdale announced.

They kept chanting the final refrain.

'Gentlemen!'

Nothing.

'My lords!' Arriet yelled. They stopped and looked. 'Greetings.'

His Majesty kept nonchalant reserve, his usual way in this moment. His forearm, however, which he was using to prop up his cocked head, was trembling.

The culoo, Larksdale realised, *he's absolutely cresting on the stuff.*

That powder had been a mistake. Osrin's gang had become outright mean on it, threatening servants and cajoling Willem Cutbill into snorting more than anyone. The poor fellow was rocking in his chair and staring at the condiments. The very sight of the untouched bowl of mustard reminded Larksdale of that lost and damnable cargo ship he had thrown all his wealth at. He put the thought aside.

'Your Majesty,' Larksdale said. 'Might I introduce Arriet?'

The men cooed. Osrin's gang slapped the table. Arriet let go of Larksdale's arm, stepped forward and twirled. Her smile shone with the candlelight.

The king shifted in his seat, unable to keep his repose. With one hand he gestured for her to approach. She glided toward him, and Larksdale was relieved she took the route around the table opposite to the leering Osrin and ever-loud Pym. Regardless, Larksdale was sure to follow Arriet a little way behind. Just in case.

The king stood up and got his sleeve caught on a chair arm. A servant helped him, fixing the sleeve and pulling the chair back across the tiles.

Osrin guffawed. His rats chuckled likewise.

King Ean looked at them and smiled. This night was a night of brothers, of good cheer. He could not be seen to take japes sorely. Larksdale suspected Ean regretted that sentiment now.

'Your Majesty.' Arriet curtsied.

'My lady.' He held his hand out for hers and she took it.

'Stunning tits!' Lord Pym cried and men laughed.

'Hers or the king's?' Osrin replied.

The hall burst into howls and hoots. Palms slapped against oak and goblets toppled. *'Hers or the king's,'* someone repeated.

Arriet smiled, lady and whore at once.

A mania flashed in the king's eyes. A stranger to true mockery, Ean. He knew not how to deflect or ignore japery as all other men do, nor call a man an ass. Instead he grinned at everyone like some mad beggar people crossed streets to avoid.

He took Arriet by the waist and drew her in. 'We'll see about that!'

He tugged at her bodice, but the thing was too tough to pull down. He did so again and the men cheered and slavered.

'Oh, sirs!' Arriet shouted joyfully but her eyes flashed wide at Larksdale.

So many lusts all upon one girl. Larksdale waved at a servant to bring on all the other women. 'Quickly,' he told him and the servant broke into a run.

Ean had stopped trying to pull down her bodice but had taken to nuzzling Arriet's neck and holding her tight. Someone flicked a chicken bone at her.

Count Osrin grinned at his absurd monarch. At his handiwork.

Someone pulled on Larksdale's arm. Damned Tibald Slyke, looking up from his chair with a smirk.

'Yes, Slyke?' Larksdale smiled at Slyke's audience, some four lords, three of whom he was on friendly terms with, the other one Lord Pym, his pig eyes staring out of his pink face from the other side of the banquet table.

'I heard a little rumour, sir,' Slyke replied. He was far from drunk, Larksdale sensed, but was happy to play to all drunk-kind. 'A scurrilous street-tale about you and your money.'

One of the lords beside him winced. Bringing up the subject of coin while in the keep was like announcing your latest bowel movement. Slyke was above neither.

'Let's not darken this feast,' Larksdale said, throwing on a grin. 'Are we having fun, gentlemen?'

'Don't change the subject,' Slyke chided, still clinging to Larksdale's forearm like the most boorish squid. 'Is it true that you've put every penny on one ship? A ship full of naught but mustard?'

Lord Rossard, sitting beside Slyke, chuckled at that. A man who had never had to risk a single coin in his life.

'Well not *every* penny,' Larksdale answered.

'Give us your financial wisdom, Harry,' Slyke said. 'What's your secret?'

Larksdale had no time for this. He looked over to the king. He had settled down a little, content to nuzzle Arriet's bare shoulder as she sat upon his lap. Arriet grinned at adjacent nobles, happily answering their ribald questions.

Satisfied, Larksdale turned back to Slyke and his chums. They were poised to mock whatever Larksdale said, but perhaps one of them might quietly see the genius in his rationale. He shrugged, smiled, lifted a full spoon from the untouched pot of yellow on the table and deposited its contents upon the side of Slyke's brass plate.

'What's that, my lord?'

'Mustard,' Slyke said with reluctance.

'To accompany and accentuate a fellow's beef.' He took an eating knife from the table, impaled a slice of roast beef from Slyke's plate and smeared it comprehensively with mustard. He offered it to Slyke. 'Please, Slyke, if you would.'

Slyke, frowning, seized the knife from Larksdale and made a point of wiping half the mustard away on his plate. This was much to Larksdale's delight, for his victim had fallen into his trap. Slyke gave the others a theatrically weary look and popped the beef into his mouth.

'Now what?' Slyke said, still chewing.

'You wiped half away,' Larksdale said.

'There was far too bloody much,' Slyke replied.

'Men miscalculate the amount of mustard they truly need when first they pop in on their plate. Whenever I spy a finished meal there is always a third to a half of mustard remaining.'

'But *you* just put it on my plate,' Slyke said.

'No man ever eats all his mustard,' Larksdale told the group, ignoring Slyke's protest. He pointed at the table. 'And that is but one plate. Think on it, sirs. Multiply this plate by the thousands. Why, men throw away near half the mustard they buy! Each half-tun a'mustard tossed to the devil! Yet man's need for the yellow marvel never abates. A seller's market, good friends! A seller's market!'

They gazed at him, their mouths agape.

'You fucking twat,' Slyke said. He let go of Larksdale's arm at last and started to laugh. The others laughed with him. 'You've burnt your purse on an idle thought.'

'An *understanding*,' Larksdale said. 'A comprehension of human behaviour. That's how fortunes are made.'

They only laughed the more.

'No, Larksdale,' Slyke replied. 'Fortunes are made on expertise and sound arithmetic, not some notion you dreamed during a post-prandial nap. And so what if people buy mustard, eat half and throw half away? Nothing about that means they buy more mustard. Nothing.'

'You haven't considered the finer details,' Larksdale said.

Slyke only cackled the more. 'Away with you.'

Arriet squealed. Larksdale looked over to her. Ean had just spanked her thigh and now did so again.

'There'll be a bastard made tonight!' a ruddy-cheeked lord yelled.

'Yes!' Ean roared, pointing at him. 'Yes!'

'Reminds me of the commrach isle,' Osrin declaimed. 'Girls fuck girls there all the time.'

Not everyone laughed but Osrin's gang hissed with delight.

Ean stared at him with a faux rage that at base was real as the keep's stones.

'Eh?' Ean laughed. 'What?'

'Banter, my milky brother,' Osrin said. He made show of shrugging and everyone laughed. 'A joke.'

'You're every inch the man, sir,' another knight shouted and he made a hard cock of his fist and forearm, ramming it back and forth in the musty air. 'Eh?'

Arriet made a mock-scandalised sound and laughed with the others. Was she scared? Larksdale had thought she was. But she was too good an actress for him to tell now.

I should do something, he thought. *Shouldn't I? Is she content with this?*

'I think…' Ean yelled and everyone quieted, 'you all need a lesson!' He snorted back a palmful of culoo and threw the rest in the air. 'Your king, sirs, is a *man*!'

The men cheered and Ean threw Arriet forward, her hairstyle toppling and her bodice crushing a pie on the table.

Larksdale was frozen. He'd no words.

Ean rifled up her skirts.

'Me next, Your Majesty!' Pym shouted. 'I'll have some of that!'

'*Me, me!*' others chorused.

Please no, Larksdale thought, *oh Pilgrim, please no.*

A yell filled the room. A man's roar. A chair flew, thrown from the other end of the table. Nobles ducked from its arc.

All sounds ceased but the man's screaming.

It lowered to a growl, its source Willem Cutbill. The big man was staggering, slapping the back of his own head with great force.

'No!' he shouted. 'No!' He grabbed a roast pig's head from the table and threw it at a tapestry, its flesh bursting against a rearing unicorn. His staggering ceased and he leered at the men. At the king.

'Not having it,' he snapped. Tears were streaming from his eyes. 'Not fucking havin' it.'

'Sir,' Osrin said, 'are you—'

'Shut it! Just fucking shut it! I won't have it, I wouldn't let my men back then, I wouldn't, and I won't have it here. *I will not!*' A realisation hit him, as if whispered by some unseen angel. 'You're lords! You're supposed to be better! Yeah?' He pointed at Ean. 'You! You're a fuckin' king, mate! Sort it out! Fuck's sake!'

Pym drew his sword. 'Take that back.'

Other men drew their blades too.

Yes, the culoo had indeed been a mistake. Larksdale opened his mouth to speak.

'She's another plate to you lot, you fuckin' lot. In't she?' He pointed at the half-eaten food on the table. He rammed his wrist up against his left eye as if trying to stop its contents from falling out. 'She's not your *fucking* plate.'

'Once a peasant,' Osrin said, chuckling. 'Someone throw him a sword. No one insults the king.'

'It's fine,' Ean said.

'It's fine,' Arriet said and she stood up, jam pie all down her front like gore. She gestured at Cutbill. 'I'm fine, sir. It was just sport, yes? I was happy with it all. Every moment.'

'But you weren't!' Cutbill pleaded. 'You just have to be. You hadn't a choice.' He wrapped his arms around his chest and began to shake. Tears were streaming from him.

'Sirs,' Larksdale said aloud, seizing the lull, 'I think our dear Willem has had a little too much… muchness.'

'You're right I fucking have,' Cutbill said.

Larksdale, arms wide, walked toward him. 'Come, friend, let us take some air. Hmm?'

Cutbill slapped his hand away and stormed off. 'I'm going. I'm…' He exited the hall.

'He'll be fine,' Larksdale assured everyone. 'He'll walk it off.'

The king stood pale. Shocked.

'Come, Your Majesty,' Arriet said, seizing the moment. She took Ean by the hand and led him out of the hall.

Larksdale looked at everyone. Some forty men, twenty with blades readied. They looked back at him.

'Great party,' Slyke said, his nasal voice flat. He was the only one sitting down.

The cast burst through the doors behind Larksdale. Forty common women in dresses their betters had worn but once and thrown away.

The men put their blades away and sat down.

Larksdale nodded at the women and pointed at the men. They began the ancient business of sitting down on laps. But all the men were drained now the king had left.

Larksdale stood alone on the wide tiled floor. He felt defeated, wretched. Miserable. Willem Cutbill was a bore and, yes, a lowly glover's son. Not to mention utterly culoo-addled. But he had done what Larksdale had wanted to do, should have done. Of course, ol' Harry Larksdale wouldn't have thrown chairs and pig heads, that was too-too much, but he could have stopped things with… a quip? Something, some child of his silver tongue.

But no.

He sighed. He walked halfway down the table until he was standing next to Pym, who already had a woman in his arms. A platter of white culoo sat near Pym's elbow and Larksdale dragged it toward himself. He picked up the slender metal tube at the side of the plate and fashioned a big line of the flour-like substance. He snorted in one go. His nostrils and throat burnt and then they felt nothing, a cold numbness. He waved at the musicians to play and then fashioned himself another line. He sat down.

Arriet had only wanted to act. He eyed the hall. All these other girls had had dreams too, probably. Better to never dream and let the world happen to you. Hope? Hope had only ever procured him a pimp's crown.

'Look at you.' It was Slyke's voice.

Tibald Slyke had no woman upon his lap like the other guests, though one hovered just behind his chair, uncertain what to do with herself.

'Looking at me,' Larksdale replied, 'is the closest you get to competency.' He hadn't the energy to be civil.

'This is competency?' Slyke nodded at Larksdale. 'You've broke the captain general, shamed the king, drenched our best men in whores and filled everyone's head with some unguessable lunacy-powder. The night's a triumph.'

'They've yet to bring dessert.' Larksdale made another line of culoo, his teeth grinding.

'They did,' Slyke said. 'The jam pie. It was crushed, remember? By your first whore.'

'She's an actress.' He leered at Slyke, the fucker. 'Say it.' He slapped the table and plates shook. '*Say it!*'

Pym and his woman stopped and looked. So did others. Larksdale cared naught for any of them.

'You're finished, boy,' Slyke said. 'All His Majesty and everyone else wants from you are the diversions you can offer them. But tastes change and appetites tire and you've run out of ideas.'

Larksdale got to his feet. 'Really? Do you know, Slykey-boy, that people ask me not to sit them with you. Do you know that? I have to move you around this table month to month. That way you're a burden eased.'

'Hey,' Sir Risbalt Quence said, his shoulders enjoying a massage from a brunette in velvet. 'Harry my fellow, I think you're overstating the—'

'Oh come on,' Larksdale said, cutting him off. 'It was you who told me to put him next to Sir Mardle there.'

'He did?' Mardle said.

'You all have,' Larksdale said. He'd a fire in his skull. He knew he was making an enemy of simply everyone but it was as if he couldn't turn the cart around. 'You all act like loving brothers of the sword but you all come to me in whispers, *"Oh don't put me near Slyke, he's a bore, don't put me near Cutbill, he's a lowly thug."*'

'We were right,' Osrin said and the woman on his lap laughed.

Larksdale sighed and snorted up the culoo he'd marshalled.

'Go back to your theatre,' Slyke said. 'Because you'll lose that soon enough. Your mustard ship's lost at sea and you're a bankrupt.'

'Cease your droning you fucking gnat,' Larksdale said.

'Give it a rest, you two,' Lord Pym said.

'Our king will discard you,' Slyke told Larksdale. 'Right after your theatre girl beds him. She's neither convincing as an actress nor as a whore.' He grinned. 'I'll bet she's giving a tepid performance as we speak.'

Larksdale scrambled on to the table and seized the platter of mustard. He drove it into Slyke's face and threw his entire weight after it, falling on to his shocked rival and toppling his chair.

Magnificent, to sit astride a supine enemy and rub yellow vengeance into his face. 'How's my performance, Slyke?' Larksdale bellowed. 'Are you convinced?' Larksdale was taken by some other's fury, someone braver and far more foolish. He didn't care. All he could see was Arriet pushed down on the table. He knocked the platter from Slyke's face and drew the eating knife from his own belt. 'I'll give you an opening night, ribs to fucking balls!'

Larksdale was lifted upright and a forearm slid around his chest. It held him in place, a crushing pressure, a vice made flesh.

Osrin was dragging him backwards out of the hall at an incredible rate. Larksdale's shuffle could barely keep pace.

Quence and two other lords had Slyke bent double, as if readying him for a crude and impromptu beheading. The man was coughing up mustard.

'I'll butcher you!' Slyke barked between retches. 'Bastard!'

'And I'll cut your cock off!' Larksdale shouted. 'Feather your daft bloody hat with it!'

Larksdale stumbled, his ankle giving way, and Osrin dragged him anyway, shouldering a door open and pulling Larksdale into darkness.

'Stop now,' Osrin hissed in Larksdale's ear. 'You're a raging mouse in a parlour full of cats.'

Larksdale was slung down the corridor, landing on his arse. The breath flew from him.

'Now fuck off,' Osrin commanded. 'And keep fucking off.'

'But—'

'I'll *break* you, queer,' Osrin warned him. 'Break you.'

The door slammed closed and Larksdale was left to gloom and a hammering heart. A lantern hung directly above him, its cheap sides smearing a dead pig's veins across the sandstone ceiling. Everything hurt.

'But it's my party,' he whispered. 'My party.'

Somewhere above him hundreds of criminals turned great wheels in the dark. He hated using the paternoster. He wished he were standing on the empty stage of the Wreath, the winter night's air on his skin.

His limbs were pulsing. The fight. The powder. He reached his regular guest chamber and turned the iron ring of the door. Inside, a single candle flickered upon the nightstand. The bed chamber, near-spherical in shape, had been someone's attempt to illustrate the universe in woodwork. The bed's four posters were the pillars of the world, with the peoples of the earth carved upon them. The posters blended into the ceiling and floor seamlessly and one could follow humanity's dead as they rose up to God and the Holy Pilgrim in the oaken dome above. Other souls, naturally, descended.

Larksdale stood upon those souls now. Hundreds of carved screaming faces peered up from the varnished floor, tormented by winged sprites painted in gold lacquer. For a moment, Larksdale pictured himself sinking feet first into the damned vignette.

He shook the feeling off. So too his boots and jacket. The bed's heavy curtains, sage green and fern as per Larksdale's colours, were drawn. Spangles of golden light quavered upon them, for the round walls were decorated with hundreds of silver studs that served both as portrait of the night sky and as luminesce, their mirrored surfaces reflecting any candle placed in the room. There were no windows. Larksdale drew back the curtain.

Gethwen lay on his front, his back bare, the top of his buttocks visible above the green sheets.

He slept. The slumber of the innocent, not that he had earned such. A liar, or at least a dissembler. Larksdale had removed Gethwen from Becken as Sister Ruradoola demanded. The keep wasn't exactly Becken after all. Another world. With another world's rules.

'You've left the door open,' Gethwen muttered.

Larksdale went back and closed it. Anyone could have entered while Larksdale mooned over this beauty. He had to be more careful now. By the time he returned Gethwen was sitting up, his knees drawn in and making a tent of the sheets, his hairless torso vellum in the candlelight.

Larksdale removed his own tights and kept his shirt on. He dropped on to the bed and stared at varnished saints above. He was weary and far too awake.

'You fooled me,' Larksdale said. 'You should have told me everything. About your mother. This… black crown.'

'I wouldn't embroil you,' Gethwen said. 'I had meant to stay a night at the rooms above the Wreath then be gone.'

'You have some power, Ruradoola said.' Larksdale scratched his beard. 'To read others' feelings, to play them.'

'I try not to. Believe me.'

'You'd say that either way.'

Gethwen did not reply.

Perhaps Gethwen had powers. Or perhaps it was all rustic superstition. Likely, that. But Larksdale wanted the lad safe and away.

'This black crown,' Larksdale said. 'You threw it in the pond at the shrine, yes? Before I caught up.'

Gethwen gulped. He nodded.

'Tomorrow, we'll dredge it up,' Larksdale said. 'Get you out of Becken.'

Gethwen said nothing.

'The banquet was disastrous,' Larksdale said blankly. 'I've made a mess of everything. My plan, my dream. And I think… I might be a bad man.'

'No.' Gethwen drew the sheets aside and clambered next to Larksdale. They kissed. 'You're a weak man.'

Larksdale chuckled, exasperated. He was in bed with Slyke.

'Listen,' Gethwen said. 'You're a weak man *here,* in this keep. You bow to people no better than you, follow ways you know are absurd. And it's killing you, sir. I see that. With my power.'

'I work with what I have,' Larksdale said, disturbed.

'But out there—' Gethwen pointed toward what he must have assumed to be Tetchford, though he was aiming toward the sea. '—you are chief. When I first saw you, Harry, I saw a great man.'

'I was working a crowd of bored housewives.'

'You *moved* them, all of us. Took us out of our lives a moment, dispensed justice to a wrongdoer.' He slapped Larksdale's chest with his fingers. 'To see you like this, in here, a chained hound?' He rubbed the spot he'd just slapped. 'I'm lover to two men, Harry. I know which I prefer.'

'Apologies for his absence.'

Gethwen kissed him again. 'He's here if you want him here.' He sat upright and began to remove Larksdale's shirt. 'Now tell me this dream of yours. This plan.'

Larksdale lifted his haunches and his shirt was dragged off. The pair of them, naked inside a little wooden universe. They lay on their sides facing one another.

'I'm not in the habit of telling,' Larksdale told him.

Gethwen's manhood was already stiff and he grinned when Larksdale noticed. 'Who would ever listen to a spineman in this place?'

Larksdale felt the culoo course in his scalp, his chest. He kissed Gethwen, long this time, and slipped his fingers around his hardness. Gethwen moaned and cupped his own hand around Larksdale's. They tugged each other gently and stared into one another's eyes.

'I want… to be master,' Larksdale said. 'Of arts and revels.'

'What's that?'

'The lord of theatre. Of craft. Beauty.'

'Slower,' Gethwen whispered. 'Gentle now.' He purred. 'Tell me. Tell me your dream.'

'I'll not rest at plays. I'll beautify the world. Art frees men, my sweet. Women, too. I've seen it in their eyes.' He felt alive. 'I'll make artists of the lowest beggar and the highest lord.'

'Tell me,' Gethwen said.

'No curtsies or beheadings. No crimes nor honours. All equal, all artists.'

'Faster. Please.'

'A golden world,' Larksdale said, fire rising, 'worthy of God. Worthy of…'

'Yes… oh…'

'Worthy of man.'

Larksdale strained with ecstasy, a saint taken by an angel's whisper. His spine curled and he moaned.

All tension seeped from his bones. Gethwen's hot seed had dappled his wrist and forearm. They had climaxed as one. A rare thing.

The pair of them breathed as one. Gently, Gethwen found Larksdale's hand and weaved its fingers with his own.

'Sir,' Gethwen said. 'In the mountains we would call you madman. We would follow you into the mouth of death.'

Larksdale smiled. He wondered if Gethwen had used some power upon him to make him speak, or if it all were simple and blessed affection.

But he could not keep his eyelids open.

21

Fwych

Fwych had missed her chance. They had vanished, Carmotta and her man. They had lain there earlier, after their mountings, lain a long time. Just when Fwych had thought them asleep one would whisper and the other laugh. But it was Fwych who had fallen asleep and when she had woken the room was daubed in moonlight and they were gone. So she'd had a shit in the bowl they gave her. It were all she could do.

Five nights till Yulenight Eve. If the boy had had the black crown taken from him, if whoever had taken it were foolish enough to take the crown into the heart of this evil place… all was over. All gone.

Perhaps the lad would prove good enough. But Fwych couldn't shake off the fear his enemies were better. Whoever sent the pennyblades to the inn had known about the meeting with Aifen-the-Tom before the meeting even happened. That she-beast Red Marie had known they were all there too. The only hope lay in Gethwen making friends, good ones.

Something crashed upon the floor. Something in the dark beyond the bed.

Fwych grabbed her bone knife. She peered into the darkness.

'Shit,' a man's voice whispered.

Feet padded across the wooden floor. A thin man in black cap and clothes burst out of the gloom, a chopping blade raised. He charged at the bed, swung down at the strewn pillows and linen. He sliced and sliced, fell on to the bed and hacked away at the side nearer Fwych. He stopped, looked at his handiwork.

'Shit,' he said.

He leaped off the bed and stalked over to the door that likely led to Carmotta's pissery. He wrenched the door open and leaped into the other room.

'Shit,' he muttered. He stepped back into the bedroom. '*Shit.*'

He stood there a moment, uncertain what to do.

Fwych hissed at him. Tongueless, it came out a rattling growl.

The thin man stared at her. He hadn't seen Fwych in her cage; likely Old Mother Moon had shone in his eyes before. That and he didn't know what he were even bloody doing. No killer, for certain.

Fwych hid her bone shiv. With her free hand she pointed at her own eyes then pointed at him. *I've seen you, son.*

'Aw shit,' the thin man said. He thought a moment, then he smiled all friendly.

He strode up to the cage, downplaying the chopping blade in his hand by holding it behind his back. He had the weakest moustache, stolen from a maiden's arm.

Fwych pointed at the lock on the cage. She shook the locked door.

The thin man stopped. 'Shit.'

Fwych pointed at the white table against the wall. The thin young man took the hint and walked over. He stared at its bare surface, uncertain what to do.

Witless fool. Fwych rattled the cage for his attention then pointed at the table's drawer.

The man nodded thanks and drew it open. He found the key Carmotta's lover had placed there when Fwych had first arrived.

The thin man waved it at Fwych and Fwych nodded back. He grinned. Daft lad.

He strode over, chopper behind his back, feigning he wasn't going to kill her for seeing his face.

Fwych readied herself. Never easy to kill one so young.

The man slipped the key into the lock and turned it. The bolt withdrew.

Fwych drove her bone spike into his eye.

It snapped.

He were as shocked as she. Both of them froze, unsure, then the thin man yanked open the cage's door and squeezed inside. He lifted his chopper.

Fwych screeched.

The man froze. Fwych knew the look. He'd been stunned by her voice. By her power.

Fwych grabbed his shoulders and threw him. His head hit the bars at the other side of the cage and then he dropped face-first into Fwych's waste bowl.

Fwych tugged the chopping blade from the young man's fist.

The thin young man lifted his head from the bowl. 'Shit,' he muttered.

Fwych swung the chopper into the back of his skull. His face flew back into the bowl and filth sprayed a halo around the bottom of the cage. He went still save for a twitching leg. She grabbed the chopper's hilt and drew it from the bone. A clean cut. Blade were worth keeping.

Something glassy rolled around the cage's metal floor. She picked it up: a glass ball. She wiped the shitty blood from it and looked. The ball stared back. It were an eyeball, real-looking, one of those wonders of flatlander craft.

So that's why her bone spike had snapped when she drove it at his eyeball. It hadn't been an eyeball at all but a clever replacement for one already lost. Must have popped out its socket when his head hit the cage.

She put the thing back on the floor and set about pulling the man's soft shoes and clothes off. They would fit her fine enough.

She made for the door out. She stopped when she saw something oblong upon the floor. One of them big framed paintings, face down. It had to have been what made the crashing sound. On the wall above it was a big square hole. A tunnel with a draught pouring out.

She stepped a little closer to the hole and saw it had iron hooks at each corner. The picture on the floor had straps on the back of its frame. A blessing that. She could climb into the tunnel and hang the portrait back up. No one would ever know where she went. Things would be on her terms.

Only then did she recall her voice. She had screeched and the lad had been stunned. She still had that power at least, if not the power to persuade in words. That was something. *She* was something.

Delaying only to leave Carmotta and her lover a token of esteem, Fwych climbed into the tunnel and sealed it with the fallen picture.

22

Carmotta

She reached the bottom of a coiling stairwell, its candle lamps fashioned from painted bats' wings – one of the Brintland's stranger decor choices – and passed along a corridor in silence.

She could hear men shouting and laughing over the strains of harps and gitterns. All of it emanating up from the stairwell at the end of the corridor. This was as close as she would ever wish to get. Carmotta wasn't that naive sort of woman who wondered what men talked about when only men were present. That was obvious enough.

If he's not being intimate with you, ask him why, the Explainer had said just before everything had turned to nightmare. *You haven't even tried that, have you?* The spike-eared devil had spoken truth.

A man was at his most honest when he had spent his seed. Ean would have sent away his whore by now and he would be in a melancholy mood. That was his way after the act, with any woman. Dulenci, however, was at his most clinging after sex. It had been draining, prising him from her side. He had sulked off to his own chambers, cursing her and the world.

The two armoured guards before the door Carmotta had expected; the skinny woman with auburn hair and sunken eyes she had not. She filled the air with cheap jasmine perfume. She had a great pink stain all down her old dress and she was shocked to see her queen.

'Your Majesty.' Skinny curtsied inexpertly. She should not have spoken.

'His whore,' Carmotta replied. 'Your name.'

'Arriet. Arriet Cab—'

'Your first will suffice.' Carmotta looked her up and down. 'I wore those very earrings some years ago.'

'At Moleford Waters?' Arriet asked. She remembered to say, 'Your Majesty.'

Carmotta gave Arriet the executioner's stare, cold and damning. In truth, Carmotta did not know what to say. That summer day at Moleford Waters, her first true public outing, had been both a triumph and a danger. She had won the court over, having got Dulenci to pay an oarsman to 'accidentally' spray her with water. She had made jest of it, announcing how the river Brint had given her land's new queen her blessing. The gambit worked and Carmotta knew she would leave Moleford that day only half as foreign to these nobles as when she had arrived.

Yet he had been there. Larksdale. The first time they had met since Manca. Surrounded, the pair of them had feigned polite interest, a little mirth. Only they could see the blades both drew. That the circling of each other had begun. Now, here was another one of Larksdale's animals, a tool lifted from those streets he wallowed in. The bastard had even told her about Moleford.

'I trust you fucked him well, Arriet,' Carmotta said.

The whore's sunken eyes lit with fear.

'You must fuck well,' Carmotta continued. 'I see no other reason you would be chosen.' She ran her hand down Arriet's side like a farmer checking his swine. 'This rake, this frail and unremarkable stick, is not a body that warriors are born from.' Arriet the whore made a strange face then, a guilty face. Interesting. 'I see you doubt it too. So we are agreed, are we not? You must be an exquisite, monumental, haunting *fuck*.'

'Your Majesty, I beg you…'

'Did *you* beg *him*? He likes a little begging.' *If only I could do this to dear Queen Emmabelle,* Carmotta thought. 'Did he ride you or he him? How long for? How—'

Arriet muttered something. She shook her head.

'What?'

'Nothing,' Arriet said. 'Nothing happened.'

The skinny bitch was telling the truth, Carmotta could tell. 'Continue.'

Arriet the whore eyed the guards behind her.

'They're just a pair of halberds, girl,' Carmotta told her.

'We kissed,' Arriet admitted. 'But he… would not perform. His Majesty is, well, out of sorts.'

'He's ill?' Carmotta asked.

'Not exactly,' Arriet replied.

'You lie. Ean never drinks to excess.'

'There was an… enervating powder the men all snorted.'

'*Bastard* Larksdale.' She pushed Arriet to one side. 'I will see to His Majesty. You shall leave.'

'Where to?'

Carmotta froze, incensed.

'Do I look like I know where whores slumber?' she demanded. 'I am Carmotta Il'Lunadella, First-Queen of the Brintland, not some pox-addled tavern madam who takes your filthy coin and gives you bedding straw.'

'My apologies, Your Majesty,' Arriet said, squirming. She looked at the two guards. 'Perhaps—'

'These men guard our king,' Carmotta said. 'You think them night porters to a whore in another woman's clothes? How dare you?' Carmotta grinned. 'And do not even *think* about begging Larksdale's madam and her girls for a room. The other lords will see you. Your presence will shame the king's virility.' It was cheap, wrecking this woman, but a whore's pain was worth a queen's pride. 'No. You must come to some other arrangement within this keep, one I simply have no interest in. Begone.'

Arriet bowed and scuttled off down the corridor. Larksdale's prettied-up animal would hate her master now. So she should: he had done nothing to secure her a place to stay the night, nor a coach home. Now Arriet the whore would be lost in the keep's many, many corridors. Alone and cursing Harry Larksdale. One had to find one's victories where one could.

She entered the bedroom and the warmth of a log fire caressed her. It blazed in a circular hearth at the centre of the chamber, a brick-and-mortar chimney above it collecting the smoke. The low ceiling was entirely covered with plates of mirrored glass imported from the isle of the commrach, for only elves could make mirrors so fine and in such quantity. Carmotta did not look up. A reflection so clear simply had to be witchcraft, despite what others insisted.

This ceiling was, of course, for the benefit of the great bed at the room's end. Women were commonly held to be the vain sex but, in Carmotta's experience, it was men who liked to watch themselves frolic. In that, Ean and Dulenci were alike. If her blasphemous dream of bedding them together ever had the faintest hope of occurring, she realised, it could only ever be in this room.

Ean was topless but still in breeches and boots. There wasn't even half a fuck in him; Arriet had been right enough there. He lay upon his side, his leg shaking, a muscled arm stretched out above his head, its hand gripping one of the bed's posters.

'Ean,' she said.

Ean's twitching leg drew up and his sculpted belly tightened. A single word from her had procured only a cringing dread.

'Oh Ean, do I sicken you so?'

'No,' he muttered.

'Let me tend to you, my king.'

His silence was acquiescence. Carmotta strutted over to the bed and, raising her heavy skirts, clambered on to its softness. This bed where he fucked all and sundry, for the blood of Neyes cannot be damned. She caressed his wrist and his bare arm shivered, the light hairs upon it already full-risen. She prised his hand from the poster and slipped her ringed fingers between his. She kissed the back of his hand, the cold flesh there.

'My love, my love,' she said.

'I'm so sorry,' came Ean's muffled reply. 'I'm sorry.'

She raised his arm to see his face. His jaw was shivering, his lips parted, and his eyes were red-rimmed and wet, a desperate boy's. She felt an intense compassion for him and a familiar contempt for Larksdale.

'Shh,' she whispered. She slipped her fingers from his and shifted her body so that he could rest his head on her thigh. *Larksdale fed him some potion to humiliate him,* she thought, *consciously or otherwise.* She caressed Ean's clammy brow with her fingertips. For a single breath she thought Larksdale might have done it at the behest of Count Osrin, but then she remembered Larksdale was simply a fool too desperate to be liked. That was his poison.

'Tonight I thought I had so many brothers,' Ean said. 'But there's just me.'

'You have me. I will never leave you, Ean.' It was true. Cornered in a passage by treacherous swords, she would throw her body before Ean. She had played the moment out in her mind many times, but in these last few days it seemed more than an idle fantasy.

'I did not want her, my love,' Ean whispered.

'We do not have to talk of that.'

'They were mocking me,' he said. 'For the milk. I should have crushed them all but I didn't. So I wanted them to see I wanted her. That I'm still a man.'

'You are.' Guilt gripped her. It had been the Explainer's aphrodisiac that had provoked him to express milk. Her own desperation. 'And their king besides.'

Her connivance had threatened his rule. What other word to give it? She had been steeped in ploys and manipulation all her life. She had simply worked with the cards given her. For lack of cock she had received no sword and for lack of sword no armies would ever follow her. But she had lost sight of things, of love. She was a compassionate woman beneath it all. For too long she had thought that weakness.

If he's not being intimate with you, ask him why.

She waited, perhaps an hour passing, maybe less. She stroked his brow and at one point his cracked lips kissed the knuckle of her thumb. It was like the old times, before the other queens.

'Could we talk, my love?' She gazed into his star-blue eyes.

His mouth parted. The powder-addled fear was rising in him, but she could not turn back.

'Yesterday,' she said, 'in your chamber, I was too forceful, too demanding. You did not want me.' She bit her lip. 'But you never want me.'

'I love you,' he whispered.

'I know. But you… fear my flesh. You did not used to. Not before…'

His jaw stopped shivering. His face was as a statue.

She forced herself. 'Not before we lost our little boy.'

He squinted. He began to scowl at her as if she had slighted him.

'My love…' she tried.

'How dare you?' he growled. 'How…'

His head rose from her thigh. He lifted himself up from the bed. His body was alive now. His eyes had a strange fire.

'You do not speak of that!' he bellowed.

'Ean—'

'You think it your king's fault? You think that?'

Fear gripped her. Would the guards come if he beat her?

'Listen, my love—'

'Not I,' he hissed. 'It was not I who failed, woman.' He almost grinned. 'You humiliated me. Your very body.'

So long this venom has festered in him, she thought. *I never saw.*

Inches above his head black lines emerged and rippled from the air. Five, like eels, snakes.

Carmotta blinked.

The lines were still there. They thickened, grew points, five points that hovered over his forehead. At the top of his skull they thickened into one mass. They were as a hydra now, floating above his head.

She clambered off the bed, to the other side of it.

Ean's leer faltered. His shoulders shook. 'Carmotta,' he said. 'I'm sorry.' He was staring at her, startled by her expression, oblivious to the blackness that hung over his skull. 'I should not have…' He trailed off.

She pointed at his head. Words could not come.

A hand. That rippling blackness was a clawed hand. Fingers thin as bone, cupping the air just above Ean's head. No detail to it, the hand was made of that same stuff as light motes in the eye, flat and featureless and almost transparent. But black, a negative space, an affront to the very air.

A trick of the light, it had to be. She looked up at the mirrored ceiling.

The hand was still there in Ean's reflection above. Like a spider riding his skull.

No, no.

She craned her head back further.

Five sharp fingers hovered above her own brow.

A scream. Hers. Carmotta tore her hairstyle apart with wild blows. She braced for the cold touch of the black hand. She connected with nothing. But the hand remained in the mirror above.

Clawing at her hair, she belted for the door. She pulled it open, saw two guards, each with a clawed hand above their helmet. She darted out between them, screaming down the corridor, wishing the world back to how it had been.

23

Red Marie

She hung above them in the dark, her gloved hands gripping the wooden faces in the ceiling, her sickles sleeping in their wrist holsters. They were beautiful specimens, the two men below her, at least in the dying candlelight. None of the thick body hair of most male humans, save for that on their crotches and the older man's chin. Smooth skin, to the point of shining. Red Marie wanted nothing more than to flay that smoothness, hold the warmth against her cheek. The younger one was her quarry. Had been since the inn three nights past. The older was Sir Harrance Larksdale, who would have to be taken care of. First things first.

She felt no ache in her limbs. Her inordinate strength saw to that and the suit carried her weight well enough. It was a different suit to that which she wore on the streets of Becken. This suit was made for the keep, to blend against its halls and chambers. The ribs, spine and helm were of dark wood, like the varnished doors of the upper corridors, the sleeves and tights were as fine tapestries and curtains. Her face-mask was of their St Neyes, that child's face carved in stone and wood throughout the great keep. Red Marie's version had wondrous fangs of stained glass. Red Marie did not have to be sealed into this suit as she did with the city variant. The ancient curse had no power to kill her inside the keep, only beyond it. But the keep wasn't half so fun to prowl through as the streets of Becken.

Harrance Larksdale stirred below, much to Red Marie's annoyance. She had hoped he had fallen unconscious by now. Not that he would see her should he open his eyes. The eye of the observer simply did not want to: the world beyond the suit a sliver more interesting. It took rare focus and effort to make a suit capable of that, to make it so formidably irrelevant. In the daylight hours between hunting and sleep Red Marie caressed each segment, each twine of the suit, chanting the words and finding the neutral place in her mind. It was her refuge, that ritual, for she had performed the act since childhood, deep, deep in those pines where sunlight never touched the forest floor and everything was windless and warm and black. She had been happy there, in the ever-night, despite her father. But she could never go back.

She had let her mind drift. Larksdale was gently snoring, worn out after all his exertions. Red Marie had followed him up from the catacombs and through the black halls, had clung to the underside of one of those coffin-like boxes that rattled and creaked up and down their strange chimney and scuttled out after him when he stepped out. The final part had been easy; the fool had left the door wide open when he had entered his bedroom. He was no challenge, this Larksdale. Walking meat. She would put pain in him. Gift him with grief.

She slithered across the ceiling until she came to hang directly above Larksdale. She tilted her head back and pressed her tongue against one of the mask's stained-glass teeth. It clicked, swung down and dangled on its hinge. Dark liquid welled in the open gum. It poured along a vein in the glass tooth, collecting at the tip. A single droplet fell into Larksdale's open mouth. He ceased snoring. Red Marie smiled.

'Boy,' she said. *'Boy.'*

The young spineman stirred.

'I am here for you,' she told him. *'And you are alone.'*

The spineman sat upright. Keen, this one, this Gethwen. The mountains had honed his edge. A fine prey. He looked at Larksdale and nudged him.

'Harry?'

'He can't help you.'

The youth looked around. 'Who are you?'

'There are those who call me the deceiver.'

'Be gone. I warn you, spirit. I have powers.'

'Your mother had powers, boy. I took her tongue.'

'You killed her?'

'Where is it?'

'Where's what?'

'Come, come,' Red Marie said. *'You know. The black crown. Where have you put the crown, boy?'*

His terror was sweet and clear. A demon who knew all about the black crown was a terrifying prospect to any spinefolk aware of the object and its history. Red Marie's masters had told her as much.

'No idea what you mean,' Gethwen said.

'Mother knew. She gave you the crown to take with you. I saw it all.' A pause. *'I'll hurt you if you tell me where it is.'*

The youth paused, uncomprehending. 'Then why should I tell you?'

'Because I'll do worse than hurt you if you do not.' That was good, she had been meaning to use that. She drank up his fear.

'I've powers,' he insisted. 'I can control you.'

'Your mother had powers of control. You only have powers of feeling. Go on, reach out. Feel what I'm feeling.'

He paused. He screamed.

She let go of the ceiling and twisted mid-air, deployed her sickles from out of her suit's wrists.

She smacked into an empty mattress, sliced into linen, not flesh.

The youth had rolled off the bed and was rolling under it.

Red Marie drove her sickles through the bed's base and sliced only wood and air beneath. She ripped her sickles out and feathers filled the gloom, bursting from the bed in a cloud. She leaped over Larksdale, toward the side of the bed nearest the door, to head the lad off. She dropped on to all fours and swiped beneath the bed. No one.

Bare feet pounded. The youth had turned back on himself and darted out from the other side of the bed. By the time Red Marie had burst out of the curtains surrounding the bed, the youth was out the door and into the corridor.

Behind her mask she grinned. Fine prey. She gave him five seconds. Then she pursued.

24

Carmotta

Running, she could find no stairs up, only down. She could not bear down, toward the black heart of the keep, and so she kept to the corridors. The mouths of her slippers bit against her feet and her long hair hung down, all the pins and fastenings that had kept it aloft swinging against her shoulders and back.

I have gone insane, she thought. *His words broke my mind.* She had never expected it to be so straightforward. Had it been so for Second-Queen Violee? *Why yes, it follows I must now become a hedgehog;* is that how she had thought of it?

She passed a statue of Neyes the Child, before the Pilgrim had worked his miracle on the boy, then another of Neyes the Conqueror holding the keys to Becken Keep, when he had taken it by right of conquest. She had passed these statues before. She slowed. She would pass a statue of Neyes on his deathbed soon. She was running in circles, knots. That or history runs into circles then knots, the actions of great men like water circling a drain.

She had to cease being insane. She had no zeal for it.

A stringed instrument played somewhere ahead, down the long corridor with its chain of brass lanterns that flickered above. A gittern, most likely, a desolate refrain.

She turned a corner and saw the gittern player through a doorway: a young woman sitting in a great chair by a roaring hearth-fire. She wore nothing, her long blonde locks obscuring her breasts, the instrument her parts. A dark and ghostly hand slumbered over her head. A figure of folk tale she seemed to Carmotta, though no tale she knew. The woman had not seen Carmotta, being so rapt with the plucking of her strings, and Carmotta had the sense she was no true musician, just capable and a little out of practice.

Carmotta entered and a warmth surrounded her. The room was huge, a hall, with a low ceiling of painted rock. The woman with the gittern had merely been to one side of it, keeping warm beside her hearth. At the hall's centre ran a long banqueting table festooned with torn food and toppled goblets. The feeding finished, men were now taking their fill of women.

So this is the room. The thought came dreamily to her. Her feet carried her forwards.

There were few men, some six, she reckoned. Most of the lords had long vanished, taking their whores with them, no doubt. She saw Lord Pym, his oak chair pulled back from the table, a woman with ginger plaits sucking upon his length, her ringed hand grasping the shaft. Pym's head was back, his balding scalp reflecting the red light of a hearth-fire, his eyes screwed tight in pleasure.

And there it was again, half-transparent in the firelight. The spectral hand, clawed and thin, floating above Pym's head.

Her belly's sickness twisted to ice.

The other men. Across the table, Sir Recimer groped at two women who pretended to laugh. He was drunk, all the time looking poised to vomit. Another hand of night rippled above his skull. More hands yet. Each weighing over a skull unseen. On the other side of the table someone she could not recognise lay atop a woman, his breeches about his ankles, his sallow buttocks pumping between her thighs. Carmotta stepped closer, saw the back of another demon's hand. Everyone. Each and every rutting man and woman, vessel to their own unseen nightmare.

She felt eyes upon her. She looked up from the tupping pair, toward the end of the banquet table.

Count Osrin. Alone, he had one boot upon the table, his body half-sunk into the ornate chair he sat in.

Ean's chair. He has seized it for himself.

The act seemed far more debauched than anything around the room. His bleary eyes recognised her. He seemed as confused as she, as if they were two dreamers realising they were sharing one dream.

Every man here is his.

She could be made to disappear, she knew, if Osrin and his gang could shake off their lust and indolence. This was their world she had stumbled into. It went without saying the hand of night was upon Osrin. A large specimen, a starving tarantula.

Osrin smiled at Carmotta, the V-shaped scar that ran from his chin to both cheekbones stretching as he did so. They knew each other in this moment, and everything she had ever thought him capable of she now knew true. He would kill Ean or die trying, this one. He would take the throne like another chair.

She ran. Ran into the corridor to her left, a long tunnel of carved rock, the stretched shadows of veins and arteries arcing across the damp stone. She heard no footsteps behind her, no charging conspirators with swords at the ready. Still she ran.

She darted around a bend and collided with a body. The pair of them tumbled to the tiled floor, their limbs flailing. They lay beside one another. Carmotta shrugged off the pain. She squinted.

Arriet the whore. Dazed, but unhurt. Her make-up ruined with tears.

And no hand above her head.

25

Fwych

She should have taken a lantern. Black as caverns and tighter still. But these tunnels had to lead somewhere. They had to have purpose, being chiselled by man. Had to have.

She crawled on all fours, the thin man's chopping knife hanging from her belt. She kept a good pace but not so fast as to tire and lose sense. Cavern discipline, that. Taught from parent to child back home in the mountains.

She sensed a wall ahead, reached out a hand and felt that that were so. But there were a hot breeze all about; this weren't no dead end. Fwych reached out left and right and found only more wall. The breeze were coming from below.

She might have gone arse-up, down into who-knew-where, if she hadn't been cautious.

Had she known, she would have gone arse-forwards down this tunnel, because now if she wanted to go down she would have to drop face-first down into nothing; nothing she could see, anyhow.

She got on her belly and leaned over the drop, stretching her arms down the hole. The hole was square and near the same size as the tunnel. No ladder, no rungs in the stone.

That suggested the drop weren't far. The one-eyed man she'd killed had climbed up it, after all, and he hadn't shown a sniff of sense, so it couldn't be that far, not with him. Still, no point risking a broken arm. She would just have to crawl backwards and—

Gethwen. She felt his fear.

He were alive. In danger.

No choice, none to be had. Fwych barked her fear out and threw herself down the hole. The world turned blind and wind beat at her face, whistled in her ears. She had her wrists out before her, braced for them to crack.

The back of her skull scraped against stone, then her elbow. The vent were shrinking. Her back and belly scraped against the walls and then she jolted, air thrown from her lungs, her arm sockets stinging.

She hung upside down in the vent, silent a moment, making sense of all the pain and the pain to come.

Gethwen. Closer now.

Arms aching, she clawed at the hot, wet walls, dragged her body down through the tightness, happy neither her ribs nor her collar had snapped. Then she fell again.

She screamed, hit a floor. Broke nothing.

She got on to all fours and gazed around. Four tunnels, forward, back, left and right. She could see them because each gave off a trace of light, a hollow square of candlelight. The junction led to four more paintings, she reckoned. Four rooms.

Which way? She reached out her energies, felt for the lad Gethwen.

Right. *No,* forwards; the lad was moving fast. Best to cut him off.

She crawled at speed, cavern discipline be damned. The square of light pounded toward her and she could see the end of the tunnel was pale wood; the back of another painting. She reached the painting's back, hammered with both fists, and it came loose and fell at once. Fwych threw herself into a candlelit gloom.

She fell on a large bed, her toes hitting the headboard. The bedroom was almost as fancy as Carmotta's but the bedclothes and curtains were torn and everything reeked of stale food and piss.

Fwych got to her knees upon the mattress and saw a young woman in white curled up into a ball at the end of the bed.

Panicked, Fwych thought. *Good.*

Fwych made to leap off the bed and bolt for the nearest door, but her feet got twisted in the bedclothes and she tumbled, hitting the floor with her shoulder. She looked up to see the woman in white scuttling toward her on all fours, glaring down at Fwych and hissing. The woman's black hair were a nasty tangle with dust upon it and a chicken bone jutting out. Her eyes were rimmed red and terrifying.

Fwych leaped to her feet and circled around the hissing woman, hands raised to show she were no threat.

The woman yipped and snorted. Father Mountain, what was this?

Fwych belted for the door. She yanked it open and found a young woman with a silver jug on the other side. She tottered forward, her ear having been pressed to the door. Fwych gave her a roundhouse punch and the girl collapsed on her back, spraying milk everywhere.

Fwych leaped over her and ran into a dark corridor. She stopped, closed her eyes. She reached out. *Gethwen…*

26

Red Marie

His own ignorance had doomed him. He was exactly where she had been driving him, at the termination of a corridor with nowhere to go. She could hear him there just before she turned the corner. Could hear his panting, his tears. Oh, and his resignation. Her sex tingled, just like that first time when she had cornered her father's hunting lynx. When it knew it could not flee.

'*There's no escape here, boy,*' she said. '*No saviour.*' She stepped into the corridor and raised her sickles. '*You're all alone.*'

The lad was a picture, a corona of stained glass behind him, a window with that haloed saint, Neyes. His eyes were red and wide, the lad, his mouth agape and his nostrils flaring. He had a marble bust in both hands, the head of some old king or other. He must have swiped it while on his furious travail.

'*You won't hit me with that,*' she informed him. '*I'm ohhh-too-swift.*' He was but two yards away. '*Try, if you like.*'

He tensed, went to throw, and she ducked. He clutched the bust tighter.

Behind her mask's glass teeth she licked her lips, the lower one first, then the upper, the harelip, that visible sign she was inferior to her fucking masters. Before they put her in their suits.

'The crown, boy. I'll let you live if you show me where it is.'

'You'll kill the world,' he said.

'No, no,' she said. *'That's superstition. We just want to know more.'* She hated explaining things.

'Liar.' He was crying. Oh he was *crying*. 'Liar.'

He spun and threw the bust through the window. The battling winds blew in but he fought against them, ran and clambered on to the jagged sill.

Red Marie went to grab his ankles but stopped. She had to be careful with her sickles. *'Stop.'*

But he was gone, stepping out and to the right of the broken window.

Red Marie jumped on to the sill, glass cracking under hoof. There was a ledge directly below the window, the width of a man's shoulders. The lad was trying to make his way along it, chest to the keep's stonework, clinging to cleft and lump. His right foot was a dark mess, leaving rivulets of blood on the ledge like an offering upon an altar. A thick triangle of glass was lodged in the arch of his foot. He was having to stand on his toes.

She stepped out on to the ledge. She did not cling to the wall. Her balance was that of a lynx. She took in the night, the wonderful view of Becken from so far up.

'You can see both bays from up here,' she shouted so as to be heard over the barrelling winds. One could even see out to the trade obelisk of the commrach with its pinpricks of silver light.

The lad had gotten a little further, dappling the ledge with his blood. He had reached the visage of a huge gargoyle and was trying to climb into its barrel-sized maw.

'It's fine to be scared,' she shouted to him. *'Just come with me.'* She wasn't convincing and she knew it. It should not have come to this.

He was struggling, not just to climb into that stone mouth but merely to stay conscious. It was all pouring out from that foot wound of his. She strode over to him and, gentle as a dove's wing, cradled a sickle around his throat.

'*Come now,*' she spoke into his ear. '*I know a place so quiet and so warm. We can talk there. You and I.*'

She never saw his expression. He slid his neck away from her sharpness and a thin line of blood sprayed across a giant stone tongue. He threw himself from the ledge, down from the keep and into the dark of its gardens below.

Her climax was stolen. She had imagined the pleasure of this night, flaying the answers her masters wanted from the lad's mind and muscles. But no.

There would be questions. She would have to answer for what had just happened.

She turned and saw a face staring at her. It was the tongueless hag, gazing out from the smashed window. She had seen her boy fall.

Red Marie hadn't the energy to grin at her. Perhaps in the moonlight it would seem her mask was doing so. Or perhaps the hag could not even see her, was staring in horror at the place where her child had only just been.

Red Marie climbed into the maw of the giant gargoyle. She would wait awhile and disappear once more.

THREE NIGHTS TILL YULENIGHT EVE

27

Larksdale

'Sir Harrance.'

Where was he?

'Sir Harrance.' A familiar voice, low and rich with gravel. 'Please.'

Willem Cutbill. Why was he waking to Willem Cutbill? Why would anyone?

'Sir Harrance.'

'Fine, fine,' Larksdale relented. 'I shall open my eyes. Happy now?' He did so and saw Sir Willem Cutbill standing above the bed, a lit candle in hand. His eyes had bags under them and his lips were chapped. All else was darkness.

Larksdale was naked under thick blankets. His shoulders were freezing. The hearth-fire must have gone out.

'What time of night is it?' he asked.

'Midday.'

What? He could not have had a full night's sleep, for his skull was a groggy bowl of fog. Could it be midday? Like many rooms deep inside the keep, his chamber had no windows. Illumination depended on the hearth-fire and the candles and the many polished silver studs along the walls. Gethwen had delighted in all the room's 'shiny stars'.

Gethwen.

Gethwen wasn't here. Perhaps for the best, given Cutbill's presence. Larksdale smiled. He and Gethwen had saved a night from the jaws of despond and raised it to… well…

'Why the smile?' Cutbill asked, face grey as winter.

'No reason.'

'I'm here about your page,' Cutbill said. 'Gethwen. That his name?'

Larksdale sat up. What had the young fool done now? 'Where is he?'

'Outside.'

'Well bring him in.'

'He's outside the keep.' Cutbill studied him, as if he were looking up from the groundlings of a theatre and Larksdale were alone on the stage. 'He's dead, Harry.'

Larksdale snorted a laugh. 'No. You're…' But Cutbill had no sense of humour. 'No.'

He slipped his hand under the sheets to where Gethwen had lain, hoping he would find some warmth there. None, none at all. Just a deep gash in the mattress that had not been there before. He elected not to show it to Cutbill.

'I'm sorry for your loss,' Cutbill said.

'Take me to him.'

'That wouldn't be wise.'

'Neither's standing in my way.' The anger was sudden, a lump in him.

'He's been manured already,' Cutbill explained. 'They thought him an escaped convict. From the paternoster wheel.'

Chopped to pieces. Larksdale drew his finger through his hair. He cradled the back of his head. Gethwen had feared the keep. Now he would never leave its flower beds. Come spring he would be a violet.

'Captain of the palace guard is a drunken fool,' Cutbill said. 'The lad's body needed investigation, with me, over at Wessel Bridge. And a burial thereafter.' He stared at the carved floor. 'This bloody place.'

'How…' The feeling he might awake soon was receding. 'How did it happen?'

Cutbill paused and it was then Larksdale knew Cutbill had been studying him this whole time. Studying the surfeit of bed feathers too, which mysteriously littered the room.

'Murdered,' Cutbill said.

Larksdale met Cutbill's stare. Anything else might seem guilt.

'How?' Larksdale asked.

'Sliced throat.' Cutbill said. 'Thrown from the keep.'

'I appreciate your manner, sir,' Larksdale said ruefully. He wiped a tear, held back more. 'The quick jab being the kindest.'

'You were the last one seen with him.'

'Slyke,' Larksdale snapped. 'He's the one you want.' Well who else? The weaselly shit had killed Gethwen. 'Slyke and I bickered last night. Said he'd kill me, get revenge. At least I think he did. It's all a blur.'

'You were the last one seen with him,' Cutbill repeated.

Larksdale tensed. 'You think me the killer? Hmm? I adored the fellow. Slyke *knew* that. He's your man. Sir Tibald Slyke.'

'Did Gethwen say anything to you?' Cutbill asked. 'People saw him enter here.'

'We made conversation.' *Love, too,* he thought. Such love, where Larksdale had opened up, explained his life's secret plan. 'He sat over there, tending the hearth.' He pointed across the room. 'I must have fallen asleep while we talked.'

The big bull could see he was lying. Larksdale was struck with a fresh memory. Cutbill had been wrecked on the rocks of culoo powder, the rage he had known in the heat of a hundred battles suddenly there for all to see. That was why he looked so terrible now.

Yes, Larksdale thought, *the rage has never left this man, nor the guilt of surviving where others died.*

'Well,' Larksdale said, 'if I cannot see...' A lump caught in his throat. Gethwen in a flower bed. In pieces. 'If I cannot see him, I suppose I had better get back to my theatre.' *For there one can weep.*

'You cannot go,' Cutbill said.

'I'm for the clink?' He could picture his cell already. 'For the rack?'

'No,' Cutbill replied. 'I haven't the power to do that, Larksdale. I'm captain general of the city guard, not the keep.'

'So why the *fucking* questions?'

'Habit,' Cutbill offered. 'That and the palace captain won't bother.'

'So what man are you to tell me I cannot go?'

'A man commanded by our queen. She commands your presence.' He looked Larksdale up and down. 'You had better get dressed.'

'So *she's* head of the guard here now, hmm?'

Cutbill's brow creased in the candlelight. He seemed uncomfortable as well as tired. 'It's a delicate matter,' he said. 'Her Majesty won't leave her chamber. She's even locked her cousin out.'

'What's any of that buffoonery to do with me or poor bloody Gethwen?' Larksdale demanded.

'She won't leave until you offer her your presence.'

'You're joking.' He waited. 'No, of course you're not joking.' He could make out his shirt on the floor. He gestured for Cutbill to bring it to him. 'Does the king know?'

'I'm trying to keep things discreet.' He passed the shirt.

'Do you mean the murder?' Larksdale asked. 'Or the queen's behaviour?'

'Both, now you ask. Though more the latter.'

Larksdale put his arms through his shirt sleeves and began to button up. 'I see. Well, after we're done with that we shall talk to the palace guard, eh? Because, *damn it*, Slyke killed that poor sweet lad. I'll see him in chains. And worse.'

'You won't,' Cutbill replied. 'Do you hear guards banging at your door, Harry? Your lad was a commoner, a spineman to boot. This is Becken Keep, where the great and the good reside.' Disgust passed across his face. 'No one cares here, not about the likes of him. At best he's the latest gossip about someone else. You.'

'But it's murder,' Larksdale said.

'No, Harry,' Cutbill said. He smiled sadly. 'Just bad form.'

In the gloom and rattle of the paternoster, Larksdale found he could cry a few tears, one for each day he had known Gethwen. Cutbill said nothing as compartments above and below their own collided occasionally with the walls – they were noisier when empty – and each bang sounded like a judge's gavel.

Two palace guards stepped back to let them through and another two let them into the antechamber of the queen's chambers.

Dulenci was in there, striding back and forth in front of the locked double door. Larksdale did not think people did that in real life, that such was the acting of utter hams, but here it was.

'Get in there,' he said to Larksdale. 'Quickly.'

Larksdale stopped before him. 'She does not wish to see you? I do hope your popularity isn't waning.' A little cruelty thrown at Gethwen's betters eased the raw grief.

'You're one to speak,' Dulenci replied. 'They say your boy threw himself off the keep to escape your thirsts.'

'And the boys in Tetchford say you do not stop at your thirsts,' Larksdale replied. 'You're straight on to your seconds and thirds.'

'You have been following me,' Dulenci said with no malice. 'Your taste is commendable.'

'Why am I here, Dulenci?'

'Our queen will not leave her chamber until you speak with her. Now do as she commands. Swiftly, before the whole keep notices. She has engagements to fulfil this day.'

Larksdale shrugged. 'We've spare queens.'

'Spare *queen*,' Cutbill piped up. 'Second-Queen Violee has escaped again.'

'Really?' Larksdale said.

'This time she punched a handmaid.'

'Better than last time, I suppose,' Larksdale replied and the other two men nodded in agreement. 'Fine, I'll do this.' He had a sudden image of Gethwen falling, his blood on the melting snows. *Oh, Geth*. 'But I likely have quite the day ahead of me. I cannot be at this long.'

He walked over to the double doors and knocked.

'Larksdale?' Arriet Cabbot called out.

'*Arriet?*'

Oh. This could not be good.

The doors unlocked and the left one opened slowly. No candlelight beyond, only daylight through half-drawn curtains. The air hung stale with used perfumes. Beneath that was the whiff of something less palatable. Something of the drains.

Arriet Cabbot looked pale and spent, her eyes more sunken than ever.

'I forgot to get you home last night,' Larksdale said. 'That's unforgivable.'

'It doesn't matter,' she replied. She touched his hand. 'I heard. I'm so sorry.'

'Bring him here!' Carmotta snapped somewhere behind Arriet. 'And – hell's fuck, why not – the others too!'

The men entered. The great windows at the opposite end of the room made Larksdale squint, the sky beyond them white as wool. The pinewood floor below his feet was the size of the Wreath's stage and halfway along it squatted a leviathan of a four-poster bed. Chairs and tables stood here and there like actors, and under the far windows was something like a cage. Carmotta's chambers were everything he expected they might be: furnished with that resplendent ugliness of old Brintland nobility and garnished with Mancanese art in an acceptably insipid way. *You betray the girl you were, Carmotta. But that's to be expected.*

He mistook the queen for another saccharine *objet d'art* at first, perhaps a lumpen bronze. She was sitting in a high-backed chair in the middle of the room, a silhouette in the window's light. A footstool stood before her, quite unused.

'Sit,' she said. She could only mean the footstool.

Larksdale did as she said, lifting the tail of his long jacket to do so. The stool was small and his knees jutted upward, tight in their hose.

Carmotta leaned forward. Her hair was wrapped in a samite turban, a style quite unlike her, as if she had not bothered to dress her raven locks. Her stately dresses had vanished too, replaced with some sleeping gown and scarf. Her eyes were veined and her make-up had gone to wherever her dresses had decided to die.

She stared at Larksdale's hairline and he wondered if he had got some cobweb in it. For a breath there was fear in her reddened eyes, then a terrible sadness, a look almost of defeat. She closed her eyes.

'Something the matter, Your Majesty?' Larksdale said.

Her eyes opened once more and she glared at him. *Our shared game has resumed,* he thought, *with a fury.*

Willem Cutbill drew breath. His shoes creaked upon the pine floor as he shifted his weight. He was looking at the cage at the end of the room. Without asking for the queen's leave, he strode toward it.

Larksdale looked at Arriet, standing by the bed. She would not meet his gaze. He looked at Carmotta again and she was still staring at him. Damn it. Time for ol' Harry Larksdale to take charge of matters.

He got up and followed Cutbill. Dulenci, never one to keep his nose out, followed Larksdale.

At first, Larksdale thought the cage home to some monstrous beast too freakish for even the keep's menagerie, a cyclops from shores unknown. Not so. The thing was a naked man bent prone over a wooden chest, his hindquarters very much on display to the room. A pale blue human eye peered out from between his buttocks. A glass replica, clearly, for to imagine it anything else was the road to lunacy. The man's head and shoulders lay on the other side of the chest. Something reeked here, despite Carmotta's obvious attempt to conceal it with perfumes.

'Is he dead?' Dulenci said.

'Ask him,' said Larksdale.

'Split skull,' Cutbill said. He had made his way to the side of the cage and was squatting to get a better look.

'Do you see who it is?' Larksdale asked him.

'His face is in a bowl of excrement,' Cutbill replied.

'At least he got a last meal,' Dulenci said. He chuckled.

The other two men looked at him.

'What?' he replied. 'Whoever this is, he broke into our queen's private chambers. In my opinion he has got off very lightly indeed.' He looked back over his shoulder. 'Did he hurt you, my queen?'

'He was like that when I got here,' Carmotta replied. Casually, as if this murderous diorama was the least of her troubles. 'I had been visiting my husband.'

'A warning, maybe,' Cutbill said. 'A message.'

'An eye in an arse?' Larksdale replied. 'What on earth would it be trying to say?'

'Look behind you?' Dulenci offered. He was serious.

Cutbill sighed. 'We'll only really know once we see his face.'

Oh no.

'We haven't the keys,' Larksdale said.

Cutbill reached down and picked up some iron keys by the dead man's feet. 'Here you go.'

Larksdale turned to look at Dulenci but he was already stood by Carmotta's chair. She reached out and held his hand.

'Fine,' Larksdale said. He seized the keys from the big man's fingers. 'I'll open, you turn him over.'

The cage door opened easily enough and Cutbill stepped in. He turned the naked man over and laid him on the floor. The reek had risen to a stink now but the old soldier showed no disgust. Camp life, Larksdale suspected.

'You got a cloth, Sir Harry?'

Larksdale grunted and passed a handkerchief. 'Keep it.'

Cutbill wiped the face down. A young face, somewhat guileless. He was missing his left eye, its hollow socket crammed with filth.

'Makes sense,' Cutbill muttered.

'Something had to,' Larksdale said.

Neither man recognised the corpse's face.

'This has to be connected to Gethwen,' Larksdale said. *Yes, and with Tibald Slyke, the spider at the centre.* 'Too much of a coincidence not to be.'

The queen called out, 'My thoughts exactly, Larksdale!' She had always possessed the most irritatingly good hearing. 'Now get back over here.'

He gave Cutbill a look and wandered back over to the queen in her chair. She nodded to the uncomfortably small stool and he sat back down upon the wretched thing.

'Sir Willem,' Carmotta said, never taking her eyes off Larksdale. 'You would be wise to arrest this man and put him to the question.'

'Are you commanding me, Your Majesty?'

'If it were a command,' she barked, 'I would have spoken it so.' She took a breath. 'That's the curse of being royal: everyone takes your orders but never your advice.'

She was a fraught and haggard mess, Larksdale saw, a woman barely holding things together. Quite unlike her. He would not have believed a mere corpse with a glass eye in its fundament would wreck her so, though admittedly he had never given the scenario much thought. Carmotta was of firmer stuff. There was more here.

But sweet, sweet Gethwen was dead and so – if Cutbill was not going to take him to Wessel gaol, which he seemed disinclined to do – Larksdale did not care.

'Your Majesty,' Larksdale said, 'are you implying I crept in here and gifted you that cadaver?'

'Word reaches me your mountain youth was murdered in the early hours,' she replied. 'Like as not the same time this man here perished. As you say, too much the coincidence. Believe me, Larksdale, if this man—' She pointed a finger behind her. '—was the sole corpse this morning I would place a hundred braver and more capable men as the likely hand behind his slaughter. But given your lover—'

'Majesty,' Larksdale said, 'if you were not queen I would call that slander.'

'Oh cease the act, man,' Carmotta said. 'Do I look a priest? Do any of us here?' She continued. 'But given your *lover* has also passed from this vale of misery, it rather draws suspicion. Hmm?'

'My queen,' Dulenci said, 'we men desirous of men are prone to most amorous fury.'

Larksdale had never heard such rot. To hear it from another man-lover, even one so crass as Dulenci, was maddening. One could find ten women murdered by a man's passion before one found a man.

'Larksdale's cowardice,' Carmotta said to her cousin, 'outweighs his passion. Always.' She let the words hang, to be understood between her and Larksdale alone. 'He hired or cajoled the caged man to kill his lover and then hired another man, I presume, to kill the killer and leave his body here in the chamber of his enemy.'

Larksdale nodded with as much sarcasm as he could muster. 'In a cage.'

Carmotta nodded. She was clearly as unsure of this hypothesis as anyone in the room.

'Why is there a cage?' Larksdale asked.

'Parrots,' she answered without a blink. 'I am expecting a flock.' She looked down. 'Though sadly with the Hoxham situation I have been made to wait.'

Same as my mustard, Larksdale thought.

'So, my hired killer,' Larksdale said, 'my *second* hired killer, carried my first hired killer naked to this place, opened up your polly-hutch and – now here's a puzzler – decided to leave a bowl of his bowel movements?' He shook his head. 'Or is that a birdbath? I'm lost here, I'll admit.'

'Who knows the sick minds of the scum you patronise?' Dulenci said to Larksdale. 'The second killer probably told him if he shat in the bowl he would permit him to live. Then, despite his compliance, he drowned him in it. As you commanded.'

'Absurd,' Larksdale said.

'Is it?' Dulenci asked. 'I think it has that singular theatricality we've all come to associate with you.'

'You're a simpleton,' Larksdale said.

'Your Majesty,' Cutbill said, nipping this farce at the bud. 'We'll have a far better understanding of what happened once we talk to the guards who were outside your chamber last night.'

Carmotta's expression flickered, as if she were running some equation in her head. She looked to Dulenci.

Dulenci looked at his feet. 'I bade them leave.' He waved a hand. 'They would only have got in the way. I and my servants were bringing the cage up here and putting it together and so forth.'

'And you did not think to bring them back once you were finished?' Larksdale asked.

'Why bother?' Carmotta said and she grinned. 'Cousin Dulenci is worth ten guards, such is his prowess.'

'My weapon is unmatched,' Dulenci added. 'Many a man will tell you that.'

He made a camp little swagger and Carmotta giggled. It struck Larksdale as strange, crass and wholly inappropriate, but he supposed such was the general tenor of the morning.

'Your Majesty,' he said. 'My respect for the Crown is unrivalled. But I have had more than any mortal man can bear. That I am thought that sweet boy's killer I find unbearable. He was a dear soul, too unique for this world.' He could see Gethwen smile. He had smiled only hours before. 'The other day…' he had to pause, to hold back tears, 'I lost him in the gardens around the keep. When I found him again, he was by the pond in the forest shrine, staring at the statue of Neyes and the Pilgrim.' Only Cutbill was listening. Surprisingly raptly, in fact. 'Gethwen was lost in the art, the grace. A grace the rest of us walk by daily.' A lie – he had only gone to throw that damned crown in the water – but Larksdale wanted it to be true. Rage crackled in him. 'How dare you, my queen?' He met her eyes. 'How bloody dare you?'

'Get out,' she whispered. Larksdale thought she meant him but then she looked to the others and shouted, 'Get out! I'm perfectly safe! Leave us!'

Cutbill and Dulenci headed for the doors. Arriet, whom Larksdale had forgotten in all the farrago, followed them.

'Arriet,' Carmotta said. 'Remember what I told you.'

Arriet stopped, looked at the queen and then Larksdale. She curtsied and left.

This was all very concerning. 'Making new friends, Your Majesty?'

'Shut your lips.' Carmotta's madness evaporated, as if Larksdale's skill for irritating her were a tonic. 'Or I will make certain you never open them again.'

This is not our game, Larksdale thought. *What has Arriet told her?*

'Do not fake rage for your lost boy,' Carmotta said flatly. 'You never loved him. You are incapable of that.'

Larksdale frowned at her.

'Stop it,' Carmotta said. 'You convince yourself you are wildly in love because the idea of wild love consumes you. Like all good actors you are the last to realise you are acting at all. If only it made you a danger to none but yourself.'

She was a joke, this bitch. All the court thought so, though none spoke it. He pictured Gethwen's smile again. How dare she? This joke. This bitch.

Larksdale coughed. 'Perhaps His Majesty will—'

'His Majesty is a greater man than you,' she said, cutting him off. 'Even as the lowest peasant he would be greater than you. I see you, Harry. I see how you idolise him, how you want to be him, you wisp of a shadow. But Ean has honour, he has restraint, and above all he has *presence*. That's what you truly hunger for. Because all you've ever possessed is *charm*.' She hissed the word like it were the name of some plague. 'Charming men envy men of presence, for a charmer has to constantly be in motion, dazzling and caressing folk with his tongue. But a man with presence only has to stand in the same room and all flattery is his. You shrink to *nothing* in Ean's presence. Pilgrim's heart, it seems to me now, watching you here, that you shrink to nothing even when you do not speak. It's why you speechify and gesticulate and command your peasants to act and dance. Stillness reveals how inconsequential you truly are.' She chuckled.

'Now I see it, it is obvious. As plain as that too-long nose upon your face.'

Larksdale found his gloved hand was digging into his knee. This was all just too-too much, just utter. He rose to stand.

'Sit,' Carmotta snapped.

He did so. She was queen, after all.

He smiled sardonically. Scorn had never come to him easily, but by God he tried it now. For the moment had come.

'I really hurt you, didn't I?' he said.

Her face kept still but her belly quivered a half-second. She had dreaded a moment like this, he knew. She could have him executed, certainly, but she would have to explain why. So it followed she could not. She knew that. Always had.

'Too much pride, Your Majesty.' He wagged a finger. 'Haughtiness is the most garish of shields and ultimately as flimsy. Face the truth of it: I left you waiting on a poxy dockside like a poxy dockside doxy. But we've all been made to seem fools, my dear. Get over yourself.'

Her brown eyes lit up. She leaned forward in her chair.

'I was kept to my bedroom for a year.' Her words came out clipped. She was furious. She was beautiful. 'I could have mentioned your name, you worm. But I didn't.'

'Oh don't play the heroine, Mottie.' He had not said that name in years. 'If you'd mentioned a man, we would have both been for the block, such being your Mancan honour. Your father's pride exceeds his ample estates and you are far from his only daughter.'

'Cold bastard,' she whispered. 'I should have seen you were a cold bastard. I was *seventeen*.'

'And I nineteen. You had all the gullibility of that age and I the pomposity. The difference is I have learned maturity's chief lesson: that we must laugh at the absurdity of our own selves.' He waved at all the chintz and silk in her room. 'You've been cocooned by all this, Mottie. A monarch never grows up past the age they were crowned and you had ceased growing up before even then. Despite your plots and your airs you are still that naïve, slack-mouthed girl. Waiting at that dock.'

Silence. Her brow became pinched, her lips flat as a shore.

'Arriet,' she said.

Larksdale shifted in his seat. He tried to look nonchalant.

'I made acquaintance with your friend Arriet,' Carmotta said. 'A pure soul.' She paused a moment, as if recalling something. Then her ice returned. 'She kept me company all night after we found that.' She nodded behind her, toward the corpse in the cage. 'We had many hours together. Two frightened women can share much of their lives. You saved her from her husband, she says. But I see you only did so to make her another whore.'

'It was nothing like that,' Larksdale said.

'It wasn't? Well then you are truly the most spineless of men, defenceless against even yourself.' Carmotta smiled. 'I got much out of her. I'm good at that. I'm the queen. She was happy enough to open her legs for you, Harry, and accept the man you want to be's cock. But she wanted so *badly* to be an actress. She did not want his seed.' Larksdale tensed and Carmotta grinned. 'So you offered her a bottle of that elf-stuff. That isle potion. Hmm?'

'What in heaven are you talking about?'

'Slather.' She hissed the word. '*Slather.* To kill the holy seed of St Neyes before it finds soil.' She cupped her chin and looked quizzical. 'Now, I am no theologist but… is not such an act a sin? A blasphemy? Tell me, Sir Harry, what is the punishment?'

'The words of one woman,' he said. 'One liar.'

'Yes.' She stood up and walked over to one of her dreadful chests. Pulling open a drawer she produced a small book and opened it. 'Jane Chiswell, Tanner Lane. Abercine Habbaz, Hollowlyve Road. Rainhouse Wyldest…' She looked up. 'What a name! Rainhouse

Wyldest, Golden Pig Inn, Tetchford.' She closed the book. 'Twenty-eight names. Twenty-eight whores you proffered to my man. You think I wouldn't find out who they all are?'

'I'd have thought you above such things,' Larksdale said.

'Then you do not know women. You do not know a woman in love. Because I *love* him, you bastard. Now ask yourself if even one of these ambitious prostitutes will hold silent for you. Hold silent with all the weight of this keep upon them?'

The book may as well have been a crossbow. An executioner's axe.

She shook the book. 'I've been waiting. These names were my latitude, now this talk of slather is my longitude. You are on my map, Harry. I *have* you.'

'Really, now. I'm hardly worth a queen's rage.'

'Agreed.' She blinked. She looked at the top of his head again. 'But all manner of plots surround my husband and the Crown. The fact of the matter is I have no more time for our insipid game. You are a triviality, Harry. A distraction. Go to your theatre and stay there. Never return to this keep.'

'You cannot do this,' he said.

'I am doing it,' she replied. 'If I see you inside the keep I will begin a process that can only lead to your head spiked upon Wessel Bridge. Do not think that I won't, not now I have spoken it.' She dropped her little book back into the drawer. 'Go. I am finished with you.'

Larksdale stood up. 'Perhaps… some time away would be salubrious.'

Carmotta merely stared.

Larksdale – furious, trapped – nodded and smiled. 'Yes.' It was all he could think to say. 'Yes.'

He exited her chambers. She gave him an enigmatic look as he did so. Larksdale could have sworn it was disappointment.

28

Fwych

She had wept within dark tunnels before but never when so sane and sober. Only when she had eaten of the cap-of-the-way, when the madness and truth of Father Mountain took her. She were far from him now and her tears too clear-headed to be Father Mountain's gift. Gethwen were dead. She had seen him die.

She were thirsty. Hungry besides. *Oh Mountain.*

How had she ended up back in the tunnels? She had wondered that more than once. Her mind must have given out when she saw the lad fall. When she saw… *her* again. The beast. *But my body must have known what were best for me.*

She must, she realised, have replaced the painting in the crawling woman's bedroom when she climbed back into the tunnels. Otherwise, men would be in these tunnels now, searching for Fwych, jabbing with their damned spears. Fwych were amazed by herself, to think of doing that and then to forget.

He had been no good for hiding, that Gethwen. He were a dazzler by nature, liked to shine. He could read people – such being the powers of a tricky-man – and he had always played up to that. A good lad really. But too much the dazzler.

She had to wipe her eyes again, had to move. The world hung

waiting. She had to find the black crown. It hadn't been on him when he died. Where would he have put it? In all this place? Why had he come here? The very heart of all wrongness. He should have…

She had to move.

If she thought too long about the impossibility of it all, the size of this place, the smallness of the crown, the difficulty of asking anyone anything now she had no tongue, she knew she would go quite mad. Madness could not save the world. It never had. She simply had to trust in Father Mountain.

Her tunnel ended in the back of another painting. Fwych was sure she had not seen this one before. She put her ear close to where the painting's wooden back met the stone wall. Not a sound. But there were candlelight beyond.

She hadn't the strength to turn back. So thirsty. Her face came to rest against the back of the painting, then her weight and the painting fell and she with it.

Fwych lay awhile. She opened her eyes. A small room, this. It smelled of old candles and soup. Most every object in the room were covered over with blankets save one: a tall padded chair, its back to Fwych. Someone were sat in that chair. She could feel them when she reached out her senses.

The chair-sitter got up. An old woman in a dusty dress and wimple.

'Ooh now,' she said. 'Who are you?'

Fwych couldn't reply, of course. No tongue. She pointed at her open mouth.

'Hungry, right?' the old woman said. 'I'll bet you're thirsty too, stuck in all them tunnels.' She squinted. 'Did someone send you to kill me? Is that it?'

Fwych shook her head.

'Well you won't be needing that chopper, then.' The old lady pointed at Fwych's belt. She waddled toward Fwych, bent to the sounds of much cracking and wheezing, and took Fwych's stolen blade. She studied the pale steel. 'Nice work, that.' She tapped Fwych's nose with the tip. 'Queen Carmotta sent you, that it? Kidnap me to get my son's attention, I'll bet. She's eager, that one. No better than she ought to be, mind, that's for certain.' She tapped again. 'Speak up, then. Use the tongue God gave you.'

Fwych opened her mouth wide again.

'Ooh,' the old woman said. 'Nasty. Did she slice it off so you couldn't tell tales?' She frowned. 'No, too clever for her. I'll bet Count Osrin's mother is behind this. Told me her son Osrin was planning to take the throne. She's regretting that, so she sent you I'll bet. Still, have to play nice when next she comes for high tea. Appearances and all...'

The woman wasn't all that old. The same age as Fwych. She just seemed to gather age about her. A woman of dust.

The woman of dust were deep in thought. 'I could use a double agent. Gives one an edge about these parts.' She looked down at Fwych. 'You've still some tongue back there, you know.'

Fwych nodded.

'About as much as a butcher's parlour after feast day,' the woman said, 'but still enough. I could teach you to talk again.'

What?

'You haven't even tried, have you?' The woman laughed. 'You don't need a tongue to talk. I mean it *helps* but it's not fundamental. Common misconception. High lords are always like, "Take this man's tongue!" And I want to shout at them, "Don't be daft. You're daft, you daft prannet."' She were barking these words to the wall, to some made-up man. '"He'll just learn to speak again and he'll sound funny but he'll still slag you off in public and more will listen now on account he sounds so funny."' She shook her head. '"You daft prannet."' She looked at Fwych once more. 'I used to teach diction before I came here. If I teach you to speak, will you help me with a few chores?' She looked around, then whispered, 'I mean to put my son upon the throne.'

Fwych nodded. Anything for water, a little bread.

'You're in the circle now,' the dusty woman told her and she winked. 'Let's get you some soup.' She headed for some other part of the chamber.

Fwych nodded thanks. She would get out of this madwoman's chamber as soon as she got her strength. She had to keep moving, searching.

But to learn to speak again? Were it possible? If she could… she would be Mother Fwych again. A mountain mother with her voice of power.

A growl came. Fwych got up on her haunches though her back stung from her fall.

The animal woman. She had scuttled out from under one of the blanket-covered pieces of furniture and was nearing Fwych on all fours. Her black hair was still a bramble bush, her dress still torn and stained. Her nose twitched as if smelling the air.

'Eh!' the dusty woman barked. 'Leave her be! Friend, Violee, friend.' The dusty woman turned to Fwych. 'That's Second-Queen Violee. Thinks she's a hedgehog. I found her out in the hall last night. Do you see? We're in the big game now, my dear. High stakes. We've a royal hostage.'

29

Larksdale

His Majesty was kind enough to lend Larksdale a box palanquin out of the keep. It would be the last kindness, he supposed. The last regard. The journey back to Tetchford was long and odious and quite comfortable. He had drawn the window curtain of the palanquin. He had no use for the day and its people. Arriet, sitting in the palanquin's opposite seat, had not drawn hers.

'Harry,' Arriet, his ruination, said.

He cut her off. 'Leave it. It's no matter.'

She returned to gazing out of her little window, at the streets of Tetchford and all its iniquities. A good woman. Kind and captivating, but no match for Carmotta's guile. A night sitting beside Carmotta would draw mortar from brickwork. He had tried to get an audience with the king. He had known himself a fool to even try. Between the disaster of the party and the lover fallen from the keep, Ean had removed his presence from his bastard brother. He just had not told his bastard brother. Ol' Harry Larksdale had had to work that out for himself as he fretted and strutted about the keep's halls. He had seen the same happen to other men.

'The Wreath,' Larksdale said, still gazing out at the street. The palanquin lowered to the cobbles.

'I'm sorry,' Arriet said. 'For Gethwen. For it all.'

Gethwen. The name spoken was as a lash. *My sweet love...*

Larksdale nodded and she climbed out, helped by one of the bearers. Larksdale waved his own bearer away. The street smelled of roasting acorns and the River Tetch's filth. He'd rather missed it.

Arriet had already scuttled off into the Wreath. He let out a misted breath and stared at his theatre. They would be in there now, Tichborne and all the rest, rehearsing for their king.

How to break it to them? he wondered.

Across the street someone was screaming about Red Marie, about how the bodies were piling up in the alleys of Becken while the keep frolicked. Larksdale headed for the Wreath's doors before this preacher-of-the-cobbles saw his finery.

The cast's first dress rehearsal. The costumes were delightful. It only pained his heart the more.

The actors stopped all a sudden. Tichborne, directing from the groundlings in his wheeled boat and blankie, twisted to get a look at what everyone was staring at, which was Larksdale.

Clearly, they all knew about Gethwen.

Larksdale smiled. 'Carry on!' he commanded. He gestured at them and their stage. 'Absolutely wonderful! Simply orgasmic! Keep it up!'

Uncertain, they all did so. He made his way to the office. He had intended to cry inside there but it was already occupied.

'Marla!'

She was standing behind the desk, a clutch of papers in hand.

She grinned. 'I'm gone a day and a half and your filing goes to shit, boss.' She threw the papers to the floor, ran over to Larksdale and hugged him as if he were about to vanish. 'Oh Harry...' she muttered. 'Harry.'

'They let you go,' Larksdale said. The joy in him was as a tonic.

'When they knew Gethwen was nowhere to be seen in town.' Marla stiffened. 'I mean...'

'It's fine, I know what you mean.' He let go of her and stepped back. So fine to see her cheery face. 'I had ensconced him in the keep. A mistake. In hindsight.' He felt tears well. He pinched the bridge of his nose. Gethwen was dead. Oh, he was *dead*.

'Please, boss...'

'I... do not suppose it matters all that much,' Larksdale said. 'I do not suppose any of our lives matter really, not in the great scheme of things.'

Marla pulled out a handkerchief and gave it him. 'Then the great scheme of things shouldn't matter to us either, eh? He was a good soul.'

'But not a good soul for me,' Larksdale admitted, wiping his tears. Marla did not contradict him. He only liked her more for that. 'You look fine,' he told her. Which was true enough, for she wasn't a severed head in a box or the like. 'They treated you well at Fleawater?'

Boathook Marla grinned. 'Time of my life. Them fleas can roister.'

'You got them on side? Of course you did!' He ruffled her red woolly hat.

'It wasn't easy, boss,' she said. 'But once they realised I could help them out with a few of my various sidelines...' She shrugged. 'Plain sailing. Honestly, if we play our cards right we'll have an ally on Becken's west side.'

Larksdale nodded. He had no idea why an ally on the west side might be of use to a theatre but he supposed it could not harm.

Someone knocked on the door.

'Yes?'

Arriet stuck her head through. 'The Master of Arts and Revels is here!'

'Slyke?' Larksdale said.

'With men.'

Anger consumed Larksdale. Gethwen's murderer, most like, striding about the Wreath. It was too-too utter. Just… utterly. Utter.

Larksdale barged past Arriet and made for the stage, knowing full well that would be Tibald Slyke's style: raining down proclamations like arrows upon all present. Larksdale strode on to the boards just as Slyke was ascending the stairs at stage front. Slyke's arch presence, not to mention the two palace guards following him, had already reduced the cast to slack-jawed silence.

Slyke was not surprised by Larksdale's sudden appearance. If anything, he looked triumphant. His guards were of the keep, glowing with bright breastplate and polished halberd. This, Larksdale realised, was keep business.

'I am here for your play, Larksdale,' Slyke said. 'By our king's command.'

In the dumbfounded silence that followed, Tibald Slyke rested both his ringed and white-gloved hands upon his lacquered cane, his eyes noting Larksdale had no cane at all.

I shall fly at him now, Larksdale thought, *and he shall topple backward and snap his neck upon those stairs. Let the guards do what they may.*

He felt the actors all about him, their rouge and their tights and their memorised verse. Down in the groundlings Tichborne stared up from his wheeled boat, shocked and expectant. So too the carpenters and the seamstresses and all the rest. All of them looking. All ignorant. All hopeful.

'Sir Tibald!' Larksdale let his rage pool into a wide and loving grin. 'I had not expected you so early! But I should have, you being so dogged in your pursuit of theatre!'

He embraced Slyke, ducking his head under the man's wide-brimmed hat. Slyke froze. Larksdale turned him to face the groundlings, an arm around his shoulders.

'Good news, friends,' Larksdale announced. 'I'd been meaning to surprise you all but our city's Master of Arts and Revels is here already to take charge of our play!'

Everyone just stared.

'Do you not see?' Larksdale continued. 'Our realm's foremost impresario, the very monarch of the stage, has been dispatched by good King Ean to polish our humble offering to its finest possible sheen. How *lucky* are we?' Larksdale placed his free hand against his chest. 'No! Not luck. Talent. Hard work. You have earned this, my friends, my compatriots. Each and every one of you.' He squeezed Slyke's shoulder. 'This... man, this muse, this artiste beyond compare, is what you plainly deserve. He will raise you to new heights, friends. This is a new dawn for you all! I'm so happy, so *damnably* happy...'

He made an overwrought face, as if the moment was all he had asked for since boyhood. People began to cheer. Larksdale gestured for more and they gave it, clapping and hooting.

'Slyke!' Larksdale shouted. 'Slyke! Slyke!'

Everyone followed his chant. Larksdale spun Slyke to face him and embraced the swine once more.

'What ploy is this now?' Slyke hissed.

'Idiot,' Larksdale said. 'Do you want them at their best or not? Their happiness is my duty and now it is yours. Try to keep up, eh?'

He kissed Slyke's bristling cheek and stepped away, clapping the man before the gathered crowd. Larksdale blew kisses at his people, grinned and then exited stage left.

He remembered last night. How Gethwen had called Larksdale a great man in the streets of Tetchford but a coward in the keep.

'Oh my love,' Larksdale muttered, heading for his office, 'the keep has swallowed everything now.'

He locked the door of his empty office, lay upon the bed in the corner, and sobbed.

30

Carmotta

'Stop following me.'

'I am your bodyguard.'

They were striding through the underworld once more, the keep's distended guts, making their way along the tunnels that led to the hollow. She would rather have been doing so alone.

'What enemies lurk down here?' Carmotta said.

'A bodyguard guards a body,' Dulenci replied. 'And, frankly my love, you are your own body's enemy. Let's turn back. You have not slept, woman.'

She did not reply. That might mean looking at him. He had the hand of night above his head.

They all did, bar one soul: Ean's whore, Arriet, of all people. There seemed no logic to the matter. That dark and transparent hand, skeleton-thin and clawed of nail, hovered over the skull of everyone else she knew, including herself. The hands would not go away. Carmotta had the feeling that even if they should disappear they would still be there, unseen. That they had always been there and always would. She had merely learned to see them.

Or she might just be insane.

'Carmotta.' He grabbed her shoulder and she stopped for fear he might turn her around to face him.

'What?' she said, staring at a dripping wall.

'Why come here?' he said. 'You keep coming here.'

'For answers,' she replied. Which was true. 'For this babe inside me.' Which was not. 'You think I come here for leisure?'

Dulenci paused. 'You have enormous tastes. One might say insatiable.' He drew a long breath. 'I accept you must be the king's, but… I could never accept *him*.'

He meant the commrach, the Explainer.

Laughter overtook her, a hysterical ecstasy.

'What?' he said.

'You astoundingly stupid bastard.'

He spun her to face him, and as he leaned toward her the hand above his scalp flexed.

She yelped, pulled from him. 'Keep away!'

'What's got into you?' he demanded. 'You've become so cold to me. I cannot live without your love. I cannot.'

Trust a man to make her mental collapse all about him. She reached out and held his wrists.

'If you loved me, you would trust me,' she told him.

'Look at me, Carmotta,' Dulenci said.

She shook her head.

'Why not?' he said.

Why not indeed? She could not maintain all this avoidance of everyone. She was first-queen of the Brintland, daughter of House Il'Lunadella. Her whole life she had met people eye-to-eye.

She did so now. They were still her lover's eyes, yet black ethereal talons hovered inches above them.

'Kiss me,' he whispered.

No…

She took him by the chin and planted a kiss upon his lips, then stepped away. The hand had not moved, a slumbering spider. She wondered if the hand above her own head was also still.

'I love you,' he said. 'Always.'

'Why don't you go back up?' she said. 'I need someone to take care of the cage situation.' By which she meant the mountain woman who had escaped from it.

He shrugged. 'Come now, she's probably long left the keep. Even if they caught her, well, what could a tongueless savage tell anyone?'

'What of the man?' she asked.

'Man?'

'The dead man,' she said. 'He had an eyeball in his arse. Surely that left an impression on you.'

'Oh, him,' Dulenci said. 'I thought you meant the dead man who fell from the keep.'

Larksdale's youth. He had been pretty, that one. She could see the attraction. Perhaps it was true Larksdale had murdered him in a passion, as most of the court were saying, enough for Ean to keep Larksdale at a remove. She had not thought so until she saw him earlier. Larksdale had the hand of night above his head too. For some reason that felt like a betrayal.

'The cage-man must be someone's spy,' she said. 'Some bribed servant killed by his own curiosity. Whatever, a man with a fake eye will be identified soon enough.'

'One hopes,' Dulenci said. 'For myself, I cannot recall the face of a single servant beyond those who dress me. Can you?'

The truth of that unnerved her.

Carmotta was not surprised to see the hand of night above the head of old Jans. He had guarded an evil threshold for decades and, though the door had shaped the man, the man had not had the slightest effect upon the door.

Old Jans stifled a squeal as Dulenci pressed him against the wall beside the door.

Carmotta gave Jans a shushing gesture, then she inspected the black door. She had a theory about its mechanism and a modicum of skill in lock-picking, the latter being one of the seven secret 'accomplishments' Mancan noblewomen learned from their mothers.

'Key,' she said.

Dulenci passed Jans's keys to her and she slipped it into the lock. She turned it slowly, mindful of any slight and sudden resistance. She pulled the key as she turned, so that its teeth pulled the lock toward her and held the door tight against the sill. Difficult, to be both delicate and forceful at once, but anything less would play into the Explainer's defences.

There: a soft pressure against the key's teeth. She stopped. She had guessed right: the Explainer had not settled for a spring wire against the back of the door. His curiosity had led him to prise open the ancient lock and experiment with its innards. Likely he believed his modification to be far beyond the ken of humanity. But he had reckoned without Carmotta's mother: she had taught her child well.

She pushed the door open. She looked at Dulenci.

'Do not turn this key any further,' she told him. 'Hold him here. I'll be back shortly.'

Carmotta slipped through the doorway and closed it shut. The lunar glow enveloped her, the silvery light of the Explainer's hanging clay moons. She made her way down the stairs and out into the cavernous hollow.

The keep-within loomed over her, its walls of talon-shaped stones ghostly in the silver light. Carmotta felt only curiosity. Had her exposure to the keep-within's sorcery normalised its presence? It had altered her very senses, after all…

The Explainer was nowhere to be seen. He could only be in his tent, which she knew to be in the dark at the other side of the great vault. Perfect. She meant to get the upper hand and there would be no better advantage than to surprise him at slumber.

She kept to the edge of the great vault, stepping over broken masonry and pebbles in the gloom beside the walls. She had an instinct the keep-within would be no threat for a while, not since it had unleashed its energies, and that seemed to be the case. Without that instinct she would not have come here. She would not have risked her child.

The child. Her likely doom. Though there was still ample time to bed Ean and claim the babe his, she knew he had no wish to ever touch her flesh again. Ironically it was her failure to produce a living child that repulsed him. Regardless, her body would grow all the same, her belly ripening into an executioner's block.

She could see the Explainer's tent, a boxy shroud in the dark. Moonlight emanated from the slit of its door. He had offered to remove her problem, the Explainer. A simple matter, quick and painless, given the commrach arts. But a mortal sin, passage to the darkest hells. *Still,* Carmotta thought, *it would not be a sin to ask about his process, to understand what my life would be like as a woman of that peculiar isle.*

Her heart beat faster as she reached the tent. She drew back the flap.

He wasn't there.

A single moon tile hung from the tent's ridge pole, casting deathly light upon a thin mattress and a rolled-up blanket. There were few other objects: a couple of chests and a writing table with its stool. How could anyone live like this? She stepped inside.

A white face glared at her, its mouth stuffed with fangs. She stepped back, near-toppling on to the mattress. A hand over her mouth muffled her scream.

Her own hand. She relaxed, almost laughing at herself.

The white face was not alive. It was part of some kind of

sculpture. Blasphemous sculpture, for the face was a likeness of Neyes the Child, its eyes of stained glass. Neyes' parted lips had been festooned with savage fangs. The teeth were jagged slivers of stained glass, ground into points.

The face was part of an ornate helm that hung from a hook on the tent's rear right pole. Below the helmet was an entire suit of armour. Of sorts. Its varnished wood and blackened flax seemed impractical against spear and sword.

She made the sign of the Pilgrim upon her chest. God only knew what use the Explainer put this armour to. Some experiment perhaps, a means of getting close to the keep-within. For a second she hungered to know what he had seen, wearing that suit. They had a shared insight now, she and him. A most damnable bond.

She hardened her heart. Here was an opportunity to rifle through one of her adversaries' things. A spare key for his neck disc would be stashed here somewhere. Doubtless he had one. It was impossibly easy to take the original key from Jans, and if the Explainer hadn't before, he most certainly would have since she had threatened him.

The largest chest was unlocked but it contained no key. Some clothing lay in it, all patiently folded and finer than anything the Explainer normally wore, finer than most men's apparel.

A small chest was sitting on the edge of the writing table. Already Carmotta pictured the Explainer's face when he discovered the key in there gone. She opened it and was greeted with a waft of perfume: rosemary. Third-Queen Emmabelle's scent. The chest contained several dainty scrolls, each bound with a piece of twine. Carmotta took the top one, pushed it down her corset and closed the lid. Here was no place for idle reading.

Carmotta made for another chest, a large one set away in one corner of the tent. When she opened it a cold draught hit her chin and face, a sensation wholly at odds with the humidity of the hollow. Nothing but blackness greeted her eyes. The chest had no bottom, only a square-shaped hole that led down who-knew-where.

She shut the lid. He could only be down there in the dark. In his tunnel.

Time to leave.

She took a path closer to the keep-within, closer than she would like, crossing the vault's floor in the direct light of the Explainer's tripods with their many moon tiles. If she got out of the hollow now the Explainer would never know she was here. She refused to look at the jagged tower directly as she passed it, but it had a way of making itself paramount even as one kept it to the edges of one's vision. Always there, even when you blinked. A colonisation of your inner world.

She stopped walking. She was not sure why. She turned to face the keep-within's door. Ageless bronze, embedded in the black stonework of the tower, like a sun sinking into twilight. Featureless save for a knob of bronze at its very centre. Carmotta had an intense sensation that the door would open any moment, that a pair of eyes would glint at her from the darkness inside, that some wet mouth would hiss.

'Hey!'

Carmotta jolted. The Explainer's voice. He was walking out of the dark, from the direction of his tent.

'How did you get in here?' he asked. He stopped some five feet from Carmotta and she noticed he had a slender blade in his hand. A surgeon's knife.

'Jans,' she replied. 'I... asked to be let through.' When the Explainer's eyes glanced in the direction of the hollow's entrance, Carmotta knew he felt exposed. His clever little alarm had failed. 'Is everything fine, Explainer?'

He smiled. 'Yes. I had drifted off into a nap in my tent.' He waved his little blade with a flick of the wrist. 'Your footsteps woke me.'

'You commrach have sharp ears,' she replied. They did, quite literally. Slender and tapered. 'I meant no insult. I meant you have good—'

'I understood you,' he said. 'How strange. You almost apologised for something.'

'I was deliberating whether to disturb you,' Carmotta said, ignoring his barb. 'I assumed you would be in your tent.' She did not like the way he stared when she said that. For some reason she recalled the strip of human skin that had been attached to one of his queer devices. Better to change the subject of their conversation. She gestured at the keep-within-the-keep. 'But something about the door took my interest.' She looked at it again. Nothing about it was threatening now. Well, no more than usual.

'And what was that?' he asked.

She looked it over for some detail. 'The, er, lump there. The knob at its centre. Is it decoration?'

'Apparently not,' the Explainer replied. 'If you stood really close to the door, which I would not recommend, you would note the two indents, one either side of the "knob", as you quaintly put it.'

'Indents?' she asked. 'What for?'

'It's a door. So they're probably the housings for a knocker.'

Carmotta laughed. 'That is funny, somehow. Inappropriately… domestic.'

'Whatever it once housed is lost to the ages,' he said, his face blank. 'But I don't imagine you came here to talk of door-knockers. To what do I owe the displeasure of your company?'

He stepped closer and she saw a great spider nestled in his hair. Yet another hand of night. His demon blood had not protected him from the curse.

Realisation hit her. 'You see this, don't you?' She pointed just above her head. 'You have seen them all along.'

A sadness took his elfin features. 'I was rather hoping you would not.'

Carmotta nodded. 'What is it? What do these hands mean?'

'A symptom of contamination,' he replied. 'You had a heavy dose, if only once. So there's much hope for you I think.'

She thought of the life inside her. She put the thought aside.

'Why are there hands above everyone's heads? They have not been contaminated as you and I. And I saw one woman, Explainer, with no hand above her at all. What could make her so unique?'

The Explainer flashed a fang-rich grin. 'You really don't get out much, do you?'

'Hypocrite,' she said, looking about the hollow.

'Walk through the filthy city beyond the keep's walls and you will see a thousand heads free of the hands. Oh, you may see one or two so cursed, but so too will you notice their fine clothing or servant's garb. Knowledge of this...' he pointed his blade at the keep-within '...results in this.' He pointed the blade at the ghostly fingers in his wild hair. 'Presumably these hands play some part in dooming any person who speaks of the keep-within outside of the greater keep's grounds.' He shrugged. 'Selfish of me, I know, but I'm relieved someone else can see them. It's moderately less like madness.'

She wanted to ask him where he had seen these people without the hand of night above their heads. He never left these catacombs, after all. But she thought of the tunnel beneath the chest and the scalpel in his hand and thought better of it. He was a monster, a dread warlock. She could not forget that.

'My child,' she said. 'Will they see the hands? Will they see them all their life?' A terrible notion. The more she waded through it the more she sunk.

'I really do not know,' he replied.

'But you want to, don't you? You want to know everything there is.'

'Certainly,' he said. 'But it is tenet among the order of Explainers that the wishes of whoever carries the potential child comes first.'

'Potential child.'

'This early on,' he replied, 'potential is very much the operative word.'

So cold, these commrach. Facts, not faith: that was their doctrine. The notion scared her, she who had kneeled before altars and spoke the Pilgrim's prayer since she could first walk. Yet the commrach had studied the mechanics of nature for millennia. They knew truth in its finer details, though not God's boundless wisdom. The child was but potential, they said. Nothing else. Was it possible?

'Your Majesty,' he said. His inhuman eyes looked concerned. 'You seem troubled.'

'I want to keep it,' Carmotta answered. 'Despite the dangers to it, despite the dangers to me.'

'I see,' he said. His expression held no judgement.

'Not from fear of some holy law,' she said. 'Not any more.' She glanced at the keep-within, sighed and looked down at her belly. 'The ugly fact is… I feel so alone. I *know* I am, at heart, alone. But in that loneliness I find have an incredible love to give, if only another could comprehend it. I think a child could.'

'Love,' the Explainer muttered like a physician repeating a patient's complaint.

'As a reply to dread.'

He nodded, then glanced at his scalpel. 'I apologise if I scared you just now. Good day. If day it be.' He headed back for his tent, the lone inhabitant of this silent underworld.

She watched him slink into the darkness. There had been no key, she realised. He kept no spare despite constant mortal danger. He wasn't stupid, he was just true to the promise he had made when he first came here.

The most principled man in Becken Keep, she thought, *and he's not even a man.*

She turned and made her way back to the black door. To all the dangers beyond.

31

Red Marie

'An inspired idea, that,' Count Osrin said, 'giving him leaky tits.'

'That was not us,' Mard'Kem replied. 'The first-queen threatened our Explainer and our Explainer panicked.'

'How so?' Osrin asked.

'She wanted an aphrodisiac for the king and he gave her some random potion of his.'

Count Osrin's laughter filled the pale hall of the trade obelisk, reverberating off its many sleek pillars. Red Marie watched him from behind one such pillar.

If Count Osrin had any fear being here it did not show on his scarred and handsome face. Such serenity was obscene, against the natural order. Any human animal should have been cowed by the splendour of this commrach hall, should have babbled at its milk-glass walls rising into a dome of green and lilac glass, at the pewter vines and flowers that lined the walls and seemed to undulate in an unfelt breeze, such was their artistry. But not Count Osrin. He merely sat at one end of the long table, bereft of guard and blade, and gazed at his hosts as if they were new visitors to *his* home. Red Marie hated to see comfort in any creature at the best of times, but smugness was the repugnant scent of comfort's putrid flower and Red Marie would be all too happy to prune this complacent shit.

'Carmotta,' Osrin announced with a shake of his head. 'That sow really is fucking hopeless.'

'The Explainer thinks her cunning,' Mard'Kem said.

'Your Explainer needs to find some balls. Carmotta is a fat, miserable bitch. The only time she lights up a room is when she steps away from the window. Your Explainer found out which brave soul got her knocked up yet?'

'No,' Mard'Kem replied.

'Honestly? I'd shake the man's hand. The sheer resolve—'

'You haven't long here, Count Osrin,' Mard'Kem reminded him.

'I know,' Osrin said as if he were being criticised. 'So this lactation thing: could we get His Majesty to do it again? Maintain the flow, so to speak?'

'No.'

'You're no fun,' Osrin said, 'you know that?'

'Duly noted,' Mard'Kem said.

Red Marie circled the hall, keeping behind the pillars. No one in here could see her. Not Osrin, certainly, nor Mard'Kem and their two guards. Red Marie was wearing her suit of the city at large, the one that was entirely sealed so that the keep-within's curse could not get to her. The Explainer really was a visionary and an artist. Though this modified hinter-suit was primarily made for the slums and alleys of Becken, it could still dissuade the eye even in a hall of the trade obelisk.

She had reached the end of the hall directly behind Count Osrin. She always liked the gloominess there, plus the strange animal bones on display in the little glass boxes. Now this place had an added bonus: she could not see the count's insufferable face.

Mard'Kem was quite visible though, their white tunic and silver hair braids almost glowing beneath the light from all the moontiles above. Sinti Mard'Kem, steward of the trade obelisk, was of rarefied blood. Not the evolutionary pinnacle of the Cal families, the true highbloods and rulers of the isle, nor the blood of the Sils, that swaggering warrior caste, but as finely bred a commrach aristocrat as a lowly forest feral like Hoom would ever be permitted to see.

But Hoom is dead, Red Marie thought. *I am Red Marie, the terror of all men.*

Behind her mask she licked her upper lip, feeling the gap there, her harelip. A sign to any commrach who saw her hidden face, clear as the moon and stars: *Here is a face of lowest breeding, of blood unrefined, whom no one bothered to stitch the lip of as a babe.* She preferred her truer face. Red Marie's.

'Speaking of Queen Carmotta,' Mard'Kem said. 'Perhaps you might lend me some insight as to why a dead man was found in her bedchambers.'

'Suicide, I imagine,' Osrin replied. He chuckled at his own joke.

'My dear count, if you do not my mind my saying, it has the scent of your infamously impetuous idiom upon it.'

'My what, now?' Osrin asked.

Mard'Kem sighed and straightened the plaits of their asymmetrical hairstyle. 'Throwing a fresh corpse into your rival's bedroom has an audacity to it reminiscent of your ploy only the night before. The one you had us seed for you.'

'It worked, did it not?' Osrin countered. 'That Larksdale fop took the bait and stirred up a wonderful false alarm. "Treason!" he squeaked. "Regicide!" All the while pointing the finger at me and the boys. You really should have been there: it was a hoot.' Red Marie heard him lean forward in his chair. 'And now, having been accused of treason falsely, I am the last man in all the realm to be expected to do so.'

'Your king could have killed you on the spot,' Mard'Kem observed.

'Too cautious,' Osrin said. 'Too timid, though in appearance he evokes strength and conviction. I know my brother. And *that's* why, Mard'Kem, my...' He trailed off. 'Actually, Mard'Kem, I'm sorry to have to ask you this, but are you a man or a woman?'

'That's really none of my business,' Mard'Kem joked dryly.

'Commrach,' Osrin muttered with disgust at the isle's genderspan. *Barbarian.* 'Why did you bring me here?'

Mard'Kem nodded to a guard and she walked down the hall toward Osrin. The guard reached for her sword belt, paused a moment, then produced a parchment. She placed it before the count.

Osrin grunted and began to read.

Boring. Red Marie studied the skull in the glass case before her. A skull like a donkey's but larger, its snout slenderer. An extinct relation to the donkey, the Explainers said. Red Marie adored the idea of an entire species dying. She tried to imagine every species dying all at once, baying and screeching. She had to stop. It was too exciting a thought. She might get carried away.

'Oh,' Osrin said, discarding the parchment upon the table's surface. 'I do not know this name. I know her calling though. Killing one such would not be popular.'

'You do not have to kill them,' Mard'Kem explained. 'Merely approach the captain general of the city guard with the information. Then browbeat him with your status: he'll have no choice but to let you lead the arrest. You may need to suppress a lot of people.'

'Doubtless,' Osrin said. 'There's hundreds of those scum.'

'My superiors suggest you do so during King Ean's baptism of the River Flume. That way it will outshine the king's presence among his subjects.'

'Nice touch,' Osrin admitted.

Red Marie had gotten bored of her favourite niche. She walked past the skull on its plinth and, still keeping behind the pillars, approached the western wall with its pewter dolphins. *Dolphins are mammals,* the Explainer had told her one time as they made their way along the hidden tunnels and up into the keep's hollow heart. Red Marie had feigned being impressed then, because the Explainer liked to impress with facts. The truth was she had not even known what a dolphin was.

She did nowadays, and these playful creatures cast in precious alloy, leaping in and out of the marble relief waves, were most assuredly dolphins. They were freshly imbued, likely by the obelisk's lower staff, and seemed to sport and splash when one did not directly look at them. The conscious touch of a commrach hand lent singular qualities to material objects – Red Marie and the Explainer had spent many an hour in the keep's hollow caressing the two hinter-suits into a state of extreme irrelevance to any but the keenest eye. No doubt servants had been made to imbue these dolphins so as to impress Count Osrin, not that he had looked at the wall sculpture even once.

'I won't say it's not appreciated,' Osrin was saying, 'but it is adding more complexity into an ever-shrinking amount of time. Yulenight Eve is but three nights hence.' The human had his elbows upon the table, his fingers steepled. 'Perhaps we should be kinder to ourselves, hmm? Does this coup really have to take place on Yulenight Eve? *Really*? My king can be stabbed as easily on any of the other three hundred and sixty-eight days of the year.'

Mard'Kem looked exasperated with all the stupidity. The same look Red Marie's father would give her whenever she returned to the hut with no catch.

Her suit's sickles twitched and one of the two guards looked in Red Marie's direction. Red Marie kept quite still and the guard looked away.

'What?' Osrin was demanding of Mard'Kem. 'It's a perfectly valid question. I'm tired of your affected superiority, man. Woman. What-have-you.'

'High steward,' Mard'Kem corrected him. Their face was as blank as their tone.

Osrin grunted. 'Fucking commrach.'

'We've been through this before, my dear count. The king's death at midnight on the longest night of the year will have tremendous impact on the subconscious of your people, especially when slain by their ancient nightmare "Red Marie". It will possess a psychic resonance so mighty that your own act of slaying Red Marie immediately after will render your bastardy irrelevant and place – nay, hammer – you on to the sacred throne of Neyes. It's a performance, a re-enactment of humanity's earliest agricultural ritual: death and rebirth of the spring king, the vegetative god.'

'What *absolute* twaddle,' Osrin said. 'Every time I hear it I think you've been picking mushrooms from the wrong side of the pig shit; I really do.'

'The order of Explainers,' Mard'Kem said, 'has been studying this manner of thing since before you people invented bricks.' Mard'Kem shook their head and looked to their two guards. '*Siln teberu'li tila.*'

'*Siln edra ni dou,*' Osrin shot back, his Commrach poorly accented. Yet even Red Marie had to admit it was a fine riposte.

Mard'Kem straightened their tunic and took a deep breath. 'Please. Indulge us this eccentricity. It is… just a time and place we would be very gratified to see you act out the, er…'

'Regicide,' Osrin said.

'Quite. You must remember that we are going all out to help you, dear count. At considerable cost and risk. Your visit to our isle endeared you to all the highest families. I may be out of turn here, but I suspect my superiors see you as a son. Of sorts. They want what's best for you.' Mard'Kem smiled. 'Because, I think, they see a king.'

Count Osrin pushed his chair back and stood up. He walked toward Mard'Kem, one finger tracing the long table's surface as if checking for dust. He came to a stop before the high steward's seat when the guards placed a hand on their rapier hilts.

'I did not know,' Osrin said, 'you held me in such low regard as to feed me that saccharine speech. I'm hurt, steward, really I am. Be honest now. You elves do not want to see a wise and beloved king on any human throne. You want to see a mainland in flames, same as you always have. King Ean is a man of peace, a soul of conciliation, and your rulers can't bury that kind of fucker quick enough. And I'll help you, have no fear of that. And I'll do more. I'll give you true discord. I'll set the mainland alight with war and bloodshed because it's what a king is *meant* to do. Neyes the Conqueror knew that. As do I.'

'You are his blood,' Mard'Kem said.

'And I do not spill it at leisure,' Osrin warned them. 'I'll indulge this plan of your superiors. But the whole performance hinges on this killer of yours. This Red Marie. That concerns me.'

Red Marie's attention perked up.

'Red Marie is a consummate murderer,' Mard'Kem said. 'The commoners of Becken live in abject fear of her blades.'

'Anyone can stab beggars,' Osrin said, the V-scar on his face tightening. 'Killing a king? That takes an artist. Or a damned maniac.'

'We have both,' Mard'Kem replied.

Mard'Kem tapped a finger on the table. The sign Red Marie had been waiting for. She swept toward Osrin, slid behind the human and placed a sickle against his throat.

Count Osrin went still.

'Oh, she's here now,' Mard'Kem said. 'Our hand within the city, diligently working the populace into a new terror over old folk tales.'

And your hand within the keep too, Red Marie thought, *but let's not tell him that, eh?*

'My dear count,' Mard'Kem continued, 'you are wondering how our agent remained unseen even as she embraced you.'

'Pray tell,' Osrin mumbled, alert but unafraid. Red Marie hated that.

'She wears a hinter-suit,' Mard'Kem explained. 'The cutting edge of commrach artistry, crafted and imbued in such a way as to be... the opposite of decoration. Our forest folk invented hinter-suits millennia ago to stalk prey, but our order of Explainers and the high artists of our cities have perfected that concept. Not everyone can wear one, of course.'

'That's fashion for you,' Osrin said.

'Takes a true hunter,' Mard'Kem said. 'One born to the leaves. There is a forest shunned by normal commrach, its canopy so thick no sunlight ever touches the forest floor. A tribe live therein, so demented and pale that even our lowest-blooded abhor them. Said tribe exiled this one for unknown horrors when she was a child. She spent several years feeding upon the rural folk, ever hiding in shadows.'

Hoom felt sudden rage. Red Marie held that same rage back.

'Evidently she was caught,' Osrin said.

'No. She got bored, handed herself to the Explainers for study.' Mard'Kem looked at Red Marie. 'Lowblood, you may speak one sentence, if you wish.'

Red Marie did so.

'*I am at a loss*—' She indicated Osrin. '—*as to why this one should be worthy of the humans' "sacred" throne.*'

'Because I'm pure of heart, arsehole.' Osrin drove his elbow into Red Marie's belly.

Red Marie felt nothing and Count Osrin yelped. The two guards chuckled at Osrin's pain. Mard'Kem indicated for Red Marie to step away. She did so.

'My funny bone,' Osrin hissed. He shook his arm to dispel the discomfort. 'God, I hate that...'

'Not only does she wear a sealed suit,' Mard'Kem said, 'our Explainers have been pumping her full of serums these last few years. She possesses incredible speed and, I'm certain you've just noted, absurd toughness. I dare say you could slice her in half and she would still crawl to get you.'

Osrin turned to face Red Marie. He could see her now his blood was pumping.

'Sealed?' he asked, looking her mask right in its glass eyes. 'Why's she sealed like that?'

'You would have to ask the Explainer in the keep,' Mard'Kem replied. 'Something to do with whatever goes on in there that you people cannot tell anyone about.'

'I could tell you, Mard'Kem,' Osrin said.

'But I do not think you will, my count,' they replied.

Mard'Kem looked uncomfortable for the first time. Red Marie liked that. Behind her mask she licked her harelip. Even referring to the mystery of the keep's hollow heart could prove unhealthy. Mard'Kem knew that much, despite not knowing a jot about the keep-within-the-keep. *To speak of it outside the grounds of the keep is death,* the Explainer had told Red Marie. Red Marie could, though; it was another unique power, unique to her in all the world. The curse could not get her when she stalked through the city, because she was sealed in her extra special hinter-suit. The curse was airborne in some way even the Explainer did not pretend to understand. Red Marie, in all the world, could tell someone of the keep-within and never suffer the consequences. It just meant she could never be outside her sealed suit, not outside the grounds of the keep at any rate. A small sacrifice. She could whisper the truth into an ear and that ear's mouth might spread it to other ears.

'Fine,' Osrin said, knowing better than to pry further. 'I am satisfied. Mostly. But the plan requires me to kill Red Marie.' He looked her up and down. 'You appreciate my dilemma should she elect not to die.'

'Red Marie is dying already,' Mard'Kem said. 'There's a reason we do not pump the Explainers' serums into every one of our warriors. The body cannot take such strength and celerity.' They looked at Red Marie. 'Lowblood, how long do you have?'

'A *year, maybe less,*' Red Marie replied. '*So the Explainer tells me, high steward.*'

'That's a year longer than if she follows your plan,' Osrin said to Mard'Kem. 'She might agree to it now, yet sentiments fade when blades are drawn.'

Mard'Kem smiled. 'For a man who spent a year upon the isle, you know little of its natives. We believe an individual's life should come to a finer point than even their sword. A life must be polished into a bright finish. It must be a story.' They nodded toward Red Marie. 'Few lowbloods have the opportunity to become such a tale.'

'The tale is not her own,' Osrin observed.

'*It is better,*' Red Marie said. She remembered herself and dropped to her knees before Mard'Kem. '*Apologies, high steward. I spoke without permission.*'

Mard'Kem ignored her, which was practically forgiveness. 'You had better take the tunnel back to the keep,' they told Count Osrin.

Osrin stepped forward, until he stood beside Mard'Kem in their chair. The two guards touched the hilts of their swords. Osrin leant forward, took Mard'Kem's hand and kissed it.

'Farewell, my dear high steward,' he said. 'Let's hope our performance succeeds, otherwise we'll be the wrong kind of story. The cautionary sort.'

With that, he strode from the hall.

'You have permission to leave,' Mard'Kem told Red Marie, who was still on her knees. 'Be about your terror, lowblood.'

Red Marie arose and nodded. She took the servants' entrance, all the servants' corridors, until she was out in the trade obelisk's gardens with its paths and low hedges, a shadow in the gloom. Snow had begun to fall, sharp against the night, each feathery clump made silver by the light of the obelisk's moontiles.

Beyond the garden lay Becken Bay and beyond that the lights of the city. The closest lights, which were few and sputtering, were of the Hook, where Red Marie was worshipped as a devil. She leaped into the slumbering waves of the bay.

She did not feel the freezing shock of the water, nor taste its tang of salt. She did not even have to keep her head above the waves. She was all-powerful in this suit, could swim the bay and not even tire.

I'll be a story, all right, she thought, pounding through the waves and licking her harelip. *But not theirs. I'm Red Marie now. Not Hoom. Red Marie.* She would kill King Ean, just as they commanded. But she would murder Osrin too and all the soppy, bloated court of Becken Keep. Then, still not sated, she would swim back to the obelisk and kill all the highbloods. Mard'Kem she would save for last, a long and ecstatic violation.

Red Marie would reach it then, that golden vibration she had sensed her whole life but never quite reached. That vision, that orgasm, that rebirth that would place her at the centre of the universe upon her throne.

She would die then, she was certain. But she would be a story, the only one worth telling.

TWO NIGHTS TILL YULENIGHT EVE

32

Carmotta

She ordered her handmaids bring her fourth favourite winter coat. A grey lilac, its collar and sleeves were trimmed with sable furs. More importantly, the sleeves could be drawn back. Ideal for a lady who meant to use a bow.

Two guards escorted Carmotta and her handmaids to the butts. She would have felt safer with Dulenci beside her, but he was off across the city with his boys, having been careful to announce as much to all nearby, as was his custom. A crack was opening between her and him. They had not enjoyed one another's bodies for almost a day and a night. A sadness for her and absolute hell for Dulenci who, when all was said and done, was a walking erection.

She had found she could not touch him. Nor Ean, nor even herself. How was human love possible with her new insight, with those *things* forever upon every brow? The question of her pregnancy was becoming ever more insoluble. Almost.

'Greetings, sister wife,' said a woman's voice as Carmotta's entourage turned a corner into a wide stairwell lit by candles inside hollowed deer skulls. It was Third-Queen Emmabelle and her entourage: two more guards and three handmaids as blonde as she. Each person had their own hand of night upon their head.

'Sister wife,' Carmotta replied, as both entourages descended the stairwell together, 'I did not think you would be taking part today, given your God-blessed condition.'

'Where my family hails from everyone knows how to wield a bow.' Emmabelle snorted with laughter as if it were a joke. 'In Duxby, a day at the butts is considered healthy for an expectant mother.'

'I see.' Carmotta could see her skills were real. Not only did Emmabelle's blue coat have the retractable sleeves like Carmotta's own, Emmabelle was already wearing the leather protection thing – Carmotta knew not its name – on her wrist. 'We Mancanese have scant familiarity with the longbow.'

'Crossbows over there, isn't it?' Emmabelle said. 'I suppose that's easier: crank and pull a lever. Anyone can do that.'

'For my people,' Carmotta replied, 'that's precisely the beauty of them.'

'Of course, I won't be using a longbow,' Emmabelle said, bored of the conversation's direction. Her rosemary perfume wafted to Carmotta's nose. 'I'm too petite, too much a lady. With your arms you might have been all right, though. Your shoulders, too.'

Little bitch. Carmotta smiled. Barbed insult or idiot stumble, Emmabelle's comments would not get the better of her. Carmotta was in the process of owning Emmabelle and Emmabelle had not the faintest clue. It was her rosemary perfume upon the letter Carmotta had stolen from the Explainer's chest. Her handwriting too, though she had been careful not to sign her name at the bottom nor address the letter's recipient at the top. But the body of the letter? Oh what a gift. *I cannot stop thinking of when last you held me, were last inside me. I touch myself as I write this, my love, and I pretend it is you.* That manner of drivel. That letter would open the way for Carmotta. She merely had to discern who the letter had been written to.

It could not be the Explainer. Too much to hope for, a halfbreed in her belly, a caliban. More likely she was leaving letters with him to pass to another, his tent in the keep's hollow acting almost as a money vault. Likely Emmabelle's paramour used the same system to send letters to her. Indeed, that chest was likely full of torrid correspondence. Carmotta wished she had seized more scrolls from it; she had thought of returning to the tent on some pretence in order to steal more. But Emmabelle's paramour would be diving into that chest soon enough, if not already.

'I hate this weather we're having,' Emmabelle said.

'I rather like snow,' Carmotta replied. 'In winter it is the only brightness.'

'Has there been any news of our dear sister wife?' Emmabelle asked.

'No. Violee has not been spotted, much less caught.'

The poor girl had been a fragile thing the day she came to court, and life in the keep's gloom had broken her. Violee had been no rival to Carmotta, merely a victim of highest birth. Of *human* birth. Violee would have been happier scuttling about some forest floor.

Carmotta took Emmabelle's hand and patted it. 'Have no fear. Our sister wife has escaped her quarters many times and always returns home safe and happier for a little run.'

'Oh,' Emmabelle said. She forgot to hide her disappointment.

What a little shit you are, Carmotta thought. *And stupid, you rosemary-reeking fool.*

Yes. Emmabelle would have to be crushed slowly and, ultimately, publicly. Not only would it be so very satisfying, it was Carmotta's last hope. For Ean would simply *have* to pretend the seed in Carmotta's belly was his own, would he not? After Emmabelle's was shown to be a likely bastard, the 'milky king' could never risk being seen to be cuckolded twice. Not with all these quiet threats to his crown.

Put like that, Carmotta thought, *it is Emmabelle's child or mine.*

They walked out of the double doors into a white world. Carmotta had known little of snow as a child and almost as little of its bite. She never tired of its simple crisp… nowness. Yes, that was it. A landscape of snow made one feel the very present, made one more awake than awake. The keep's many lawns were purity itself, untouched by any boot. The pathway they took to the butts had been covered with dried rushes so that users might not slip. The rushes crunched pleasantly underfoot.

Halfway along the pass they crossed over the vast bronze circle that lay embedded in the earth. Carmotta remembered the women in her vision, their blood pouring into the molten alloy. She braced for some unholy force as she stepped over, if only a tingle. But she felt nothing.

The men, some twenty plus three times as many servants and adjudicators, were already about their sport. Arrows stuck out of the six painted targets and were soon accompanied by more as the noblemen let fly. Iron braziers had been set to the rear of the field and less eager participants warmed their hands and chatted amiably.

Carmotta and Emmabelle passed through the gate into the butts simultaneously, mindful not to upstage or be upstaged in turn.

Ean passed his bow to whomever might take it, which transpired to be big Willem Cutbill. King Ean, glorious in a long red coat lined with ermine, stepped forward and took his queens' hands, kissing Carmotta's first, Emmabelle's second. After that he drew them both closer, kissing Carmotta on the cheek and then turning to do so with Emmabelle, who met Ean's lips with her own.

Carmotta stepped back, as dignified as she might. In truth she was happy to get away from both their night-hands.

'Your Majesty,' Lucine, her leading handmaid, said, and she

passed Carmotta a bow, one smaller and narrower than that of the Brintland noblemen.

Carmotta nodded at one or two of the participants. This event was meant to be a distraction for herself, Ean and Cutbill, which was to say an attempt to make Cutbill feel appreciated. It paid to have the captain general of the city guard a friend. The big man was no conniver but he would be pliable to others who were. Besides, there had been some consternation with Cutbill at that wretched banquet of Larksdale's. He had made a lout of himself and Ean wished to bandage the wounds, so to speak, with a little time at the butts. Unfortunately, as with any distraction Ean decided upon, this morning's archery had accreted guests and their hangers-on.

'Your Majesty,' Willem Cutbill said, bowing. He wore a dull winter coat but no hat upon his shaved head. An old Brintland soldier, he was inured to a cold morning. The dark hand over his skull was the only one on full display. It was transparent as dirty water in the morning's sun. 'Your cousin did not come?' he asked of her.

'Dulenci is about his pursuits in the city,' she said aloud so that others might hear. It was vital never to stop insinuating Dulenci was a homosexual. But, by the Pilgrim, it was tiring.

'Tetchford, I expect.' Tibald Slyke's voice. 'Had to wade through those parts only yesterday.'

She turned to face him. He was not wearing his typical wide-brimmed hat but a thing of badger fur with long earflaps. That was not the startling thing about him, however: it was the hand of night above his head. The fingers were more curled than the others, its sharp fingernails almost pointing at the floor.

'Your Majesty?' Slyke blinked. 'Oh. This?' He shook a long leather case that hung on a strap from his shoulder. 'With your indulgence, Your Majesty,' Slyke said, 'let me show you. I think you will appreciate it.'

Before Carmotta might reply he had set the case upon the snow and opened it, an ageing man as eager as a boy.

'An import, just arrived.' He pulled out a crossbow. 'One of a kind.'

'Be careful, good sir,' Carmotta said.

'Quite safe, quite safe,' he assured her. 'Hasn't been loaded.' He grinned. 'This will be my first go of it.' He stood upright and hefted it in his arms. 'Constructed in Vergamo, Manca.'

'It is a beauty,' she said. It truly was. Black lacquer and gold inlay. The quality rivalled those in her father's collection. It came with a steel gaffe lever – a newer, easier manner of cranking – and the bow itself was of some treated horn. 'Have you much experience?' she asked him. Carmotta had wielded her first crossbow as a little girl.

'They're self-explanatory,' Slyke replied.

She looked back at Ean. He still had Emmabelle in one arm, his other hand cradling her large belly. A mawkish scene. Carmotta looked away and signalled to an adjudicator she wished to take her first go.

People were watching Count Osrin as he took his stand and Carmotta delayed her own to watch him. His aim was considered, focused. But between loosing he displayed none of that theatricality that usually drenched his martial displays. His second shot was almost dead centre, but when those watching drew breath, he did nothing to address them.

'Ma'am,' an adjudicator said beside her, indicating her arrows were ready.

Carmotta nodded and turned toward the butt some ten yards away. She pulled an arrow out of the ground, notched, aimed and loosed. She hit far off the centre mark, but her mind had ignited in the moment she had released. She took her next two shots in quick succession, with only the second being of any merit.

As the adjudicator walked up to the butt and measured each hit's distance, Carmotta allowed the thought in her to blossom. Osrin was a man with no wish to draw attention to himself today. He had no wish to be noticed while Ean embraced Emmabelle. Osrin was Emmabelle's lover. *By the Pilgrim,* Carmotta thought, *is it not obvious?*

It explained much. The count loved danger, thrived on it. Emmabelle's pregnancy was his spur to action. If the crown were his he could marry Emmabelle and the babe would be no bastard, for King Osrin would have the power to legitimise it. He might even openly admit his amorous treason. Many would see it as part of his audacious legend, the actions of a vigorous and warlike monarch. The sort of thing the old king, his father, might have done.

And Emmabelle? No more third-queen. No more Carmotta. Yes, she might just be stupid enough for that, stupidity being its own breed of audacity. History was rich with examples.

The more Carmotta thought on it, the more it made sense. Those two were blatant enough for such a ploy, their supporters powerful enough to indulge it. Pym and the rest of the Osrin gang were just the tip of the conspiracy. Who knew what other warmongers and financiers waited in the wings.

The adjudicator announced Carmotta's score: five. She nodded thanks and walked away from the stand, her bow in hand.

But there will be time, she told herself. Yes, for this was winter and would be for some months. The supporting lords in this conspiracy possessed the largest armies in the Brintland but they would have to muster said armies and, more to the point, move them. All the roads to Becken would soon be impassable slush and the canals of the old empire were already freezing over. The sea would be too arduous and all ships lay in the hands of the Crown and the merchant guilds, not the barons.

She looked back at Osrin and Pym, talking to one another, discussing trajectory and damning the morning's breeze. *A hard season for them,* she thought, *all this waiting for spring.*

Little boys with a big secret. Winter was their weak spot and they lived in hope no one had noticed. But Carmotta had. Winter was her sword to wield. An excitement filled her, the likes of which she had never known. Because if she were good, very good, she could thrust the point home, right into the heart of all the king's enemies. But she only had two nights to prepare.

King Ean had called for some wretched peasant play to be performed before the entire court at midnight on Yulenight Eve. The thing would be cancelled just as it began, Carmotta would see to that. She would give her own little performance, guards in tow, and by the end of it Emmabelle and Osrin would be taken away to be put to the question. Ean and her baby would be saved.

Big Willem Cutbill was on the stand. He had the meanest-looking longbow, unpainted and unadorned. His aim was competent enough but each arrow caused the target to shudder.

'Maybe we should help him,' her handmaid, Lucine, said in Mancanese. The other two giggled.

They were talking about Slyke, Master of Arts and Revels. He was on his knees now, beside his box, fumbling with the gaffe lever and the string. Carmotta considered helping but something about his night-hand's pose, the tightening fingers, gave her pause.

'Wait here,' she told her handmaids and she made her way toward Cutbill, careful not to get too close to Emmabelle and Ean, who were still deep in doe-eyed conversation. A good man, Ean, but a terrible judge of conspiracies. All presence and no guile.

'Your Majesty,' Cutbill said, mist billowing from his bearded mouth.

'Willem,' she replied. 'Might I call you Willem?'

'As Your Majesty pleases,' he said uncomfortably.

'Relax, I will not request you call me Carmotta.'

He nodded, his eyes looking about.

'Captain,' she said. 'I should call you Captain. For you are of the king's army.'

'I serve the Crown with my life,' he said without emotion. 'Both the king and his father before that.' He was uncomfortable speaking to young noblewomen, simply everyone knew that. They had never been part of his world. 'The old king raised me up from nothing, Your Majesty.'

'Not from nothing. Your actions as a young man may well have saved the Brintland.' Nosford Vale. Cutbill's flank attack had turned defeat to victory. This common-enough man had only been in command an hour after his lord had drowned leading the regiment into a bog. 'Glory only gifts itself to the gifted.'

A pained smile twisted at his jaw, an ugly thing, a spasm. Almost as ugly as the hand of night above his head, which – to the connoisseur Carmotta's eyes – was rather unremarkable among its kind. Cutbill stared at his feet. 'There was no glory in it. Not that day.' He frowned. 'Not there.'

'Forgive me,' Carmotta said. She reached out and touched his bow wrist. 'I had not meant to stir up…' She stopped. She had stumbled down a bad lane here, the pain of the battlefield had never left him. 'My husband speaks only fine words of you. He grew up in admiration of your deeds.'

'Your Majesty.' He looked toward Slyke, still no further with loading his crossbow. Cutbill was eager for anyone to get him away from this young and exotic queen.

She had to work fast. 'We speak little, Captain. I should like to change that.'

Cutbill tensed. Behind him, over on the range, Emmabelle was readying, reaching for her first arrow.

'I and my cousin' Carmotta said, 'like to make afternoon prayer in the south-west chapel. You know the one?'

He nodded, less tense now Dulenci and a little worship were part of the prospect.

'Meet us there tomorrow.' She smiled. 'I should like to talk of your future, Captain.'

'Surely that's a matter for the king's conscience.' He shook his head and the hand above it followed perfectly, as if fixed by a nail. 'Apologies, Your Majesty. I mean I am happy as captain general.'

'My opinion means much to my husband,' she said. 'Though of course he—' She stopped when she saw Emmabelle's arrow fly dead centre into the target. Men watching cheered and Emmabelle turned back and grinned at them. Carmotta looked back to Cutbill. 'Captain, I will paint my words no more.' She looked to see if anyone was near, then whispered, 'I am worried for my husband. For the Crown. I need to speak with you.'

Concern crossed his leathered face. 'Now?'

She shook her head. 'Midday tomorrow. The chapel.' She pursed her lips, willed her eyes full of fear. 'Please.'

He nodded. 'I had better go.'

'Help Slyke with his crossbow,' she said.

'Your Majesty.' He did so.

Men cheered Emmabelle's final shot. Carmotta did not look. Had she gone too far with Cutbill? The promise of advancement had failed, only the cliché of the scared damsel had remained. But in truth that was hardly a performance. She *was* scared. Willem Cutbill was a vital piece in all this. He was of the city guard but his legend among the soldiery was such he could walk into the keep and command any palace guard therein.

He could be trusted. If he were of Osrin's pack their treason would be successful by now. Cutbill would have locked down the keep and then the city. Strange, she reflected, and worrying, that the royal family's safety should be in the hands of a glover's son.

Mulled wine was brought forth and everyone huddled around the braziers. Carmotta stood beside Ean, enjoying the warmth of the goblet in her hands and the smell of the spices.

The men were talking of Larksdale. Ean had mentioned his disappointment in the man and the rest proceeded to savage Larksdale's reputation like a pack of lampreys.

'When I arrived at his theatre,' Slyke announced, 'no one had the slightest clue what they were doing.' He still had his crossbow with him, holding it by the stock and pointing it at the ground. Apparently, he could not put it back in the box now it was readied. 'Everyone there hates him.' He coughed politely.

'It's best he's kept from the keep,' Osrin said.

'Boot him all the way to the Far Isles,' Slyke said. 'Dump him wherever that foul powder he acquired comes from.' The men all moaned with the memory of the stuff. 'I'm sorry, but the man has always irked me. Never trusted him. The folk-play would never happen if I had not stepped in.'

The hand of night was tighter over Slyke's skull. Carmotta could see the tips of the translucent claws were embedded in Slyke's forehead. She drew breath.

'Are you well, my sister wife?' Emmabelle said from nowhere, lifting her head up from Ean's other shoulder.

'Yes,' Carmotta replied. 'Just the cold.'

'But you look so well insulated,' Emmabelle replied, waving at Carmotta's apparel. And body.

By the time I'm finished with you, Carmotta thought, *I'll wear your skin as a surcoat, bitch.*

'Then there's the dead lad,' Cutbill was saying to the other men. 'Either he killed himself because of Larksdale or… well, I never did see the body.' He looked pained at that. Denied some answer only he cared about. 'But I get above myself, Your Majesty.'

'No, no,' the king replied, surprised anyone would have the crudity to mention the death itself. 'It is healthy to voice one's disappointment. Indeed, I'd have cancelled the folk-play if Sir Tibald had not volunteered to save it. Larksdale is my brother. But that night… revealed a side to him.'

The men nodded. Carmotta suspected that wretched banquet had revealed something of each of them. Men set naked before one another soon find one of their comrades to blame. It kept the pack's pride. Good Pilgrim, and people thought women capricious.

'Am I right in thinking he's a queer too?' Emmabelle asked the gathering. 'What with the young spineman and everything and the little breath fresheners he keeps in that box he carries about, well, he just seems queer.'

'Yes, Your Majesty,' Slyke replied.

'Only he's danced with women,' Emmabelle said, 'and charmed away their virtue, so it's said. But that would mean he's a real man, surely?'

'In the theatrical world it is possible to be both,' Slyke explained. 'As a director one has to come down hard on that sort of thing before it spreads. Naturally it's as a plague at the Wreath.'

'Larksdale's bound for hell and its fires then,' Emmabelle said, tittering.

'He'll be made to watch his own productions,' Slyke muttered.

Everyone guffawed. Carmotta just smiled. She abhorred Larksdale but it seemed a jejune sort of joke.

She spoke to Slyke across the other side of the brazier. 'There is something I do not quite comprehend, Sir Tibald.'

He coughed. 'Your Majesty?' The claws were pushing deeper into his skull now. She could almost see them moving. But he seemed not maligned in the slightest. Whatever could it mean?

'Larksdale,' Carmotta replied, trying not to appear unsettled. 'You said the folk-play would not have happened if it had been left to him. But if so, how had his previous productions occurred? Am I missing something?'

He looked pained a moment, then smiled. 'The work of the professionals around him.' He hefted his crossbow and checked it. There was a bolt loaded.

'Sir Tibald,' Carmotta said. 'Two things. Firstly, you should not be carrying a loaded crossbow here. I suggest you call a servant and have them unload it for you. Secondly, if Larksdale has these professionals around him, where were they this time?'

Slyke coughed. 'In answer to your first question…' He lifted the crossbow up so that its talking-end was pointing just above everyone's heads. 'This specialised crossbow is fitted with a safety hook of a design Your Majesty may not be aware of. It cannot misfire.' He coughed, snorted. The hand of night above his head was mostly *in* his head now. It was almost – almost – a fist. 'As to the second question, well, they all absconded when Larksdale refused to pay them.' He chuckled. 'More coin elsewhere.'

'I've barely touched a coin in my life,' Carmotta said, 'but I would be fascinated to know who could pay them more coin than a king.'

Slyke looked pained for an answer.

Good. Carmotta did not enjoy anyone ruining Harry Larksdale but her good self. An unpleasing eccentricity she had hitherto never noticed.

'Sir Tibald,' she added, 'might I also ask if this safety hook is configured to latch under the string as opposed to over it? That is a manner of crossbow I *am* aware of, seeing as it maimed my uncle in a hunting accident.'

Everyone around the brazier stiffened. Tibald glanced at his darling crossbow and gulped.

'Perhaps', Ean said, 'you should point it at the floor, Sir Tibald. So as to not perturb the ladies present.'

'Your Majesty.' He lowered it, pointing it harmlessly at the snow. The hand above his head was a fist now though it did not seem to affect him.

Carmotta relaxed.

'They know much about the crossbow, the Mancanese,' Osrin said, trying to lighten the mood.

'And queers,' Emmabelle said. 'Dulenci, for instance. Doomed to hellfire, doubtless, but, oh, he *does* make me giggle so.'

Slyke coughed.

'Slyke,' Ean said. He pointed at Slyke's face.

Yellow slop ran from Slyke's nose. He wiped it off with a white-gloved hand and studied it, astounded. More yellow came. He opened his mouth to speak and a bubbling mixture of the slop and his own saliva poured out, matting the fur of his coat.

'I've a handkerchief,' Emmabelle said, offering a tiny thing.

Slyke's chest shuddered and Carmotta thought he was going to laugh at Emmabelle's comment. Instead he puked.

Yellow, all of it yellow and bubbling. The stuff sizzled on the brazier, sending up a pillar of acrid white smoke, its stink oddly familiar. Slyke's eyes went wide, then the rims of his eyes went yellow. He was crying sloppy yellow tears.

Slyke spasmed and sprayed more yellow. Carmotta was certain a dollop had flown at her hat. Emmabelle screeched. She and the king had caught a volley of the stuff on their midriffs.

Slyke fell forward. His face hit the brazier and its red-hot coals. He screeched like a piglet and the morning reeked of burnt hair and the acrid yellow pong.

Cutbill and Osrin pulled him off the brazier and Slyke collapsed backward. He hit the snowy ground and a yellow fountain disgorged from his mouth. A crossbow bolt's feathers jutted out of Slyke's codpiece.

'His balls!' Osrin shouted. 'God, his balls!'

Servants were running over.

Slyke's face was a mass of braised flesh and putrid, bubbling yellow. *He's drowning*, Carmotta thought.

Slyke shuddered. He stopped. The fist of night, its knuckles jutting out of his head, evaporated to nothing.

'He's dead,' Carmotta announced.

The servants were gathered around Slyke but no one knew what to do.

Carmotta had to step away from the stink of the brazier, as did the others.

'By the Pilgrim,' she heard Osrin say. 'What *is* that smell?'

'Mustard,' Cutbill replied. 'I think it's mustard.'

33

Larksdale

Young men in winter coats and gaudy tights leaned against the Carnation's pillars. They cheered upon seeing Dulenci who, flicking a half-eaten apple from his dagger and sheathing it, nodded back to them. Four of the mollyboys swaggered over and he embraced them all.

'Rushed by beauty!' he proclaimed, his words filling the square. 'How am I, Dulenci Il'Lunadella, ever to choose?'

'*Me!*' one mollyboy said and then the others repeated it. '*Me! Me!*'

Such scenes made Larksdale cringe. 'Too-too much,' he muttered.

'Sir?' Marla asked behind him.

He ignored her and kept his eyes on the streetside clownery.

'Oh, but I cannot choose!' Dulenci declared to the entire square. 'I can never choose! Come, once *again* I shall take you all in my libidinous arms!'

He passed out silver, two pips apiece, and his acquaintances squealed. His arms akimbo, the mollyboys threaded their own through his and escorted him inside.

'There you go,' Marla said behind him. 'That's what he does. Let's be off, eh?'

'I have to know,' Larksdale replied. 'I have to go in there. See for myself.'

'Erm…' Marla paused. 'Sir, I'm… worried for you. This is…'

He turned to face her. 'Marla, Marla. My mind's not broken just yet. Trust me.' He tussled the woolly red hat upon her head. 'Have the rest of the day off, eh? I'll be fine.'

'I'll wait over there.' She nodded to a bench by a leafless tree.

'I'll be some time,' he said.

'And I'll be here.'

He nodded and strode toward the Carnation. It was Carmotta who had set Larksdale to act. Her scathing words had set him alight. She could not just throw him away, banish him from court. No, not ol' Harry Larksdale. By the Holy Pilgrim, no.

He hoped so, at least. All he had left was Dulenci and his pursuits outside the keep. Inside the entrance hall, in a hearth that had once been an alcove for some nabob's statue, a fire burnt high and giddily. The Carnation had been the lobby of a counting house in centuries past. Larksdale took down his hood and relished the warmth upon his face.

Earless Mundt, the Carnation's proprietor, was sitting upon his fine but long-broken couch. A rake of a man, folk had long named him Earless on account any secret was famously safe with him, right up until the day it wasn't and some villain, in an act of ironic reprisal, had made Mundt's nickname very literal indeed. He now hid the scars either side of his head by brushing what little hair he had left to him downwards. He grinned upon seeing Larksdale.

'Harry, me boy!' he declared. 'Long time no vada. How fares the playhouse?'

'It fares,' Larksdale said. He sat on the couch beside Mundt. 'And for that I am thankful.'

'Thank God for the punters, eh?' Mundt kissed an icon of the

Holy Pilgrim he had on a chain about his neck. 'What would we be without them?'

'May their tastes never coarsen.'

'And fuck the bear pit.'

'Oh yes, fuck that *bloody* bear-baiting pit.' Larksdale shook his head. 'I mean, come on now, it's the same every week. It *never* changes.'

'Fuck 'em.' Mundt lifted up a clay jug and offered Larksdale what was presumably wine. 'Right in the furry muzzle.'

Larksdale waved away the offer. 'Mundt, old pal, I've something of an atypical request.' Larksdale pressed on. 'The gentleman who just came in—'

'No.' Earless Mundt laughed. 'I've no more ears to lose here, Harry.'

Larksdale looked around, sat closer. 'I have no wish to know who he is.'

'Then what?' Mundt asked.

'I was hoping I might be audience to your own theatrical enterprise,' Larksdale said, embarrassed. 'So to speak.'

Earless Mundt chuckled. 'Nothing to be ashamed of. Who wouldn't want to vada four young dillies and their bona paramour?' He poured out a wine and passed it to Larksdale. 'Problem is, Harry, that gentleman you've taken a shine to isn't just some Tetchford well-to-do. He's keep. Like you. Surprised you haven't met him, actually.'

'I do not frequent the keep these days.' Which was true, or soon would be. He sipped the red wine and found it bitter. 'Fine, Mundt. I'll give you what I've always denied you. Send a few lads to the Wreath. They can work the groundlings.'

'Blimey,' Mundt said. 'You'd let me queer your pitch? You are *lovestruck*, dolly-doo.' Mundt sipped and swirled his goblet. 'No. There's something else I want. I want to look down on one of your plays.'

'From the upper stalls?'

'Just once, Harry,' Mundt said. 'Sit up there in the gods with the well-to-dos and vada a drama.'

'Mundt, come now.'

'I'll dress me finest, Harry,' Mundt protested. 'And you know I'm not one to spit nor fart.'

'A quality I've always admired in you.' Larksdale gulped down all his wine and set the goblet on the floor. 'Done.'

Earless Mundt led him to a thin door at one corner of the hall. He took out a clutch of keys, selected one and turned the lock. The two men stepped through into a thin, dusty corridor, its walls of wattle and clay. Mundt lit a candle, closed the door behind them and led the way.

The right side of the corridor was lined with plain wooden doors. Mundt stopped at the third, opened it and gestured for Larksdale to step in.

Larksdale did so. It was a small dark space with naught but a stool in it. The opposite wall was made of wood and had a line of light at its centre from ceiling to floor. He could hear Dulenci talking beyond it.

'This is a wardrobe,' Larksdale said. 'The inside of an inbuilt wardrobe.'

Mundt shushed him. 'Camouflage,' he whispered. 'Part of the room.'

'What if he opens the doors?'

'While fucking four rent boys?' Mundt countered. 'He's hardly in need of a parasol. Anyhow, you'll find a panel that slides across on the door there. You're done when he's done, all right? Enjoy the show.' With that he closed the door. He opened it again. 'Is it true the king's grown massive tits?'

Larksdale closed the door on him. He stood in darkness. He removed his winter cloak, felt the door behind him and found a few clothes pegs above it. He hung his cloak up, then found the stool in the dark and sat down.

Dulenci was a crass and empty performance of a man and thus Larksdale had always tried never to contemplate the fool. Yet Carmotta's cruelty had forced him to consider her interminable cousin, and that had set ol' Harry Larksdale's mind aflame.

He had an instinct about Dulenci, an instinct so deep that it had never risen to become an identifiable thought. Not until now.

Larksdale found the knob and slid the panel open. He stared into the room beyond his cupboard.

And saw his instinct true.

34

Fwych

'Peh ah cah,' Fwych said.

'Pet the cat,' Lady Larksdale said.

'Peh ah cah,' Fwych tried again.

'Pet... the... cat.'

'Peh ah cah.'

'Well, you tried,' Lady Larksdale said, sat on her high-backed chair. 'Anyway, I don't suppose you pet many cats where you come from.'

Fwych, upon a stool, looked over at Violee for support, but the second-queen were busy lapping up milk from her bowl. She seemed happy: her bum were wiggling in the air.

Fwych felt much better now, given a day and night to rest in Lady Larksdale's quarters. It had been vital to rest. She had lost time, yes, but what good would she have been elsewise? And to take this woman's help, a woman who believed Fwych would speak again even without a tongue? It sparked hope, it did.

The man with the false eye, whoever he had been, had been paralysed by just Fwych's bark. She had that power at least. That were something. But those powers she used to enjoy, those powers to command others to action... with those powers she might save the very world. All she needed to be was understood.

'Mil bohl,' she told Lady Larksdale.

'I beg yours?'

'Mil bohl.'

'Erm...'

'Mil bohl.' She pointed at Violee's milk bowl, now mostly empty.

'Violee,' Lady Larksdale replied. 'Vie... oh... lee.'

Second-Queen Violee looked up, her nose all milky.

'You carry on, love,' Lady Larksdale told her. She looked back at Fwych and smiled.

A strange woman this Lady Larksdale, even for a flatlander, with her plots and plans and her big talk of her son, how he would be king if he just forgot about his nonsense. This son of hers were surely a scoundrel, for he should have kept her in his hall. But even if Fwych had had a tongue she would not say so, for a light filled Lady Larksdale's eyes whenever she mentioned him.

Now, far too late, Fwych wished she had permitted such a light to come out from her own self whenever she had spoken of Gethwen. Though it had been a duty of a mountain mother to raise one of his kind, though she had had no choice, she had cared for him. In her way. A silly lad, all told. He'd thought a roadside inn a thing of great beauty. Beauty were his weakness. His fault.

'Oh, petal,' Lady Larksdale said. 'You're crying.'

She was. The misery of it all. The loss. She closed her eyes to stop the weeping.

Arms cradled her. Lady Larksdale's, up from her chair and leaning down to hold Fwych.

'There, there,' she cooed.

A scuttling came and then a familiar musty smell and another pair of arms embraced both Fwych and Lady Larksdale.

'Aww,' Lady Larksdale cooed. 'She wants to join in.' She put an arm around Violee and the three women hugged. 'Well, isn't this nice?'

Fwych nodded through tears and Violee growled low with delight. They hugged for some time.

'That's enough now, girls,' Lady Larksdale said. 'I've got something to show you.'

She let go and stepped away. She was more spry than Fwych had first thought. Excitement put fire in her limbs. She sauntered over to a chest that, like all the furniture in these chambers, were covered over with a white blanket. Lady Larksdale took out a roll of material, some beige and blue weave. She brought it back over and sat in her chair.

'Can you guess what this is?' she asked Fwych.

Fwych could not place it. She shook her head.

'It's the official material of a servant of the keep,' Lady Larksdale said. She reached down and picked up a leather bag. 'And I've the skill to make you a servant's dress. Do you see? You won't just crawl through all those nasty tunnels in order to act out our plot. You'll walk the hallways unmolested too. Take my word: none of the finery ever notices a serving wench.' She looked around as if someone might be listening, then said, 'Truth is, neither do the guards around here. Plenty of lords have died at the hands of assassins dressed as serving waifs. But no one learns their lesson. Know why?'

Fwych shook her head.

'Because to do so would be to admit that a serving wench is the same flesh as they.' She nodded. 'Then where would we all be?' She opened her leather bag and pulled out needle and thread.

This were heartening. Fwych needed to get about this place unnoticed, if she were ever to find the black crown. To walk about the hallways and grounds of the keep, using Father Mountain's gift, she could open to sensation. If she got lucky, got close enough to the black crown, she would sense its presence.

Gethwen would have been in a rush when he hid the thing; it

would be near where he'd died. That, or, had he had time, he would have…

A knock at the door.

Lady Larksdale stood up. Violee stopped scratching her head with her leg. Fwych drew the chopping knife at her belt.

'Who's that?' Lady Larksdale shouted.

'Have no fear,' said a reedy female voice. 'It is your friend, the Countess Osrin.'

Oh not her, Lady Larksdale's face seemed to say. 'Now's not a good time, my dear,' she announced.

'I would speak but briefly,' this Countess Osrin said. 'Please, I am an ageing woman and it is cold out here.'

Lady Larksdale growled under her breath. 'Give me some moments, Countess. I'm not decent.'

'Of course,' the woman's voice replied.

'And I cannot spare long.' Larksdale gestured to Fwych to help her get Violee into the back bedroom.

'Oh come now,' the countess said through the door. 'Where have the likes of us to go?'

'Affairs of state,' Lady Larksdale said, shooing Violee. Violee's nose wrinkled. She looked ready to bite.

The countess laughed. 'You amuse me so, Lady Larksdale.'

Lady Larksdale grimaced at that. But she focused on helping Fwych get Violee into the back room. They locked the door.

Fwych ducked under a couch that had tall wooden legs. The blanket over the couch hid her well, as did the gloom of the corner it sat in. She did not sheathe her chopper.

'I brought a little something,' the voice behind the door said. 'I hope it's not too early.'

Lady Larksdale perked up at that. She opened the door.

Fwych, lying on her side beneath the couch, let the blanket hang in front of her. Footsteps creaked upon the pinewood floor.

She heard Lady Larksdale sigh as she got back into her chair. Someone else sat upon the stool where Fwych had just been.

'Hmm, rather warm,' the rasping female voice said.

'I was just sitting there,' Lady Larksdale lied. 'I'm trying to vary my day.'

'Very wise I am sure. Now, have a sip of this, my dear.'

'Ooh.' Lady Larksdale made a swallowing sound then coughed. She spluttered and retched. Fwych readied her blade to save her friend, but then Lady Larksdale said, 'That's revived my sinew. I'd better have another sip, mind. Just to be sure.'

Her visitor giggled. 'Certainly.'

Lady Larksdale went through the process of spluttering and retching again. 'Delightful,' she said.

'I was concerned for you, dear,' her visitor, this countess said. 'For your poor son.'

'You need never worry for him, Countess,' Lady Larksdale said. 'Forgive my candour, but it is your own sweet boy you should be concerned for. Have they thrown him in the gaol yet? I assumed so, for that Ean lad is still king. I know that much.'

'Oh *that?*' the countess said, a hint of delight in her raspy tone. 'He decided against a coup in the end; he just wanted to see who he could call upon should the time come. But March is the time for coups, so he says. Everyone has that certain spring in their step.'

'He should ask my boy,' Lady Larksdale said. 'He would be good in a coup, he would. Just needs a shove.' She paused to swig and splutter. 'What did you mean, "poor son"?'

'Haven't you heard? Your son's boy died. Leaped from the keep.'

Gethwen. He had been playing lover to Lady Larksdale's son?

'Oh,' Lady Larksdale said. 'Was he that ginger lad?'

'*Yes,*' The countess's rasp gained an odd honey a moment and something about it put Fwych on edge. '*Yes,* that's the one. You talked to him, yes?'

'Handsome lad,' Lady Larksdale said. 'Quiet and polite.'

'And always with a little bag on his shoulder, eh, Lady Larksdale? Quite the eccentricity.' The guest laughed.

Fwych froze. The bag. The bag had had the black crown in it, back at the inn. Here were the enemy. Scheming on a stool.

'Well, I do not know about eccentricity,' Lady Larksdale replied. Her tone had changed, Fwych realised. Not her own but more like this countess's. She had been doing it since the countess entered. 'But he certainly possessed a bag.'

'They did not find it upon his person,' the countess said. 'Which we have all thought strange. He wouldn't have left it here, by any chance? The royal court would be in your debt if you could produce it.'

Lady Larksdale grumbled. 'I cannot say as I have. But, well, I shouldn't say...'

'Have another sip my dear.'

Larksdale swigged and spluttered again. 'Well, I did sneak a look inside his bag. While he was helping my son affix a... I mean move some furniture. He had put his bag down and I thought it prudent to have a bit of a glance.'

'Of course.'

'From outside I thought it might be a weapon or something, that Harry's new squire was a potential assassin. Fat chance. Just some big ring of iron, Countess Osrin. A bloody great door-knocker as far as I could tell, size of your head. I mean, who carries a door-knocker around, eh?'

'Indeed.' The countess sighed. 'Well, my son and I wished to give our condolences to your sweet Harry. I know you have mentioned he oversees the Wreath Theatre in the city. But I am also aware of his houseboat along the Tetch. Which does he spend the night at? Because I've heard different sources saying he stays at both.'

'Ooh, you do not want to visit either of those, Countess. Oh no.'

'It's the least I can do,' Countess Osrin replied.

'Oh no,' Lady Larksdale said. 'Do not bother going to Tetchford, oh no. I wish he'd spend his time here, I really do.'

'Lady Larksdale, I really *do* want to visit Tetchford. *Really.*' Something cold hissed in her tone. 'But you see, I need to know where in Tetchford he stays. The Wreath… or his houseboat. I haven't time for both.'

'The Wreath,' Lady Larksdale muttered, shame-faced. 'In Tetchford. I don't know why he insists on sleeping there.'

'Thank you, Lady Larksdale,' Countess Osrin said. 'Well now, I *really* must be going.'

'Oh.'

'But you may keep the flask.'

'Ooh.'

Fwych wanted to kill this minion of evil. But it would upset Fwych's host. A mountain mother could never violate a host's other guests, the greatest taboo. But it were vital she knew her new enemy on sight. Fwych lifted the blanket, an inch or more. She peeked out.

Lady Larksdale were already seeing her guest out. A small woman in dark dress and high wimple.

'Give my son my love, will you?' Lady Larksdale said.

The countess turned to say farewell. The upper part of her face was covered by a black veil. But her mouth were visible. The teeth seemed almost pointed and the upper lip had a slash, like an old wound from nose to puckered, painted lip. A harelip.

'I'll be sure to,' the countess replied to Lady Larksdale.

35

Carmotta

She had never seen the mortuary before. Its walls were grey and all of one piece, as if it were cut out of a vast stone embedded in the keep. There were four slabs for bodies to lie upon but only the third was occupied. Sir Tibald Slyke, Master of Arts and Revels. An ever-yellowing cloth covered him.

'There's really no need to open him up,' the Explainer said to Ean. 'My chemical tests on the yellow substance tell me enough.' He drew his long fine coat about himself, the coat Carmotta had seen in his tent, and sighed. 'May I return to the keep's hollow soon?'

'What was the manner of poison?' Ean asked.

'Mm?'

'What is it? How was it administered?' Ean asked.

Carmotta put her arm through Ean's and said to the Explainer, 'It is why we brought you here. We needed your skills, sir.' The keep's own doctors had been of no use at all.

'I doubt it's poison,' the Explainer told them both. 'Not in the sense of a conscious, premeditated affair. You gentlemen ingested culoo powder the other night, yes?' He waited for an answer.

'Aye,' Sir Willem Cutbill answered when Ean held silent. 'Two nights past.'

'Well that would give it time to ferment in the system.' He beckoned to old Jans the doorkeeper, who had followed the Explainer up here. Jans pulled out a key and stuck it in the iron disc around the Explainer's neck. 'Culoo is a highly reactive substance. It's also new to these lands, though views differ as to where it even hails from.' Jans gave him a look that said *keep still* and the Explainer did so with reluctance, like a cat being checked for fleas. Jans began turning the key that tightened the spring that stopped the Explainer from getting decapitated. 'There's enormous value in cultural exchange,' the Explainer continued, 'but also occasional danger. You Brintlanders have never encountered culoo before and, conversely, the distant people of wherever culoo comes from are not accustomed to mustard. Unfortunate that, for our cadaverous friend here might be walking around now were all the facts known.'

'What are you saying?' Ean asked.

'That an admixture of culoo and mustard fermented in his gut. Then, at a certain time, expanded exponentially.' He tapped Slyke's charred face. 'With bleakest results.'

Ean shook his head. 'You're saying it was an accident?'

'Let us be thankful he was the only one to touch the mustard pot that night.'

'No,' Carmotta protested. She was surprised to find Cutbill said the word at exactly the same time.

Ean chuckled despite himself and the Explainer squinted like he'd demanded to see everyone's academic credentials.

'Your Majesty,' Cutbill said to Carmotta, gesturing for her to speak first.

'The curse,' Carmotta said. 'Slyke must have spoken about the keep-within-the-keep while out and about in the city.'

Ean shook his head and Cutbill dipped his own. But both men had hands of night above their heads they could not even see. But Carmotta saw. She saw better than them all, save the Explainer.

'It was brutal enough,' Carmotta persisted. 'The sort of payment the curse infamously demands.'

'He died within the grounds,' Ean said. 'The curse gets people when they are beyond the walls, not within. Slyke's death was bizarre but hardly diabolical.'

She could not tell them. Not about the hands of night. They would think her insane. And if the Explainer backed her they might think her glamoured by dark commrach arts.

'Perhaps Slyke did not believe in the curse,' she said. 'He was a cynical sort.'

'Carmotta, please.' Ean let go of her arm. 'I've little taste for talking about the curse of our keep. Poor Slyke died on safe ground, there's an end to it. Sir Willem, you have something you wish to say.'

The big man crossed his arms. 'Your Majesty, I cannot believe this death mere accident. Nor do I believe it diabolical: it's all too human in intent. Larksdale has coveted Slyke's position a long time. So there's motive. Add to that the fact they never got along. More to the point, Larksdale shoved a plate of untouched mustard into Slyke's face and mouth. With intent.'

'You are wrong,' Carmotta said.

'With all courtesy, Your Majesty, I don't think I am. Larksdale's connections in the city run deep. We might not know about the effects of mixing culoo with this and that condiment, but Larksdale must know the people bringing culoo in. Between the docks of whatever land it comes from and the docks in Becken *someone* would have discovered the mustard hazard. And he's a poet, Larksdale. Or he's a taste for it. Kill Sir Tibald with the very thing Sir Tibald mocks him all over court about.'

'Larksdale has not the...' She could not think of the word in these people's tongue. 'Has not the temperament.'

'Certainly, Your Majesty,' Cutbill said. 'Or he would have

picked a less glaring method. Neither would he have killed his lad and tried to make it look like suicide either.'

'You think them connected?' Ean asked.

'Most definitely, Your Majesty. A lover's rage. The lad was like to tell on him, spill the truth. So Larksdale chased him through the halls and threw him off the keep. I just—' He balled his right hand to a fist. '—wish I could have seen his body before he got manured.'

'Manured?' Carmotta asked. So did Ean.

'To fertilise the lawns and flowers around here. It's what happens to the dead of no account.'

It was? By the Pilgrim, that was horrid. Carmotta had never thought to enquire.

'Sorry to interrupt,' the Explainer said, his neck disc fully wound. 'Might I take my leave? I've matters to attend to. And, frankly, I do not like the air up here.'

Ean nodded assent and the Explainer and Jans headed out without the slightest deference.

Cutbill watched the commrach leave and made the sign of the Holy Pilgrim against his chest.

'Your Majesty,' he said to Ean, 'my instincts could be wrong, but I think it's at least worth apprehending Larksdale and bringing him into the city guard. Ask a few questions. Nothing too heavy, I assure you. He's a nobleman, after all.'

'And our brother,' Ean muttered. 'So be it. But bring him here and not to the city gaol.'

'Your Majesty.'

'Get him here before tomorrow night and the baptism of the rivers,' Ean said. 'The streets will be packed by then I've no doubt.'

'Your Majesty, I can bring him here before nightfall. I've a guard tailing him right now.' He shrugged. 'I took the liberty.'

'You do not trust him,' Carmotta said. 'I commend you, Captain.'

'Never have, Your Majesty,' he said. 'I've had a spy among his people for quite some time.'

36

Larksdale

The more nothing happened, the more it was delectable. Larksdale had been sitting on his stool in the dark for what might be hours now – for he had had to be absolutely sure – and was never less than riveted by the performance before him.

Dulenci was sitting by the fire on the other side of the little bedroom, studying his game of backgammon. One of the four mollyboys he had hired was sitting at the other side of the little gaming table waiting dutifully for his employer to make a move, and not in any figurative sense. The other three dillies – one sat upon the unused bed and the other two upon the floor perusing copies of that treasonous groat-sheet, *The Wit* – looked entirely bored.

'She does not trust me,' Dulenci said. 'She *always* trusted me and now…' He put a finger on one of the backgammon pieces, studied it, then let go. 'I would never cheat her. I have never lain with another woman in my life. It never occurred to me. I love her. I love her *so much* and it hurts. It hurts.'

Oh my. So utterly utter. A true delight. Characters doing naught but witter about their problems for three hours would never be the future of theatre, not slightly, yet to Larksdale this current performance shone greater than even the keep-plays, be it Christopher Kimble's *Two Twins of Corso* or even Hosslett's *Neyes the Conqueror.* Larksdale wanted to clap, cheer, throw roses. Dulenci Il'Lunadella was a straight-card, a breeder, a naff! A regular old lover of women and a damned boring one at that! For he loved but one maiden. Oh, but *did* he love but one maiden! Larksdale's mad instinct, that twinge he had felt whenever Dulenci loudly catcalled his fellow man or made some camp pose, had been right all along. He should listen to his gut more, ol' Harry Larksdale, he really should...

This instinct was his saviour. All that was required was to bring a worthy witness here – Willem Cutbill, say – and make them watch Dulenci's profound absence of sodomy. More importantly, they would see his florid pining for the wrong sort of queen. A pining, it seemed, long reciprocated.

Oh. This was heaven.

Dulenci's backgammon opponent bit his lip. 'Sir,' he said softly, 'love that stings be no true love.'

The mollyboy on the bed piped up, 'You didn't come up with that, Reeves. That was in a play or summink.'

'Still true,' the first lad snapped back. He returned his gaze to Dulenci. He placed a hand on Dulenci's elbow. 'You deserve to be free.'

'Don't touch me you fucking nancy-mary!' He pushed away the mollyboy's hand in disgust and got out of his seat. 'And do not say it is denial! You types always say that. It is not denial! That's why I am in hell! Can you not see? For years I have pretended to be one of you absolute degenerates, to prance around in front of all my equals – and *lessers* – at court! I've risked life and honour! Just for her! To be near *her*!'

He began to shake. To weep.

Oh poor darling. It occurred to Larksdale he would not be able to blackmail Carmotta. A shame. To see her smug face break when he told her he knew, then all those subsequent years of her pained public smiles and forged laughter? Absolute paradise. But impossible. She would merely have Dulenci never return to the Carnation or perhaps even sent back to Manca entirely.

'Don't touch me...' Dulenci blurted through wet fingers. 'Don't touch me, you fucking Gwendolines...'

The mollyboys looked at one another and the one on the bed shook his head. His colleague passed him a groat-sheet to read, though likely none of them could. Commoners just liked the funny pictures of lords and ladies. *The Wit*'s words were aimed at the more feckless type of merchant and clerk.

No. Get a witness next time cry-baby here visited, then tell the king. Ha! Then let the king witness! Sitting here in this cupboard in his mink and crown. What a thought.

Carmotta would be done for then, he supposed. No one would want to hear of her little book of Larksdale's women and the pot of slather he had given them to prevent the king's seed. Packed off to a nunnery. That was the usual way of it, the precedent. She had birthed no child so the chopping block was out and, elsewise, King Ean did not love her nearly enough to fly into a rage and order it.

Still, it would be a strange keep without her. Her dark eyes twitching at his every barb, her lips stinging him...

He would have to think.

The door behind him opened and candlelight poured in. What did Earless Mundt want now?

The cloak on the peg behind him slapped the back of his head. Silver flashed above. A sword, caught in the cloak. Someone had just impaled Larksdale's cloak.

'Fuck,' the sword's owner said as they tried to pull it out.

'Just stab the cunt,' another voice said.

Men are trying to kill me, Larksdale realised.

He yelled and leaped up. He threw himself against the wardrobe's door and burst into the candlelight, into the bedroom. He tripped and hit the floor.

He scrambled on all fours away from the cupboard and its assassins. He stopped when his nose touched a sword's tip.

Dulenci's sword.

'Larksdale?' Dulenci said, staring down at him. His face was incredulous. 'You were *watching*?'

'Wardrobe backs on to both rooms,' Larksdale lied. 'Who'd have thought, eh?'

'You were watching.' Dulenci's brow tightened, coming to realisation. A killer's brow.

The wardrobe doors swung open again and one door fell off. Three men poured out, rough as wolves. Pennyblades, by the look of them, villains to a man. Each had a sword in hand, though one of them was untangling his from Larksdale's cloak.

Dulenci was agog. 'How many of you perverts are in there?' He waved his sword at the wardrobe.

'Shit,' said the lead pennyblade, a stocky man with a scalp shaved bald. He eyed Dulenci's steel.

'No witnesses,' the second one, the largest, said. He had managed to throw Larksdale's impaled cloak to the floor.

Dulenci grinned. 'Sit down, boys.' He waved at the backgammon board. 'Join us for a game.'

The three pennyblades had clearly not been expecting an armed man. They hesitated.

'No witnesses,' the first pennyblade repeated to the others.

He lunged forward only to get a game table in his face. He fell back on to the other two, blood rushing down his stubbled chin.

Dulenci was upon them, thrusting with his sword and using a mollyboy – his backgammon opponent – as a shield.

Larksdale belted for the door. He closed it after him and made a straight run for the entrance hall. Dulenci was surely as good as dead. Despite everything, Larksdale felt guilt for that terrible arse. *But his death might have bought my life.* He had to get out, run and take Marla with him.

Earless Mundt lay still, on his back upon his old couch in the entrance hall, his face a mass of red.

Footsteps to Larksdale's right.

A man in uniform. City guard. A sergeant. His left fist and the knife in it were painted with blood, so much so Larksdale half-fancied the blade a part of the sergeant's body, like a great insect's sting. A short man, but he had that serenity of someone who knew themselves swift.

'Well, well,' he said. 'Those fools back there can't get anything right.'

He had prised the facts out of poor Mundt, judging by his bloody hands. Larksdale thought about running back down the hallway he had come from, but he knew from memory that it led to nothing but locked heavy doors. That and a bunch of killers.

'Impersonating a member of the city guard is an offence,' Larksdale said. 'Let me go and I'll see you get a light sentence. I'm the king's brother, you know.'

The sergeant laughed. Before Larksdale knew it he was up against a wall with a sticky blade against his throat.

'I know,' the sergeant said. If sergeant he was. 'Always wanted to kill a noble.' He made a whistling sound that poured cold smelly breath on Larksdale's face. 'You'll forgive me if I savour the moment, sir.'

'Like a nice cheese,' Larksdale said. The threat of painful death made him waffle, it seemed. The last fact about himself he would ever discover.

'But cheese don't cry for its mommy, eh?' sergeant said.

'I suppose not,' Larksdale replied, almost wincing. 'I can pay you, sir.' He could not.

'No you couldn't.' The sergeant said. 'What you think I am? A fucking penny*aggghh*!'

The sergeant shuddered. Then shuddered again.

'Oh no,' he squeaked. He dropped to the floor, his knife clattering on the granite tiles.

Two eyes peered out of a gore-smattered face where the sergeant's face had just been. It was Earless Mundt, his own knife in hand. He pulled out an embroidered handkerchief and covered his face.

'Larksdale, you prick,' he said.

'You're alive.'

'Pretended to pass out,' Mundt explained. 'Bastard's took my nose.'

'I'm so sorry,' Larksdale said.

'Prick. You owe me. Let's be gone.'

Larksdale nodded. Fortunate, he supposed, Mundt was not a vengeful man. Nor vain.

They ran out of the main door and into the square. The crowds were busier now: Larksdale could not see Marla. Perhaps she was still sitting under the tree across the square. He moved through the throng, snaking his way toward it. Mundt had darted off his own way, into the myriad alleys of Becken no doubt, somewhere Larksdale would have to lose himself in too.

There were two old men beneath the tree but no Marla. Larksdale looked around.

A girl screamed. No, not a girl: more like a terrified man.

Everyone in the square froze and looked toward the Carnation's open doorway. Through a gap in the crowd Larksdale saw a man on his belly dragging himself over the doorstep. It was the bald and stocky leader of the pennyblades whom Dulenci had thwacked with the backgammon table. He was screaming through his toothless red hole of a mouth.

'Pleahhh! Hehhhp! Pleahhh!'

'No witnesses!' Dulenci tottered out of the gloom of the Carnation's foyer, a granite bust of some ancient king held above his head. He'd blood on his cheek and his styled hair was now a floppy mess. 'No witnesses!'

'Pleahhh—'

Dulenci threw the bust down and the pennyblade's bare scalp split instantly, spraying red heat across snow.

Screams filled the square.

'Keep business!' Dulenci shouted to the throng. 'This is keep business, you impoverished shits!'

People ran. Others tried to drag away someone who had fainted.

Dulenci's expression turned to a grimace and Larksdale realised he had been spotted. He turned and ran.

He had to slide and dive between people, saying, 'Sorry, sorry,' all the time, but when he heard shouting behind him he began to actively barge, something he had always found abominable in others.

City guard were entering the square from the Hollowlyve Road ahead, some six in all, all brass helms and halberds. One of them pointed at Larksdale.

Larksdale squeezed himself between two wheelbarrows and raced down an alley the width of a cow. The alley was boot-deep with last night's snow, crunchy on top and slushy beneath. Once or twice he stumbled, but the shouting behind him from Dulenci and others spurred him on. Larksdale was no fighter but he was some runner, despite his abhorrence for it. Tetchford had taught him that.

The alley increasingly descended as it headed toward Becken Bay. Things were becoming even less sure-footed. A crossroads lay ahead, a wider lane cutting across the alley's path, its cobbles wet but snowless. He pressed on, wanting to sprint but knowing that would break an ankle.

Dulenci cursed behind him, his curses becoming gradually fainter. Clearly he had taken a tumble. Larksdale smiled. The Mancan wasn't accustomed to Brintland snows in Becken's alleys.

The cobbles became stairs. An open doorway into a brick building lay on his right. He dived into the entrance.

Inside, it was dark and stank of raw meat. He ran into two oiled leather curtains. He pushed them apart and, still dashing, saw he was in a warehouse with openings in the high roof that cast trunks of sunlight into the meaty gloom. A thin man was dragging a dead sheep by its hind legs across the stones, its broken head leaving a line of gore like a paintbrush on vellum.

'Next one, Charlie!' the man hollered. He hadn't seen Larksdale.

Larksdale ran toward him, aiming to circle around the dead sheep and continue on his way.

Something bellowed above and Larksdale looked up to see a sheep falling from a trapdoor in the roof. Larksdale threw himself forward, on to his belly, sliding in the water and gore, and a sheep's scream was cut short behind him with an ugly thwack. Warmth splattered on the back of his neck. He got up.

'Fuck,' he heard the thin man say.

Larksdale ran once more. *Funny,* he found himself thinking, *you never think about how it gets to your plate.*

He ran between lines of crates, the stink of raw meat in his nostrils. The backs of his tights were slick with warmth. Sheep's blood. Just utter, just too awfully utter. He turned left between two crates and down some steps.

He had to stop. He was gasping for air, his side riven with

a stitch. He was in a cellar of some kind, with only the light of the doorway and another doorway the other side to illuminate anything. Various meats hung from the ceiling, all of it cured. The finer morsels. The room was salty to the nose, cold to bare flesh.

He heard men shouting away off, where he had just come from. He thought of running but he was quite done. He needed a minute. The shouting drifted away and no one came.

He waited, bent double and panting. Why were people trying to kill him? And who had ordered his death? Carmotta, most likely, or Slyke. But why were the city guard in pursuit too? The brass-tops arrived suspiciously quick to the scene. Had the man in the sergeant's uniform been a genuine guard? Or had it been a disguise to fool the Carnation's proprietor? Not that Mundt had bought it.

'Good man, Mundt,' Larksdale whispered. 'A good man.'

Larksdale heard a sword unsheathe from its scabbard. He stood up.

'Sir Harrance Larksdale.' Dulenci's voice. 'Quivering in the dark.'

Dulenci was silhouetted in the light of the doorway at the other side of the cellar. He prowled closer and the light from the doorway behind Larksdale illuminated his tanned face.

'Come here often?' Larksdale said. He smiled, best he might. It was impossible to kill a man making light of an absurd situation. In an ideal world.

Dulenci grinned. Then his grin vanished.

'Nothing personal,' Dulenci said. 'Well, apart from trying to watch me fuck, you sick man. Otherwise you are a fine enough soul. Yet I can permit no witnesses.'

Larksdale drew his eating knife from his belt.

Dulenci sighed. 'Have some dignity, man.'

Larksdale turned and fled. Back through the door from whence he'd come. He ran past the crates and turned right, into that open area of the warehouse once more.

'Hey,' the man who had dragged the sheep carcass earlier said. He moved to step in front of Larksdale, his bloody palms wide to grab him. Then the man's eyes went wide and he leaped back, scared.

Larksdale realised he still had his eating knife in hand. He could hear Dulenci's boots slapping the floor behind him. Larksdale almost slipped over the wide gore stain where the sheep had fallen. Crossing it, he stopped and turned to face his pursuer, knife lifted in a style that, in stage productions, evoked a man who knew what he was doing.

Dulenci stopped and laughed at Larksdale's attempt.

'What a stance!' he exclaimed. 'I've heard of a "fool's guard", but that's an "imbecile's gait".' He shook his head and laughed again. 'Come on, let's get this over with.' He stepped forward and lifted his blade.

'Next one, Charlie!' Larksdale shouted in a rough accent.

Dulenci frowned.

Dulenci had just enough time to see the screaming sheep fall toward him, both he and the beast open-mouthed with shock.

A vicious *crack* sound filled Larksdale's ears as he closed his eyes and turned. He dropped his knife upon the floor and ran.

Two beggars were screaming at one another. It was the manner of thing Harrance Larksdale would have walked past earlier that day, would have taken in his stride. It was all part of Tetchford's rough charm. Now, as he stood beneath a house's overhang to avoid the drizzle, his hair wet and his ears cold, Larksdale had time to give this two-man performance his full focus.

'Cunny 'ole!' the taller tramp was shouting. 'Fackin' cunny 'ole!'

'I never ripped yer,' the shorter, much older tramp pleaded. 'I wouldn't.' With his bald pate and grey beard he looked the ancient philosopher of Cykanos or Manca, but his shoes were tied sackcloth and his fingers were black.

'Yer a rip-off prick, mate!' the taller countered. 'Cunny 'ole, look at yer! It's dirty! Cut wi' shit!'

The rain bothered neither man.

It bothered Larksdale. He had walked the city, uncertain of what to do. Now the evening was drawing in. He could not go to the keep, of course. And the Wreath, he was certain, would have city guard all around it. It had been no accident they were outside the Carnation. They had been after him from the start, he knew it. Ol' Harry Larksdale was a hunted man. It was not as romantic a role as one might think.

The old tramp walked away but then he circled back again. 'I never,' he pleaded again.

The taller tramp became only more incensed. He began to wave his arms and scream.

Marla. Was it she who had pointed the way? Betrayed him? Either to those foul pennyblades or the guard or – and the thought struck him oddly – both? That last pennyblade had even dressed as a brass-top. Could it be possible he actually was?

He did not want Marla to be his traitor. Though, classically, it was always the person you trusted most. The thought she was as underhand as any of the keep's court made him want to be gone from this loveless world entirely.

You should hand yourself in, fool, he thought, mouthing the words. The sensible option, proof he was guilty of nothing. But somehow he knew he would not even make it to trial. Whoever had paid the pennyblades would see to that.

'Carmotta,' he whispered and the word sounded like the rain upon the filthy ground.

The taller man slapped the other's shoulder in rage. 'Fuck off!'

They wouldn't harm one another; Larksdale knew a performance when he saw one. Still, they might attract the city guard with such antics. Larksdale stepped out in the cold rain.

The two tramps turned to him as he passed.

'Got lulu sir,' the old greybeard told him. 'A pip for a pop. Good stuff it is.'

Larksdale stopped. 'Lulu?'

'The powder,' the taller one answered. 'Foreign. Puts a spring in your step.'

They meant culoo, the powder he had served to the king. Was that what all the tramps in Tetchford fought about? Culoo seemed far less fun down here in the streets.

'I'm trying to give it up.' Larksdale walked away.

He stepped out on to the westside quay of the River Tetch. Aside from a few river men unloading barrels from their barge, there was no one about.

He walked along the quay, keeping close to the warehouses' walls, partly for reasons of stealth and partly for cover from the insistent drizzle. The sky was a blank grey page, yet, set against its greyness, beyond the ships on the Tetch, the high new buildings of Tetmouth and the rotten church spire upon the Hook, stood the black splendour of the commrach trade obelisk. He had always admired its strange beauty, though whenever he did he rather shivered. Sitting upon a reef in the bay since before the city existed, it was the furthest outpost of an unknowable realm, its eldritch inhumanity looming over the bay's daily life. He doubted he would find sanctuary over there, at least none he'd remotely like.

He passed a high-sailed barge and there it was: his houseboat, its windows and entrance reassuringly untampered with. No home to winter in, this, though tramps occasionally had. A lonely place to summer in, too, especially when the joys of the

Wreath and its companionship were so close. Some years past he had thought to have the houseboat pulled away from Becken and made some rural home, though he knew he would never leave the city. Others had suggested he sell it but he had not the heart. It belonged to Mother, after all.

The thing had two floors above the low wide hull. It had carved decorations all along the woodwork, all of it covered in fading, cracked and once-gay paint. A winged lady, an angel perhaps, rose from the prow. She held a rusted iron crown in both outstretched arms. The crown had once had a chain through it, so as to pull the floating house all the way from the Brintland's north to this very spot on the quay, where locals cheered and the old king's chamberlain waited. It had not moved since.

The closer one got, the more one could see its crudity: the roughness of the angel's skin, the ill-educated impersonation of classical patterns within the woodwork. This riverboat was the labour of skilled yet simple country folk, the aggregation of a small town's wealth. Its lone sin was its sheer ambition.

Mother had first arrived in Becken on this boat, at that very spot. It had been built to carry her and, more precisely, the life in her belly the old king had bestowed on her while about a royal tour. She had never set foot back on the boat. She had never returned to the country. Neither had Larksdale.

'Father,' came a voice behind him. Someone tried to cover him with something.

He dipped his head and made to run.

'It's me,' Marla said, then louder, 'You forgot your coat, Father!'

He did not entirely trust her, but the sheer warmth of the heavy coat and its hood she was placing over him, the protection from the rain, was a voluptuous ecstasy.

'Keep walking,' she whispered. She said more loudly, 'Let's get you home, me duck, eh?'

She might be leading him into an alley and a blade, but he was done with doubt. He was too damp for it. He would trust her as he always had. He put on the gait of an ageing man.

'Did you have to call me "father"?' he muttered. 'I'd have been *nine*, for God's sake.'

'One day on the streets has aged you.' She paused as she led him around a corner and then another. 'Still, nothing a swig of sherris won't sort out.' She passed him a leather flask.

He took it. They came to a stop behind the brick rampart of a particularly imposing warehouse. It blocked out most of the rain and the drumming on his new coat's hood lessened. He uncorked the flask.

'Where did you go?' he asked her. He took a gulp of sack and the sweet warmth filled him like the light of the Pilgrim.

'I waited,' Marla insisted. 'Hours. But I'm only human, boss.'

'Loyalty has its limits,' he conceded.

'I mean I needed to piss. When I got back you were being chased around the square by that bigoted Mancan prick.' She was referring to Dulenci of course. 'I tried to follow but with all the guards—'

'It's fine.' He took another swig and passed it back. So good, so very warm. 'I cannot comprehend what is going on, Marla.'

She looked at him with piteous eyes. 'Can't you?'

'No,' he insisted. 'But you do, clearly.'

'They say you murdered someone.' Her words made him feel like the sherris had been all for nothing. 'Poison, up at the keep.' She gulped. 'No one can say who.'

'I've killed no one.' Depression hit him and his shoulders sank. 'Actually, I... may have killed Dulenci.'

'How?'

'With a sheep,' he replied. 'Self-defence.'

She stared at him incredulously.

'But that happened *after* they came for me,' he explained. 'So it's not for him they want me.'

'We'd better keep you from the brass-tops for the time being,' Marla said.

'People generally,' Larksdale replied. 'Some pennyblades tried to kill me back in the Carnation.'

'What?'

'I'm as perplexed as you are, dear Marla.'

This was all too-too utter. Within half a day Larksdale had gone from being exiled from court to inches-close to besting the queen to being the most wanted man in a city never short of villains. Dulenci was dead, and even if he were not dead he would never be foolish enough to frequent the Carnation again. Larksdale's hold on Carmotta had gone. Now that was the least of his ills.

He rubbed the balls of his eyes with his wet gloved hand. 'I need time, Marla. A night's rest to reflect and a day to marshal my resources. The theatre is being watched, I presume?'

'Absolutely,' she said. 'Brass-tops turned the Wreath over looking for you. We all feigned ignorance, which wasn't hard, and they might have taken a few of us for the rack if the king, bless him, didn't still want his play. Tichborne's looking after everything now. He's terrible but at least he's there.'

'Slyke has done nothing?' Larksdale shook his head. 'Typical. How did you know to come here?'

'Well you wouldn't go to the Wreath, would you? You're not half as daft as you pretend to be.'

He nodded, though he had never pretended to be daft in his life. 'I'll have to write a letter,' he said. 'But how to place it in the king's hand? I would have trusted Cutbill, but I've no idea if his guard have been given misinformation or someone beneath him is working for the damned queen or what.' He sighed. 'I suppose I have time to plan.'

'I don't think there's any going back, boss,' she said.

That chilled him more than the rain. At first he thought she might produce a knife and be done with him, but that was silly of course. Marla's statement chilled him because it was true.

She passed him the sherris once more and he glugged down a fiery deluge. He spluttered and coughed.

'The king discards me,' he said. 'His queen wishes me damned, which is fortunate for her, because now I am wanted for a noble's murder. My lover lies dead. I've no friends at the keep and my Tetchford friends risk their lives to know me. I put all my wealth into a cog full of mustard that has almost certainly sunk. My part of the Wreath, that houseboat and all these silly bloody rings on my fingers I'll have to give to my debtors, presuming I do not die first.' He took a smaller swig. 'Tell me if I'm missing anything.'

Marla crossed her arms.

'Marla, please don't cry.'

'You deserve better, boss,' she snarled. 'It's not…' She pinched her brow, drew a long breath and breathed out a cone of mist. 'You deserve better. That's what I think, anyhow.'

He took a long look at the riverfront. His home. He tried to speak, but for the only time since he could remember, he had absolutely nothing to say. He passed the sherris back.

'There is something, boss,' Marla almost whispered. Her words seemed the crash of a lazy wave. 'I might know some people.'

'In my experience, Marla,' he replied uncertainly, 'you almost always do.'

She did not smile. 'You know I have lots of little occupations, yeah? I've one sideline I never told you about. I get a couple coins now and then. From a man who knows people. He pays me—' She paused, winced. '—to tell him about what's going on around here and at the keep.'

It was like fingers upon his neck. Soft now, but getting tighter. 'These people your employer knows – they're in Hoxham, yes?'

'Yeah,' Marla said. 'Yeah, they are.'

'You're a spy, then? A traitor to the city that took you in.' He wanted to be angry. He was too cold and tired and giddy.

'In a... really not particularly bothered sort of way,' Marla explained. 'I'm supposed to tell them stuff you've said or done but... well, you're not exactly the king are you? All I can tell them is new plays and bad investments. I don't know why they keep paying me. But I'd never tell them anything that would get anyone hurt. I swear.'

'Oh Marla, dear,' Larksdale said, 'it never works out like that.'

'Maybe not. But, I'm thinking, you know... they could use a brother of King Ean over in Hoxham. You could give them advice, you know? They'd give you some nice digs, some coin.'

A traitor then, and well-pampered. 'Some very fine playhouses in that city, so I'm told.'

'I could ask about that,' Marla said.

It was all too much to take in, sitting on a cold river beneath a colder sky. 'Let me think on it. And, your secret is safe with me, whatever happens. I want you to know that, Marla.' She wiped a tear and smiled and Larksdale felt better for it. 'But right now we need a rowing boat.'

'I'll be doing the rowing, right?'

'The second to last favour I'll ask of you.'

She frowned.

He smiled. 'I require your social connections, Marla. There is really only one last place for me to hide.'

37

Red Marie

That is meant to be me?

She gazed down from the Wreath's thatched roof at a man in red face paint and hood waving two sickles of bent chaff above his head as others on stage lay about clutching their throats.

'I am the death that you all fear!' this 'Red Marie' bellowed. 'I terrorise all, both far and near!'

He began to jig.

I should flay him, Red Marie thought.

There was no sign of Larksdale.

Her suit only worked in gloom or at night, and so Red Marie had to be tactical with her time. She had a sacrifice waiting at Knucklebone Smones's tonight and a powerful hankering to gut some random family as they slept in their hovel and lay out their intestines in an alluring way. With all this in mind it had been necessary to wear a dress and veil and converse with that awful hag, Larksdale's mother. It was not all fun, being Red Marie. But mostly it was.

Dressing as a veiled noblewoman had been her idea. None of her masters at the obelisk had thanked her for it. In fact, they had gotten angry. But Mother Larksdale absorbed all the rumour and hearsay in the keep and Red Marie's masters soon learned to make use of it, oh yes. They and Osrin had thought themselves very clever when they had Red Marie feed nonsense to Mother Larksdale on the night before her son's regular visit. But exploiting Mother Larksdale had been Hoom's idea – no, *Red Marie's* idea – and her masters should have recognised that. She was a far better mummer than anyone here tonight, that much was true.

'Stop it!' a man in a wheeled rowing boat screamed at the stage. 'Jack Poyter, you ludicrous shit-heap! My very *mind* is capsizing!'

'I was promised Dickie!' the false Red Marie hissed in a man's voice. '*Everyone* promised! If I have to be Red-fucking-Marie, then by God sir, I will *jig*. I'm Jack Poyter. To jig is in my blood.'

'So's booze,' the boat-man declared. 'I'm certainly in no mood to fellate you, you puffed-up turd, but the truth of it is only you know Red Marie's lines. No one in this feeble troupe has the skill to learn them before the performance save one and he's a broken ankle. So, I am stuck with you, Poyter, and you are stuck with Marie. I'm sorry. Life's harsh, mate. Harsh as your face.'

'Tichborne,' a woman said.

'Silence, Arriet!' this Tichborne snapped. He looked back at Poyter. 'No jigging.'

'You're a tyrant,' Poyter said, starting to cry. Arriet got on to the stage to comfort him.

'Tyrants make art happen,' Tichborne replied. 'And if you so much as canter I'm nailing your feet to the boards.'

'My Red Marie jigs!' Poyter said.

'*Dickie o' the Green* jigs!'

Two men in green leotards and leaves in their hair came out from either side of the stage. They cavorted and danced sideways and toward one another, grinning at where the audience was meant to be.

'*You're not on yet!*' Tichborne screamed. 'And that's not the way Larksdale described it!'

The two green men careened into one another, toppling in a verdant heap.

Up in the thatch, Red Marie had never seen such prosaic misery. She was almost entertained.

'Pilgrim's arse!' Tichborne yelled into the night sky. 'You're dragging me down, all of you! Every man-jack and hussy! If we fuck this goose, people, we're for the chop. Literally, at the king's displeasure. And, frankly, I'll be ecstatic because my wish is to see theatre thrive. You're all guileless, talentless shite-carts and I'm sick, *sick* of your gawping faces.'

'You cannot talk to us like that,' the Arriet woman said. 'We're professionals. We're the Wreath!'

'*I* am the Wreath!' Tichborne yelled at her, slapping his chest. '*Me*, you farcical parasite!'

'Fine,' Arriet said. 'Keep your theatre.' She looked at all those assembled. 'Let us leave this place. The keep calls and we have earned the right to perform there. Each of us. We'll rehearse in an inn's garden if need be.' She jumped off the stage. 'Who is with me?'

The crowd cheered. Arriet headed for the great doors and the others followed, many patting her shoulder.

'It's my play!' Tichborne shouted.

'You called it a turd, tyrant,' Poyter said as he passed. He threw a chaff sickle into Tichborne's boat, did a little jig, and followed the others into the wintery night.

Tichborne started to cry with that genuine misery of the completely bereft. Red Marie watched him for some time, allowing that tingling feeling to smoulder in her parts. *He's a broken ankle under that blanket,* she thought. She licked her lips. Broken things were such fun to toy with.

She stopped herself. She hadn't the time. She had to locate Larksdale to find that fucking black crown her masters so sorely wanted but never explained the rationale for. Then again... tickling the whereabouts of Larksdale out of his friend would be more efficient than trundling over to that houseboat to look for him, surely? Yes…

She crawled along the curling roof, then down past a thin window. She hugged a wooden pillar and slid her way down to the mucky, sludge-rippled floor of the pit.

Tichborne wept into his palms. Then he sniffed the air. Once, twice.

Red Marie stopped. Was it possible she stank? In her sealed suit she had no idea. She lifted either hoof-shaped boot and checked the underside. Nothing, not even pigeon shit.

Before Tichborne knew it, she was behind him and his silly boat, a sickle over his jugular.

Tichborne went still as a gargoyle of the keep. Not the sort of man to fight, but not the sort to beg either. The paralysed kind, made dull matter by the glint of a blade.

'*Larksdale,*' Red Marie whispered. '*Where?*'

Tichborne relaxed slightly. 'I already told you people.'

'*What?*'

'Please, there's been some confusion. I told your colleagues Larksdale was going to the Carnation, the mollyboy place. Went with the foreign-looking girl in the red hat. Your colleagues must have him by now. They're supposed to come and pay me.'

None of this pleased Red Marie. More complication over this black crown. More knots to untie.

'*What colleagues?*' Red Marie said.

'What?'

'*What men have taken him?*' Red Marie demanded. '*Where to?*'

Tichborne said nothing. Paralysed again.

Red Marie needed to get moving, but she knew she would have to be patient with this fool. He was the only way through this new complexity, whatever it was.

A heavy door slammed. Tichborne drew breath.

The big doors rumbled with the sound of a chain being dragged across them.

'Oh Pilgrim, no,' the young man said.

'What?'

'You cannot smell it?' He winced. 'We have to go. Back door behind the stage. Carry me!'

Red Marie sliced his cheek. *'What smell?'*

'Please…'

The thatched roof above the big doors was smoking. An orange luminescence dappled the night sky behind it.

Red Marie kicked the rowing boat on its side and Tichborne rolled out on to the mud. He screamed to see Red Marie's painted face, that ship's figurehead, its mouth festooned with nails. She stamped on his ankle and snapped it once more, his screech filling the Wreath. She retracted a sickle and grabbed him by his shirt with her fist, holding him aloft.

'Hold on to my neck,' she hissed at him.

He had seized up again. The pain. The fear.

'You want to burn to death?' she said. *'Hold on to my neck!'*

He saw sense and wrapped his elbows around her.

'Legs up.'

He did so, presumably squeezing his thighs around her midriff though she could not feel it. He mewled with his fresh agony.

'The other door?' she demanded.

'Stage left.'

She turned around, his weight no weight at all, only to see smoke pouring from stage left. She ran toward it anyway. No use. There were drapes of some kind, golden with flame, lighting up the walls. Red Marie might make it – with fire she was not so certain – but the young man and his knowledge would choke and die. She ran to the timber pillar she had descended from and began climbing it, sickles and hoof-spikes slicing into wood.

A cruel trick, she thought, *trapping someone and burning them.* They had no idea who they had dragged into their little banality. Now they would be the ones to suffer.

She reached the roof and clambered up the thatch. Some thirty yards away it was already burning, spreading from the thatch above the entrance. She mounted the arch of the roof.

A small man with an eyepatch was up there, between her and the burning thatch. He had a clay jug and was pouring its black contents on to the thatch beside him. He stopped pouring and looked toward Red Marie.

He could see her. Of course. She had a groaning man hanging off her.

The one-eyed man threw the empty jug down into the pit and drew a long-knife.

He was surely one of these people Tichborne had just been alluding to, come to kill the thespian in an 'accident' instead of pay him. But a closer, better source of information.

'I'm going to leave you here,' Red Marie told Tichborne. *'You're going to burn to death.'*

'What?'

'It's really painful,' she informed him eagerly. She tore him off her and dropped him to the thatch.

'No,' he pleaded. 'Please!'

She charged at the one-eyed man.

The one-eyed man was a fighter by profession, she could tell. But he could see his nightmares racing toward him. He made one thrust that she parried with ease.

'I am the deceiver,' she squealed. *'The blooded blade!'* Her sickle slid through the palm of his hand. *'I am Red Marie!'*

The man pulled his hand away in terror and it split in two.

He staggered, fell down the thatch roof and slammed into gloom-shrouded cobbles below. Voices yelled out of the darkness.

'I've plays to write!' Tichborne shouted. 'Please!'

She leaped down. She could not help herself. Such was her fury, her joy. She paid in pain, a little, shooting up her legs. She staggered and righted herself. She would heal soon; the changes in her body would see to it. But she had been lucky: she might have unsealed her suit.

There was a ladder propped against the Wreath's outer wall, the splattered corpse of the one-eyed man beneath it and two other – still living – men with torches in hand, staring wide-mouthed at their colleague. One was blonde and bearded, the other brown-skinned. Both were blessed with old scars.

'I'm Red Marie!' she yelled and threw her right sickle into the blonde man's face. It popped right through his skull and lightning jumped in Red Marie's chest and feathered in her tummy. She drank down his confused stare as life left his brain and vanished forever. She glared at the dark man.

He drove his torch into her face.

She laughed and readied to take him prisoner but it seemed her face was on fire. The mask. The painted mask.

Her vision turned gold, orange. She pulled her sickle from the dead man and swung the other at her assailant. She hit nothing. She could not see.

Something jabbed at her torso. A blade, trying to find a gap somewhere. A weak spot.

'Never heard of you!' her assailant shouted in an accent she didn't know. 'Never heard of you!'

How dare he.

'I'm Red Marie!' she screamed, slashing, hitting nothing. 'Your nightmare!'

Something hammered the back of her helm. 'Never heard of you!'

She blocked his blows with her gauntlets, flames raging in her face, brighter for her movements. She kicked and her hoof-spike ran deep into something solid.

She had him impaled. She slashed and slashed, tearing through bone and flesh.

'I'm Red Marie! I'm Red Marie!'

She could hear the screams of many people, people who had come to gawp at a fire. Red Marie remembered to beat the flames out on her face.

She could see again. A gathering of folk were staring at her.

'I'm Red Marie!' she told them. She paused a moment, uncertain what more to say. She ran off into the night.

BAPTISMAS, THE NIGHT BEFORE YULENIGHT EVE

38

Fwych

Fwych gawped. She had never seen the like. It were of a height with waterfalls and canyons but with patterns and faces and beasts upon the skin of its rock. Carved stone it were, but so carved and sanded that this hall seemed not built by man but grown from the very earth, like some dream in the skull of Father Mountain. This, she knew, had to be the keep's greeting hall.

And she had to be gone from it. Gone from the keep and into the city, to the hall Lady Larksdale had called the Wreath. Find her son. Sir Larksdale had the black crown now, had to, if the forces of evil – Countess Osrin or whoever she were – hadn't grabbed it already.

There were many folk about the greeting hall. Servants dressed as she, and others beside. No one paid her much attention. Mother Larksdale had said as much when she had sewn the dress, that it would protect Fwych from prying eyes. Almost a spell this, being a servant. A ward of unseeing. It had been a torture, waiting for Lady Larksdale's old hands to make the dress, knowing the evil countess were a day ahead of her. Soon as getting it on Fwych had practically run out of the room, had gone down stair after stair after stair until she thought she were mad. But now the way out were clear. Two great doors of oak, open to the sunlight.

She stopped, looked around the hall and then took the parchment from her pocket. It were covered in inky lines – writing, apparently – and had a doodle of a strange animal. A message to the king, Lady Larksdale had said, unsigned, saying that the writer had the hedgehog girl in their possession and would soon send another message with their demands. That weren't the clever part though, not according to Lady Larksdale. The clever part were that she had written the message in the language of Queen Carmotta. They would think Carmotta the kidnapper. And the doodle of the animal. The animal – a 'lionfox' apparently, but to Fwych it looked a russet badger – were the symbol of Count Osrin, son of Countess Osrin. *Do you see?* Lady Larksdale had asked Fwych, laughing as she did. *It will confuse all our rivals, set them against each other. We're sowing dissent!*

Fwych weren't sure of any of it. But Lady Larksdale had saved Fwych and given her sanctuary. The least she could do were carry out her bidding. Fwych placed the parchment on the base of a statue then made for the great doors and the daylight beyond.

Someone were looking straight at her. A girl, twelve or thirteen, in rough white cloth with a black stripe running down the front. She were stood before a great pillar. Her hair were red and braided, like Fwych's had been at that age.

A mountain mother, Fwych realised, *an adept*. Fwych could tell from the pale blue tattoos along her arms. Servants passed the girl by, uninterested. Then one passed straight through her. A spirit, this girl. A vision. Far from Fwych's first.

As she stepped closer, careful not to draw attention of others, Fwych saw it was no black stripe upon her tunic but a line of thickest blood that ran from the girl's sliced throat.

Fwych drew breath and reached her own spirit out to meet the dead girl, to soothe her. No spirit reached back. The girl was a hollow thing, a vessel. But something held that vessel. Behind that empty girl writhed a vast power.

The power grabbed Fwych. It seized her spirit, hooked it like a fish.

The girl drifted backward into the daylight beyond the doorway and Fwych felt her own body follow.

Sunlight engulfed Fwych, white and warm, though the air blew cold enough. She felt these things both in her body, which were now a remote thing, and in her essence, which poured through the air as an unseen mist. She felt the tiled path and the grass besides and the air above.

The further she got up the path, the more the power drawing her thickened. It were like being dragged into a gale but a gale made from screams. The strangest thing. A serving man passed by Fwych's walking body, ignorant of the scream-winds all about.

Ahead of her, embedded in the path, were a great curve of brown metal. Bronze, by the look. The power had its source there. It poured out from the metal like a spring from a mountain's crack, ceaseless and mad.

The land and sky darkened the closer she stepped toward the bronze curve. The tiles became dead earth and rock, the skies full of black cloud and the morn became dusk. The world were shifting upon itself; she could feel it. All the things of the keep – the outer walls, the hedges and the lawns and the people – were gone and the land were bare. Steam rose from the bronze curve in the ground and the air turned hot as from an oven. The curve glowed now, its bronze molten and fresh. On the other side of it were the girl and many other mountain mothers. All ages, all in the same pale tunics, their throats uncut.

Fwych were in her own body now, but it were like a body in a dream, present but unstuck. She turned her head left and right and saw, half-veiled by the rising steam, more women, hundreds of them, each woman a few feet apart from the next, a line following the molten curve into the dark distance. As one, the women dropped to their knees, their faces lit by the molten glow before them.

Demons prowled from out of the dusk. Fwych had never seen the like. Slender and short, they were bound in black armour from face to heel. Black daggers in their fists. Each one came to a stop behind their chosen woman and the women closed their eyes and smiled.

Fwych tried to shout, to move, but it came out as a murmur, a stumble.

Throats were slit and bodies pushed forward, lifeblood pouring into the cooling metal. Hair were set alight and flesh blackened.

A roar, as of a great beast, came from behind Fwych. She turned herself around, an act that took all strength, all focus. The great keep had vanished. There were a much smaller castle, three storeys high, upon the blasted plain. Ruddy light were pouring from the spaces between its stones. The light were the source of the roar, Fwych knew.

A figure stood before the castle, a silhouette in the red glow. Its long hair and robes danced in the winds. It raised its arms aloft.

Fwych screamed and turned. She could not hear her own scream in the endless roar. She were carried by the air off of her feet. Like in dreams. She fell into the heat of the molten bronze.

It took her in. Her body vanished and she were racing through bronze, travelling along the great circlet at the speed of thought. She understood it, were at one with it. It were a reservoir, a raging circle of that power she had once carried upon her tongue. The power to compel and the power to understand others' feelings which, Fwych suddenly perceived, were really one and the same. A thousand mountain mothers, their power locked in, bound as one. Holding the keep's evil in place.

Fwych reached out to them all. An honour, that. An honour a thousandfold. But like the girl they did not reach back. Not truly. They had ceased to be women, to be themselves. There were no folk here, no spirits, just a racing, churning torrent of feeling and smashed memory. The great circle were nothing but a single urge, a thought with no true thinker. *Keep evil in.*

But even that were not enough. The evil of the keep still seeped out in drips, staining the streets and minds of the city. Now, the stars being all wrong this Yulenight Eve, a flood would come. If mortal hands opened the way. And hands there were, unseen and willing and knowledgeable.

Weird lightning beat at her. The power, hammering her essence. Changing Fwych, making her an alloy.

It needed a pair of living hands, the great circle. That were all. It knew where the black crown lay. It knew the thing had to be gone from here.

Fwych let the circle know she were willing.

She could see her body again, stood under the morning sun. It had not moved from where she had left it, its eyes staring at the bronze curve that cut across the tiled path. Her body seemed happy enough. She might have felt it even, but her essence was a tumult, throbbing with strange power not its own, coming to terms with a newness. She would never be the same.

She were vaguely aware of her body turning around and heading back along the path, then turning down another. She could not take it in because she were beset with flashes, images of things that had never happened. The nail-fanged face of Red Marie rising from below a river's surface, the hand of someone unseen, readying a blade to meet Red Marie, to stab hopelessly at her chest. A skinny man hanging upside down, clothes and skin grass green, his hair russet as a spineman's. A burning wax candle studded with nails.

Fwych were aware of her body once more. It had walked some distance along the paths and were soon on no path at all, waddling across lawns green and wet and dotted with snow. Ahead stood a copse of trees.

Gethwen were running toward it. Fwych's heart bounded, but almost as quickly she realised it were another vision, a thing shown to her by that near-mindless circle of power. Though Gethwen ran beneath a morning sun, the light upon him was of the moon and stars. He had run this way on some night before he had died. The great circle had seen it.

The Gethwen-vision had the bag upon its shoulder. The bag with the black crown inside. Oh blessed Mountain, the black crown lay within the copse of trees! She were being guided!

A man were chasing Gethwen. Similarly cast in moonlight and in the fancy wear of a rich flatlander. Whoever he were, he had some part to play in all this.

She could feel her body now. She were deeper in its bones and muscle. But it still walked toward the trees despite her.

39

Larksdale

It proved to be a fresh morning, a cloudless sky above Fleawater camp, and Sister Ruradoola insisted he sit outside so that she might shave his beard off and cut his hair.

He was sitting on an old carpet atop two small crates that stood upon the stony earth between two caravans. To his left lay the greater part of Fleawater camp, with its fleet of caravans and braying donkeys, and beyond all that the barricades. The place was silent as a mortuary. To his right was a shallow decline that led straight to the shore of the River Flume. The river's detritus collected there: rotten planks, broken glass. Harry Larksdale. Dear Marla had quickly convinced the fleas to host him. Tomorrow she would return here to take him to her spymaster. A life of comfy treason awaited. Pilgrim's mercy.

'Take your top off,' Sister Ruradoola told him.

'That's rather forward for a holy Perfecti, Sister,' he replied. 'Should you not at least take my confession first?' He grinned at her.

Her face, dark as umber, flashed a smile within her grey wimple. 'I suspect we'd be here all day,' she replied. 'You theatre types collect fewer sins than most but those you do generally require much explanation.' She drew a silver blade from somewhere in her ragged vestments. Larksdale noticed her fingers: covered in dried black ink. Interesting, that. He did as she ordered, though typically he preferred his toplessness be a thing of candlelight.

'Thank you.' She stepped behind him. 'I am going to give you the hair of a young flea.'

Flea, fleawet, these names were an insult, he had discovered, though deep in his heart he had always known as much, he had just never given it much thought. These people called themselves 'spinefolk', or more precisely 'the wandering sort', given that they had ventured from that range of mountains that ran down the length of the Main like a backbone. He had to wonder at Sister Ruradoola, someone clearly not of their blood, bandying such insults in their very home.

She began to slice his dark locks off at the back. Almost made him weep, that. But what did another insult upon his person matter? Especially one that might help him hide.

Staring at his feet, he said, 'What is this hair of a young, er... this style of...'

'A young flea? Most the skull a half-inch short and the front locks kept long.'

He recalled the two lads with the donkey had had that style, the day he, Gethwen and Marla visited, the day he had first met the sister.

'With their forelocks to cover their upper face,' Ruradoola replied, 'the young men become hard to identify. That's what suspicion and disdain teaches us, Sir Harrance. Never stand out.'

Her fingers splayed against his scalp and she sliced.

'You say "us",' he replied. 'You do not strike me as a woman of the spines, Sister. The Church sent you, yes?'

'I minister here,' she answered. 'They are devotees of God, the wandering sort, despite what people think. But it's their own manner of devotion, rich with the worship of Father Mountain. It is quite the task, to place a Perfecti in their midst. We have the same powers as their mountain mothers but they believe us broken and tamed. They're right, of course.'

This was damned unholy talk, beyond that of a playhouse libertine, let alone a Perfecti. Perfecti began as young girls living in the foothills of the Spine Mountains who showed powers of verbal control, and it was vital they were found fast and pressed into God's loving arms, otherwise they would assuredly be lured by the devil's trickery up into the mountains. To join his daughters the ban-hags.

'I feel like I should be taking your confession, Sister,' he said, uncertainly. 'What you say is unorthodox. To put it lightly.'

'Dangerous, too,' she replied. 'I've spent time among these people, Sir Harrance. I've seen what the Church and your blessed keep has done to them and, lately, I feel great affinity with ban-hags. I've never been so respected as here.'

A heretic with a knife to my head, Larksdale thought. Still, he rather liked her. She had both toughness and a sense of humour, which at root were the same thing.

'They accept you because you do not look like them,' he observed.

'Ironic, isn't it?' She sliced again.

'I mean no insult, but how is it you have the power of a Perfecti or, indeed, a ban-hag? You, well, seem the last person to have the blood of the spinefolk.'

'I grew up far away on the plateau of Ammu. The tongue-power's source is not a question of ethnicity, Harrance, but one of altitude.'

'Closeness to God,' Larksdale replied and he pointed at the sky.

The sister harrumphed at that and went to grab a stool nearby. A woman had come out of the caravan in front of him and was now sitting on the step before its gaily painted entrance. All the caravans were painted brightly and were immaculately clean, something Larksdale would not have expected. The woman, her eyes red raw and her jaw tight, had a wooden spoon and a bowl with something pale in it.

Sister Ruradoola placed the stool before Larksdale's feet and sat upon it. She spun her little knife between her ink-stained fingers.

'Time to shave that beard off,' she said.

'Oh that's too-too much,' he said. Yet he relented.

She gripped his beard and sliced. 'Please, you must tell me what happened to the black crown.'

'I never even saw it,' he said. Which was true. 'I've no clue where it is.' A lie. It lay at the bottom of a pond in the keep. He would only tell Ruradoola this when he left with Marla. He had no wish to be mixed up in dark superstitions and, besides, it would make for a useful leverage should Fleawater suddenly elect to take his life.

Of course, she could take the facts from him simply by using her voice. But she did not. It seemed she believed his faux ignorance.

The woman with the mixing bowl got up and walked away, leaving the receptacle within reach of Sister Ruradoola.

'A remarkable blade,' he whispered, as if alluding to the thing in Ruradoola's hand might protect him from it.

'Commrach steel. A gift.' She turned his head a little, slid the sorcerous metal down the other side of his throat. 'The commrach have been after the crown for some time too. Which is bad enough, perhaps, but decidedly better than the other, more mysterious group with an interest in it. Of whom I know absolutely nothing save they're well-versed in the subject and intend the end of the world. Alchemists, perhaps.'

'Or intensely jaded academics,' Larksdale added.

His face was smooth now, smoother than it had ever been. It was said commrach metalworkers dripped demon blood into molten steel. He shuddered to think what evil might have sunk into his pores. She sat back down on the stool and placed the bowl on her lap. The pale gloop inside the bowl looked like porridge. It stank, like bladder-water but… somehow purer. 'This stuff's a bleach,' she said. 'Turns hair blonde, though with your black locks it should come out ginger.' She nodded. 'You'll make a good ginger.'

'Is it always so quiet around here?' he asked. 'I'd have expected a flea camp to be riotous. Something isn't right, is it?'

'It's not a healthy subject, Sir Harrance,' she replied. 'You would not thank me.' She frowned and, with an oiled rag, scooped up some of the piss-porridge and rubbed it into his scalp. It burnt and he wanted to leap up, but if she had not slit his throat yet this stuff was likely safe enough. 'Funny thing, the black crown,' she said, going about her porridge-rubbing. 'They say the story of its creation is untellable, that no language has the capacity nor any mind the acceptance.' She worked the strands of his surviving forelocks. 'Anyway, the crown was kept in the Spine Mountains in some profane cave, but it made its way by human hand to this camp a few centuries ago. The camp chief back then sent word to the mountains and a mother came along with a tricky-man. They returned to the mountains with the crown – the tricky-man carrying it and the mountain mother to watch him.'

'A what now?' Larksdale said.

'Tricky-men are shunned creatures,' she replied. 'That's why your Gethwen was shooed off from here: he had no mountain mother to counter his evil.'

'There was no evil to that youth,' Larksdale said. Damn her.

'There was manipulation,' the sister replied with no malice. 'Men born with his powers cannot help it.'

'You did not know Gethwen.'

'Your defensiveness suggests he worked you well. I'll bet you found a strong friendship with him, eh? That you could confide in one another? You're what the spinefolk call a trick-hound. Following on a leash.'

'Nonsense,' Larksdale said, an anger rising.

'Gethwen was trying to survive as best he could,' Ruradoola said.

Larksdale said nothing. It *had* been strange, the way he had opened up to Gethwen. He had never told anyone of his life's plan, of his mad hunger to turn the world gold with art. Yet Gethwen had sucked this truth right out of him. Had it all been a lie? Every moment of it? *Did you think me a hound, Gethwen?*

'Are you well?' the sister asked.

His lip quivered. 'Tell me of this crown.'

Sister Ruradoola stood up and walked behind him. She began to massage the back of his head with the burning gloop. He held back his tears.

'The black crown was returned to its cave,' she said. 'Placed upon "Father Mountain's head" which, they say, only a tricky-man can do. Ten years later it made its way back to this camp, carried again by human hands. Presumably in a bag.'

'Who exactly?'

'Several people,' Sister Ruradoola said. 'All of them with perfectly good reasons at the time that, had you or I been there, would have been perfectly understandable. Well, another mother and tricky-man collected it and went back and two decades later…'

'It came back here?' Larksdale could make no sense of this tale. 'Are you saying the crown has a mind? That it seduces people?'

Ruradoola laughed, warm and full-throated. 'A cunning trinket? That's absurd. No, it is this city that seduces, and the spider at its centre.'

'The keep,' Larksdale said.

'You barely feel its evil,' she said. 'But we Perfecti feel it, believe me.' She slapped on a little more of the acrid porridge. 'It drew its trinket closer, again and again, into its little larder. Until the people in its larder relented and just buried the crown at the centre of Fleawater camp. Then, about two months past, people started dying around here. Horribly and inexplicably. Thus the silence you noted.'

Larksdale's shoulders tightened. Death stalked here. A death that stank of the keep-within-the-keep, that devil tower in the hollow heart.

'This coming yulenight is important to the spinefolk's religion,' the sister continued. 'Indeed, it was important to everyone in ancient times. This will be the yule-of-yules, the winter where powers align.'

'In what sense?'

'Fucked if I know,' she admitted. 'But that and all the strange deaths put our camp into fear and fury. Aifen-the-Tom had the crown dug up and bagged for transport. He left the city under cover of night and passed it to your friend Gethwen and his mountain mother, a meeting Aifen never returned from.'

'More death,' Larksdale said.

'I think digging up the black crown and trying to send it back was exactly what the keep wanted. The time is right and it desires its little morsel long buried in its larder by mortal fools.'

'I've lived in that keep for many years, Sister. It's full of pampered boors. Nothing more.' A lie, of course. But he was scared of blurting the keep's hidden truth. 'I'd show you around there but my popularity is somewhat waning of late.'

Behind him, Sister Ruradoola fell silent as a field in winter. Her fingers stopped moving through his hair. 'I'm not talking about its outer hide,' she said. 'I mean the keep-within.'

What? How could she know? She had executed herself with her own tongue. He dared not speak a word. How much or how little *could* one say? How close a reference or allusion could one actually make before the curse saw you?

A dead soul walking. She knew it too.

'All done,' she said with finality and it took a second for Larksdale to realise she meant his hair. 'I'm afraid you will have to suffer its irritation an hour. Then we'll wash it out.'

He was cold. The weather must have turned. He pulled his shirt up and buttoned it.

'The bleach will drip on your shirt,' she said.

He stood up. 'I've stopped caring.' He looked at her. He wanted to express sympathy, to say something that might make her fate incrementally less terrifying. But he was scared to even do that.

She smiled sadly at him. *She can read me,* he thought.

'Come along,' Sister Ruradoola said. 'There is someone you should meet.'

40

Carmotta

'You are not well. You should not accompany me.'

'I am your sworn sword.'

'You cannot even hold one, Dulenci.'

They were descending in the paternoster. Every bump and bang of the box they stood in made Dulenci squirm with discomfort. His sword arm was broken and in a sling.

'Still I must try,' he replied. He looked dejected, his round eyes a mewling puppy's. 'Else I am nothing.'

'Oh, my sweet, my sweet,' she said. 'That falling sheep did not break your cock, eh?'

He did not smile or make a pass. He was in a pit of unhappiness, her sweet Dulenci.

He had returned to her on a stretcher, in complete agony and with a bizarre tale to tell. He had discovered Larksdale 'in a cupboard', watching him in the act of non-sexual relations with several youths. Some thugs had then materialised and set upon everyone. Dulenci, having despatched the thugs and the mollyboys, then chased Larksdale into a slaughterhouse wherein Larksdale had, by the sounds of it, outwitted him with falling mutton.

Carmotta honestly had no idea what to make of any of it.

Dulenci had always been lousy at relaying facts and the servants who had brought him back to the keep had left before she might speak with them. Dulenci had been alarmed about Larksdale when first he was carried in before Carmotta, for now someone finally knew the truth behind Dulenci's erotic facade. Carmotta had had to reassure Dulenci that Larksdale was a hunted criminal now and that no one would believe such a story, for he had no evidence: all the youths had died and their pimp had vanished. Dulenci had calmed on hearing that. Honestly, Carmotta had a growing suspicion the whole tale was a lie. She had always trusted Dulenci implicitly but this story was simply too much. It was then she realised, with a little guilt, that if Dulenci *were* to lie this was exactly the manner of flamboyant drool his brain would come up with. Something had happened to him in Tetchford, undeniably. But not Sir Harrance Larksdale in a sex-cupboard with a pack of mercenaries.

Another woman, she had thought then. She did not want to think that. But she did. He was a man, after all, a handsome one. With handsome men it was only a matter of time.

She kissed her fingers and placed them gently on his lips. 'I am glad you are alive, my love. I could not live without you.'

He almost smiled.

A silence fell, one which she tried to pass off as comfortable. High above them men were toiling to death making this paternoster work day and night. She wondered if they had the hand of night above their heads too.

'Count Osrin,' she muttered.

'What about him?'

'Remember when last we rode this paternoster? He was waiting on the floor where we got out. You manhandled Lord Pym, remember?'

'Yes.' He did not smile. He normally would have laughed.

'Then we met that bitch Emmabelle down in the catacombs. I never considered she was about to use the paternoster to go up as we had used it to go down. That Osrin and his toads were waiting for her.'

'What does it matter?' Dulenci said. 'You already have her love letter to him.'

She had that letter on her now. Her weapon within this very hour.

'I know,' she replied. 'But I should have comprehended as much at the time. Her presence and his. I am not as quick and clever as I think I am, Dulenci. I still do not even know who sent that one-eyed assassin. I should. If I am not clever I shall die.'

Dulenci frowned.

'What?' Carmotta asked.

'Cleverness would be to leave this misery entirely. My love, let us away.'

'Oh Dulenci.' He was a fool, holding to this nonsense. He had taken a throwaway sentiment of hers and made of it holy writ. 'The Explainer was right: we haven't the skills to live among the common folk.'

He grinned, almost giddily. 'We won't need to. Carmotta, the Wreath burnt down last night.'

Larksdale's theatre. 'Was everyone fine?'

'Who cares?' He frowned when he plainly saw she was concerned for Larksdale, but continued. 'The land it's built on is now empty. Our land, Carmotta. Already my man in the city has been inundated with offers. For many… er, coins.'

'You're typically more interesting than this, cousin.'

'Don't you see? We can take those coins and run. Live free. And if we need more coins we'll just burn down another building.' He grinned. 'I think I may have an instinct for this line of business.'

This had to end. She was torturing him by not ending it.

'Dulenci, I am the queen. We are never leaving the keep.'

He reached out for her cheek. 'Who cares for that when our love is the world?'

'Our love is *in* the world.' She pushed his hand away. 'You can leave, Dulenci. I will not. This is my life.' She could not be so cruel. 'Though I'd rather you remain and love me.'

He sniffed, his lip twitching. 'I am always going to have to pretend not to love you.' His eyes watered. 'Aren't I?'

She made no reply.

To speak of the devil brings him near. It seemed the same was true for Count Osrin. He was standing on the chequered floor in the hallway before the ancient chapel in the west wing, talking with Willem Cutbill.

Both men saw her and Dulenci enter and bowed. The hands of night were above their heads, of course. Carmotta wished Osrin's was squeezing down on him like it had poor Slyke. But no.

'Please, sirs,' she said a wave of the wrist, 'we are all equal before God and his Pilgrim.' She indicated the archway of the chapel with its fine carvings of the nine stages of the Pilgrim's death. 'Will you be joining us in prayer, Count Osrin?' She hoped not. Was it remotely possible he already suspected her plan?

'I am afraid not, Your Majesty,' he replied. 'I am a man of action called to action.' He eyed Dulenci's broken arm in its sling and smiled.

'How exciting,' Carmotta said, feigning a girlish insouciance she hardly believed herself. 'What action?'

'The king forbids we speak of it,' Sir Willem Cutbill said, 'till it is done. Forgive us, Your Majesty.'

'Of course,' she replied. A matter for the city's guard, surely. Why else would Osrin approach the lowborn Cutbill?

'It'll be finished by tonight,' Osrin said, an eager expression upon his V-scarred face. 'No secret by morning.'

His face seemed too earnest to be mocking her. Whatever he had planned was giving him a child's glee, not a conspirator's serenity. It would be of no threat to Ean or herself. Likely a city matter, a crushing of common folk, as happened sometimes. Tiresome and vile.

'Let us not keep you,' Dulenci said to Osrin, no verve in his tone.

Osrin half-smiled. 'Of course.' He walked away from the group then, turning, said, 'My apologies to you and His Majesty, by the way. I shan't be able to make it along to the tri-baptism tonight.' He bowed and left.

The baptism of the three rivers was a yule ritual that required the king and his queens to leave the keep and traipse the city. Carmotta's least favourite duty. Count Osrin knew that.

But I have you, Count. Mock while you can.

'Shall we enter?' Cutbill asked. He meant the little chapel.

'Wait,' Carmotta said. Osrin's presence had made her cautious. 'It is a fine, bright morning. We could make prayer just as easily before the shrine on the pond. How would that sound, Sir Willem?'

The big commoner frowned. 'By habit I come here, Your Majesty. To pray for the souls of my boys.'

'Pilgrim's blood,' she said. 'You have lost sons?'

'He means his soldiers,' Dulenci said flatly.

'Back in the war.' Cutbill looked up at the stonework all around. He drew a long breath.

Carmotta touched his upper arm. 'Sir. Your boys lived their lives beneath the open sky, fighting for their realm and king. A prayer beneath that same roof would be fitting, would it not?'

Cutbill smiled. He almost looked ready to cry. 'Yes. Yes, Your Majesty. It would at that.'

'Besides,' she added, 'there is something I wish to show you both.'

The morning was indeed fresh and bright as Carmotta led the way along the path. Servants were tending to the flower beds and lawns of Becken Keep's gardens. All had a dark hand above their head. Talk of the keep-within reached everyone here, presumably too the taboo of never talking about it and certainly not beyond the outer walls.

'Are you closer to catching that untrustworthy liar Larksdale, Willem?' Dulenci asked the big man. He shook his head. 'The damned liar.'

'Unfortunately not,' Cutbill said. 'He's gone to ground but this is our city. Someone will give him up soon. It's possible he burnt his own theatre down last night. With a man in it. Three men were found murdered outside, too.'

'Bodies?' Carmotta could make no sense of that.

'This man in the fire,' Dulenci said, piping up. 'He would be burnt to a crisp, yes? It could be that liar Larksdale himself.'

'No,' Cutbill said. 'We believe it to be a playwright of his acquaintance.'

'Perhaps this playwright knew too much,' Dulenci said, venom in his tone. 'Mark my words, sir: kill Larksdale on sight. No use shall come of apprehending him; his tongue offers naught but falsehoods.'

'Gentlemen,' Carmotta said, cutting Dulenci off. 'Speaking of Larksdale, a slight detour calls to me.'

'Your Majesty?' Cutbill asked.

'The thing I wished to show you. Actually, the first of two things. This way.' She turned right on to the pathway that led to the archery butts. The men followed.

Halfway along the path she indicated for the party to cease. The three of them stood just before the pattern of bronze, the one whose circumference surrounded the keep and much of its gardens.

She pointed at the curving metal. 'I noticed it this morning, when I looked out of my chamber window. I thought back to the morning we all practised our bow arms.'

'When Slyke died,' Cutbill added.

'Mm.' She pointed at the butts, standing silent and unused. 'We were beyond the pattern's perimeter that day. Sir Willem, I do not think it is safe to talk about the keep's curse anywhere in the keep's grounds. I think the protection ends here: a step away from where I now stand. No one knows who made this pattern, so I am told. It is unspeakably ancient. Pagan. I dare say someone would have pulled it all up by now if it were not so arduous a task.' She thought of the vision the keep-within had cursed her with, the women being sacrificed before a stream of curving bronze. 'Sir, I think this pattern, this vast ring in the earth, entraps the evil of the keep. Which, when one thinks about it, makes far more sense than those ad hoc walls beyond.'

'Your Majesty,' Cutbill said, looking at the pattern and shaking his head. 'If that were the case people would die horrifically beyond the pattern but before the outer walls all the time. Bodies would pile up. How many lords and ladies have walked those pathways beyond where we stand, or shot their bows just over there and talked of the keep-within and not died? Hmm?'

'Have they?' Carmotta asked. 'Who would want to talk of such things in these pretty gardens? People barely talk of it inside the keep. You hear it once and know yourself cursed. I know I did. It's how you become a part of this place.'

Cutbill could not suppress a dark chuckle. He knew what she meant.

'Sir Willem, Larksdale did not murder Slyke,' she said. 'How could he have ever known his mustard would commingle with some exotic powder to violent effect? And even if he did, how could he know it would affect Slyke alone? It's absurd and I'm surprised a man as observant as yourself does not think it absurd too.' Yes. She could see it in his face. He had his doubts. 'But I'll tell you who would know. *What* would know. The curse.' She eyed the top of Cutbill's shaved head, where the dark and translucent hand of the keep-within sat so brazenly. It did not stir. It had reached into Slyke's skull the moment he had died and no one but she saw.

'You miss one thing, my queen,' Cutbill replied.

'And that is?'

'Let's say the curse murdered him. But for the curse to, I don't know... want... to murder him, Slyke would have to have talked about the keep-within at some point nine days before his death. That's the rules, yes?' He waved his gloved hands about with uncharacteristic nonchalance. 'When you said he murdered himself you mean he made the mistake of talking about the keep-within while standing beyond the bounds of this here pattern—' He pointed at the curving bronze line that sliced through the path. '—but not beyond the outer walls over there.' He pointed at the outer walls of the keep with its hodge-lodge of brickwork and granite, barbicans and walkways.

'Perceptive, sir.'

'Obvious,' he replied. 'Tibald Slyke was not so suicidal to go talking about you-know-what whenever he visited the streets of the city.'

She liked this version of Cutbill that had emerged. Lost in thought he had quickly forgotten his deference. That said, she would not wish it all the time.

He continued,'But you just said no one speaks about the curse when walking the gardens. You defeat yourself.' He stopped, his face paling. 'Your Majesty, I mean—'

'It is quite fine, Sir Willem,' she said. 'That quandary had struck me too. And the answer, I suspect, you will comprehend better than I. Slyke wished to talk to someone about the curse, someone he would not wish to be seen walking the keep with. Tibald was a noble and very aware of the fact. He defended his reputation as fiercely as any.'

'A commoner,' Cutbill said. 'Is that your meaning?'

'A commoner he thought to make a weapon. He told them *of* the keep-within, but he did not tell them not to *speak* of the keep-within. He made this commoner a bolt of death-bearing gossip.'

'A thought, that,' he conceded. 'But what would be the remotest use? It's too random, too wide.'

'There you have me, sir,' Carmotta said. 'My only question to you, Captain General, is has there been an outbreak of strange deaths in this city of late?'

'Some exceedingly bloody murders,' he said. 'Blamed on Red Marie as always.'

'Who?'

'A folk tale, Your Majesty. A local demon. People imagine seeing her, in fact some drunkards claimed to see her last night.' He shook his head. 'Anyhow, there's been no plague of weird accidental deaths, at least nothing that anyone's put together. Just grizzly street murders.'

She had no reply. She had rather depended on an outbreak.

'Your Majesty,' Cutbill said, 'I know you have known Sir Harry a long time. Perhaps—'

'She has no love for him,' Dulenci snapped. 'None.'

Cutbill looked taken aback at the fury of his words. Then he looked curious.

'Sir Willem,' Carmotta said. 'If you think my theory wrong then, by all means, step over the threshold at our feet and talk of the keep-within.'

He stepped over the pattern. He looked her right in the eyes.

Carmotta tensed.

'Your Majesty,' Cutbill said. He waited a breath. 'Let's go to the shrine and pray.'

It was now time to show Cutbill the second thing. Yet since she had seen him in conversation with Count Osrin, her already uncertain confidence had been shaken the more. But what choice had she?

They had returned to the path that led to the little shrine. The copse of trees, where the shrine and its pond lay, were close now. Two of the trees were cypresses, a common sight along the old roads and canals of Manca. She pictured her family estate outside Sant Ribot. She was of House Il'Lunadella, was she not? Raised to fearlessness.

'This other thing,' she said, never looking at Cutbill beside her, 'is not another theory of mine. It is but a simple question.'

'Your Majesty?'

'Are you a patriot, Sir Willem?'

'My love for the Brintland and its people I cannot even describe,' he said. 'But words are words: cunning things I've no talent for.'

'What of the Crown?'

He looked puzzled.

Before he might answer, she said, 'Dulenci, the letter please.' Her cousin handed it to Cutbill and the big bull looked apprehensive. No easy thing, she realised, to take parchment from royal hands: the contents could as easily be death as reward. She would have to remember the casual power of it for future use.

'One of a series of letters,' she told him, 'from my sister wife Emmabelle to – I strongly believe – Count Osrin, our friend back at the chapel just now. It is her side of a correspondence passed to the commrach Explainer, held by that creature in confidence and then passed to Osrin. Presumably it happens the other way too.'

They were passing into the shadow beneath the canopy of the trees. Without the sun directly upon her the day revealed its chilly truth. She crossed her arms.

Cutbill stopped walking. Carmotta and Dulenci did likewise. Cutbill's lips trembled as he read. He was half-mouthing the words and Carmotta knew him for a man who had learned to read at a late age.

He rolled the letter up. She was careful to prise it from his hand.

'There's more?' he asked.

'Plenty. In the Explainer's tent.' She almost stopped herself. The Explainer lived within the shadow of the keep-within, after all. But where they were standing now, she remembered with comfort, was safely within the radius of the brass ring. 'But the letters I have are enough. It is Emmabelle's handwriting. Emmabelle, a queen of the Brintland, her royal womb heavy with child. But whose? Your guess, Sir Willem, is as good as a tossed coin.'

'This bloody keep,' Cutbill muttered. 'This is not my business. Show it to the king.'

'I'm taking precautions before I must,' she replied. 'I'm ensuring the high ground belongs to Ean before he commits to battle. A soldier understands that, yes? Osrin and Emmabelle are poisonous as vipers and similarly as quick. Unless we prepare, Ean will fly into a rage upon reading these letters and Osrin and Emmabelle will have ready answers for him.' She stepped closer. 'Ready your guard, sir. Be ready to lock down this city.'

'Your Majesty,' Cutbill protested. 'I'm a peasant, a glover's son. I'm out of my depth.'

'Learn to swim,' she told him. 'And fast, glover's son. Osrin is popular, more popular than Ean in some lordly quarters. You know this.' For a moment she was tempted to use a little fragility, even tears, but she knew Cutbill was a man who could see through all that. He needed facts. He needed his own power explained to him. 'Come spring, Osrin's faction will move against the Crown, using the pretext of their war with Hoxham. They have immense martial power. But they do not have this city nor the keep. You do, oh sleeping giant. The city's guard is yours and the palace guard hold you in highest esteem. Many of them served under you at Nosford Vale.'

Cutbill tensed. 'Without his knowledge it all seems so—'

'I'm asking you to protect my husband.'

Cutbill's face fell blank.

'Someone is here,' Dulenci said. He was squinting, gazing toward the sunlight behind the line of trees. To where the shrine and its pond were.

A figure in a dress stood in the pond that surrounded the little shrine with its statue of the Pilgrim and St Neyes. A serving woman, if the clothes and headdress were any indicator. She was standing still with her arms out wide, as if she were bracing to fall.

'Why's she in the water?' Cutbill said.

Carmotta walked a little closer, keeping to one side of a tree. Dulenci kept close.

It was impossible to tell the woman's age: her head was down, gazing at the pond she was standing in. Sacrilege aside, something was fundamentally unnerving in the vignette, even if the pond hadn't housed a shrine.

The woman, Carmotta realised, had no hand of night above her head. The last person Carmotta had seen without a hand of midnight above them was Ean's whore Arriet. Which proved the rule: she had come from outside. An innocent. Carmotta felt drawn to her. She stepped out from behind the tree and made her way toward the pond and its occupant.

'Wait, cousin,' Dulenci said. His breathing was strained as he marched after her.

'She may be unwell, Dulenci.'

'That would be her problem.'

Carmotta stopped at the edge of the pond, a handful of yards from the serving woman. Carmotta still could not see her face but her hands were visible. The hands of a woman of middle years, likely older. The ingrained dirt made it hard to tell.

The woman was muttering under her breath. Something repetitive.

This had been a bad idea. Carmotta looked around. There were no servants to help.

Cutbill had vanished.

She sensed Dulenci freeze beside her, and when she gazed back at the serving woman, the woman was staring back.

The ban-hag. The tongueless one they had kept in the cage.

'Oh,' Carmotta heard herself say.

Realisation came to that tattooed face with its piercings. An animal's fury poured from her eyes. Her mouth opened.

She barked. A bark that poured through the air and smothered Carmotta with a heat that was no heat. It pushed her back. *Compelled* her back: she felt her own legs scuttle to get away, felt herself topple to her haunches on to the grass. The cloudless sky filled her vision.

Dulenci's scream brought Carmotta to.

The ban-hag was standing over her, staring down. A chopping knife in her fist. She grinned.

A meaty palm covered the ban-hag's mouth and her eyes went wide. Cutbill: he had come out of nowhere behind her, had her knife-arm by the wrist.

Carmotta got to her feet, recalled her father's lessons and threw all her weight into one punch. Her knuckles stung but the ban-hag got it worse, a crack to the left orbital.

The ban-hag dropped her knife. Utterly dazed.

Pilgrim's blood, thought Carmotta, *I am a street brawler now.* She was glad none of the royal court had seen her haymaker. She would have never heard the end of it.

Cutbill made quick work of tying the ban-hag's wrists. He had some leather binds at hand, which was rather disturbing but undeniably handy. Carmotta passed him a handkerchief and he shoved it in the ban-hag's slack mouth.

Dulenci was lying on his back upon the floor, his face contorted with pain.

'I need a moment,' he said, wincing with the pain in his broken arm.

'Good shot, Your Majesty,' Cutbill said, tying up the ban-hag's wrists.

The creature had used her devil powers, despite not having her tongue. A mad shout that had done nothing more than stun Carmotta and Dulenci. She had been saving that, the ban-hag, for the right moment. Which explained, if only somewhat, that dead man in the cage.

'I'd better find a guard,' Cutbill said.

'Where did you get to?' she asked him quickly, buying time to think. 'You disappeared.'

He was looking over the ban-hag, checking she was unarmed. 'I circled around the other side of the pond, just in case.'

'Thorough.'

'Thorough holds back the grave, Your Majesty,' he said.

'I am fine,' Dulenci announced sulkily. 'Thank you for the concern.'

'Oh, cousin.' She held a hand out for him to grab. She gave him a look, too: *Say nothing. We know nothing.*

Cutbill had to step over and help get Dulenci back on his feet. The young man groaned but he seemed right enough, all things considered.

Cutbill stroked his beard. 'Interesting coincidence.'

'How so?' Carmotta asked. The man was making connections already, putting this savage into Carmotta's chambers the night the one-eyed man was killed.

'She's spinefolk,' he said. 'The same blood as the Fleawater crowd.'

Carmotta relaxed. She had no idea where he was going with any of this but it seemed to be in the opposite direction to her bedroom.

'Go on, Sir Willem.'

'Count Osrin is raiding somewhere in the city tonight,' he said. 'A place full of people like her. But I'm not supposed to talk of it...'

'I think this, whatever it is—' She feigned confusion. '—has altered that vow.'

'Yes,' Cutbill said. 'Osrin has an informer who told him the locality of the treacherous printer, someone who's been filling the streets of the city with groat-sheets and lies. I've given Osrin the use of a guard platoon. He wanted the glory and I wanted no part of it.' He remembered who he was talking to. 'Your Majesty, I only meant that this city's spinefolk community are dear to me. I served with many of their men.'

'It's fine, sir.'

Cutbill nodded at the unconscious ban-hag. 'Our friend there has got word of it and came here to kill Osrin.'

'That makes sense,' Carmotta said.

'What else could it be?' Dulenci added. He chuckled.

Damn it, Dulenci.

A brief silence followed. Cutbill looked over his shoulder, checked their prisoner was still motionless.

'Sir Willem,' Carmotta said. 'You have not given your answer on the, er, other thing. The thing we were discussing just now.'

'You've my total commitment.' The fight seemed to have stirred his spirit, had put that old soldier iron back in his spine.

Strange, how quickly that could happen. 'We need to do it quick. Tomorrow evening. Before the play. We can seize his friends too.'

'My thoughts exactly.' She liked this new alliance. The best thing about a conspiracy is one never feels alone.

'We need to get this creature out of here,' Cutbill said. 'Out of the keep.'

'What?'

'If Osrin hears word someone tried to kill him, he may change his daily behaviour, even leave the city. It's a variable we don't need, Your Majesty.'

It seemed a needless bother. The keep had enough dungeons. But Cutbill's belief in this plot of savages, she supposed, stopped him sniffing out the truth of the cage in her bedroom.

'Of course,' she said. 'How do we do that?'

'The menagerie,' Dulenci said. 'They have wheeled cages. We put a cage under a tarpaulin and wheel it out along the path to here. Then load her up and head for the west gate. I have bribe-disposed friends there and in the menagerie.'

'That's brilliant, Dulenci.' It genuinely was.

'Am I ever less?' he said. Then that sulky sadness from earlier passed his face.

'Let's do it,' Cutbill said.

'I'll come with you to Wessel Bridge,' Dulenci told him.

'Sir,' Cutbill said, 'that's really not necessary. Interrogation is an ugly business.'

'You're hurt,' Carmotta told Dulenci. 'Stay here, dear cousin.'

'I want to see what this ban-hag has to say.' Dulenci gave her a look that Cutbill would never read. *Let me protect you, my love,* it said.

He was right. The hag must die. She had no tongue, of course, likely could not even write, but she had ways, this woman. Tenacity enough to sink them both.

Carmotta nodded.

Cutbill looked worn out, as if his lair was being trespassed upon. 'Of course, Your Majesty.' He smiled sadly. 'Dulenci, help me hide her in the bushes over there then I'll wait while you get this cage of yours.'

'I was about to suggest as much,' Dulenci replied. 'Your Majesty, you had better leave. Stay out in the open until you can find a palace guard to protect you.'

'Of course,' she said. 'Good fortune, gentlemen.'

She turned and headed back for the path. She got ten paces then looked back to them both.

'Larksdale,' she said.

Dulenci looked up from grabbing the ban-hag's leg with his one good arm. He frowned and Carmotta knew his jealousy had been aroused once more. So too the fear of losing her, she sensed. The sweet fool. She had been too cruel back in the paternoster.

Sir Willem Cutbill looked merely curious.

'He is no murderer,' she told them both. 'At heart, he is just a madman.'

She made for the path.

41

Larksdale

The shed's roof was the wreck of an old riverboat. The gaps in the walls' wooden panels were stuffed with rags, presumably to keep out the cold.

'Do not speak in there, Sir Harrance,' she told him. 'Conversation could prove lethal.' She walked up to the shed and opened the door.

The darkness and the stink engulfed Larksdale as he entered, obscuring the smell of the burning gloop on his head. Human waste and rotten milk and flatulence and mould. His eyes watered with it and he almost backed out into the air again. *She means to show me corpses,* he thought.

A candle fluttered to life. Sister Ruradoola's wimpled head and shoulders emerged from the darkness, her eyes glassy in the flicker. They gazed at Larksdale then looked to a corner of the shed that was piled up with old rags.

'Who's that?' a voice said and Larksdale froze. The rag pile was a man. The pile shuddered and winced.

'We should go,' Larksdale whispered to Sister Ruradoola so that the man-pile might not hear. 'Bad air.'

'You're quite safe, Larksdale,' the sister replied, 'if you remember not to speak.'

'Larksdale?' the man's voice said. It was hoarse, failing. But it seemed familiar.

'Have we met?' Larksdale said.

'Stop speaking,' Sister Ruradoola hissed.

He mouthed the word *sorry*.

'Where's my bloody cane, Larksdale?' the man in the corner said.

Cabbot. This man was Cabbot, Arriet's husband, the brutish landowner that Marla had beaten for the crowd's edification four days ago.

The sister stepped closer to Cabbot and lowered her candle. This man, this thing, looked nothing like Cabbot. And he could see that Cabbot did not lie beneath rags. Rather, he was naked. His skin was a tapestry of scabs, brown and cracking lumps that sat uneasily upon weeping flesh. No clothes could fit him now. Great lumps grew from his already portly form, some resembling deformed breasts while others were like plate fungus, like one saw on trees. These growths were brown and wet as bark after rain. Things moved all over him: string-thin and slithering and black. Worms. Of a breed Larksdale had never seen before.

Ruradoola offered Larksdale a handkerchief and he grabbed it. He placed it over his nose and mouth but still the stink came.

'Come to gawp, Larksdale?' Cabbot said. His breathing was deep and heavy. 'Made me a fool before my wife, you did.' He stared deep into Larksdale's eyes. His left eye was a red ball and his right had something moving in the white. Maggots. 'I should have taken ill at home.'

'But you came here to mock us,' Sister Ruradoola almost snarled. 'To laugh about all you had done.'

'It's my land,' he hissed back. 'Still is. My money.' He winced. 'I'm burning up. Sweet Pilgrim, but I burn...'

'Tell him,' she said. 'Tell him what you did to us.'

Cabbot tittered soft and mad. He eyed Larksdale like an underhand deal. 'You know of the keep, I'll bet? Of the keep within it?'

'Say nothing,' Ruradoola warned Larksdale.

Already Larksdale knew Cabbot's warping could only be the genius of the keep-within's curse. Cabbot was trying to draw Larksdale into that same mistake, even now. Cabbot had learned nothing in life and this curse only brought the stupidity out more.

'I'll bet you know of it,' Cabbot said, never taking his eyes off Larksdale. 'All you nobles do.' He grumbled, though perhaps it was a laugh. 'I was let into your secret. And here's my payment.'

'Tell him,' the sister said.

'To hell, you blackened sow,' he said.

Sister Ruradoola leaned forward and set the candle to a raw wet outcrop that might have once been a foot.

Cabbot screamed like the falling sheep back in the abattoir. His scream slithered down to mere wincing and then there came a squelching sound. The smell of fresh shit hammered at Larksdale's handkerchief.

Ruradoola stepped back and covered her nose, but her eyes shone with glee in her candle's light. Oh but she was as cursed as this man-pile, was she not? She had spoken of the keep-within quite openly just earlier. The keep's cruelty was blooming in her veins.

'Slyke,' Cabbot said. 'Sir Tibald. He put me to it. I was to go into business with him.' A pride almost arose in that mass of scabs and worms that was a face. 'I would have all the flea-scum here cleared. Prime land this, prime, right by the river. A little ambition and the land along the Flume could be gentleman's territory. Ambition, yes. Vision.' He nodded and worms slid down over his chest. 'Saw that in me, did Slyke.'

Slyke. Larksdale had to stop himself from hissing the name. He let Slyke's toady continue.

'Would have cost me, though. I'd need a regiment of willing men, pennyblades and the like, to clear the camp. Bribes too, of course, to councilmen and the city guard. But Sir Tibald had an idea that would save us coin. He invited me – me, the son of a butcher – to the keep itself.' That prideful look raced through him again and Larksdale had to wonder whether Cabbot was relating this tale or repeating it to himself. 'To the butts there, to play at bows. Then he told me. A keep within the keep. I merely had to announce this secret to the fleas, gather them around their landlord and announce this hidden keep. They would talk about it to me and then to each other and… a week or more and the land would be good as empty.'

'You fool,' the sister said. 'You devil's fool. I was there the moment you first uttered its existence. I remember you smiled as I asked about it. As I and the others repeated its name.'

'I did not think it would *work*,' he replied. 'But Slyke was a lord. You have to do as they suggest. That's how it all works. Anyhow, they began to die.' Scabs squeezed together in a frown. 'But I would be fine. I would be fine because I had stood within the grounds of the keep. I had been invited to the keep and being so chosen, so blessed… the curse could not touch me.'

But it had, of course. To speak of the keep-within outside the greater keep's land was death however you first heard of it.

'Pilgrim save me,' Cabbot said, staring down at his own wormy mass. 'Save me. I did everything. Everything that was asked. I worked hard and saved coin. I wore the clothes of a man made good, I dressed as well as our laws allow a man of my place. I did everything the world asks. Everything required.' Cabbot wept.

'And you die like the rest of us,' Sister Ruradoola said. She turned to Larksdale. 'He has the poog. I had to look it up at the abbey outside Becken. It's a rare ailment. Very rare, legendary in its way. The Church believes it rises up from the fissures in the earth whereas Becken folk tale holds that it comes from the web of an enormous she-spider that slumbers within the belfries of the keep. Either way – or neither – of itself it is not contagious.'

Larksdale pointed at Cabbot and waved around, indicating Fleawater camp.

'Some caught poog,' she answered him. 'Not many. The curse enjoys drawing the pain out with some, I think.' She looked fearful then and Larksdale wanted to hold her, tell her she was fine, though to say so would be a lie. 'Most it just kills quick and very painfully indeed. The terror is… never knowing how we will meet our end.' Her spare hand tightened to a fist.

No, no. He knew all this, of course, or suspected as much, but it was unbearable upon the lips of a victim. He reached and gripped her shoulder, met her eyes with his own.

She smiled then stepped back from his grip. He had gone too far, touching her like that.

He stepped back himself.

'I think the keep-within chose to give him poog,' she said, paying no heed to the moment just between them, 'because it takes time to infect a body, and when it does death waits patiently, allowing Cabbot here to spread the word.'

'Best kill me, then,' Cabbot said.

'No,' Sister Ruradoola said. 'I do not think that at all, Cabbot. Not for you. By the way, your master Tibald Slyke is dead.'

'What?' Larksdale could make no sense of it. She was lying to torture this diseased lump, surely.

'Poisoned,' Ruradoola explained. She seemed to have given up on keeping Larksdale silent. 'Was he a friend of yours?'

'Oh, closer than that: an enemy.' *Is he the one they think I killed?* Larksdale wondered. He would be a fine fit for the job, after all. A known rival, an outsider now. Would Carmotta have poisoned Slyke so as to frame ol' Harry Larksdale? Was she capable of such?

He could not equate it with the young woman he had left at the port in Sant Ribot, the woman he had spent that sunny day with. But he was not certain any more.

'The curse got him,' Cabbot said. He laughed and his blood-red eye caught the light. 'I hope he suffered for what he has done to me.'

'I've seen enough,' Larksdale said.

'Not yet,' Sister Ruradoola replied. She looked at the squalid mess that was Cabbot. 'Tell him. Tell him what you were to build here once we were all dead.'

'A playhouse,' Cabbot said. 'The largest in Becken. Slyke's idea.'

Larksdale laughed, bitter and loud. Slyke had never had an original idea in his life. *Now his dullness kills the masses.*

Cabbot was laughing too. He stopped, then said, 'I loved her, sir. My wife. I… want you, or someone, to know that. I did love her.'

A fury took Larksdale. He kicked open the door behind him and let the fresh air in. The light.

'No,' Larksdale said, his voice flat. 'No, you did not.'

A bar of daylight stretched across Cabbot's ruin of a face and the thin worms in its running sores twisted with pain. But it was the one still functioning eye that Larksdale knew would haunt him, for it contained true terror: the realisation of a life built upon nothing. No, on mere *things*. Land, coin, a wife to show for it. All gone. His was a little soul falling into the pit of its own stripped self.

Larksdale stepped into the day.

The chapel was full of clutter. There were the items of worship, of course: more homemade hooks and a large one forged from brass which he assumed had come to Fleawater with Sister Ruradoola. There was a cooking stove to one side beneath a chimney made of broken clay bottle necks, piles of cheap paper, and something tall covered with a blanket that Larksdale assumed to be a lectern. In one corner there lay a bed that looked very lived in. Daylight streamed in through the window of bottle-glass shards, turning all the clutter blue and yellow and green. Sister Ruradoola, it seemed, was something of a hoarder.

'Where does the congregation stand in here?' he asked, rubbing his short wet hair. He stepped over some discarded clothes. 'Or should that be, what do they stand on?'

She smiled and picked up a hand mirror. 'You'll find a towel on that hook there. And no, no one gathers in here. The wandering sort prefer to worship in the open. Honestly, I think that's a good idea.'

'Easier for God to see, right?' He started to towel himself. His hair felt odd, dry somehow, and his scalp sensitive to the touch even though all the gloop had been washed away.

'Such blasphemy,' she said without malice. 'Come over here.'

She was standing before a waist-high table beneath the mottled window. She held out the hand mirror for him to take.

He did not recognise this man in the polished metal. His chin was pointier than he remembered it. But his hair was the real shock. It was not ginger exactly, though he might pass for a Fleawater man. To the sides and back it was an inch short, quite brutish and common-looking, but still long at the front, enough to cover his eyes if need be.

'Your own mother would not recognise you,' the sister said.

'She would feign not to.'

She giggled at that. There was something suddenly nervous about her. She placed her fingers with their dried ink over her mouth. Yes: she was nervous he was in here.

He looked about the room. Everywhere, paper.

'Sister,' he said, 'if I were to lift the blanket off that lectern over there, I would find no lectern, yes?'

She stiffened. 'I do not suppose you would.'

He eyed her fingers again. 'A printing press.' He remembered the groat-sheet Marla had brought to the Wreath. The image of King Ean leaking milk from his royal dugs. He recalled other sheets he had seen in the last few years, the same style of block cut, the same acid wit. The same targets: landlords, moneylenders, gentry. The keep and its king. 'You're a bigger seditionist than I.'

She nodded. 'I haven't long on this earth, but I'm thinking you could take my place.'

'That's awfully forward,' he said.

'You've wit, sir. And there's work to be done. A keep to topple.'

He laughed.

'What?' she said. 'The old empire toppled, why not the keep?'

'It will not be toppled by a few printed sheets.'

She shook her head ruefully. 'Even now, hunted like a dog, you defend your court of wolves.'

'No,' he said. 'I simply run. Tomorrow I'm to meet a man who'll take me to Hoxham.'

'Another crown,' she said. 'Don't you ever dream of change?'

I used to, he wanted to say. *I had thought it possible.* He found himself thinking of Carmotta. He put the thought to one side.

'I wish I had known you longer, Sister Ruradoola,' he said eventually.

'I'm scared,' she said. 'Terrified, actually. I haven't the poog like Cabbot. So I suppose that means a quick and agonising death.' She placed a finger on his shaven lips. 'Do not answer, you fool. You're clean still.' Her face curled up with pain. No: frustration. 'Fuck it,' she said.

She pulled off her wimple and revealed a clean shaved head, pleasing in shape. She jerked her robe and it fell off. Sister Ruradoola was altogether naked.

He didn't know what to say. This was blasphemy or heresy or some sin no one had even invented a name for. She was a Perfecti, a voice of God. He a sinner, for he could not avert his gaze from her humble beauty.

'I am thirty-four,' she said. 'The Church has kept me a maiden, Sir Harrance. No man of Fleawater would take me, for they think me their mountain mother.' She crossed her arms over her chest. She had the look of someone very much regretting a recent decision. 'And I am to die. You see my quandary.'

'And the rest. You put me in an… intractable position, Sister Ruradoola.'

'I certainly hoped to,' she replied.

Larksdale laughed. He put his palms upon her smooth shoulders and urged her down, so that she was sitting upon her table. Then he pushed her, quite gently, so that her back lay flat upon the wood.

'Wait,' she whispered. 'What are you doing?'

'There is something you simply must try,' he told her. 'Trust me.'

He lowered himself to a praying position, so that his head was level with her knees. He parted her thighs.

'Stop me the moment you have reservations,' he told her. 'I won't be insulted.' Then he began.

Sister Perfecti Ruradoola did not stop him. In fact she was so impressed she requested a repeat performance barely an hour later.

42

Fwych

A ceiling. Black timber and white daub. She had not seen the like in the keep. Simple-looking, for flatlander houses anyhow.

The world around her coming into shape. She had a gag in her mouth. She knew her wrists would be bound before she even checked. Ankles, too. She lay on a wide flat plank that kept her body not quite lying flat but not full upright either.

Dusty, the room, with cobbled walls. Squares of criss-crossed sunlight stretched across the wooden floor and rose up the wall on the other side of the room. Most like from windows behind her. Not a big room this, smaller than Lady Larksdale's. In one corner were an alcove with a big long lump under black cloth that sat upon a wheeled table. There were an alcove too in the other corner, this time with an empty bench. Between both alcoves, at the centre of the wall, were a heavy-looking door of iron and studded oak.

A small table stood beside Fwych. Tools on it. Pliers and hammers and such.

Fwych sighed. Well, the daylight were a blessing, at least. The sort of thing she would soon be put through almost never happened in so much sunlight.

Her body had been stumbling under sunlight, hadn't it? She remembered it all. The slaughtered women in the great circle of bronze, the journey they had sent her on. A copse of trees, where Gethwen had run to.

Fwych struggled against her bindings. They had shown her, the slaughtered women. Shown her their memory of Gethwen throwing the black crown into a wide pond. It had landed with a splash just before a statue at the pond's centre, a statue of two men. The black crown lay there right now!

She bellowed into her gag, struggled and shook. Useless. She ceased and her wrists ached.

A weak old woman, Fwych. You were doomed from the outset.

She heard steps beyond the door, talking. The door shuddered with the turning of a key.

On the bench in the alcove to the right of the door, something appeared. The slaughtered girl with her red hair and dress of dried blood. She were sat upon the bench with her knees drawn up to her chest, her arms around her shins. Her eyes met Fwych's. Then she vanished.

The door swung open. A big man with shaved head and neat grey beard stepped through. Seen a few years, that man, but those years had only wrinkled his bark, not rotted his boughs. Fwych could tell.

'You were right,' he said. 'She's woken.'

A man came in after him, thinner and younger. Fwych recognised him: Carmotta's lover, the one with the arrogance and the big cock, the two being likely connected. Dulenci, that were his name. His right arm were in a sling. Both men had blades at their belts.

'I should like to speak to this ban-hag alone,' Dulenci said.

'She's no tongue, sir,' the big man said. 'You'll learn nothing from her.'

'Still…' Dulenci said as the big man closed the door. He looked upon Fwych with frustration. 'Still…'

Dulenci, the idiot, had no reply to his comrade. He had some secret intent, pathetically hidden. She could sense it.

'I'll open a window,' the big man said. 'Let some fresh air in.'

'At least let me stay,' Dulenci said to him, never taking his eyes off Fwych. 'I would be interested to see you interrogate her, Sir Willem.' He placed a finger on the pommel of his long thin blade. 'I hope for all our sakes she is an excellent mime.' He chuckled, then he frowned, as if his jest had become a serious thought.

'Please,' the big man said as he walked around Fwych on her plank, 'call me Cutbill. Everyone does.'

'Indeed,' Dulenci said. He eyed this Cutbill and looked to Fwych again.

Of course: Fwych had seen him mount his queen, seen everything. Now Fwych was out of her cage and outside his control.

Fwych grinned at Dulenci and his brow knitted tight.

'It's not an interrogation as such,' Cutbill said as he tried to get the window open. 'To be frank, sir, I'd rather you left it to me alone.'

'The queen's order,' Dulenci said. 'I have to be here.'

Cutbill got the window open. The air was blessed. Fresh, for this city anyhow. She could hear the sounds of crowds, a bell too, all of it distant. Fwych wondered where they were.

'Why do you want to speak to her alone, sir?' Cutbill asked.

Dulenci shrugged, checked the sling on his injured arm. It was obvious he had expected the bigger man to just nod and do as he said once he had given that command.

'They have powers,' Dulenci said eventually. 'She could heal my arm and shoulder.'

'Old wives' tales,' Cutbill said as he stepped back into view.

She could have. Once, anyhow, when she could speak words to heal flesh. It only struck her now that that was the power she really should have missed. But she had not thought of it at all. Red Marie had been right. Fwych relished the control.

'Well then, let me help you,' Dulenci said to Cutbill. He took his working arm and lifted one of the tools – a pair of pliers – up from the table beside Fwych.

He means to kill me, Fwych realised. *Slice an artery and claim mishap.*

'We won't be using those,' Cutbill told him. He reached out gently and took the pliers from the young man's hand. He placed them back on the table. Fwych had to wonder whether he knew the other man meant to kill her too. He seemed the watching kind, Cutbill.

'No interrogation,' Cutbill said again. 'An identification. Via witness.' He walked over to the alcove with the wheeled table, the one with the long lump under dark cloth, and began to push it toward Fwych. When it were level with her feet, Cutbill removed the cloth.

A body, covered from skull to toe in bandages. It lay on its side with its covered face to Fwych. The bandages were bone-white; they were fresh, but so were all the dried blood about the belly and thighs and crotch. Yellow there, too, fresh pus.

The body breathed. A woman.

Dulenci uttered something in his foreign burble, then said, 'Who is this witness? A prisoner?'

'An employee,' Cutbill told him. 'A hired hand.' With a delicacy Fwych wouldn't have credited his big fingers with, Cutbill rolled back the bandages on the woman's face.

Pale as death with dark brown eyes, wet and scared and struggling to blink. No nose. No lips.

Selly. Selly the pennyblade, the one with the crossbow back in the inn, who had wounded Fwych in the shoulder. Who Red Marie had hung from a hook and left to bleed out.

Selly's eyes set upon Fwych. They widened with terror. With recognition. Selly wheezed a scream like a kettle over a fire.

Cutbill had sent them pennyblades. It was he who wanted the black crown.

'There, there,' the big bastard whispered to Selly. He stroked her brow. 'You did good, girl. There, there.' She stopped screaming and he pulled out a brass flask and unstopped it. He tried to feed its contents into her lipless mouth. Selly hadn't the strength. He stopped pouring and took a swig himself.

'What is this?' the young man asked.

'A conspiracy, sir,' Cutbill said. 'To awaken the keep-within-the-keep.'

The young man's face was all shock. 'Fool! You're not supposed to say that out here!'

'As I understand it,' Cutbill replied, stopping for another swig, 'I've anything up to nine nights before the curse gets me.' He tossed the flask to Dulenci and the young man caught it with his free hand. 'That's nine more nights than you.'

He drew his sword and jabbed it into Dulenci's throat. He withdrew and slid it back into his scabbard again.

Dulenci's neck hissed out blood. It pattered on the floor like rain. He dropped the flask, went to reach for his own sword, then realised he had to cover the wound in his throat. He did so and stumbled toward the door.

'I only need tonight and tomorrow,' Cutbill told him, 'I think the keep will give me the time. I'm helping it out, after all.'

Cutbill got to one end of Selly's table. 'Time to give you what you keep begging for,' he told her.

He pushed Selly's table out of Fwych's view, somewhere toward the windows behind her. Selly moaned and Cutbill's breathing grew strained while Dulenci tried to open the locked door with his one good hand and only succeeded in pissing out more blood.

The young man dropped to his knees and clutched his neck again. There came a distant splash, somewhere far below the window. Cutbill came back into Fwych's view again, pulling a wheeled table with no more Selly on it. He smiled, almost, at Fwych.

'Not as young as I was,' he admitted to her. 'You understand that, I reckon.' He pointed to the window behind Fwych. 'That was you who just fell to your death,' he explained. 'You stabbed *him*.' He pointed at the young man, currently trying to stand up. 'And leaped out the window. Either they'll never find Selly's body or, if they do, no one at the keep will even check it's you. Can you bloody believe that?' He grimaced. 'You killed the queen's cousin and lover, for fuck's sake. They never check, these nobles. And we spend our lives trusting them.'

At the mention of the queen, Dulenci let go of his throat and drew his sword out, though clumsily. The door's studded oak were sprayed with red.

'I'll need you for Yulenight Eve,' Cutbill told Fwych, ignoring the dying fool. 'Well, not *need*, but I reckon you'll play a part. That's why it's drawn you here, hasn't it? We're part of the plan, you and me.'

Demon, Fwych thought. You could see cold madness in his eyes.

The young man turned and levelled his sword at Cutbill's back. It took all his ebbing strength. Half-hunched, he waddled toward Cutbill.

Fwych pretended not to see him. *Come on, boy. Do it!*

'I had to be sure,' Cutbill told her. 'That you were the one at the inn. I could see Selly recognised you. So we're good, eh?'

Dulenci fell on his face. He breathed, but shallow.

Cutbill turned and looked down on him. 'Good for you, lad.' He turned back to Fwych. 'And I thought he was all bluster.' He looked out the window and a strange calm took his eyes. 'You never can tell a man at his last. Never.' He shook his head. 'Shit. I'm no good at this explaining malarky, woman. But it feels good to share after all this time. Best to you, eh? Tongueless you. What was it took your tongue anyhow?'

'Please,' the young man said to the floor, blood pouring from his mouth. 'Leave Carmotta. Please. With child…'

Cutbill's eyes widened to hear that but he did not turn around.

'You were at the pond to look for the black crown, weren't you?' he asked Fwych. 'Because your lad, Gethwen, he threw it in there, right? This right fop – you wouldn't know him – he told me Gethwen found the shrine there beautiful. Sacred. But I didn't know he was the *exact* lad, nor that you were the ban-hag back at the inn. I had to be sure, before I went draining a big pond on royal ground. I'm cautious like that.'

He stepped over Dulenci and picked up the flask from the floor.

'I'm no good at this,' he said, 'this talking, explaining. The point I want to make is, though, the point is, I'm in a unique position. Between worlds.' He put the flask to his mouth and found it empty. He popped back the stopper and returned the flask to his inner jacket. 'All those Ruperts at the keep would never deign to talk to your lot at Fleawater, so they've no clue about the crown your people hid there so long. But me, I had many mates with spinefolk blood, back in the army. They loved telling a tale—' He chuckled at the memory. '—and I like to listen. But, on the other hand, you lot, you spinefolk, you can't read. Not many commoners can. They fear commoners who learn to read, the nobility. And in my case they're fucking right to.'

Dulenci had stopped breathing.

'Eight libraries in the keep, you know that?' Cutbill told Fwych. 'You can learn things in there while the Ruperts caper and hunt and dance. You'd think someone would have already, some secret ancient order. You'd think, wouldn't you? Knowledge of the black crown is all fucking there, mate. But no. Just me. Me and a few loyal veterans and a big bag of stolen money to pay shitty pennyblades. You know, it's not even a crown, this black crown. Never was. It's a door-ring.' He laughed. 'A fucking door-knocker.'

He walked over to the heavy door and grabbed its ring. He shook it. He laughed at Fwych and shook it again. 'A fucking knocker!'

He opened the door, walked out, and locked it again.

Fwych stared at the door so fiercely she didn't notice the slaughtered girl had appeared on the bench once more. She only noticed when the girl drifted toward her.

43

Larksdale

'I wish I'd done that before.'

'If it's any consolation, Sister, you've certainly made up for lost time.'

They were lying upon her rickety bed in the chapel, he on his back, she with her head upon his shoulder. The sun through the mottled window had given way to moonlight hours ago. She had drawn several blankets and eiderdowns over their naked bodies and they had dozed off once or twice during this anxious and wonderful day, only to awake and immediately make love again.

'For the first time,' she said, 'I feel an intense closeness to God.'

'You're not so bad yourself,' he said.

'I mean the act raises us above the meanness of the world.'

He kissed the top of her shaved head. 'Would that all days were spent so.'

Larksdale had never taken anyone's virginity before. He had always imagined it an awkward and guilt-drenched act. Yet deflowering an eager virgin of thirty-four years, it transpired, was as simple as it was rewarding. He had never felt so… useful.

'Why print all those groat-sheets?' he asked her. He had meant to ask her for some time. 'It's not like you live in a hole along the Hook. Even here in Fleawater you could ask the Church for anything.'

'You know why, Harry,' she whispered. She sailed a fingertip around his nipple. 'We all heard about you and Cabbot. About your "trial by combat" at the Wreath. We want the world decent, you and me.'

'I haven't your strength,' he said. 'Never had. I thought if I pleased the king enough I could change the keep for the better.' He tensed with the frustration and humiliation of it. 'The things I did...' *You fool,* he thought, *you scurrilous fool.* 'Well, tomorrow I'll be gone. Marla's man will take me to Hoxham and I'll be as helpful there as here.' He shook his head. 'A convenient bastard.'

Gethwen had used him too. Another Ean in his fashion. *Did you love me, Geth? Even a little?* Larksdale recalled that moment by the pond, the shrine. It had seemed genuine. And if it had seemed so then it had been. Larksdale had been dazzled by enough plays to know that true. Theatre was truth. He smiled.

Something strange had happened before that clinch, he recalled. Gethwen had practically flown backward on the path, dragging Larksdale over too. His strength inhuman.

Larksdale sat up. The air in the chapel was cold.

Gethwen had run then. To the shrine with its pond. Had thrown away his bag and its contents.

'Harry?' he heard Ruradoola say.

'That strength wasn't his.'

She sat up. 'Are you quoting some play?'

He looked in her moon-rimmed eyes.

'The black crown,' he told her. 'It's trying to get to the keep, right?'

'Yes.' He could feel her body tense.

'If it did end up on the grounds, would... I don't know... some power prevent it from leaving?'

She slapped his shoulder. 'Are you seriously telling me it's exactly where it shouldn't be? Damn it, Harry.'

'I'm sorry,' he said. 'I lied. It's in a copse of trees on the keep's grounds. Under the surface of a pond. But, before, when we tried to leave…' Gethwen had been crossing the brass ring of the keep's gardens when it happened. That was the border, not the outer walls. 'Oh, mercy. It's all true isn't it? The thing has power, actual power. It's all true isn't it?'

'Pilgrim's arse, have you even been listening?' she barked. 'Of course it is! A mortal hand is needed to carry it, for no pure evil can.' She slapped his chest again. 'You and your lad have done half the bloody work! We have to get inside, Harry! It's Yulenight Eve tomorrow.'

He felt suddenly aroused by her nakedness and her energy. Strange how these things worked. He paid it no mind.

'The play,' he said. 'The Wreath's men are putting on a play tomorrow night. At least, I think they are.'

'Harry, we—' She stopped. 'Do you hear that?'

Men's shouts carried through the night. Indistinct, blurring with the sounds of the river and its ships.

'Come on.' Ruradoola leaped out of her bed.

Larksdale felt a sudden cold at his chest and limbs. He drank in Sister Ruradoola's back and shoulders as she clambered into her vestments. This little isle of theirs, this warm and human reprieve, was already vanishing. He was determined to savour these last few seconds, for the real world had found him again, he knew it. He would be swallowed up soon enough. To appreciate the splendour of a lover's naked back was a small victory against it all, a foolhardy stand.

'I said come on!' She was dressed now and already making for the door.

He found his unders and breeches and put them on. He could

not find his hose nor his socks. His boots he stuffed his bare feet into, the leather inside feeling cold and oily.

She had left the door of her chapel swinging. He threw his shirt on but he could not remember where he had left his jacket – outside somewhere – so he stole one of her vestments that lay on a mound of paper and ran outside.

A haze of torchlight painted the night, in the direction of the camp's barricade wall. The shouting was coming from there. He trotted toward it.

There came a great tearing sound. He could not see what, his view being obscured by a row of caravans, but the shouts were turning to screams.

He reached the end of the caravan line and slipped in mud as he turned the corner. Ruradoola was standing just before him, a snowman in her white habit and robes. Some fifty yards ahead the gate of the barricade wall was in the process of toppling. Iron hooks dug into the wall's rubble and wood. One local was sliding down the wall now it was leaning. Likely he had been trying to remove one of the hooks but to no avail. The man dived back into the growing crowd, joining the body of silhouettes.

The wall collapsed with a wicked screech and roar. Dust flew up and men ran back. Torchlight filled the waste ground before the fallen gateway. Shadows of men beyond, black figures in the dust and flame. Larksdale could make out clubs, helmets. The city guard.

They raced forward and a great flag was raised behind them, the image of a rearing beast upon it. The lionfox, that ridiculous and self-designed crest of Count Osrin.

The count appeared from between the brass-tops as if his own flag had summoned him. Full-armoured he was: breastplate, helm and greaves, his form golden in the torches' glare. He'd a club in one hand, a shorter one in the other and his stance was identical to when he had tourneyed under the canopy back at Grand Gardens.

One local charged him, swinging a chain, and two comrades followed. Osrin caught the chain's bite with his short club and brained the man with the other. He drove the long club into the second man's belly and headbutted him to the floor. The third man broke and turned and Osrin chased him into the Fleawater crowd as if they were as dangerous as a cloud of gnats. The brass-tops followed him up.

Ruradoola turned and grabbed Larksdale by the shoulder. 'They want you.'

Not me. Larksdale could not take in the horror of it. *I'm not worth this.*

She ran and he followed, down the shallow slope of the camp toward the river.

'Can you row?' she barked.

'I'm keen to learn.'

Orange light filled the sky above, orange as a lionfox. Something bright arced high over them and descended. A fireball.

The fireball crashed into a shed on a rise to their left. Cabbot's shed. In a blink it was a bonfire.

A trebuchet. Osrin was all about the subtle approach.

Ruradoola stopped but Larksdale pressed her on. This was no place to idle.

The river's edge lay ahead, empty rowing boats sitting upon the mud. He was sure there were more than earlier. His jacket lay on the boxes and barrels where she had shaved off his beard.

'Get in that boat,' Ruradoola said. 'The small one.'

'Join me,' he replied.

She shook her head. 'I'm their Perfecti.'

Uncertain what to say, he went to get his jacket.

'You're surrounded,' a voice said. It was male, loud and almost drunk-sounding.

Larksdale froze, watched his breath drift into the night air.

A brass-top with a crossbow stepped out from the gloom between two caravans. Ruradoola drew sudden breath: she had been startled by another crossbowman and a sergeant beside him, stepping out from behind the opposite row of painted homes.

A pincer attack on the camp, to block anyone making for the river. It explained the extra rowing boats.

Sister Ruradoola glared at them. She lifted her hand in the air and spoke.

'*Runnnn…*'

Her voice. Her power. It was not directed at Larksdale but still his bones wanted to scuttle off into the night, away from her voice's overwhelming warmth.

The brass-tops remained where they were. Their sergeant, a man with pretentions of being a gentleman if his long moustache was anything to go by, grinned and pointed at the flaps of his metal helmet. They were padded, blocking all hearing.

'They're after *me*,' Ruradoola muttered.

Larksdale felt relief of a most selfish kind. This attack was not his fault. These men had no clue who he even was.

The full repercussions of that last part became clear when the officer pointed at him, indicating for him to be shot.

He braced for the pain.

The first crossbowman flew into the air and vanished into blackness above. Seconds later he came down. Twice. His hips and legs fell on the gritty earth between the men and Ruradoola, his intestines shooting out with the impact like a nest of disturbed snakes. His upper half fell on the boxes and barrels where Larksdale had been sitting earlier that day. The torso landed upright, as if he were waiting for a shave.

The other two brass-tops looked about. The sergeant drew his blade. None saw the growing shadow behind them.

'Behind you,' a sweet voice said.

The brass-tops did not turn around. They could not hear.

'Suit yourselves,' the voice said.

The second crossbowman's head toppled from his body. The sergeant had time to stare in disbelief before a spike burst out of his guts. He stared in disbelief at that too.

Sister Ruradoola ran for one of the smaller rowing boats. Larksdale yearned to do likewise, but he did not want to expose his back to whatever was eviscerating people.

He shuffled backwards and stepped on something: a crossbow. He snatched it up and back-shuffled again toward the rowing boats, aiming at the shadow behind the dying sergeant.

The sergeant shuddered. Larksdale sensed the shadow was keeping him upright. The spike jutting out of his sternum sliced its way down his jacket and through his breaches. His wet bowels poured out and his face turned white. The spike retracted into his body and he flopped lifeless to the stones.

'Hold there!' Larksdale shouted.

The shadow tittered. *'What if I choose not to, Larksdale?'*

It knew his name.

He had to keep it talking. 'Then you will suffer my disleisure,' he replied.

The shadow lifted its hand. A sickle. *'You mean displeasure,'* it said.

'No,' Larksdale replied. 'Disleisure. Less formal but decidedly more unkind.'

The shouting and the torchlights were getting closer, though far too slowly.

The thing tittered again. It stepped forward and Larksdale could see its lower body. Was that armour? Its limbs were decorated with the flotsam of Becken's streets: smashed pottery, roof tiles, broken chair legs.

'I'm going to kill your friend there in a moment,' the monster said. *'Then I'm going to steal you away. I'm going to torture you, Larksdale. Do you like that idea?'*

'Stay back!' He could at least protect Sister Ruradoola while she got into her boat. That was something. He had to smile at the thought: that bullied little boy of the keep's weapons yard, the wet rag who could barely lift a sword, laying down his life in combat for a maid.

'You cannot hurt me, maggot,' the shadow said. *'You've never been so useless.'*

'You should hear me play the lute.' He had to keep buying time. This thing liked to brag. 'Who are you anyway?'

The shadow tittered again, drew its hooked hand down the side of its shadowed face.

'There are those who call me... the deceiver.'

'How do I know you're not lying?'

The shadow seemed to sag. It tilted its head. It did not take well to being mocked. Not in the slightest. A small soul, this, for all its horror.

'I'm the striding nightmare,' it hissed. *'The well of all miseries.'*

'You're Monday mornings?'

'Silence!'

Larksdale pulled the lever and the bolt flew. It hit the shadow in what he hoped was the throat. He dropped the crossbow and was about to turn and run when the sky lit up.

The figure was illuminated from above. A demon, a beast of scrap iron and lacquered wood, as if born from Becken's loins. But under all that was some strange material, black and metallic, an armour like a thousand beetles' shells, sleek and rippling.

But the face. Framed by braided hair of singed rope, the face was once-painted wood, now blackened by fire damage. The carved face of a woman on a ship's prow. Rusted nails jutted from the lips.

'Red Marie,' Larksdale heard himself say.

'*Who else?*' With one sickle hand she severed the bolt shaft sticking out of her collar. Then she waved the sickle at Larksdale, as if admonishing him for his ballistic presumption. '*I come from the keep-within-the-keep.*' She tilted her head to one side. '*You know of which I speak.*'

He had no comeback to that. It was chilling. She feared not the curse. Not in the slightest.

There was a reason the sky had brightened. A payload of burning pitch was coming to earth from way above them.

Larksdale turned and threw himself on the ground. The world burst white and hot. It roared and then it rattled and cinders filled the air. Hot dust covered him, stinging his skin and flooding his nostrils.

Before the heat abated he was on his feet and scrambling for the rowing boat. He had to use this advantage, this luck of the gods. This idiocy of Osrin's.

The boat was already unmoored. Sister Ruradoola was aboard, her body curled up like a hedgehog, arms protecting her head, her robes covered with ash.

He jumped in and the boat dipped and rose. 'It's me,' he said. 'Row, woman!'

She did so. At first he thought she was hopeless, but he realised she was turning the boat about so that its prow was facing the opposite bank. Their destination.

'Come on, come on,' he could not help but say. He was terrified. He could see Sister Ruradoola was in shock too.

She had got the rowing boat around and Larksdale could see the riverbank. The falling pitch and rock had clearly smashed into the nearest of the caravans where they had been standing. No sign of Red Marie, but half the planks of a wooden caravan now raged with flame where once she had stood.

Red Marie. The nightmare hag of Becken folklore, mother of all the city's evil. She who kept a hut beneath the rivers and took the innocent below, never to be seen again. A story Larksdale knew all about: she was, after all, a vital component of most folk-plays. A villain second only to the devil, of whom she was said to be wife.

They were making some distance now and Larksdale began taking long breaths. The chill of the river air was replacing the heat of the shore.

Yet the thing Larksdale had seen was no story. Stories did not kill, at least not directly. Every year the poor of Becken claimed Red Marie stalked the streets and alleys. Every vicious murder was blamed on her, every drowning too. This year had been particularly gory. Apparently it was not all hearsay.

'Armour,' he said aloud so that Sister Ruradoola might hear, though he sensed she wouldn't listen. 'Not a spirit. Some… armour.' Saying it made it real, true. Someone was playing the part of Red Marie as much as any actor at the Wreath. Ol' Harry Larksdale knew a thespian when he saw one.

'We'll have our vengeance,' Ruradoola snapped. It made Larksdale shudder. 'Those bastards will suffer for their sins. I'll see to it.'

He might have said that such earthly revenge was not fitting of her vestments, but it was clear Sister Ruradoola had not been orthodox for some time.

'Yes.' It was all the reply he could muster. 'Yes.'

The burning caravan was distant now. They were halfway across the Flume. He removed his stolen vestment, put on his jacket, then put on the vestment again. His breath danced up to the stars.

Back on shore, a figure stepped out of the wreckage and flames. It stared at them from the shore. A silhouette with sickles for hands. It leaped, leaped higher than any human could. It dived into the waters.

'Shit,' Larksdale said. 'Row faster! Seriously!'

Red Marie was swimming inhumanly fast, churning up the river's waves. Maybe it wasn't someone in armour. Armour would sink.

'Faster!' Larksdale shouted. But already it was hopeless.

The boat slowed. Ruradoola had stopped rowing.

He clambered around to face her. Ruradoola was quite calm. She was staring out into the waters. Toward the monster.

'Take the oars,' she said. 'Go.'

'What?'

'This is how it happens to me,' she said. 'It's violent enough. This way, I almost get to choose it.'

'No!'

She pulled out her little commrach knife. 'Do not stop me.' She met his gaze. 'Understand?'

He did. He did not like it. He found himself, ever the coward, climbing on to the seat and taking the oars.

'Thank you, Harry,' she said. She looked over her shoulder and smiled at him. 'You gave me the second-best time of my life.'

He nodded. 'The first?'

She looked out to the waters again. 'That's for me to know.'

She screamed and leapt over. She barely made a splash.

Larksdale rowed away, fast as he might. The seat was still warm with her body's heat.

44

Red Marie

Interesting. Larksdale's comrade had thrown herself into the river. Self-sacrifice, perhaps? The desire for death to have meaning was powerful, even in these animals.

An animal acting strangely should be treated with caution. She had learned that long ago in the night-forests of home. She slowed her strokes. She would not sink. Her suit was remarkable, the cutting edge of commrach craftsmanship, with all the wonderful inventions the order of Explainers could dream of. Despite being entirely sealed from the outside, the suit took days to run out of air. A phenomenon that also meant Red Marie was not walking along the river bed but floating. The Red Marie of human tales was said to live in the rivers of Becken, leaping out to kill as she pleased. What human gibbering had dreamed up, commrach ingenuity had made real.

The woman was swimming toward Red Marie, one hand bunched in a fist. A knife, probably: the source of her confidence. Red Marie relaxed. No human blade could penetrate the suit.

Red Marie pounded through the waves toward her eager victim.

The woman had stopped swimming, her head above water. She thought herself sly, her blade hidden beneath the water. How sweet.

Red Marie swam straight at her, then, a yard away, lifted her masked face above the surface. Red Marie's face would be terrible in the moonlight.

The woman shouted. '*Flee.*'

Danger. Warm terror flowed into Red Marie's ears, a treacle-sound all fight-or-flight. Red Marie splashed and sloshed around and away. She had to get to safety.

Wait. Why flee? *No.*

The woman was one of their priest-things. Their voices could control, like the mountain mother back in the inn.

How dare she? Hoom was the one who ran, from father, from village, into that cold and weeping dark. Not Red Marie. *Never her.*

She called upon that energy innate to all commrach, the imbuing, that source of their superiority, that turned matter to their will. It crackled from her skin and blended with the suit. A million bubbles poured from her and she descended, a little. Enough.

She turned and saw the woman's torso and legs. She had stopped swimming again. Uncertain, anxious, unable to use her filthy tongue. The woman had thought herself capable. Now she was just any other human.

Red Marie drove a sickle's point into the woman's belly and the water turned black.

The woman shuddered. She jabbed her blade against the suit again and again. It did nothing. Red Marie rewarded her by slicing the skin of her belly in a perfect square. She peeled it loose. The bowels curled out with little encouragement.

Red Marie swam past the woman. Any other time she would have remained to admire her own handiwork. It was a trick, an art piece. The victim floats in the water face-up with their intestines swirling like tentacles. Red Marie called it her 'jellyfish' and the victim took at least an hour to die.

But, of course, fucking duty called.

Red Marie broke the surface and searched for the rowing boat. There: twenty strokes ahead. Larksdale was awful at rowing. He would be worse still when Red Marie pulled his arms off and forced him to eat every finger. His mouth was full of insolence and she would make him suffer.

She raised her left arm to begin swimming.

The suit. A metal strip in the armour. It felt loose.

If the suit was not airtight, the keep's curse would have her. No. *No!*

She brought her arm down slowly. There were leathers below the armour, layers of leather. They had kept sealed. The layers had to.

Outside the keep the curse would get you. Only the suit protected her from that. How had that jellyfish bitch damaged it? How?

No sudden movements. She could not risk tearing the leathers. She could not die of the curse. It would give her only iniquity, obscurity and filth. Her death was bound to midnight at Yulenight Eve, surrounded by every corpse, her body vibrating on the throne of the universe. That was her destiny. Her meaning.

Larksdale would be easy enough to track again. She had done it before. She had to get back to the keep's heart and the Explainer's skills.

The woman moaned as Red Marie passed her, water filling her open mouth. But it was scant joy to witness.

45

Carmotta

The Flume, the Brintchild and the Tetch: these were the three daughters of the great River Brint, mother of all Brintland, that passed through Becken. It had always been vital for the Crown to be in their good graces. Which is to say, to be seen to be so.

Carmotta sat beside Ean, the pair of them carried aloft through the streets upon an open palanquin of ash-wood and bronze. Beneath them twenty men in green doublet and hose marched, their shoulders straining and their faces blank. Carmotta felt she was atop some great centipede. Guards with halberd, helm and breastplate lined either side of the palanquin and beyond either line of guards marched men with lanterns upon sticks.

She and Ean were all in white. She wore a veil of white gauze that allowed her to see everything of immediate necessity – Ean, proud in his fine whites and gold, the nearest guards and lantern-keepers – but turned everything beyond that – Becken's ugly streets and its even more repellent crowds watching the procession – into mere nocturnal haze. If only gauze could obscure scent.

Many shouted the king's name; a few called for war with Hoxham. Ean was at his best before his people, serene yet vital, the very mirror of his ancestor Neyes the Saint, the magnanimous. No man could touch Ean for sheer bearing. Not even Osrin was close, not for all his martial renown and savage good looks. Carmotta only hoped that her own presence was no barnacle on the hull of Ean's glory. She was not of these people, of course, and though Manca had not been to war with Becken some forty years, old men bore their scars. The life of the father becomes the story of the son, always, and women never do well in tales. All she could do was act the devoted wife and hope.

Behind them trailed two more open palanquins. Each had a mannequin of Ean sitting upon the left side, full-size and dressed identically to the real king. Third-Queen Emmabelle was inside the second palanquin, to Carmotta's chagrin. Emmabelle's womb had bumped her up the queue at the expense of Second-Queen Violee, whose own palanquin bore not a living soul but two mannequins in royal finery. In truth, Violee's Baptismas palanquin had always been so, even before her troubling disappearance. After all, no hedgehog likes to be paraded through a nation's capital.

Emmabelle had decided to fix a small prince's crown atop her belly. The temerity. Such a custom was reserved for monarchs still in the womb. Yet Ean had found the little crown adorable and had laughed with all the idiocy of a man still new to the flesh of a younger woman. Carmotta had said nothing. She had wanted to bellow at this playful admission of treason. Emmabelle was as stupid as she was ravenous and flagrant, and Carmotta was sure it was she who had sent the one-eyed assassin. Ean could not see her awfulness. But he would. Tomorrow. Just before midnight.

They were turning into a bend when someone to Carmotta's right amid the crowd shouted, '*Good Queen Emmabelle!*' Others followed, '*Emmabelle!*' '*Prince's mother!*'

Ean put his hand upon Carmotta's own. 'Nearly there, my love,' he said.

She almost smiled.

They were vulnerable up here, she and Ean. She felt intolerably soft, her nerves sensing where the arrowhead would enter and when. The veil was worse than a greathelm's visor. An assassin would have to be sitting on the palanquin itself for her to spot him.

She had asked Ean, once, about how to keep the fear of assassination at bay. He had said you had to pretend to know it could never happen.

Sea air filled her veil, the smell of the Flume widening to a bay. *By God,* she thought, *we've three of these watery bastards to baptise tonight.*

The palanquin slowed to a stop. Voices rose in the distance and guards barked orders to the crowds.

'What's happening, Ean?' she said.

He did not reply. He held his dignified pose.

She lifted her veil. Some way ahead of their palanquin the lines had broken down. A mass of commoners and merchant-types congregated before the ancient jetty where the baptism was to be held. This crowd had no discernible intent, some looking toward the palanquin, others out to the river. The palace guards up there were not doing their job. They were talking with the crowd.

The crowd beside her palanquin were gawping at her like she was a beast in a menagerie, their faces grotesque in the gold of so many lamps. One old woman actually wore a sack and on someone's shoulders sat a child missing her upper lip. The ugly, squashed buildings behind the crowd were no better; a greybeard with a jug of something looked down at her from a window. This man could pour his jug and there would be nothing she could do.

Get moving, she pleaded to no one. Motion lent godliness. The more the people looked at her, the more they must realise she was but a human. She had to be first-queen, a daughter of House Il'Lunadella. She was no flower: she did not prosper in this dirt.

But you did once, eh? a voice said. *You painted that pot and your fingers became green. The sun above and the songs of fisherman and everything was so right that it was a sin.*

She tore that picture from her mind. *Never think of that. You were not yourself that day.*

She took her veil in both hands and pushed its corners into her wimple.

'Guards!' she shouted.

Ean tapped her thigh. 'What are you doing?'

She ignored him. 'Guards!'

Two guards and a lamp-bearer came over, their faces uncertain.

'What's holding up the king?' she demanded.

'We don't know,' the shorter guard said. 'Forgive us, Your Majesty.'

To the devil with it. 'Lower the palanquin. He will attend to the situation.'

'Your Majesty?'

'Do as I command, man.'

They got to it. It took minutes for them to convince the bearers to lower their palanquin.

'Carmotta, what are you doing?' Ean asked, still looking ahead.

'You are taking charge of the matter,' she told him. 'Lead me to the jetty, my love.'

He did so. By the time she met him at the front of their palanquin Ean had acquired four guards and two lamp-bearers. She herself had accreted three and two. All were uncertain of this new turn of events.

'Forwards,' she announced. 'Keep a circle around His Majesty.' Somewhere ahead they would find the parade master. Surely he would know what was happening.

The line of guards ahead of them, still talking to the crowd, suddenly realised their charges were approaching. They lifted their halberds and threatened the folk they had been conversing with moments before.

'Careful now!' Ean commanded. 'Touch not my subjects.'

The guards tried to both hold the people back and not touch them, their halberds held like quarterstaffs. The mob tried to comply, stepping back, pressing into those behind them. As she reached the jetty Carmotta heard splashes and realised people were falling into the water.

'People!' Carmotta shouted. 'Make your way along the sides,' She pointed at the pathways created between the guards' halberds and the walls of buildings either side of the street. 'Along the sides!'

The guards repeated her orders and people began to do as they were told. Though the jetty did not entirely empty, there was space enough to proceed.

Carmotta saw the reason for the hold-up: flames rose high upon the Flume's opposite bank. A motley of blazes over what appeared to be waste ground. The shouts of men and women carried on the chill air.

'What is this?' She turned her head to look at one of the guards and instead saw a little man, his face painted green and his head crowned with two horns made of dried flowers.

'Your Majesty,' he said, looking at the silver tray he carried with its two silver jugs.

Dickie o' the Green. Dickie was a folklore character in the Brintland and, much like Manca's Il Panupto, was both rascal and harbinger of spring. The man playing him now was some commoner guilty of crimes small and tawdry. The king would pardon him once he'd played his part in the baptism of the rivers. Which, as Carmotta understood things, was a better deal than his distant precursors had received. The earlier, pre-Church Dickies had had their slit throats poured into the currents.

'Speak,' Ean said to him.

'That's Fleawater camp, Your Majesty,' Dickie o' the Green said. 'Where the spinefolk live.' He made to bow but remembered he had a tray in his hands.

Count Osrin's assault. Carmotta could have laughed. Osrin had timed his assault to occur when the baptism of the Flume began.

The night sky on the other side of the Flume lit orange and something like a comet rose in the air and fell down upon Fleawater camp, illuminating many boxes that Carmotta had to assume were hovels but were more akin to wagons. As one the mob drew startled breath.

'A trebuchet,' Carmotta muttered in Mancanese. 'Ostentatious prick.'

'Who?' Ean asked beside her.

'Osrin.' She gave him a smile that said, *We must be rid of this man.*

Ean understood that look, she could tell, but he chose to gawp at the camp instead. 'What's that?' he said.

A standard was being raised, one so large it looked more like a ship's sail. A white background made orange by the light of burning hovels. Now full-raised, the crest upon it was of a rearing lionfox. The count's taste in heraldry was in reverse ratio to his ambitions.

Naturally it was working. People in the crowd were already saying his name.

'Where's the parade master?' Ean asked.

'Your Majesty,' Dickie o' the Green answered, 'I think he fell in the river.'

'We'd better see to this,' Ean told Carmotta. He stepped further along the jetty, then raised both arms.

'We salute you, Count Osrin!' Ean cried.

Carmotta gestured at the Dickie to follow her and she made her way beside Ean.

'Osrin crushes our enemies!' Ean proclaimed. When the people cheered him he set them about chanting Osrin's name.

Carmotta wanted to cringe. Ean thought he was doing the right thing, absorbing Osrin's triumph into his own presence, but in truth he was making himself a flunky. Rumour of the lactating king had already raged through the city. This scene was not helping.

He has no skill for seizing happenstance, she told herself. But she had known that all along.

Folk were gazing at the river. Carmotta cupped her hand over her brow to block out the far shore's flames. She squinted at the dark waters of the Flume.

A single figure in a rowing boat, rowing frantically. They disappeared behind the jetty's edge and then people were helping them up. The figure fell on their knees and Carmotta could see it was a man. He had the ginger hair of the spinefolk, the locks hanging over his eyes. He wore mud-stained robes. He gibbered to the people around him.

'Fellow's worn out,' Dickie o' the Green said.

Carmotta looked at Dickie and the criminal immediately gazed downwards at his tray.

'The milk,' she said to him. She held out her hand.

On his tray sat a jug of bull's blood and one of cow's milk, to be poured into the river by the king and the first-queen respectively. They represented Dickie o' the Green's blood and seed which, in the original ritual, had been... well, it did not bear thinking about. Tonight's Dickie passed her the jug of milk.

Milk jug in hand, she made her way to the panting spineman. He still shivered upon his knees and though his hair covered his face, a long nose and pointed chin were discernible.

She squatted before him and, seeing her, the spineman stopped gibbering and froze, keeping his eyes upon his own knees. For all his savage blood, he clearly knew Carmotta, his queen.

'My fellow,' she said to him, 'what is happening across there?'

'Burning, ma'am,' he said, his accent comically thick. 'Killing, ma'am.'

'Here. Drink this.'

She offered the silver jug and its milk.

He cupped his hands and she poured. His palms full and leaking, he lifted them up and guzzled their contents down.

When she looked up it was not surprise she saw in the people's faces but admiration. For her kindness. She had not expected that. Moving to her left a little she poured more milk into the palms of the spineman, so that others might see.

Osrin had stolen the night. But tomorrow, when gossip flickered across the city, the tale of Osrin's triumph could not be told without mentioning the kindness of the first-queen. She knew it already. It was in all these people's faces.

I should have walked these streets before now, she thought, *met with its people.* All this time she had been fighting without a queen's full arsenal.

'Perfecti,' the spineman blurted. Anger spiked his voice and for a moment Carmotta thought he might assault her. 'Killed tha' Perfecti, they did. Sis'er Ruradoola, they killed her.' He winced. 'Body in river. River...'

He said more but his accent was too thick to discern.

Gently, she guided him on to his feet by his shoulders. She turned to a guard and announced, so that those nearby might hear, 'Here, take him to the nearest inn and let him rest.'

Two guards grabbed him by the arms and carried him away. The poor wretch was clearly dead on his feet, as the Brintland saying had it. His head never lifted.

Carmotta turned toward Ean, who was standing some yards away. He had not moved from the spot.

'My love,' she said aloud. 'They have killed a Sister Perfecti! The blessed of God! Osrin's men have *killed* her!'

Shock passed through the crowd as if her voice had been thunder. She put on a shocked face herself. She was no actor, she knew that well enough, but this newfound script practically performed itself.

YULENIGHT EVE

46

Hoom

'Is something bothering you, Explainer, sir?' Hoom asked. She was not Red Marie right now. Nor Countess Osrin, nor anyone else. Hoom was out of her suits. 'You look perturbed, if you do not mind me saying, sir.'

The Explainer did not look up from his work. He was fixing the damaged suit. 'I have mislaid something. Some… some letters.' He eyed Hoom briefly. 'You did not pick them up did you, Hoom?'

'I know of no letters, sir,' she said. She did not. She kept stroking her suit's left sickle with her bare fingers, passing that energy peculiar to all commrach into its alloy.

The Explainer frowned a moment, then smiled. 'I believe you, Hoom.'

With anyone else she would be annoyed. Lethally so. But the Explainer had a consistency of terms that the other commrach, those over in the obelisk, always ignored. They just called her 'Hoom', her old name, the name her father gave her. But the Explainer called her Hoom when she was out of her hinter-suits and always, always, Red Marie when she wore them. She respected that. It showed respect to her.

They were sitting outside the Explainer's little tent in the keep's dark hollow. As soon as the suit was damaged by that woman in the water, Red Marie had swum with all haste upstream to the tunnel that led straight inside the Explainer's tent.

The sickle was getting as sharp as Red Marie's sickle should be. All commrach could sharpen things with their concentration and their touch. They could do many things with their powers of imbuing, but sharpening was the truest. All commrach were killers at heart, as much predators as the panthers and lynxes of the forest. Hoom, despite her lowest birth, despite her lowness visible to all on her very face, that harelip no Explainer had bothered to heal, was the truest commrach that ever lived, for she was forever in need of sharp things. She was the sharpest thing.

No one understood that. Not the Explainers, not the stewards in their obelisks, not the highblood families in their towers of onyx and iron and pewter. Civilisation had taken all of them from nature, had simmered them to self-important sauce. Even her father, with his life spent beneath the night-dark canopies, had failed to see her. He should have known; of all people, he should have. Should have embraced her that night, adored her, but he had vomited when he had seen the six unborn kittens in a pattern around their mother's head. No true commrach, Father, not for all his talk. It had taken peerless talent to keep the mother lynx alive with peeled womb and ribcage. With sliced eyes. Father had seen only meat.

You failed me, Father.

He had bound little Hoom, he and the whole tribe. He had taken her to the Explainers in their forest observatory, for that is the custom with all children who play with the hot flesh of beasts, who know ecstasy in gore-soaked hands. She was prodded and pulled and inspected. Children like Hoom were best killed or made use of, so the Explainers said. Hoom had been the latter. A weapon, aimed at things outside the Isle. She never saw her father again.

'Are you well, Hoom?' the Explainer enquired.

'I won't kill you,' she blurted out. She laughed. 'I mean, I would never kill you. So you should not fear me, Explainer, sir.'

He smiled but his eyes shone nervously. She hated that, when people said one thing and their eyes said another. She wanted to kill him. But now she had said she would never she had better not. Vows were important. And she did not want to kill him, not really.

His nervousness ebbed. 'I think I understand. It is your way of saying you hold me in high affection. Am I right?'

'Yes!' she said, delight filling her. 'I want you to know that. And if I did not tell you now then you would never know, would you? I wanted you to know that before I die tonight, when I kill the king and Osrin kills me.' A lie. Red Marie would murder everyone. Just not the Explainer. He was an eloquent man, after all, and would tell Red Marie's story.

'Thank you, Hoom,' the Explainer said. 'I hold you in high regard too.' He turned his eyes back to his work: fixing the metal strip where the knife had nearly opened up the suit.

'I could have died last night,' she said. 'Before my hour of greatness.'

'The majority of us do, Hoom,' the Explainer said. 'But not you, eh?'

'I've been thinking,' Hoom said. 'The curse kills you within nine days? If you mention the keep-within-the-keep to another person outside the boundary, yes?'

'So folklore insists,' the Explainer said. 'Yet some victims have lasted somewhat longer and others have died immediately. Here's a lesson, Hoom: folklore is almost always wrong. In truth, I suspect the keep's curse waits for a death it finds especially pleasing and the nature of our world means it never has to wait all that long.'

'I've used my time up, haven't I? Long ago. Red Marie's been telling people in Becken city for years. She tells them and the survivors tell other people and then there's little outbreaks that people blame on Red Marie. But I'm fine because I'm sealed inside Red Marie. But if Red Marie became unsealed… the curse would be instant, yes? I've a debt, surely, because I keep telling people and, though that's naughty, I always get away with doing it. Am I right?'

'Honestly?' the Explainer asked. He looked out across the hollow, to where the keep-within loomed. 'I have no idea. But best to be safe, eh? Why don't you get a little sleep in my tent?'

'On my last day of life?' Hoom tittered and shook her head. 'Red Marie has to leave and go to the Hook soon, once you have her fixed. Mister Smones is offering me one last sacrifice.'

'Why risk it?' the Explainer said.

He had a point.

'It's the principle,' Hoom replied. 'Red Marie is important to the city. It would not be fair if she did not commit one last extraordinary bloodbath.' *Before the final bloodbath in here,* Red Marie thought.

The Explainer chuckled. 'I will miss you, Hoom.'

She wanted to hug him but he would scream if she did that. 'We have had good times, Explainer, sir.'

'That we have. That we have.'

'Like the other day,' Hoom said, 'when you asked me to carry the big lady out of here.'

'The queen?' the Explainer said. 'She is substantial. Good thing you turned up, hmm?'

'I suppose so.' Hoom felt good. She could not tell him of Red Marie's coming slaughter, but she could admit a little of it. 'Red Marie's going to butcher that queen.'

'Eh?'

'Red Marie's to kill the king so really she should kill his queen. Not the pregnant one, she's vital. Red Marie will leave her,' Hoom lied. 'But our masters said nothing of the big queen. Osrin will kill her anyway, so Red Marie may as well. It's poetic, to do that. And, to be honest, Explainer, sir, when I carried her body to the spare chamber and put her on the table there, I looked at her sleeping face, a very pretty face for a human, and thought, *I want to butcher you.*' Hoom shed a tear. It had been a tender moment. 'I want to butcher her, sir. So Red Marie will. For me.'

The Explainer's face was blank. Hoom didn't like that. But then he smiled and she did too.

'I do not see why you should not,' he told her. He looked down at the patch of suit he'd been working on, where the knife had nearly opened it up. He was silent a moment and then said, 'Get yourself some sweetmeats from my tent, Hoom. I… just have to fix the last of the damage here. Then Red Marie will be good as new.'

'Yes!' Hoom cheered. 'Gracious yes!'

47

Larksdale

Against all probability he had had a good night's sleep, long and deep. It had been criminal to escape from that inn so early, both in the figurative sense and the literal (he had stolen a thick jacket on the way out), but needs must when the Crown wished you incarcerated.

He walked the cold morning streets with arms crossed. A sea wind was picking up, cruel in its promise. Sister Ruradoola had predicted a storm only last night. Full of wisdom, Ruradoola, such light in her beautiful eyes.

Everything I embrace dies…

Gethwen too, Pilgrim preserve. Yet Gethwen knew himself caught in this strange web, whatever it was. Sister Ruradoola would have been fine if he had not sought sanctuary at Fleawater. Fine and ready to die of a horrific curse. Perhaps she had.

Let us not think on any of it. There would be time enough hereafter. Besides, neither of his lovers would have wished him to give up, to weep. They had both understood the danger of this black crown better than he ever could. To retrieve it, to send it far away, would be to sate their spirits. He took it as read one could not destroy the wretched thing.

Back to the Wreath, he kept telling himself. With luck, no one would be lurking outside the theatre for him. Indeed, would they even recognise ol' Harry now? Carmotta had not. The trick, he was learning, was to act down to the level nobles expected a commoner to be, all rough deference and startled muttering, never taking one's gaze from the mud. Still, a close shave that. He had been shocked to see Carmotta, almost as much as he had been to see Red Marie suddenly real. The game had seemingly been up, Carmotta being sharper than Larksdale would ever admit, but she had a blindness to the urchin and the peasant.

The Wreath's men would be preparing to bring Tichborne's folk-play to the keep this night. Larksdale would secrete himself among their number as they made their way past the keep's outer walls. And then? Well, he would just have to wade right into that damned pond and find the crown. Better yet, he'd persuade some of the stagehands to find it.

Snow billowed above the roofs of the street ahead. Peculiar that it should be so localised.

The snow was drifting up.

A fear clutched Larksdale and he began to run toward the snow. The fear was not something he could string into words. To think the thought would make it real. He could not see the thatched roof of the Wreath. It had always peaked behind the row of tall houses.

'No… no…'

He could smell the stale smoke, the charred and rain-soaked wood.

'No.'

He turned a corner into a square of ash. All of it. Ash and charred timber and blackened daub. It was as fog, the grey ash: everywhere, carried in the twisting winds, a gritty white. The ash engulfed him and he let it.

'No.'

Cold cinders dappled his lips and tongue. He stood in a whiteness. A nothing.

A third lover dead. His deepest, truest. Nothing mattered now. Not a thing.

Something hard tapped his shoulder. He wiped his eyes of tears and ash and turned to face another fool.

Knucklebones Smones. His black-rimmed eyes shone from below his crooked hat.

'This yours, sir?' he said, waving a black lacquer cane with a brass bird at its top. He clubbed Larksdale across the face with it.

48

Fwych

They feared her tongueless mouth. The man that come to feed her wore his brass helmet with the cheek pieces tied tight together and with stuffed cloth in 'em.

Cautious, that scoundrel Cutbill. Had seen what she could do with a mere bark from her gob. He were right to be careful. But Fwych were more now. Much more.

A gale outside, the air and the waters angry. Windows banged in their frames.

'Dahn't try anythink!' the guard near-shouted. He had a tray in hand with a miserable porridge on it, a cup of water beside. 'Gah,' he said, nose ruffling, 'look what you gone dahn!'

He nodded at the piss and she smiled behind her gag. She had had no option, her bladder not being what it were when she were young, but to spite these scoundrels were an extra blessing.

'Well I ain't cleanin' it ahp!' he barked. He put the tray on the little table of tools and turned a crank beside Fwych. She jutted a little more upright. Enough to swallow and not choke.

The slaughtered girl were sat on her bench in the alcove. She stared at Fwych and the guard like they were the cold horizon. Fwych had dreamed of the girl last night. She had dreamed of all the women in the great circle. They were long dead or they hadn't been born yet and they were hollow, empty vessels, but their hollowness was full of the great circle's powers.

'Right, me lav!' the cloth-eared guard barked. 'Let's 'av no trabble, eh? None ah yer mouth. Else it's goonight, ta ta.' He tapped the club on his belt. He pulled the gag from her mouth.

She drew the air in hungrily, fresh and full, carrying the taste of old dry blood on it, a taste she had got used to this last week. The windows shook again, as if gagging for the same air.

'Uhngiig ee,' she said in the tonguing voice, the voice that controlled.

He did not even notice, his eyes upon the tray, his ears covered.

Didn't matter. She were just warming up, were Fwych.

The guard lifted a spoon full of stodge that had long stopped steaming. She let it in her mouth. She still had a sense of taste at the back of her throat and the root of her tongue, but this porridge tasted of nothing. No one could make something so bland by accident.

'Unbigh ee,' she said and the stodge poured from her mouth. She was putting Lady Larksdale's teachings to practice, what she had called 'diction'.

'Aww, look what you gan dahn!' the guard said. 'Look atcha: all piss n' porridge y'are! Fackin' savage!' He gouged up another spoonful from the bowl. 'How'd I get this fackin' job anyhow?' he muttered.

'Unbiign muhh,' she said.

The guard laughed. 'You tryin' ya wizza-wazza? That it?' He slapped his cheek guard with its stuffing. 'No use, innit? Give up!'

Weren't you I were talking to, Fwych thought.

The slaughtered girl darted through the air, swift as if she were chasing a mouse. Noiseless, she stopped beside the guard and, with one hand cupped to her mouth, she leaned forward, her face drifting inside the guard's cheekpiece as she whispered inside his mind.

Fwych knew what she whispered: *Unbind me.*

The guard's eyes went wide as coins and his chin quivered. He pulled the knife from his belt and began to slice Fwych's binds. Her left wrist, then the right.

'Gick,' Fwych said. *Give.* The slaughtered girl whispered it into the guard's head.

He had passed his knife to Fwych before he even knew it.

She slipped two fingers up between his chin and the knot that held his cheek guards together. It would stop his jaw from moving. Him from screaming.

He had that moment they had, when they knew they were being controlled but hadn't the wit to fight against it yet, the sensation being so new and strange.

She popped the knifepoint into the inner side of his socket, sliding in between the bone and the eye itself. The round jelly popped out its lids like meat from a burst sausage. His jaw pushed against her two fingers but that wasn't him. Not really. Just the dance of the already dead. She pulled out of him and he dropped.

Fwych undid her ankles from their bindings, the black blood dappling her toes. She got on to her feet and stretched. *Oooh.*

The new corpse would shit itself soon. She started working the clothes off. Good disguise, that, a guard. Better than a servant even, Fwych reckoned.

She told the slaughtered girl to float out beyond the door and have a look who was there. It would be tricky, walking out of here, but easier than leaping out the windows to that dirty old river below. That had killed poor Selly the pennyblade.

The day was already getting dark. Mother Fwych had work to do.

49

Carmotta

Her tears ran black with mascara and by the time they dripped on her collar they were cold. Her corset choked her. She had loved this dress this morning but now it was a weight, heavy as iron, and her tears were cold and Dulenci lay on a cold table quite dead.

'Beautiful boy,' she whispered. 'Beautiful boy.'

She touched his face again and pulled away. She could not stop herself from doing so, despite the horror, the flat deadness of it.

They were in the mortuary again. Tibald Slyke still lay on his stone table. Beside Slyke was another new body, the Perfecti whom they had pulled out of the Flume. The sheet that covered her had a great stain of dried blood at its centre.

One of her handmaids – she did not see which – handed her a handkerchief. Carmotta took it and rubbed it across her face.

Dulenci's eyes were closed. A red slit in his throat, long dried. But the hand above his head was gone, that deathly hand of night.

You died protecting me. Protecting our love. Even when I was so cruel to you.

'Sir Willem,' Carmotta said. She snorted back more tears. 'You say she fell to her death?'

'The ban-hag leaped out of the window. It's a drop to the Brint below with much to hit on the way down.'

'Good. And her body?'

He was late to answer. 'With the bodies of other scum.'

'Bring her here,' Carmotta said.

'Your Majesty?'

'Bring her here. Her head will be placed on a spike, like you do with all the murderers at Wessel Bridge. No, her body entire.'

'Your Majesty, that's not custom at the keep.'

'*I do not care!*' Her yell bounced off the walls. Her handmaids jumped in their skin.

'Your Majesty,' Cutbill said. 'We shall bring her tomorrow.'

'You will bring her now! Damn you, man!' She punched his shoulder and the big man barely flinched. 'You were there and you let him die! You let him die! You peasant! You jumped-up *paisadino*!'

'Your Maj—'

She slapped his rough cheek.

'I will have you flogged, you bumpkin! You're a general, a fighter, and you let that savage kill him, you hapless fucking rantallion!' She broke, sobbing, a whistling sound coming from her lips she was too furious to stop. Her face fell into Cutbill's chest. He smelled of perspiration and cheap scent.

Cutbill stood there rigid. She could feel his arms raise a little, uncertainly.

Never looking up, she pulled his arms around her and sobbed the more. It felt good to be held.

'Everybody leave,' she said, her voice muffled against cloth. 'Wait outside.'

The handmaids' wooden heels clacked away. The two guards by the door were a little slower, but they trudged off soon enough.

Dignity has forsaken me, she thought. *That will not do.*

She pulled away from Cutbill's chest and his arms dropped from her shoulders.

'I apologise, captain of our city's guard,' she said. 'My words were unworthy.' She smiled as best she might. 'As queen I must always be above anger.'

Which was true. Today more than ever. But without Dulenci…

'Have your men ready for the seventh bell,' she told Cutbill. 'Have them on hand at the court session. I want a guard at every doorway of the true throne room.'

'Your Majesty…' Cutbill said, looking around a second. 'Your Majesty said we were to apprehend Count Osrin at midnight, with the play.'

'That may yet occur,' she replied, 'should he fail to be condemned by my husband and his court. Our plan changes. Last night his men killed a holy Perfecti.'

'My men,' Cutbill said. 'He used *my* men. And I let him.'

'He abused your trust, Sir Willem. Thus, you will beseech our king to address Osrin's violent impiety.'

'Your Majesty, I wouldn't know how—'

'You will not?' She looked up at him with pleading eyes, with cheekbones sullied by kohl.

'I've never stood before the king and demanded anything,' he said.

'You shall have a script. Fear not. The worst that can happen is he is not arraigned then and there.' He would not be, doubtless. 'But he will be on show before the whole court. It is then he or his Emmabelle shall anger and make their mistake. It's then I bring their intimate letters into the light.'

'His Majesty still has no clue about them?' Cutbill asked.

'Better that way,' she replied. 'His reaction will be natural.' In truth Carmotta was depending on the support of the court at large. Ean needed the shock and outrage of the entire court to drown out his fear of Osrin and his – albeit assuredly ebbing – lust for Emmabelle. All surface, Ean. This week had proved that much, though that surface enthralled her so.

Cutbill drew breath. 'Very well, Your Majesty.' He shrugged. 'I already have a few guards prepared for the play. Should I keep them on hand, in case we end up going with the original plan?'

'Naturally.'

'With your permission, then, I should like to take command of the palace's entire garrison. Osrin might have his own allies among their number.'

She nodded. 'You can do so discretely?'

'A quick chat, Your Majesty.'

He had risen for good reason; she could finally see that. But she could not quite reconcile it with the man who had let Dulenci be murdered, who had not even seen the ban-hag's hidden blade.

'Do so,' she answered. 'If your beseeching has little effect we shall resume with the old plan. An arrest in the great welcoming hall. Midnight, as the play begins.'

'Your Majesty,' Cutbill said, 'the play will not be held in the welcoming hall. Osrin and his friends convinced His Majesty otherwise days ago. There's a surprise for the court, a sort of… wheeze.'

'Wheeze?' she asked.

'The play is to be performed in the great hollow.'

Carmotta stared in disbelief. 'Before the keep-within?'

50

Larksdale

Water drilled against his throat for a second, then expanded into a warmth that poured downwards, over his chin and cheeks, soaking his blindfold. The stink of ammonia reached him and he struggled to pull his head away, to cover his nose and mouth with a hand and defend with the other.

Useless. All was piss in this upside-down world. His temples pounded.

The piss ceased and cackling followed.

'That's woken him, boss,' a male voice said.

'I was already awake!' Larksdale thundered, his voice echoing. 'Have been for some time, what with all the hanging upside down and all. Hadn't you bloody noticed?'

Another jet, this time filling his nostrils with warmth. He waved his arms about to break the little torrent and lifted his chin to let the piss drain from his nose. The unseen pack guffawed.

'Somewhere in this city,' Larksdale said, 'people pay good coin for this sort of thing.' He braced for more piss. None came. 'Be luvvies and let me down, eh?'

'He's the very Holy Pilgrim, boss,' the voice said, 'all hanging like that.'

True enough, though Larksdale's captors had been considerate enough not to jab a hook through his ankles. Larksdale had instead been given a pair of manacles, their inner sides fitted with something like stuffed hessian. He could hear rains batter a roof above.

'Take his blind off, Squints,' Knucklebones Smones said.

Rough fingers removed the soaked cloth. Larksdale could see the world again. He liked none of it. There were Smones's hobnail boots, of course, plus the tip of the black lacquered cane that had once been his own. Either side of those were other pairs of feet: to the right, two great heaps of bunion and canker wrapped in sackcloth; to the left, daintier moccasins.

'I haven't a care what you do to me,' Larksdale said. 'I've lost everything.'

'No you ain't,' Smones said. 'Not slightly.' He spat on the floor. 'But you've come to the right place. This your first time at the Hook, Sir Harrance?'

The Hook. The rotten promontory that severed Becken Bay. The plank floor below him was webbed with lichen. Blackened water lay in pools there too and he realised that that was these men's piss. The Hook's filth saturated its inhabitant's bodies.

'Red as beetroot, he is,' Squints said. 'He needs rest.'

'Best make him a hammock,' Smones replied.

The big thug with the dead face on his neck creaked the warped floor as he lumbered forward. Great hands took Larksdale's wrists and he was lifted up by them, the warehouse's half-lit ceiling filling his vision. Someone passed a hanging rope to the thug and the monster tied Larksdale's wrists in the same manner as his ankles. His limbs tugged at their sockets with his own weight. Yet the blood running from his head was a delightful feeling.

'Obliged,' he muttered.

'Lil' Meg!' Smones shouted. 'C'mere darling!'

Larksdale peered in the direction Smones had shouted toward. He was startled to find there were some twenty figures standing before the warehouse's timber wall, all clearly denizens of the Hook with their characteristic bad posture and gaunt stare. One of them, a waif of perhaps thirteen with a bundle of cloth in her arms, scampered forward.

The big thug picked her up and placed her upon Larksdale's solar plexus. The weight pressed his spine and squeezed his lungs. He made fists as a bulwark against the manacles' increasing bite.

The waif gazed down upon him. Her face was a child's and her hair a hag's, grey and knotted. Her expression was blank, as if she had long discarded every emotion. She clutched a sleeping babe in mouldy rags.

They had, indeed, made Larksdale a hammock. He hoped no further Hooksies would come rest upon him.

'I shouldn't have to tell ya this is ya last day alive, sir,' Smones said. 'Your corpse we'll throw into that great cemetery the sea. So take heart you won't sleep alone.'

'And the Pilgrim will call to those lost souls of the sea,' Squints quoted. 'Souls numbered beyond count.'

'Fitting,' Larksdale said. Against expectation, he was adjusting to the weight atop him. 'I lost all my coin to the sea. A hold full of mustard, the seabed its table, most like.'

'Well if it ain't already it will be tonight,' Smones said. 'Devil of a storm outside. Still, if it's consolation, your end's for a good cause, Sir Harry.'

'I would not have thought you'd need cause to slaughter.'

'You wound me, Sir Harry,' Smones said. 'Everything I do has its purpose. Besides, won't be me slaughtering. It'll be her. Old Red Marie.'

The chorus of Hooksies murmured her name. A liturgy for a goddess more feared than loved.

Smones chuckled and wiped oily phlegm from his lips. 'You surprise me, Sir Harry. The first thing that comes out most our sacrifices' mouths is that she don't exist.'

'We're past introductions, she and I,' Larksdale said.

'And you're *still* alive? Cor! Slippery fish, ain'tcha?'

'There were… others in my shoal.' Sister Ruradoola had thrown herself at Red Marie with no fear, or her fears tamed. He would have to face death too now. He hoped he would face it like her. He was trying to. The loss of everything he had enjoyed in his life certainly took the sting out of its imminent end.

'But you're the one she wants, sir. She's had us running about for you, right after she killed your lad. She had us after him before, of course, as you might recall last time we met.'

'Gethwen?' He had thought his murder Sir Tibald Slyke's callow vengeance.

'For that crown of his.' He leaned forward, to Larksdale's ear. His breath stank of cloves and lichen. 'I could do you a favour, sir, seeing as you've always been a gent to Smones. Tell us where the crown is right now and I'll dose ya soon as we get it back here. You won't feel so much as a tickle when Marie plays with your guts. Can't say fairer, eh?'

'No,' Larksdale said aloud. *Why should I be spared both my lovers' agonies?* 'No.'

Smones rose back to full height and gazed down on Larksdale. 'Think you're some martyr, is it? A fackin' saint?'

Larksdale gave Smones a look. 'Relatively speaking. You've a reputation, Smones, and you've only ever lived down to it.' He eyed the girl with the still babe in her arms. He nodded at the crowd of timid souls. 'You ply trades even the devil would eschew. You feed off the very weakest. Your throne is wrought from nothing save the limbs of the needy.'

Smones laughed, a sound like nails thrown against a pot. 'And you keep-boys don't? I'm you writ small, mate. Your king in ragged trousers.' He shook his head. 'Have a look at this.'

He snatched the babe in its swaddling cloth from little Meg. Meg screeched and tried to grab the babe back. Larksdale juddered and swung, pain lancing his sinew. Smones booted the girl off Larksdale's chest and she rolled across the floor. Larksdale took in deep breaths, his body lighter and his ears full with the child-mother's screaming.

'Word gets to me,' Smones said to Larksdale. 'They say Sir Harry gave a most *wonderful* party for King Ean, full of fine victuals and sweetest tup-girls. Culoo too, they reckon, that marvellous foreign powder that vitalises the senses and bones. Not the street stuff, mind, not the culoo cut with flour and who-knows-what that the beggars and bawds imbibe. Oh no, the *good* stuff. The cleanest, straight off the boat.' His grin stretched to his eyes. 'It ain't off no fackin' boat. Never was. Comes straight from the keep itself.'

The babe was not sleeping inside its rags. It was either dead or no babe at all.

'A sewer runs along the Hook,' Smones said, 'right out to sea. Becken Keep's sewer, built who knows when. They didn't even do us the kindness to bury it in the Hook's earth. Brickwork sticks half out the ground. Old, it is. Leaks. I'll wager half its contents never makes it to the sea, just sinks into wood and stone and steel. Has for centuries. I mean, no one's gonna come here and fix it up are they? It's no one's problem.'

Larksdale had had some idea. He would be shocked if anyone else at the keep knew or cared.

'Plenty of piss and shit, o'course,' Smones continued, 'rich in spices and honey and all the world's wonders. But worse too. Never been in your keep, sir, but I know it's fat with evil. I know because it ends up here, black and stinking. All those centuries of fanciness and cruelty, pouring into the Hook's bones. But it has its gifts,' Smones noted. He looked down at the swaddling clothes and smiled like a proud father. 'We're all twisted here, the "Hooksie look" and all that. Especially those of us born here. But some ain't even born.'

He stepped closer to Larksdale and peeled open the swaddling clothes.

It looked like dry soap that had once been left to soak, or a chunk of that powdery cheese from Manca. It had the features of a newborn babe, the face a perfect cast of a sleeping cherub. Limbs, too, fat and tiny. But its feet were gone, powdered to nothing.

'Meg's second, this,' Smones said. 'She's a good worker, right sorta womb. But we've others. I make sure there's a constant supply.' He rubbed a filthy finger on the calcified babe's ankle and powder broke off. 'It's a seller's market, mate.'

He shoved his thumb between Larksdale's lips. Filthy that thumb, but there was another taste too. Sharp and numbing, familiar. Culoo.

Larksdale fought against his bindings, tried to retch. The veins in his temples pulsed with the culoo's vigour. The atrocity of it. The atrocity.

'I should thank you most humbly,' Knucklebones Smones said. 'You completed a loop I always dreamed of – feed the keep its own shit.'

'Devil!' Larksdale shouted. 'Devil!' He could think of nothing but the night of the party, the babe-stuff running up his nose. Into his body.

'It's simply too-too utter,' Smones said, impersonating Larksdale's voice. All his cronies laughed. 'Be honest, Harry, you never cared. You were happy enough to believe any old tale of foreign powders and what-not. So's everyone else. Why question a luxury? Hmm?'

'If I'd have known—'

'You'd still do it, happily, if your king deemed it fine,' Smones said, cutting him off. 'Or your fackin' Church. You think good and bad comes bespoke out your own head? Comes from those above, always has.' He grumbled. 'Ah but this is – what's the word? – semantics. Here, Meg, me darlin'...' He tossed the babe over to Meg, who grabbed it out of the air. 'You look after your boy there, you hear? He's special, he is.'

'Kill me,' Larksdale said. He meant it. He thought he did anyway. The trouble was he felt distant, all spent. No theatre, no loves, neither wealth nor regard at court, an enemy of his nation. An actor still upon the stage, his scene over. His lines all spoken. 'Kill me, man.'

'Not as easy as that, is it?' Smones said. 'We want this crown, remember? Our Queen Marie is pretty fackin' insistent.'

When Larksdale said nothing Smones gestured for everyone to leave. Soon, the two men were alone, the sound of rain and wind battering the oily wood of the warehouse.

'You've seen her, then?' Smones said. The showmanship had vanished from his tone.

Larksdale nodded. His head was racing from the culoo, the child-dust. The air burnt with colour.

'I know she's not really Red Marie,' Smones said. 'I wouldn't want you to think I didn't, Sir Harry, not now you've seen her too. Fancy suit, ain't it?'

'Remarkable,' Larksdale said.

'Never out of it. Not once. Must get hot in there.'

Larksdale thought about that. Red Marie had mentioned the keep-within, right out in the open. Perhaps... oh, it mattered not.

'I gotta know, Sir Harry,' Smones said. 'Purely academic like. She's from the keep, yeah? All that armour and such...'

'No,' Larksdale replied. 'We've nothing like that.' There remained but one option. He recalled Ruradoola's knife. 'Commrach,' he told

Smones. 'Has to be commrach made. They have the sorcery to warp metal to their bidding, it's said, a magical touch.'

'Them's from sprite island?' Smones sighed. 'Never considered elves. Then again, I'm not an educated man like you.'

And there it was. Leverage. 'You've been working for powers inhuman, Smones. Sprites. They think of us as animals, you know. They've played you for a fool, my man.'

'Hardly matters,' Smones said with a finality that blew all hope of a ruse away. 'Whoever's in that suit, Red Marie's taking her over. She always does.'

'I don't understand, Smones.'

'Red Marie ain't no bogeywoman. She's a state o' mind. An essence. She's in the black filth from the pipe. Seeps out and infects a person from time to time. I've seen it, Sir Harry. I've helped her every time she's possessed a body. Have my whole adult life, I have, which is a lot longer than you might fackin' think, believe me. Well, she's picked a real beauty this time round and no mistake.'

'I thought you a plain thug,' Larksdale said. 'But you're insane, Smones. You need help.'

Smones stepped closer and combed his dirty fingers through Larksdale's hair. Larksdale hadn't the strength to draw his head away.

'Sir Harry, the problem I've always found with you – if I may humbly say – is you believe in the brotherhood of man and the sisterhood of woman. That's why you'll never accept something like Marie. You're a well-known do-gooder around town. As if good could ever be done.'

'Good can always be done,' Larksdale said. This lunatic's words, his air of amused pity, was infuriating. 'And how, I beg you, is a belief in the decency of people a weakness? Kindness, sir, is a strength.'

'I wonder if I ever thought like that,' Smones said. 'I really can't remember. It only takes one look about this city, any city, to see any good done is like plaster slapped on a bad wall by a poor workman. It never dries. It crumbles, and the brick and wattle, the truth of man, is always exposed. Understand that fact, see it for what it is, and you'll live a long life my friend.' He eyed Larksdale's hanging form. 'Quad erat fackin' demonsratum, as them ancients would say, sir.'

'All right, I suppose I've time,' Larksdale said. He could feel the culoo pounding in his chest. 'Astonish me with this truth of yours.'

Smones took out a clay pipe and began filling it with some weed or other.

'We're dog and rabbit, we men,' Smones said. 'Hunter and prey, all in one race. More besides: the dog and the rabbit and the green, green grass. Man's the only creature really like that, see? We got so good at killing every other animal, bending them to our whim, we had to become an animal kingdom all our own. Man feeds on man, sir. Even dresses so as to look like different beasts: your nobles in their finery, the merchants in a little less, your poorest in sackcloth.' He took the pipe to his mouth, lit the weed with a flint device of such beauty it simply had to be stolen, and imbibed. He breathed out vile smoke and continued. 'You can't see that, Sir Harry, and now you're very much its victim. There can be no brotherhood of man because at heart we're not even the same animal, not in our heads. Hound and rabbit and the green, green grass. And if you *could* somehow shake it all up – not that you could, mind – we'd only start to make layers again, with different people up and down. But still those layers.' He took another drag on his pipe. 'Hope I'm making sense, mate. I'm not one for speeches.'

'Actually, you're quite the orator,' Larksdale said.

'Really?'

'The very definition: you make the contemptible acceptable. And your first victim was of course yourself, eh? Look at you, you regent of a rookery, tyrant above the tired. Of course you have to spin bleak justifications.'

'I just give people what they want deep down,' Smones said. 'You ask anyone in your keep, you ask the fat merchants of the town, all the fine folk, ask them to picture what manner of man runs the Hook and in their minds they see someone like me. They sleep safer knowing a rotten man runs the pit of this city. You do too, and all the bleeding-hearts like you. I pour myself into that mould you fine men dreamed up.'

A calm crossed Smones's face. There was a sobriety to him Larksdale had never seen in anyone before, a nightmare sanity.

'You're weak,' Larksdale snapped, lifting his lance against this dragon. 'There *is* a brotherhood among all men, though it slumbers too often. It wakes when men of heart steel themselves to be kind. You, sir, never possessed such steel.'

'Not enough men of heart, not enough steel.'

'One day,' Larksdale said. 'Mark my words.' He looked down at his hanging form. 'Though I shall not see it.' *My,* he thought, *I really am going to die, aren't I?*

'That would take a change in the human fundament, hitherto unseen.' Smones pushed Larksdale slightly, allowed him to swing. 'And if yer fackin' Pilgrim ain't done it, nor his Church, nor any king, what hope is there for a kinder world, hmm? What's even left?'

'Art,' Larksdale said. 'It lies in art.'

Smones met his eyes. He laughed, his chest shuddering with the violence of it. It faded into a coughing fit.

'Marvellous,' he said, wincing. 'Fackin' classic, sir. You're a gem.'

'I bloody mean it!' Larksdale shouted. 'You insipid wretch, of course I mean it!'

'Blimey,' Smones said, 'I shouldn't ah given you all that culoo.' He smiled. He poured the burning fibres of his pipe upon Larksdale's bare throat. 'Go on: paint your way outta that.'

The cinders gnawed unseen below his chin, the ash-stink filling his nose and mouth. Larksdale tried to twist this way and that, but the burning would not cool, would not roll off from him. He tried blowing at it.

Two fingers rammed into his nostrils, filling them. They stank of cheese. Smones lifted him by his nose. The pain in his back flowed straight to his nose and boiled there.

'Sing yourself free,' Smones said. He pulled his fingers out.

The pain flew from Larksdale's nose and rushed to his spine once more, but angrier now. Above him the rotting beams swung left and right. His neck ached and he wanted to vomit.

'Dance yourself still,' Smones said. 'Can't even do that, can you?' He pressed a palm against Larksdale's side and the swinging ceased. He brushed the cooling ash from Larksdale's throat. 'Art? I don't know much about art, Sir Harry, but I know you'd do anything not to die. There's the only rule. S'why we cower before the strong and eat up the weak. You can't paint over that with yer fancy brushwork.'

'Art is the compass to a finer world,' Larksdale insisted, forcing back the pain. 'The best we can be. This world *is* possible, Smones. I have always known so, as if God had whispered it to me in my cot. My life's work. Damn your tepid mockery.'

'Your dream,' Smones said. 'A made-up world only you've seen.'

'No!' Larksdale shouted. 'I have been there!' He saw her smile back then, her marvellous serenity. 'And I was not alone. I saw it with another.'

The manacles on his feet were being removed. Knucklebones Smones lowered his legs to the floor. A small ecstasy, to stand upon mouldy boards and cooling piss. His arms remained bound above him. Outside, waves kept beating along the Hook. The gale was ceaseless.

'Would you take my confession?' Larksdale asked.

'All right,' Smones said. 'But don't think the irony is lost on me.'

Larksdale could only look at his own feet. The nail on his left big toe looked as if it would blacken soon. 'I was… nineteen I think, she two years younger. Soon to marry the king and seal a peace between two kingdoms.' He glanced at Smones, expecting to see surprise, but the rascal's face was placid. 'I had been sent to the duke of Il'Lunadella. A prenuptial hostage, as royal bastards often become, though here it was pleasant formality and a chance to learn of the larger world. She greeted me on the day I arrived, as is custom. Her parents and siblings too. Ravishing, their estate. It made me wonder why we all don't just decamp from the Brintland and live in that warm, green land instead. But the estate's fascination was as nothing, *nothing* compared to her.

'Her eyes, Smones. Her smile. I had been an awkward lad, bullied by half-brothers in the keep, lectured to by Mother, but in this young woman's curtsy all that simply evaporated. Her eyes held a detached amusement with the moment and its formality, with the world entire. I had often felt that in myself but never dreamed I'd see it in another. I was charmed beyond sense.'

A sheet of rain hit the warehouse like a lady's slap.

'Go on,' Smones said.

'I knew she saw it in me too. Trouble was the duke, a man shrewd as he is cold, saw it before either of us. He kept us apart aside from formal events, but she had stirred a new confidence in me, one that became apparent to the whole family once I was caught in flagrante delicto with Señor Balmeri, my language tutor. The duke exiled him.'

'And you?'

'My Mancanese went downhill, that's for sure,' Larksdale replied. 'But I never could get my tongue around the harder parts. The main thing was the duke relaxed. To him I was a pure lavender, no threat to his four daughters. Now he was fixed upon keeping me from his sons and his dreadful little nephew. Strange how some cannot conceive of a soul who loves both sexes.' He shook his head. 'Carmotta and I began a heavenly summer. Arm in arm through the gardens, jokes whispered to one another at the banquet table. Each morning I awoke hungry to taste each minute of a new day. Each night I bathed in sweetest dreams, with the perfumes of the estate's flowers pouring through an open balcony, the scent of Carmotta upon my skin.'

'So yer facked the queen?' Smones asked. 'Nice work, pal. Quite the confession.'

'No. No, that's precisely the point I'm coming to. I *thought* I wanted to. It had to be lust, I told myself, for what else could this consuming fascination be? I had no other context. Neither did she. I knew she was obsessed, lost in the calm of standing by my side. Months passed. We never kissed. Then came the week before I would leave for Becken, a full eight months before she would be wed. One last adventure, but our greatest. We would venture beyond the estate unaccompanied. To the port town of Sant Ribot nearby, dressed in the clothes of Manca's commonfolk.

'We bought pendants from stalls, capered to a fisherman's song outside a tavern.' Larksdale heaved a laugh. 'We chased a seagull along the seafront. We were free, young, with no history and no responsibilities. Paradise, that. Paradise. It was then Carmotta spotted a... I don't know what one would call it... a pottery-house, I suppose. There was a long table outside where people were making pots from clay and painting ones that had already been fired. They seemed the natives of some happier land. They welcomed us readily. Looking back, I'm certain they knew who we were. They were older than us, most of them, and must have known the tricks of the young and titled. I fancied working with the clay itself, it seemed such a messy fun. Carmotta was taken with the brushes and paints. Neither of us minded our borrowed clothes getting dirty.

'What happened next… I cannot truly explain in words. It was a sort of spell, hours golden and conjured, cleaved from a dream more than life. For I was a potter, she a painter, and we were lost in creation. The rest was dust and detail, all of it, the estate and our titles and all the kingdoms of the world. There was but the act of making, of being with another soul who made.' Larksdale's eyes watered. His jaw shivered. 'Hours passed and they had fired the first terrible pot I had made. She would have no other paint it but herself. It was then we… we looked at one another. We knew we were not lovers; that was beneath us somehow. We had entered another world, that world which all humanity will someday know. I never saw that pot of ours come out the kiln. The hour was late, the spell unwound. We ran back to the estate before we were missed. But this world was not the same. We could never return to that estate nor I to the keep, not in our hearts. We elected to run away. To live free. A potter and a painter.'

'But, sir,' Smones's voice said, 'that ain't what happened, is it?'

Larksdale sobbed. Tears flowing like blood from so many wounds.

The gale howled. Rain hammered the roof.

Knucklebones Smones walked off into a dark corner of the warehouse, abandoning Larksdale to his tears. To his greatest shame.

You ran, you coward, he thought. *You have never stopped your running.*

Smones returned carrying a bucket. Larksdale could only just make him out, his vision being so very blurred.

A splash of cold gloop and Larksdale screamed. He was covered, dripping with green paint.

'For the ritual,' he heard Smones say. He dropped the bucket and pulled out his pipe. 'Hey, I don't make the rules…'

51

Mother Fwych

The dead had drawn her to the houses of her people. Most of it stood burnt and broken, their camp's walls all torn down. *This is what happens when you leave the mountains of your forebears,* she thought. Yet she did not think them fools. She felt only anger.

Cutbill's scoundrels had done this, wearing the costume she now wore. All through the streets of this terrifying place – here, where folk lived atop folk and no one knew peace – the people had stepped aside to let her pass. It were like a spell, this soft armour and brass helm she had stolen, a power beyond that of her lost tongue.

She passed a dead ox, the rain pooling red around it. This were a bitter gale, but it had put out the fires. So many fires there had been.

Fwych had never seen so many cart-homes. Painted things on wheels, lovely in their way despite wheels being flatland things. Their decoration had kept true to old ways, telling stories of Father Mountain and his children in patterns impossible for outsiders to discern. All smashed now, burnt, their innards lying about in the mud and the rain. Clothes, pots, keepsakes. Fwych had never seen a place of such tears.

She passed the slaughtered girl, atop one of the wooden

wrecks. The slaughtered girl looked toward one of the pathways between the cart-homes and Fwych turned down into it. Pointing the way, the slaughtered girl in white had led her here.

Burnt cloth flew by. A loose spoke rattled in its wheel. Shouting ahead, wavering in and out of the howling wind. Fwych ran toward it.

There were a building that were an upturned boat. It had the damned Pilgrim's hook atop it and little glass windows. One wall had been torn down. The path beside were covered in paper, most half-buried in mud and flapping in the wind like grass. There had been a bonfire too, in the middle of the path. Charred wood, blackened metal. Little blocks of wood there were too, big as a finger. Most charred, but some fresh. Flatlander sigils on 'em.

Movement in the gloom of the torn house. Bodies moving, struggling. Stepping off the path, Mother Fwych could see men of the wandering sort, a few women too, their clothes soaked and dirtied. They had a small woman by her blonde scalp and her left leg and they were shouting at her. Others still were shouting at the ones shouting. The woman were shouting at everyone, swinging her fist.

I approach, Fwych thought at the blonde woman, and the slaughtered girl appeared among the huddle in the broken house. The slaughtered girl whispered in the woman's ear and she stopped her struggle. She looked toward Mother Fwych in the rain. The wandering folk who held her stopped and looked too.

They were scared of Fwych. All of them. They feared the dress of Cutbill's men. She unstrapped the brass helm and threw it in the mud, threw off her cloak so they might see her tattoos.

The blonde woman broke free. She snatched a red woollen hat from the fist of one of the women and pulled it over her own scalp. She picked up a satchel that had a stick poking out of it and stepped out from the torn house and into the rain, toward Fwych.

A big man followed her. One of her persecutors.

'Where is he?' he bellowed after the small and slender woman. 'He killed her, yer bitch!'

Enough, she thought to him and the slaughtered girl whispered in his ear.

The big man clutched his skull and dropped, writhing in a puddle. The others looked at him then looked back at Fwych. One of the women dropped to her knees and lifted her arms in supplication, in the old way.

The woman in the red hat had closed in on Mother Fwych, her hands open and empty. She looked like no one Mother Fwych had ever seen, her skin and her eyes different. But Mother Fwych recognised her resolve.

'Where is he?' the woman said. 'Where is he?'

The air, the world itself, seemed to stretch, widen. Mother Fwych staggered on her feet, a vision coming. In her mind she saw a church of the flatlanders with its spiked tower. Rundown it were, evil, leaning out over stormy waves.

'Larksdale!' the woman in the red hat shouted. 'Sir Harry Larksdale!'

Power lashed Fwych's skull. It tasted of the great ring around the keep. She dropped to her knees in the mud and wet ash. In the back of her skull a man was hanging by his arms. That green man, that suffering man. He had appeared to her before, in her visions by the pond under the trees. He hung in the gloom of a dark hall and Fwych knew it were the temple.

Red Marie, she thought, *Red Marie comes for him.*

Mother Fwych screamed into the rock-grey sky, felt rain pool in the cave of her mouth.

She arose. She stretched her tattooed arms wide, stretched her mind out wider. Unseen by all save Fwych, the slaughtered women of the ring emerged from cracks in the air. Some hundred or more.

They whispered in the ears of all there. Whispered to every soul inside this broken camp, hiding in their ruined homes. Whispered Mother Fwych's words, of who she were and what danger waited at the midnight hour. She whispered to them her plan.

It would not take them to the keep, that plan. Not directly, anyhow.

52

Red Marie

Her last night leaping across the roofs, her city, her hunting grounds. She lost herself to the joy of each bound, to the scratch of sickle's point against wet slate. She was impervious, terrifying in her unseen splendour amid this storm and gale. She would live past this night, for she had left these roofs and all below them a legacy of exquisite terror. She was Becken's nightmare tonight and for ever! Red Marie!

The ninth hour of night was drawing in. Soon the bells would ring at Becken Cathedral and Knucklebones Smones and his congregation would cower in their usual awe. He wasn't such a bad sort really, Smones. Unctuous, yes, wheedling, certainly, but… oh, who was she kidding? She would tear his spine out right after the sacrifice. Murder the lot, then back to Becken Keep to slay King Ean as her masters wished.

And the rest… his big queen and his little queen and the lord who would usurp him. This was Red Marie's final performance, *her* play, written in everybody else's blood.

The streets were empty. She had hoped to slash a few citizens on the way to the Hook, spray gore upon wattle and daub. Damned weather. She settled for smashing a tiny window in the arch of a roof. The people inside screamed to see her nail-fanged face peer through.

'There's a castle within the keep!' she screeched at them. *'A keep within the keep!'*

She bounded off, over the roofs. They would talk of her tomorrow, mention her words to others. So many would die, painfully absurdly. She liked to do that from time to time: tell the big secret. Months could pass before such plagues burnt out. She only wished she had spread the word more, but the Explainer frowned upon that sort of thing.

She reached the base of the Hook, its promontory reaching out into the wave-wracked bay. The roofs were skeletal along here, peppered with holes that led into darkness. She ceased her bounds and settled for stalking. The spire of the wooden church rose from a blur of rain and waves.

She could see movement. The inhabitants of the Hook, weaving like packs of rats between the shacks and around the mouldy brickwork, their bodies obscured by oiled cloaks. So many, Red Marie had never thought there were so many. Her sickles would feed tonight.

A step from the roof of the old warehouse to the roof of her church, though this time she had to lean into the winds which were almost a hurricane in intensity. Climbing up and into the spire was hard but her sickles found purchase in all the slices they had made before.

Her name was being chanted by tired and frightened throats. Bells rang from far off. The ninth hour.

The bells finished and Knucklebones Smones began his mummery.

'Children of Marie! The red hour be upon us!'

Red Marie sickled her way down the inner walls of the church tower. Reaching the floor, she concentrated and removed that power of her body, her commrach imbuing, from the material of her hinter-suit. She became visible to all eyes. She stepped into the church's hall.

'She comes!' Smones, in priestly robes, announced. He waved a black cane in one hand. That part was new. 'Fackin' heck! 'Ere she is!'

The congregation was lined either side of the hall, their hoods and coats slick with rain. So many, twice as many as any other time Red Marie could recall. They lowered to their knees, though some were slow in so doing. This night had drawn even the Hook's less devout.

'Bring forth the sacrifice!' Smones yelled.

Smones's two lackeys, the midget and the big man, came forward, a man between them. The man's body was smeared in the appropriate green, symbolic of the fictional Red Marie's yulenight victim. They set the victim down on his knees before the far wall that, though usually ornamental in its decrepitude, looked downright dangerous tonight. Sea water kept spurting through. But what of it? Red Marie would survive any storm.

She prowled down the aisle. She rubbed her sickles together and sparks flew.

The victim, a ginger and clean-shaven man, looked up.

She recognised that face. The long nose, the arched eyebrows. Larksdale.

She smiled. Oh but she had not failed in hunting him down. Her threats had pushed Smones and his gang to untold heights of competency.

So much fun! She would prise the truth from this awful man, this Larksdale who had mocked her so haughtily back at Fleawater camp. She would take her time with this one, as much as schedule allowed, find out where that black crown that her masters were eager to own actually was. She would wear it at midnight as she tore her own body apart. As she vibrated with the universe upon her bloody throne.

'It is I, Larksdale,' she announced. *'Red Marie.'*

'Well who else?' he spat.

She was above him, gazing down on his kneeling form. *'You will know such agony, fool.'*

You afraid? A girl's voice. Right in her ear.

Red Marie turned her head toward the voice. There was no one there.

No one can save you, the girl said in Red Marie's other ear.

'Who said that?' Red Marie demanded of the congregation.

The inhabitants of the Hook stared at her blanky. Smones shrugged.

'Is this a joke?' Red Marie shouted at them. *'I do not appreciate jokes!'*

They were all as unkind as the rest. As her father, her village. All of them.

Just a scared little thing, the voice said in her ear again. Almost a whisper. *A baby wrapped in iron.*

'No!' Red Marie snapped. *'I'm Red Marie! Red Marie is never scared!'*

The congregation was too stupid for this. It had to be Larksdale. A theatre man, with tricks to change his voice and cruelly throw it. She looked down at him again. Strangely, he was staring not at her eyes or the floor but at her chest plate. He seemed fixated on it.

No one ever loved you, the girl's voice said to Red Marie. *And you'll die alone.*

Red Marie darted around the rear of Larksdale and put a sickle under his chin. Larksdale tensed.

'I'll die in glory!' Red Marie screamed.

'Don't let us stop you,' Larksdale said.

'Who's your friend?' Red Marie demanded of him.

He shrugged. 'No one here.'

I see now, the voice whispered in her ear. *Yes. Strange ways you had. They shunned you. Sent you away.*

'It was just a lynx!' Red Marie bellowed. *'I just wanted to see its babies, Father!'* The congregation stared at her. *'I'll kill you!'* she yelled. *'Show yourself!'*

Show yourself, the girl's voice said. *Step out your shell, you scoundrel.*

'I'm Red Marie! It's I who rule here! Show yourself!'

One of the congregation stepped out into the central aisle. They were hooded, cloaked. They walked forward.

Scared, you are, the voice said. *Always and for ever.*

'Show me your face!' Red Marie bellowed.

S'why you scare others. I should have seen that from the start.

'Show me!'

The figure dropped the hood. It threw off the cloak.

The mountain mother. From the inn.

Red Marie laughed. *'You've no tongue. I took it. You're nothing.'*

You're less, the voice said.

The girl-voice screamed in Red Marie's ears. It filled the inside of her helm, vibrated her mask. Or seemed like it did. The mountain mother's lips never moved.

Trickery. There was no sound, none. These bitch-mothers and their tricks. She had to concentrate. She was better than this tongueless crone, better than all these creatures. She pushed her mind back at the endless scream filling her world.

A woman in a red hat charged out of the congregation, a hooked sword in both hands, raised above her head. She swung at Red Marie.

Red Marie parried the sword easily, though the scream still echoed through her mind. She took her other sickle away from Larksdale's neck and readied to puncture the red-hat's chest.

A pull on her torso. A feeling like one's ear popping but with her entire body. The scream had stopped but the timbre of the whole church had changed.

Red Marie looked down.

Larksdale was still on his knees but was looking up at her. He had something thin and metallic in his fist.

'How could I resist?' he said.

Commrach steel. A strip, a rib-piece from her hinter-suit, a piece of torn leather hanging from it. It was the rib the knife had slid under, that the Explainer had fixed. Along its length, written in the human language by an imbuing commrach finger, it said:

PULL HERE!

The Explainer…

No.

Red Marie could feel the curse. Actually feel it. A cresting wave with teeth.

'*Daddy,*' Hoom muttered in commrach.

The wall behind her roared. Splinters and dust engulfed her. Everyone was running.

It burst from her chest before she felt it tear through her spine. A ram, a great length of dark and polished oak, smooth and round and wet with the sea.

She was lifted from the ground, rising, like a saint in the humans' stories, into the heavens. She stopped a few feet above the floor. The smooth pole that skewered her juddered and she shook. It stopped moving.

This wasn't happening. It wasn't.

She forced a little imbuing into her helm. Her mask with its wooden face and rusty fangs dropped to the floor below. The air was heavy with sea salt. Then hottest puke filled her mouth and nose.

Blood. Blood with all kinds of bits in, bubbling at her chin and running down her front, rolling over the pole and raining down upon the dead church's floor.

No. This wasn't happening. She'd a destiny. She was meant to… to vibrate.

No.

The green man stared at Hoom. Hoom wanted him to make it not so. Because it wasn't. It couldn't. Not right. Red Marie was meant…

Meant to have a point.

53

Larksdale

She was dead, all right: she'd a bowsprit through her chest. At least Larksdale thought that was the term for it. This particular bowsprit, as with the majority of bowsprits, was attached to the front of a sailing ship.

A big one. The ship had, as far as ol' Harry Larksdale could see, just smashed through the end wall of the church. Likely carried on a wave in the storm which, quite noticeably, was abating with preternatural speed.

The church floor was a mass of splinters, broken glass, dust, sea water and stunned souls. Larksdale himself was covered in pieces of wood and dust, all of it adhering to his fresh coat of green.

A bearded man clambered on to the ship's forecastle, gripping his wide-brimmed and rakish hat as if the storm were still raging.

'Oh thank you, Holy Pilgrim!' he shouted to the church ceiling. 'Thank you, sweet lord! Alive! *Alive!*' He leaned against the railing and sobbed. Only then did he take in the hundreds of people looking at the ship.

'Welcome ashore,' Larksdale said. He wasn't certain what else to say. This was the work of the curse. What else could it be? He had known the suit had protected Red Marie, or Red Marie's actor, from the curse's powers, though how the suit did so was beyond understanding. Red Marie had been able to proclaim the keep-within's existence anywhere she had wanted – she had done so at the camp that first time Larksdale encountered her – without fear of a monstrous and absurd death. Until now.

He still held the strip of steel in his fist. Fine commrach material like Sister Ruradoola's knife. But the hastily scrawled message upon it was artless indeed. *Pull Here!* For a moment he had believed it some double-bluff of Red Marie, but then he had recalled his fellows in the keep when he was a boy, how they had written *Kick Me* on his back. Similarly, Red Marie could not have seen the message on her own armour. A wretched trick, all told. But every soul in Becken would be thankful.

Red Marie's true face hung exposed. Ghastly pale, the eyes wide and golden-green as no human's ever were. Dark gore ran from the nose and mouth, glittering with silver motes that were already in the process of fading. He had read somewhere that the blood of the isle-folk glittered. It was the power behind their sorcerous touch.

He had killed this commrach in the most roundabout way. He had likely killed Dulenci in just such a convoluted style. Perhaps he *had* murdered Tibald Slyke like his accusers were saying, he just could not see the obscure and multiple bonds. Was he some puppet? Some tool of the keep's curse? How very utter.

Larksdale wondered about the individual behind the savage and fallen mask. The commrach's finest, no doubt, given their wondrous armour. An aristocrat of one of their gleaming towers.

'Kill the fackin' witch!' Smones shouted.

The Hooksies were getting to their feet, their sallow faces masks of shock and bewilderment at their dead god.

'Do it!' Smones yelled, threatening the Hooksies with Cabbot's cane. 'Kill!'

Many among the parishioners threw back their hoods and pulled out knives and clubs. Larksdale recognised some of their faces from Fleawater camp.

'Stay your hands, friends!' Larksdale shouted. 'Our opponents mean no harm.'

The Fleawater folk could see that was true enough. The Hooksies were bereft, open-mouthed and out of sorts. One or two of them were rather smiling at Red Marie's corpse.

'Friends!' Larksdale announced to the hall, his arms wide. 'Are we not all this city's damned? The disdained and overlooked in our own separate ways? The outsiders…' He gestured at the large spineman who had once threatened him. 'The downtrodden.' He pointed and smiled at the closest Hooksie. 'In that, at least, can we not be brothers?'

Everyone looked at one another. Weapons were being sheathed.

'Thank you, friends,' Larksdale said. 'You came for me. Risked your very lives.' His heart was fit to burst. He looked at Smones. 'Do you see now? Hmm?'

Smones glared at him. Larksdale grinned back.

'Ah, fack this,' Knucklebones Smones said. He shook his head at Larksdale, tossed the black cane on the floor and sauntered out of the church. No one stopped him.

Been looking for you, son, said a little girl's voice in his left ear.

Larksdale looked around but could see no child on stilts.

'Did anyone…' He stopped speaking. This was exactly what Red Marie had been doing before her demise. Hearing voices.

I'm the crone on the floor, the child's voice said.

Larksdale kept a wide grin for all the onlookers. Ah, there was indeed an old woman lying on her side in the church aisle, two fleas kneeling over her. Larksdale wandered over.

'Are you well, my lady?' he asked her.

I've no tongue, lad, the child's voice said in his ear. The woman, her face full of piercings and her braids a greying flame, opened her mouth to reveal a reddened stump. *Aside from that I've never been happier.*

'She's speaking to him,' one of the Fleawater folks kneeling over her, a young woman, said to the others. 'She's a mountain mother, sir. She's come to take the black crown, she has.'

Witchcraft and madness. Larksdale felt at home with both this night.

You know a Cutbill? the little girl's voice said. It had not got any less disconcerting.

'Willem?' Larksdale replied. 'Captain of the city guard. A dependable sort, if gruff.'

He means to destroy this world.

'Hmm,' Larksdale said. 'I guess you never can tell. Can you be certain, ma'am?'

He told me. After he killed a man – Dulenci – and thought I'd soon be dead too. The Fleawater folk helped her to her feet.

Dulenci murdered by Cutbill. Larksdale would have been agog if he hadn't thought he'd killed him already.

The mountain mother looked worn out, drained. *He knows the black crown was left in the pond by poor Gethwen. We have to get to the keep, man. Before midnight.*

She tottered to one side and her friends held her. She indicated she was fine.

'How does this crown work?' he asked her. 'Who is to be coronated?'

No crown. A knocker. For a door.

Larksdale had seen the keep-within but twice in his life, once on a young man's dare and once so as to procure a pot of slather from the commrach Explainer. He could picture the circular bronze door well enough, just below the window slit. As memory served, there had been an embossed bump at the very centre. Could that house a door-knocker? What was it Ruradoola had said: only a mortal hand could wield it. To what end? A knock?

Larksdale looked about the hall. 'Friends!' He called out. 'Ever wanted to visit the royal keep of Becken? I'm a theatre man and tonight I need a troupe. Our king commands a play and, besides that, the world needs saving.'

No one cheered. For a moment he thought himself a fool, but then he realised no one in this hall was the sort to cheer. They were not buoyed by flag or nation, rather they were wholly unchained: they'd nothing to lose. There was a shared strength inside this broken church, of a kind invisible to him but days ago.

'Green suits you, boss.'

He turned to see Boathook Marla, a strange curved blade hanging from her right fist.

'Marla!' He embraced her. 'You tried to save me.'

'S'all right, me duck.'

'I don't think I'll be going to Hoxham any time soon, my dear friend.'

'I got that impression, boss.'

'Harry,' he insisted. Why had he let her call him 'boss' all these years? 'So… what was the plan?'

Marla shrugged. 'Just, you know, smack the monster around until she stopped.'

'Really? No attempt to make contact with me before? A wink or secret message or something of that nature? Some ruse like that?'

'You're the ideas man, Harry.' She shook her head. 'Fuck's sake.'

'No, no, I'm not complaining. All's well, after all.' He grinned. In truth he was sheepishly grateful for his unknown ally with their *Pull!* instruction. 'I'm proud of you, Marla. Truly.'

'Excuse me,' a man's voice called out. It was the bearded ship's captain, still up on his forecastle, rope in hand. 'Could someone tie this to something? I think she's fair lodged but best to be safe, eh?'

'I have you,' Marla said. She walked closer and Larksdale followed.

The sailor threw down the rope and Marla began tying it to a wooden pillar.

'What is this ship?' Larksdale asked the captain.

'*The Flagrant Bess,*' the captain replied. 'A merchant cog.'

That name! Joy sparked in Larksdale's breast. 'Sir, might I ask what's in your hold?'

'Mustard,' the captain replied, a spark of pride in his tone. 'Naught but mustard, sir. Tonnes o' the stuff.'

'Really?' Marla asked, beaming. 'Y'know, you can't get that anywhere right now. Not for love nor money.'

Larksdale looked at the ship a moment, with its speared commrach offering at the front and its torn and sagging sails. He grinned like a loon.

54

Carmotta

She closed her eyes and pictured the dock of Sant Ribot. The quay.

She had never waited for a man before. She had never waited for anything.

It had seemed to her then that an undiscovered island awaited, though, in truth, she and Harry would set sail for Ralbride or Talonshire or wherever the first passage would take them. It mattered not. They would craft such a place from whatever raw clay they found. She was where she needed to be with Harry Larksdale beside her and her him.

And so she had waited in her most ordinary of dresses, which she had believed humble until it drew the eyes of arriving sailors. She had ignored them, picturing her future, a life making things with her hands. She wanted callouses, like the gardeners had. She imagined Harry's face when he arrived, his smile, his delight when he saw the bowl in her bag.

For he had made it with his fingers only the day before and she had decorated it straight from the kiln. She had not let him see her brushwork, nor her choice of subject matter. They had had to return to the estate before it might be taken out of the kiln.

The sun rose higher. Another ship arrived. She fancied this would be their ship. Two disembarking sailors eyed her. They told her good day and she nodded and they asked her how much and she asked what they meant. When they laughed she asked again and one announced she was a tease. Other sailors gathered.

Harry, she had thought. *Harry will be here soon.* He had a way with men, Harry Larksdale, for putting them at ease with words. This moment, she could see, was the first test of her new life. She had known it would have its difficulties. She would endure.

Men were saying dirty things about her body, about what they would do. Some of the things she did not understand.

Please, she had said, still smiling. *Leave me to myself, good sirs.*

Men laughed. They passed a green bottle. They had laughed at her.

A hand groped her buttock. She screamed. She punched the man to the floor, like father had taught. Then all the man's friends were shouting, some picking him up, his mouth bloody, others pushing her shoulders, slapping the back of her head until her high hair came loose. The world had claws and it hated her. She screamed and held her forearms up and they took mocking fists. Someone grabbed her elbow and dragged her away and she screamed and yelled the more. Bodies colliding, men fighting each other now. She fought against her abductor, but he and his new accomplice were too strong. They dragged her through a doorway. Into the dark.

They locked the door and she fell upon cold tiles. The men outside were kicking at the door, shaking the blinds that blocked the windows. She braced for the worst, for the things commoners did to women when they lost control. A hand gripped her shoulder and she yelled again. She stopped when she saw the hand was a woman's. An old woman shushed Carmotta, told her to be calm. That she was safe.

The siege lasted an hour, the men throwing clay bottles at the house. She shook the whole time. Yet true terror seized her when she heard a horn blare. Father's men, with their crossbows and swords. Eight sailors lay dead by evening. Eight souls. Save for those who saved her, every man in Sant Ribot was flogged. Harry Larksdale, she discovered months later, halfway through her confinement to her chambers, had taken canal-barge to Becken the morning of the incident.

I never told anyone, Larksdale. I was true to you, even then. But the years passed. I can be a fool no longer.

She ceased her false prayers. Her arms fell to her sides and her hands balled to fists. She was sufficiently angry for the task ahead.

Her chief handmaid, Lucine, took this as a sign Carmotta was ready to leave the quiet hallway and enter the throne room. She told the two footmen to open the doors.

A horn sounded and a footman announced her.

One could have held a jousting tourney inside the primary throne room; the brasher kings of the Brintland occasionally had. The place was a forest of curling pillars rising to a vaulted ceiling so high it would have been drowned in darkness if not for all the gold leaf. There were no windows save one, vast and round and all of stained glass, its subject St Neyes with his crown and furrowed brow. It hung like a harvest moon above the true throne, a bronze marvel dappled with precious stones and set upon a dais. The thrones of the queens seemed to grow from its magnificence, each taking lower places on the dais steps.

Ean was already sitting, an earthly simulacrum of the stained-glass king above. For a half moment, as she glided down the aisle watched by every courtier and page and footman, she felt as though Ean's sheer presence might burn her belly, eviscerate her bastard with holiest flames of truth.

People bowed and curtsied as she passed. Solemnly, in deference to the black of her dress. *My sweet Dulenci, how much easier this walk would be with you beside me.*

She curtsied before the true throne and made her way up to the highest throne a queen could sit upon. Ean turned and smiled. He took her hand.

'My love,' he said.

'My love,' she replied. She was grateful for his kind smile. She only had Ean now.

Queen Emmabelle approached, her own handmaids in tow. She still had that gaudy little crown tied above her belly, above her bastard. She passed Count Osrin, whom Carmotta had somehow missed earlier. If he and Emmabelle had heard about the murdered Perfecti in Fleawater, neither showed sign of it.

Carmotta looked for Sir Willem Cutbill. She found him on the opposite side of the aisle to Osrin. He had never fitted in with the rest of the court, Cutbill. Something in his poise as if he were for ever observing a battlefield. This night he was particularly luminous.

Emmabelle curtsied to Ean and made her way up the dais, assisted by a handmaid.

'My deepest condolences,' she told Carmotta and extended a dainty hand.

Carmotta took it. 'Thank you, my sister.'

Emmabelle smiled at Ean and then, quite brazenly, took the throne of the second-queen.

The bitch had no right to that seat: it belonged to poor Violee, though mad and vanished. Carmotta wondered whether Violee's disappearance was Emmabelle's doing. Killing a mad innocent for the sake of vanity? Perfectly Emmabelle. So too the one-eyed man in Carmotta's chamber. All redolent of Emmabelle's crude intrigues. No matter. By midnight she would be gone.

The high steward read out a list of honours and prizes. Few matters of import ever took place on these occasions. But, just occasionally, in those moments of high drama that only happened once or twice a century, they did.

She had to maintain her fury. Fury kept tempered minds sharp. She thought of Larksdale again, of Sant Ribot. They were not those same two creatures any more and never could be again, not with the realities she had weathered and he… he had weathered too. The ideals of that young man must have choked long ago, pimping for a king.

What had it even been, this thing between them? It had not been carnal. That was the uncanny part. Back at Grand Gardens days earlier he had stolen a glance at her breasts, which men did all the damned time of course, but from him it felt like a betrayal. But in truth? Once, when Ean did not call for her and Dulenci dared not risk visiting, it had been Larksdale she had imagined above her in the dark, a fantasy she had found flesh-creeping afterward. Whatever had been between them that lost day had decayed, had normalised itself into ordinary hate and occasional lust. It was all that remained.

Something so fragile was gone from the world. She could feel it, in her body. It never even had a name. A tear ran down her cheek that should have been for Dulenci.

Those hundreds watching must have thought so. Each noble brow and styled head had a hand of night above it. Carmotta had never seen so many. Up here on the dais it was unmissable. The trouble with being able to see hell's hands was that you soon got used to them.

Ean arose and addressed the throng. She could barely concentrate. At one point he spoke kind words of Dulenci, genuine words, and if she had heard them she would have appreciated their honesty and taste. She loved Ean, she really did. But in her trepidation of the coming moment she couldn't take him in.

'Now,' he said, 'our fellows, our friends.' This was it. 'As is custom, who among you would bring matters or grievance to us on this, the last night of the year?'

Cutbill made a step but an old lady swung herself out into the centre of the aisle.

'Pardon my son Harry, Your Majesty!' she demanded. 'Stem a mother's tears!'

This was Lady Larksdale. Carmotta had never seen her before.

'He must answer to the charges, good woman,' Ean told her. 'He is wanted for the murder of Sir Tibald Slyke.'

'He's a good boy really,' the lady tried. 'Ever so polite.'

Osrin and his gang sniggered to hear it. Others looked askance.

'Lady Larksdale,' Ean said, 'we cannot pardon your son.'

'Your father would have,' Lady Larksdale protested. 'He had gumption.' The court drew breath. 'I'm just saying what you're all thinking.'

Carmotta touched Ean's hand.

'Forgive her, my love,' she said, desperate to put her ploy to work. She looked to Larksdale's mother. 'My lady, I will visit your chambers tomorrow. We can discuss your frustrations there.'

Lady Larksdale appeared uncertain. 'Could we, er, make that your chambers? My room is… in a lacklustre state.'

'Of course.' Anything to make the woman sit down, which happily she did.

Carmotta gave Cutbill a look.

He stepped out into the aisle and dropped to one knee.

'Your Majesty,' he said. He pulled out the parchment. 'May I read something I've prepared?'

Ean gave the court a smile. *Let's indulge yet another character,* it seemed to say. 'Of course, Sir Willem.'

'Count Osrin…' Cutbill faltered. Osrin's eyes widened. 'Last night, Baptismas Night, Count Osrin led a sortie of men into the camp of our fair city's spinefolk, in Fleawater beside the River Flume. There… there his men did slaughter a Perfecti of the True Church, a Sister Ruradoola.' Whispers filled the air. 'Her body was defiled and thrown into the river. My king, Your Majesty, defender of the Brintland and this great city: such vileness cannot stand.' He got to his feet. 'It cannot stand. Count Osrin must—'

'It was *your* men!' Osrin shouted. 'Not mine! Your animals! I gave no order for…' He trailed off. He looked to Ean. 'Please, brother. Let's not ruin this night, eh?'

Ean arose. He took a step down the granite dais. 'We are aware of this travesty,' he said. 'It pains us and—'

'Your Majesty,' Osrin cut in. He stepped out and walked down the aisle to the base of the dais. 'I would see the new year in with you, see the play till its end. Let this ugly business be for the new year, my king. I beg you.'

'My husband,' Emmabelle said, 'let him see the play. We can give our loyal count that much, surely?'

What's with this play? Carmotta thought. *Why this obsession with peasant entertainments?* Emmabelle was giving a game away. These two had something planned for midnight too.

'My husband,' Carmotta said, standing up. She had not even thought what to say. 'With all love to our dear Count Osrin—' She made a show of taking a deep breath. '—the blood of a Perfecti, a priestess touched by the powers of our very lord—' She made the sign of the Pilgrim. '—cannot be put to one side.'

'Indeed,' Ean said. He looked bemused by so many opinions flying around him.

'No!' Osrin snapped. 'I mean, *yes*, of course, but…' The V-shaped scar that ran from chin to cheeks buckled with frustration. 'Please, Your Majesty,' he said, lifting both arms in supplication, 'give me the honour of sitting beside you as midnight chimes. Then, tomorrow, right after…' Yes, Osrin had plans for midnight and now he floundered to make it happen. Nothing would keep him from the keep's great hollow. Was it not he who had convinced Ean to hold the folk-play there? '…I will lead the investigation! I will find the men who killed that holy creature and I will take righteous pleasure in hanging their—'

'Shut up!' Cutbill bellowed and the whole court drew breath. 'It was you, Osrin! You led my men that night!' He stormed down the aisle and glowered at the count. '*You* made them animals! You care nothing for that Perfecti. You care nothing for anyone!'

Osrin looked to Ean. 'I think he's having one of his scenes.' He looked back at Cutbill. 'Lay off the culoo, good chap.'

Cutbill lifted a meaty fist and Osrin stepped back, half drawing his sword and grinning. No false blades tonight, not at the final court. Tradition demanded so.

'You're too old, you lummox,' Osrin said. 'Walk away.'

Cutbill stepped forward.

'Stop this!' Ean commanded the pair. 'Throw down your blades.'

Both men undid their scabbards and threw them to the floor, neither breaking eye contact with the other.

'How about now, boy?' Cutbill said, raising his fists once more.

'Gentlemen,' Carmotta said, stepping halfway down the dais, ahead of Ean. 'No violence.' She had to control this, bring it all to her victory. She looked to her husband. 'A private meeting, perhaps?'

Ean nodded. He looked down on the two men. 'A sorry scene, gentlemen. It shall not be played out before the true throne.' He looked to the hundreds watching and announced, 'Please friends, remain here while we oversee this matter of state. Wine shall be served. We look forward to seeing you all within the hour for our play.'

Two footmen blared their horns. Ean pointed at four guards to accompany him, then gestured for Osrin and Cutbill to follow. Carmotta, excited, proud, followed him toward the north-east door.

Her three handmaids were behind her, of course. She turned her head to give them leave then noticed Emmabelle was also in tow with her own three handmaids behind her.

Fine. Carmotta would keep hers.

'To our solus chamber,' Ean said. Two guards marched ahead of him while the second two waited for the rest of the procession to pass.

And it *was* a procession now, fifteen in all. Everyone made their way up four flights of stairs.

'I do not think we will all fit in your solus chamber,' Carmotta called to Ean between panting breaths. When Ean stopped, turned around and stared at everyone in disbelief, she added, 'It is some distance.'

'What are you all doing here?' he asked the two queens. 'This is between these two men and I.'

'My love,' Carmotta answered, 'the meeting was my idea. I assumed you required my presence.'

'I, the mother of your child,' Emmabelle said, 'cannot be from you this Yulenight Eve.'

Bloody woman. Carmotta sensed her own handmaids behind her, fuming at their opposite numbers, those blonde nobodies of shitting Duxby.

'I don't mind, Your Majesty,' Cutbill said. He eyed Carmotta.

'A woman's presence,' Osrin replied, looking at Emmabelle, 'may stay our hands from anger.'

'Fine, then,' Ean said, shaking his head. 'But the handmaids may leave.'

'They've come this far,' Emmabelle said.

'True, my sister wife,' Carmotta added, not to be outmatched.

King Ean stared at his wives a moment then bowed mockingly. 'Well, we cannot talk on the stairs all night.' He frowned. 'Where are we going anyhow?'

'Perhaps the hunter's lounge, sire,' Cutbill said. 'On the floor just above.'

'There's chairs and tables and such,' Osrin said.

'Very well,' Ean replied. He gestured at Cutbill to lead the way.

Cutbill did so and it was not long before they were proceeding down a very long corridor indeed, the many iron chandeliers above casting sickly cones of yellow.

'We've taken the wrong way,' Osrin said.

'Not at all,' Cutbill replied. He stopped and announced, 'Nosford Vale.'

The two guards in front turned about and readied their halberds. Ean almost walked into them. Carmotta turned to see the two guards at the rear of the procession had hefted their halberds too.

Osrin cursed. His blade lay back in the throne room.

'Sir Willem,' Ean said, 'stop this.'

Cutbill shook his head.

What is happening? Carmotta thought. *He's played me like a fool, this soldier, this simple man.*

Osrin stepped forward, standing beside the king. 'Fancy yourself lord governor, Cutbill? This is the Brintland, sir. We'll have none of it.'

'I want none of it,' Cutbill said. 'Not a crumb.' He stepped over to a heavy door and turned the key in its lock. He pushed the door open. The room beyond was silver with moonlight, the shadows of window frames stretching thin across the pine floor. 'But I will not kill our king, despite everything. Get in there. The lot of you.'

Everyone did, though Osrin had to be bundled in by Cutbill and a guard.

Standing in the hallway, Cutbill drew the door ajar.

'Can I just say,' he told his hostages, 'that you are the worst people I've ever known. Truly. And I've been shield-to-shield with men who tried to kill me.'

'Willem,' Carmotta tried, 'this is your king.'

'Who's been begging the Church for a divorce,' Cutbill said and he pointed at her. 'Because, quote, "only death comes from her womb".'

'Liar,' she said. Because he must be.

'You're no good to him,' Cutbill said. 'She is.' He pointed at Emmabelle. 'And this fool—' He pointed at Osrin. '—has been plotting with the sprites in the bay. They want the whole mainland aflame and he's willing to oblige. If it gets him the throne.' He shrugged. 'I don't know the details. Oh, and Your Majesty?'

'Yes?' Ean said, dazed.

'Queen Carmotta's womb's no wasteland. Dulenci put his seed in her. He told me as much as he begged for his life.'

'Bastard!' Carmotta shouted, glaring at him. She hadn't the courage to look at anyone else.

'I'm locking the door,' Cutbill told everyone. 'These here four guards will be outside. This room is the storage and display room next to the hunter's lounge. Those quicker among you may have noticed its walls are covered in weapons.' He grinned. 'Happy new year.'

The door slammed shut.

55

Mother Fwych

They had been walking an hour, and where Mother Fwych had thought they would lose many of their number, the crowd had only grown. This horde of the lost, of the hopeless and weak, had caught the eye of the street, of those beggars, thieves and bastards who hung about the alleys before midnight, the city being full of yulenight revellers eager to get out after the sudden death of the storm. They didn't know the purpose of this march, but they knew its end had to be something. It was heading for the keep.

We should have been stopped by now, she thought. She were braced for a fight. One of the wandering sort had given her a short sword she now hid under her city guard's cloak. Mother Fwych could only think no one stopped them because no one knew exactly what they were. The fine-sorts watching could only believe that somewhere some lord of the keep had permitted all this. That someone were in control.

Looking at him stride just ahead of her, she wondered if this Larksdale had known that would happen. Eager the whole way, Larksdale, as if he saw every step. Fwych would not be so keen to follow if her visions hadn't shown her him.

The crowd reached the keep's outer wall and turned right,

heading for the east gate where the shrine in the pond were closest. Fwych doubted they'd find the black crown before Cutbill, not this late, but she was braced for a fight should it happen. A good place to kill and die, a shrine. But for the life of her she was not sure how they would reach there. The halls of the mighty were never easy to enter.

'There's another crowd ahead,' the girl Marla said to Larksdale. 'At the gates.'

'This has turned out better than I could have hoped!' Larksdale said. 'Exactly the people we're aiming to impersonate: the Wreath's men. Good Pilgrim, I've missed 'em.'

The rear of this new crowd stared at the approaching mob. They were dressed little better, though many had made a daft show of colour and lace. They were carrying stuff too, wooden poles and cloth and the like.

'Who are you?' one of them asked.

'Extras,' Larksdale said, never stopping. He started to slide between the people before him.

Marla were waving to everyone behind to stop and wait. Fwych decided to follow the leader, so to speak. She snaked through this new bunch in their bright tights and nasty perfumes.

'Where's Tichborne?' Larksdale asked people as he passed, but they merely stared in shock.

'That Harry?' one muttered to another as Mother Fwych passed.

The gatehouse's big doors were open and guards were blocking entry to the gardens beyond. A frail-looking woman with high hair was trying to convince them to let everyone enter.

'We're late as is,' she said to the guard with the tallest helmet. 'His Majesty the king expects us.'

'We're awaiting confirmation, ma'am,' the guard said. 'My fellow will return soon.'

'This is ridiculous.' The woman gestured at the crowd behind her. 'What, you think we're all rogues impersonating a troupe?'

'Hardly likely,' Larksdale said and he placed a hand on the woman's shoulder. 'Arriet.'

This woman, Arriet, almost said his name aloud but checked herself. Her eyes widened when she saw her 'troupe' had trebled in number.

'The gang's all here,' Larksdale said.

Six guards before them. One more up on the gatehouse wall above, stood beside a great iron horn.

Fwych looked up, commanded the slaughtered girl appear next to him and bade her whisper, *Sleep*.

The guard collapsed out of view behind his wall.

'Why are you painted all over?' Arriet was asking Larksdale.

'Why, I'm Dickie o' the Green,' Larksdale said.

'No you are *fucking* not,' an angry man in green tights and doublet said. One of the troupe. Beside him another man in green nodded with fury.

'I'm an understudy,' Larksdale told them both. 'Fear not, your Dickies are sacrosanct.' He looked to Arriet. 'Where's Tichborne?'

'Oh, Harry,' she said.

Fwych hadn't the time to listen. She looked at all six guards and made slaughtered women stand beside them. Fwych felt her ankles go weak, the power getting harder to call upon. The living body weren't made for such.

'Oh, Harry,' Arriet were saying again.

'It's fine,' he said, snorting back a sadness. 'He would want us to proceed.' He nodded. Then stepped up to the feathered guard. 'Let us through now, Captain.'

'I've already explained—'

'I'm Sir Harrance Larksdale. Do I really have to mention you to the king, hmm?'

'Larksdale?' Captain made a gesture and the five guards levelled their spear-things. 'You're wanted for murder. Sir.'

Mother Fwych readied her powers. The guards were too focused to be ordered to sleep. She would have to tell them to think themselves aflame.

'What?' Larksdale said. '*That?*' He laughed and shook his head. 'Keep up, Captain. A minor tiff, all done and dusted.'

'You're the most wanted man in Becken,' Captain insisted.

'God's sake, man!' Larksdale snapped. 'Would the most wanted man in Becken walk up to the keep and demand to be let through? Use the brain God – or whoever he hired that day – gave you. My brother the king awaits my play, you tiresome fellow.'

Captain looked uncertain. He waved at his pals and they lifted their spears and stepped back.

'Thank you,' Larksdale said to Captain. 'And apologies. I get quite tetchy before a performance.'

'Quite all right sir,' Captain said. 'Let's not mention this to His Majesty, sir, if I may ask.'

'Quite, quite.'

The crowds started making their way through the gates.

Breaths were drawn all round, like rain pattering, again and again. These people of the city had never stood on the lawns of the keep, had never seen the horror and the glory, not from top to bottom like now.

No time for staring, she told herself. She traipsed across the wet lawn to a spot where the brass smoothness that were the great ring peeked out. She closed her eyes and slammed her boot down upon it.

The great ring met her, its whirl of memory and anguish surrounding her mind. She reached her spirit out and flew over the keep's grounds like a bird.

The pond beneath the trees were gone, now it were all mud and puddle, dead fish and streaks of weed. The statue at the pond's centre, with its two men carved from white stone, had half-toppled in the filth.

Cutbill, Fwych thought, *bastard bugger Cutbill has the crown.* She spread her spirit further. He was up there in the keep, halfway up, perhaps. Hard to tell. *Once inside I'll know,* she thought. *Then I'll have you, scoundrel.*

A body bumped into her and she were stood upon the grass once more. One of the Hooksies had broken her concentration. A dwarf.

'Sorry, me lady,' the dwarf said, his eyes barely brave enough to meet hers. 'They're leading us inside.'

It were true. The mob were being led along a pathway to the keep, their numbers funnelled by the lit braziers that lined their journey.

She felt weak again, dead on her feet. She nodded thanks at the little man then ran, well, half-ran, across the grass, heading off Larksdale at the head of the column.

There were a man striding just ahead of Larksdale, all full of himself and wearing feathered hat and bright pantaloons. Two other men followed with lamps on sticks. *Keep men,* Mother Fwych told herself, *the bowing kind.*

She met up with Larksdale and Marla and the woman Arriet. She slowed and walked the path with them.

Ahead loomed a great doorway into the keep. *The keep's wide mouth,* she thought, *its insides a furnace of yellow.* They crossed under the arch, five men high, and she saw a hundred beasts shaped from the stone – deer and dogs and creatures that were half one beast, half another. The people around her slowed a little to look up and slowed the more when they entered the hall beyond. Even though she'd been in other parts of the keep before, this were different. Fwych had never seen the like, not outside of Father Mountain's Belly, and this were all wrought by the hand of man, not gods. The ceiling were as the base of great trees, thirty trees or more, their grey stone roots intermingling. She had sat in high trees in valley forests before and looked down and this were exactly that but upside down and made of granite or the like. She felt dizzy, as if she might fall up and smash her bones against those grey roots. The dizziness did not leave her as she looked down at the walls all about. This place were but an entrance and yet it were greater, far greater, than any hall of the mountains she had seen. There were no reason to build such a room, with its stairways wider than four ox carts and its tapestries the size of a house wall.

Larksdale reached the centre of the room and waved at everyone to gather around him.

'Friends, here we are!' he shouted. 'The plays are performed in this very hall where we now stand and the four stairways there—' He gestured behind him. '—are where the court shall place their cushions and watch. I dare say good King Ean shall take his usual seat just there.' He pointed to one of the lower steps on the second right staircase.

We must move, Mother Fwych sent to him and the slaughtered girl floated beside his ear. *Cutbill has the black crown. I need to track him.*

The man in the feathered hat and pantaloons stepped through the crowd now surrounding Larksdale. A guard, one of four in the hall, followed uncertainly.

'Sir,' Pantaloon said, 'let's not dally.' He eyed the crowd with scorn, though his smile kept rigid as slate.

'This is where we perform,' Larksdale told him.

'Not this night,' Pantaloon said. 'His Majesty requires you perform somewhere far more evocative.'

'How so?'

'The keep's hollow,' Pantaloon said, his grin growing a-sudden. 'He would see you perform before the very—'

Larksdale punched him square in the face. Pantaloon dropped. Larksdale stamped on the man's face. Again and again.

The hall froze. The screams and yells began.

'I had to,' Larksdale said. He had never killed before, he had that look. 'I had no choice!'

'Why?' Arriet shouted, terrified.

'I'd rather not discuss it.'

People stumbled aside as the guard rushed at Larksdale. His eye burst with blood and he stopped running. He dropped his spear and stood quite still.

Marla had swung something into the guard's face. A sword with a hooked tip and a long wooden hilt, like the clawswords of home. Marla stared at her handiwork, startled by the guard not dropping to his arse there and then.

'Boathook Marla,' Larksdale muttered like a soul in a dream.

'Not a boathook,' Marla said, staring at the guard. He was still on his feet, his mouth making weird breathing shapes like a fish on a riverbank. 'A panabas. Sword from my dad's land.' She roared then, let out her fear and panic. 'I *hate* that nickname.'

'My apologies,' Larksdale said. 'I did not know.'

Guards were rushing down the stairs.

Fwych ran forward, kicked the upright dying guard over, then called upon the slaughtered women.

Burn! she thought, the word coming from her throat in a burble. The guards dropped, all of them rolling down the stairs and yelling.

'Forward!' Larksdale shouted. He belted toward the stairs and the mob followed. 'For Tichborne!'

People shouted the name, though Mother Fwych had barely heard of it and suspected most others hadn't either.

'Larksdale, you monster!' Arriet screamed. 'What's even happening?'

Mother Fwych ran up the stairs, leaped over a shaking guard and ran a second through with her knife.

'Take their halberds!' Marla shouted, pointing at a spear-thing. 'Use 'em!'

So that's what they were called. Fwych picked one up and charged up the stairs. She could feel Cutbill, deep inside the keep.

The hour drew near.

56

Carmotta

'The windows,' Carmotta said, looking at the thin row above, the moon a warped plate of silver in the thick glass. 'We can climb out.'

'Not all of us.' Osrin already had a sword in hand. He stood on the other side of the small room. 'I'll go.'

'No,' Ean said.

'Dear brother,' Osrin said, 'you do not believe Cutbill's lies?'

Ean pulled a halberd off the wall. 'I'm open-minded,' he said.

'It would do him no good to kill you,' Emmabelle said. 'My love.'

'Well, not now,' Carmotta replied. She had opened the lid of a crate beside her in a search of rope. She had found brass cases the length of her forearm with three feathered bolts atop one another inside. A Mancanese invention. She knew their purpose.

'What's she looking at?' one of Emmabelle's handmaids asked her queen.

'Hoof traps for deer, I think,' Carmotta replied. She lifted one up and dropped it back in the case nonchalantly so that none might get a good view in the moonlight. 'Our captors are hoof-less.'

'You've made a cuckold of me, woman,' Ean said bitterly. 'A fool. I should have known you were fucking that stupid cousin of yours.'

'Sweet Dulenci only desired *men*,' Carmotta said, meeting his stare. No easy task, that. She stepped back against the wall. She could feel the crossbow hanging there behind her. Small, a lady's model. If she could put her hand behind her back, she could find what manner of mechanism it possessed. 'Cutbill lies,' she told everyone. 'To set us all killing one another. He thinks that is all we nobles are capable of.'

'Yes!' Osrin said, pointing at Carmotta with his free hand, his short sword low and ready. 'Dulenci – bless his memory – loved no woman. And I could plot no treason. Now we have to work together and escape, then make our retreat to the great hollow by midnight.'

'Wait,' Emmabelle said. 'Aren't some men both?'

'Nonsense,' Carmotta lied. Damn this thick bitch.

'Yes they are,' Emmabelle protested. 'Sir Tibald Slyke said so, just before he died. He was talking about Larksdale, but Dulenci could be a queer and a real man too.' She nodded, as if that settled it.

'She's right,' Ean said.

'She's stupid,' Carmotta protested.

Emmabelle sneered. 'No I'm not. Your Majesty, if we all kill this foreign cow right now you won't need your divorce.'

Carmotta's handmaids seized weapons from the wall, knives and clubs. Emmabelle's did likewise and the two groups of young women faced each other from across the store room.

'Woah, woah,' Ean said. 'Come now.'

Osrin grinned at the sight.

None of the handmaids were eager to attack: each one merely wished to defend her queen. Carmotta took the opportunity to fondle the crossbow hanging upside down behind her. It had no turn crank but it had a gaffe lever fitted to one side. She could work a gaffe well enough but no one could do that behind their back unseen.

'She's made a fool of you, my husband,' Emmabelle said to Ean. 'Do you think a brute like Cutbill has the wit to make up a story?'

'Yes he does,' Osrin said out of the side of his mouth.

Emmabelle frowned at him. 'I know you're working with her.' She nodded at Carmotta.

'What?' Carmotta and Osrin said as one.

'It's in Mancanese.' Emmabelle nodded at her lead handmaid, who produced a piece of vellum she handed nervously to Carmotta. 'Read it out. Translate it.'

Carmotta read the scratchy handwriting aloud.

'"To monarch man. Your loving hedgehog be am. Second letter come. Wait."' This was terrible Mancanese. 'That's all it says,' Carmotta said. 'Aside from a drawing of… an otter? In a wig.'

'The lionfox,' Emmabelle insisted. 'Osrin's crest! In *your* language!' She looked at Ean. 'My handmaids found this ransom note in the south entrance hall. We can trust no one, Ean.'

'Emmabelle, really now,' Osrin pleaded. He remembered Ean was in the room. 'My *queen*, it's but a forgery.'

Ean pointed his halberd toward him.

'Do your conspiracies ever end?' Emmabelle said to Carmotta. 'You fat, meddlesome whore. You've cuckolded poor Ean.'

'Silence!' Ean snapped at her. He stepped up to Carmotta. 'Well? Is it true?' He shook her by the shoulder. 'Is it?'

'Whore?' Carmotta said and she tried to reach the letter beneath her corset. Struggling, furious, she pulled the lacing loose from the upper eyelets. She shoved her hand down and produced the letter. 'You'll recognise the handwriting, Ean.'

Ean snatched it from her hand.

'I have to step into the moonlight,' he said. 'Everyone stand back. Return to starting positions.'

He did so and everyone complied.

Carmotta grabbed the short crossbow from the wall, fitted the gaffe and began to tug with haste. Her bosom was on the verge of falling out but this was no courtly ceremony. This was a pantry of death.

'Whore!' Emmabelle screamed. She fumbled at the wall behind her.

Carmotta looked up to see Emmabelle throwing a quiver over one shoulder and placing an arrow against some small bow of foreign design. Carmotta worked the gaffe faster. The string slid on to the latch and she lifted the small crossbow.

Emmabelle had an arrow aimed at Carmotta.

She laughed. 'You're not even loaded, you cunt.' She eased her bow's string to a resting position, the arrow still notched.

'Easy, you two,' Ean said.

'It's fine, my love,' Emmabelle told him. Her blonde locks glistened as ice in the moonlight. 'The trusty bow of the Brintland shall always prevail.'

'Read on, my darling,' Carmotta beseeched Ean. Of course, the cowardly shit meant to divorce her but right now a most singular diplomacy was needed.

Ean read. Osrin and Emmabelle looked at one another.

They know, Carmotta thought. She grabbed a brass magazine from the crate beside her and fitted it to the already cocked repeating crossbow.

She leaned and pulled the trigger. The first bolt flew past Ean's thigh and pierced Osrin's sword arm at the elbow just as he raised it. Osrin yelled with surprise and pain. His arm was skewered to his thigh.

Every handmaiden screamed.

Emmabelle drew her bow.

'No!' Ean threw himself in front of Carmotta. His back flew into her and then he collapsed to the floor, rolling on to his spine. An arrow stuck out of his forehead.

Carmotta looked at Emmabelle. The young queen's mouth was agape.

She shot her. The bolt struck the top of Emmabelle's huge belly just beneath the little crown. Her bow dropped.

'No.' She gazed down at the bolt shaft. She mewled like a child whose birthday had been forgotten. Blood ran down her bulge. 'No.' She looked to her handmaidens with a pleading look, as if they could make it better. '*No…*'

Carmotta shot her in the face. Emmabelle flew back and knocked more bows from the wall, staggered two steps to her left and collapsed in a heap. Her handmaids screamed.

'Love…' a voice said below. 'Love…'

Ean. Still alive.

'My love.'

Emmabelle had not had the room to draw her bow fully. The arrow had pierced his skull just below his crown, but was only… a half-inch deep? 'Oh, my love.'

She heard Osrin strain.

Carmotta levelled her crossbow at the count. He'd worked his elbow free of his thigh. The bolt still stuck out of his arm.

'Drop the sword,' she ordered. She stood upright.

Osrin did so. He grinned at all the horror around him.

'Might someone see to my wounds?' he asked, nodding at his arm and thigh. 'Rather losing blood here.'

Carmotta nodded. 'Sit on the floor.'

He did so. Carmotta thanked the Pilgrim Osrin did not know how many bolts were in a repeater magazine. She had already loosed the lot.

'Drop your weapons,' she told Emmabelle's handmaidens. But they already had. 'Lucine,' she said to her chief girl, 'tear your sleeve and bind his wound.'

'The king,' Osrin said, looking her up and down and grinning.

'We can both yet save him.'

'You raised your sword against him,' Carmotta said. Never taking her eyes off the vicious bastard, she said to her second handmaid, 'Ginevra, might I ask you to…'

Ginevra did not understand but then saw her queen was no longer in her corset. She got behind Carmotta, rectified her immodesty and began retying the laces at the front.

Carmotta raised her crossbow a little higher, partly to frighten Osrin, partly to help Ginevra.

There was scuffling outside, shouts from the guards.

'Help's coming, Ean,' she told him, her eyes still on Osrin.

A look of anger overcame the count, then a devilish acceptance.

'I know what you are thinking, my queen,' he said. 'That it's best to kill me now.' He breathed deep through his nostrils. 'We're cast of the same iron. Know this: I will not bow and serve another second more. I will not pander to that weak man. That venal, soft-bellied bowl of shit.' He eyed Ean.

So here was Osrin. Fantasising over his own proud and glorious death, unbroken to the last. Crush or be crushed, that was him.

The door flew open.

'Carmotta!' Larksdale's voice. A sliver of joy shot through her. 'Oh, Ean!'

'Arrest this man!' Carmotta said.

To her utter surprise, two ginger, tattooed men soon had knives at Osrin's throat.

Ginevra stepped away from her, her work done. Carmotta lowered her crossbow and turned to face the intruders.

There was another ginger man, hawk-nosed and beardless, his face and jacket covered with dried green paint. Behind him stood a small woman in a red woolly hat. The man dropped to his knees and cradled Ean.

'Larksdale?' Carmotta said.

It *was* Larksdale. What was going on here?

'Where's Cutbill?' the woman with the hat demanded.

'He's gone,' Carmotta replied. 'And I'm your queen, woman.'

'Sorry, me duck. I mean, Your Majesty.'

Larksdale, so strange without his beard, let alone with a fresh coat of gloss, looked up and said, 'Cutbill's going to…' He made a waving gesture with his hand. 'You know where, right? Don't say it.'

Carmotta nodded. His comrades were commoners. They had no evil hands above their heads.

'Bastard,' Larksdale said. He was not talking of Cutbill. He was looking at Ean.

Of course. Larksdale's theatre troupe. By commanding the play be held inside the hollow, Ean had meant to taint them all. No, not meant. He simply had not cared.

'Carry him,' Carmotta said. She would not bear the treacherous fool to die. 'We can carry him to the paternoster, you and me, Larksdale.'

'He has no chance,' Larksdale said.

'The Explainer,' Carmotta insisted. 'He has the skill.'

'No, Carmotta.'

'I am the queen. I am commanding you to help your king!'

'Shit,' Larksdale muttered. 'Right. Fine. Then let the three of us carry him all the way.'

Another figure appeared in the doorway. The ban-hag.

Carmotta thought to reach for a magazine and shoot her. She had slaughtered Dulenci. And yet… she had not. That had been Willem Cutbill.

But the ban-hag *had* seen Carmotta and Dulenci make love. Awkward, that, but it hardly mattered now. Only one regal womb had survived and Ean would have to accept its fruit. If he lived.

'We must move,' she told everyone.

'Lady,' said one of the spinemen, looking to her for orders.

'Stay here and protect these women,' she told them, indicating both gangs of handmaidens. 'As for him—'

'Kill me now,' Osrin snapped. 'I'll only go to the gallows cursing your name!' A spineman slapped him but it only provoked his fire. 'You are a woman. Ean is weak. There will be more men like me, Carmotta. Your days are numbered.'

He was right. The Brintland was ripe with audacious gentlemen, all of them raised to fight or die. Osrin's short life and violent death would be an inspiration.

She looked at the two spinemen. 'Hold him here, friends, until my guards arrive. They shall find the best implement in this well-stocked room and, gently as possible, blind him.'

What? Osrin mouthed.

'You're to spend the rest of your days in an abbey.'

'No. Please. Please, no!'

His face was a delight but she did not savour it. She was not the type.

57

Fwych

More bleeding guards at the end of the hallway. Four of 'em. It never stopped.

Pain, she thought, and the slaughtered women whispered an agony into their ears. The men screamed and dropped, rolling around on the floor.

'Why are these guards screaming so?' Carmotta asked.

'Our friend there speaks directly into people's minds,' Larksdale said, stepping over a man shuddering and pissing his tights. 'It's quite something.'

'Oh,' Carmotta said. She sounded worried. As well she should be. Filthy woman, making a mountain mother watch her goings-on, keeping her in a cage and all. Fwych, by all rights, should push that arrow deep into her husband's head. He were slowing everyone down anyhow.

'She's our greatest weapon,' Larksdale said, panting under Ean's weight. 'I should explain we're having a sort of revolt. I think.'

'I do not like that,' Carmotta said.

'All for a good cause,' he said. 'Funny thing is, it's a little girl's voice.'

'The cause?' Carmotta said as they turned a corner.

'No,' Marla told her, 'her mind's voice. Bloody weird, it is.'

'Love…' the dying king muttered. 'Green fields…'

'He's babbling,' Marla said.

'Mean's he's alive, waif,' the queen snapped.

Fwych wanted to use the voice on Carmotta, scare her, let her know she was no longer in control. But the great circle's powers were not for such pettiness. Instead, Fwych sent *bliss* to the mind of her husband. Least she could do.

'He's wet himself,' Marla said.

They reached the alcoves with the falling and rising boxes, the ones that passed between floors. Must be what the queen meant by pater nostril. Fwych had seen them before and had kept her distance. Right now they were too swift not to use.

The three of them placed the king on the floor.

'Only four of us can get in one of those compartments,' Larksdale said. 'Me and you to carry,' he told Carmotta. 'You to cut through any resistance,' he pointed at Mother Fwych.

'Oi,' Marla said.

'Go,' Larksdale told her. 'You've done more than your share.'

'Fuck you,' Marla said. 'I'm with you to hell.'

'We haven't time for this,' Carmotta said.

Sleep, the slaughtered girl whispered in Marla's ear and she staggered and listed. Larksdale helped her to the floor then dragged her into a nearby doorway.

He looked at Mother Fwych. 'Thank you.'

Fwych nodded back. It were for the best. Likely no one would be coming back up from wherever they were going.

They lifted the dying man into a falling nostril box, all squeezed together.

'Careful not to knock the arrow,' Carmotta said.

'Maybe we should snap the end off,' Larksdale said.

'That's his *brain* in there,' Carmotta said. She looked up at the ceiling.

'What?' Larksdale asked.

'Hundreds of prisoners sweating somewhere up there,' the queen said. 'Just to make these stupid things move.' She drew a breath. 'Go on, Larksdale, say something clever.'

Larksdale sighed. 'I'm out of material.'

Fwych and the rest stepped out of the box into a hot and dripping tunnel of stone.

Something bad were happening down here. People in fancy clothes were swarming down the passageway toward them, running to the other alcove, the one where the boxes went up, filling each compartment and even the spaces in between, pushing each other aside and screaming.

'Come on,' Larksdale said. 'We haven't long.'

'What does Cutbill mean to do?' Carmotta asked him over the yells.

'To open up some hell or other,' he told her as they pushed down the tunnel. 'He has a key to the bronze door, a black crown. He'll use it as the hour strikes midnight.'

'The crown?' Carmotta asked. 'Why?'

'I don't know,' Larksdale said. 'I think he wants to exchange this world for one beyond that door, swap one hell for another.'

'His life has had its fill of pain,' Carmotta said. 'What has he to lose?'

They sped up.

Evil place, this. Fwych were wading through dark powers like they were mud. Were like her soul were choking. She weren't keen to see this bronze door.

Save the world, she told herself. *Not long. Not long at all.*

A guard ran toward them and Fwych went to use the slaughtered voice but when she did her ankles buckled beneath her and she hit the wall with her shoulder. The guard did not attack. He had no weapon. He were running, mad as the rest.

Red veins stretched across the walls and ceiling as they turned a corner. Monstrous. But she saw that they were in the skin of the lanterns, those veins. Just shadows. Ugly and – what were the word? Gethwen had explained it once – a portent.

The mob had passed them by now, the passage were empty. Almost.

A body ahead, on the wet floor. Moving, dragging itself.

'A page,' Larksdale said. 'Good Pilgrim, his back's snapped.'

Larksdale were right. The lad were dragging himself with clawing fingers, legs still as tree roots. Must have been broken in the run to escape. Trodden on.

'We haven't time,' she heard Carmotta say.

The lad looked up. Eyes wide as Gethwen's. Had Gethwen suffered so? Had he? Gethwen, the boy she raised to manhood. Not of her body, sterile as all mountain mothers, but… her son. Should have called him that. Too proud and too mean to call it more than duty. Her son. Her bloody *son*.

The world could wait a moment.

Sleep, she sent to the broken youth. She had used her voice to heal in the past. She weren't sure she had the strength for that now. A sleep would have to do.

The slaughtered girl appeared, stood above the lad.

The walls around Fwych breathed in and out. She could hear dark laughter.

The slaughtered girl did not whisper this time. She stared at Mother Fwych and grinned. Black fingers pushed out of her mouth. Her eyes too, fingers creeping from empty sockets, bony and longer than a hound's tail.

Fwych were on the floor before she knew it, her legs useless. The walls squeezed in and out like a lung, veiny and moist. She screamed and laughter echoed back.

The girl fell upon her. Fwych had no control of her any more. The underground's darkness here had seen to that, hollowing her out, making her its puppet.

Fwych howled. Long fingers drifted over her flesh, disgusting, evil. They drifted into her innards, stirring the meat.

'Guh!' she told Larksdale and Carmotta. 'Guh nah!' She used her own voice, tongueless as it were, used her lips and jaw to say the words. Like Lady Larksdale had told her. 'Guh!'

They hesitated. They could not see the finger-faced girl scratching up her soul. But they heard her meaning. The two of them went on, carrying their king.

'Gufwah,' she said as the slaughtered girl consumed her. Blood poured from her eyes. 'Gufwah. Mah suhh…'

Failed to save this world had Fwych. But she would die a mother. She knew that much.

58

Larksdale

'Do *not* touch his head!'

'I'm trying to stop it from bouncing, woman.'

'Well, don't.'

Larksdale was tempted to drop his bloody king on the floor of the sweltering tunnel. Good riddance. A child taught to stride and monarchise, to puff out his ermine chest. Beneath the crown reigned a banal man of base hungers. *Find me a woman, Harry, throw me a banquet of insipid debauch and maybe – one day – I'll raise you up.* And Larksdale had fallen for it, crawling over glass to please this king, this recipient of favoured birth. All in the hope he might be made Master of Arts and Revels and make the world that little bit finer. Larksdale had sacrificed so bloody much, and none of it his own. Sacrificed women on the altar of Ean's passing desire, had tossed Arriet, talented Arriet, into a hall of swine. How many of his friends, his good loyal friends, would have died in agony merely for Ean's whimsy? Pilgrim's arse! He should drop this bag of tepid flesh and self-regard, let it bleed out all life from its royal crown.

And yet… Larksdale thought, *and yet she loves him. And she cannot carry him alone.*

The air was hot. Ahead of them, where the tunnel turned a corner, the wet stones glowed red then black then red, as light from some living, breathing hearth-fire. Larksdale had never seen the like.

Carmotta slowed.

'You've seen this?' Larksdale asked her.

Somewhere behind her husband's dangling head she nodded. 'The keep-within,' she said. 'It is at its most alive.'

No wonder she had taken his explanations so casually. She had had her own experiences down here. This was real. So very real. Something he had regarded intellectually he now felt in his gut. Powers waited to tear down the curtain of this world.

'I'm with child,' Carmotta said. 'Dulenci's.'

'Turn back,' he told her. 'I can carry Ean.' He could not.

The scarlet light pulsed in the whites of her eyes. 'No.' She sped up once more. 'I merely wished someone to know.'

A thought struck him and he laughed. 'I'd already discovered Dulenci was a breeder, you know. I suspected right from the outset.'

'A fine performance he gave,' Carmotta said. She laughed bitterly.

'Oh too-too laboured. No knocking the commitment, though.'

'Mind his head, man!' Carmotta shouted.

'I'm minding his head!'

The black door stood wide open. The descending staircase beyond flashed from red light to silver. The silver, Larksdale assumed, from those fascinating moontiles the Explainer fashioned with his people's miraculous touch.

The stairs were a nightmare to descend, the steps barely visible and spotted with blood. They spied the source: old Jans the doorman, clutching his side and waddling down the steps. His attackers must have left him for dead.

There was no helping both he and Ean. Trouble was, old Jans was blocking the way. Larksdale and Carmotta soon caught up with him and had to slow down.

'Excuse me,' Larksdale called.

Jans did not notice, absorbed with the task at hand.

'Push him over,' Carmotta told Larksdale.

'No!' The fellow was an old man, dying to boot. Carmotta could be absolutely utter sometimes.

Carmotta booted Jans in the rear, a move that made Larksdale stumble, juddering the arrow in Ean's forehead.

The kick did not topple Jans, rather it put life into the wounded man. Jans broke into a run, cantering down the ramp with singular intent.

A scarred man in guard's helm stepped out from the doorway at the bottom of the stairs and levelled a spear at Jans.

Old Jans drew two daggers hidden in his coat. He parried, knocked the spear's tip to one side, then lanced the man through the throat. Jans gambolled over him as he collapsed.

Life in the old hound... Larksdale thought.

The keep-within was aglow, the gaps between its thorn-shaped stones roaring with a scarlet fury. Figures stood before it. The keep's light would fill the hollow's great cube, daubing the ancient stone and brick scarlet, then would fade, leaving the hollow barely lit with the Explainer's clay moons. Red and black, over and over, the gasping of an unseen god.

Rows of chairs covered the hollow's uneven floor, most of them toppled. The stampede had begun here. Larksdale saw a lady's shoe, a lord's hat. On one of the upright chairs sat the Explainer, watching the keep-within and the figures around it with some manner of spyglass.

'Come on,' Carmotta said, and they made their way around the front of the chairs, bringing themselves uncomfortably close to the glowing tower. Sweat ran down Larksdale's brow.

'Save him!' Carmotta shouted at the Explainer as they lowered Ean on to his back.

The Explainer looked annoyed. 'I'm watching the end of everything.'

'We're putting a stop to that nonsense,' Larksdale heard himself say. 'See to the king.'

Before the pulsing tower stood Sir Willem Cutbill, one moment a silhouette, the next cast in the pale lunar light of the Explainer's moontiles. The big man was topless, his chest hair matted with sweat, a knife in one hand and the black crown in another. He had two accomplices, similarly half-dressed. Veterans, most like. If any of them had spotted Larksdale and Carmotta, none were interested. Beside Cutbill flickered an obese candle on an iron stand. It was one of those candles with iron nails down one side that dropped off one by one as the tallow melted, counting down the hours. Larksdale had once owned one for the purpose of waking him up and had soon destroyed it once it proved adequate for the task. The highest nail on Cutbill's already hung loose. Midnight approached.

'He's an arrow in his head,' the Explainer said, studying Ean.

'Only slightly,' Carmotta replied in desperation.

Larksdale's attention stayed on the scene at the keep-within. It was oddly like watching a play from the pit while your neighbours chatted about something else entirely. Old Jans burst out of a dark corner of the hollow. He must have been stalking his enemies, keeping low with the broken masonry and rocks that littered the floor. The first veteran barely had time to draw his sword. Jans was upon him, right blade to the jugular and the left soon buried in guts.

The other veteran drew his sword and made for Jans with catlike grace.

'Fine,' the Explainer said. 'I've a healstone in my bag.'

The veteran swung at Jans, and at the last blink the old doorkeeper ducked. He drove both his blades between the veteran's thighs, slicing trouser and flesh. Twin arcs of blood sprayed as one and the veteran collapsed, tendons cut and arteries weeping.

'Healstones are real?' Carmotta was saying.

'Why wouldn't they be?' the Explainer said. 'The other day you thought lust-powder a thing.'

Cutbill howled and ran at Jans. Jans flailed his right blade, his left, but Cutbill parried both. He booted Jans square in the chest.

Jans stumbled backward, arms wide, a silhouette with blades for hands. He fell against the tower's stones, took flame, then burst into a cloud of cinders and ash. The hollow rumbled with a titan's moan.

'Oh,' the Explainer said, looking at the smoke that had just been Jans.

'The king!' Carmotta reminded him.

'Yes, yes,' he replied. 'Give me space to work.'

Cutbill glanced at Larksdale, as if noticing him for the first time. He surely recognised ol' Harry, despite the disguise. Sir Willem always saw the man, not the finery. He seemed to find his presence amusing, beside the point, before returning to his counting candle and facing the keep-within.

Larksdale picked up a half-brick from the ground and tested its weight. Then he thought better of it. He slung it aside.

'I get it!' Larksdale shouted at Cutbill. He stepped closer, some nine strides from the man. 'I get it, Willem. You don't even have to explain. It's a bleak farce. All of it. The bloody lot.'

Cutbill's head tilted to one side. Blood dripped from the hand that held the black crown. Well, door-knocker. Larksdale had never really studied the circular bronze door at the keep-within's base before but the iron circle in Cutbill's hand would surely fit.

'Why *not* tear it all away?' Larksdale continued. 'I might, if I were you, all those young men you've seen die for some monarch's pride. The week I've had, I'm halfway to fitting that knocker myself.'

'You don't know what I want, Larksdale,' Cutbill said. 'And I haven't the words.' He looked at the nail hanging from the candle, ready to fall. 'Go sit with the pixie, there's a lad.'

'You want an end to power,' Larksdale said. 'Am I right? You want to murder control, eviscerate order and put stature into the bosom of the earth. More, you want to destroy physics, geometry, for permitting power to exist, even as potential. I tell you, man, I grasp it.' He sensed Carmotta just behind his shoulder. 'I should have talked to you more, sir, shared dreams and woes. But in truth I'm scared. Scared the common man might have an inner light, might think deep thoughts I could not think up myself. A notion so terrifying I never even regard it.' He shrugged. 'And so I smiled when others mocked you. I should have listened.'

'Away with you, Larksdale!' Cutbill shouted, looking at his counting candle. The seconds were as decades to him. 'My friends died and I lived and found favour. So I had to *command* more friends to die. I see brilliant beggars and idiot kings and the kings become songs but the beggars just die. There's no end to it. No horizon.'

The keep-within's door shook. Even Cutbill jumped. The window slit above the door loomed black with promise.

'When that door opens it'll be an end to it,' Cutbill said. 'No more control. Even the hours won't form an orderly line, the sky won't lord it over the ground. Chaos, Larksdale. Sheer. Fucking. Bliss.'

The bronze door shook. *Thud, thud.*

The glow between the stones was getting brighter, the pulse more rapid.

'I've news for you, Willem,' Larksdale said. 'There's no apocalypse behind that door, just more of the same.'

'He's right,' Carmotta said, shoulder to shoulder with Larksdale. 'Does the presence of this tower make men less coercive, less arrogant? They're worse, man. The keep-within's poisons seep through this palace, into the mortar and stone.' Larksdale could feel her stiffen. 'It places a hand over the brow of every man.'

Thud, thud.

'Listen to it,' Larksdale said. 'Listen. It wants out. It *wants*. It *demands*. Demands you do its bidding, Cutbill! Or if not you, then some fool.'

'It is every monarch,' Carmotta said. 'Every merchant, every callous landlord and self-important bureaucrat. Believe me. I know my kind.'

'Every general,' Cutbill said, little more than a whisper. He spun around and pointed his sword at Larksdale. 'I can't believe you, Larksdale. Cannot. If I believe you then there's nothing, fucking *nothing*.' He marched forward, sword raised. Before Larksdale knew it, the tip was under his chin.

'Willem, no,' Carmotta said.

Cutbill ignored her, his face a wasteland. It was impossible to say where the sweat ended and the tears began. His eyes bored into Larksdale's.

'So why go on?' he demanded. 'If there's always cruelty and orders and the weak and the strong? If that's the punchline of this cosmic fucking joke, then why ever go on?'

Larksdale squirmed. He closed his eyes.

'Beauty,' he answered. 'Beauty and another to see it with.' He was there on that sunniest day, the tang of sea salt, the clay beneath his fingers. 'Moments that point to a kinder world, a world so fine it hardly matters if it cannot exist. Moments you'll live inside for ever. Because they were shared. Because they…'

He trailed off, waiting for his throat to part.

Laughter came. Deep and hearty and soaked in pain. The sword-tip left his chin.

When he opened his eyes Willem Cutbill was lying on the wet and lumpen floor, his laughter melting to babble. Powerless, a babe.

Will it always be thus? Larksdale wondered. Good men wrecked upon the rocks of evil? When the time was right and the stars were in their positions and another true midnight came there would be another Cutbill. The black crown would be waiting, stage left.

Thud. The door rocked, the weight of unknown universes behind it. *Thud, thud.*

Larksdale took the iron ring from Cutbill's weak fingers. His wrist jolted from the touch, the pain growing. He had but seconds.

The nail fell from the candle's melted tallow, clinking upon the stones. Midnight.

Larksdale had been a joke as a boy in the training ground of the keep. No use with sword nor spear. He had, however, been competent with discus.

He threw the black crown under-arm, straight at the keep-within.

'Larksdale!' Carmotta screamed.

A perfect throw, right into the window slit. Into the dark.

A scream beyond worlds filled the great hollow, lancing bone and brain. Then it stopped. The red glow between the stones stopped pulsating, fading to a constant pink. Then nothing.

'Larksdale!' Carmotta shouted once more. 'You threw it *in* the keep!'

'Well yes,' he said.

'We're all to die, you *fucking* lunatic!'

'Carmotta,' Larksdale said, 'evil requires a mortal hand to carry the black crown, yes? That's what the legend says. That's the rules.' He pointed at the keep-within. 'The evil in there hasn't a mortal hand to throw it back out.'

Carmotta was a picture of wild bemusement. 'You've killed us, you arrogant freak. Do you really think no one has thought of—' She mimicked throwing the black crown. '—all this time? Do you?'

She had a point. Larksdale made an expression that said, *Let's see, shall we?*

They watched the keep-within for some minutes, sensitive to the slightest perceived movement. Every time Larksdale blinked, the keep-within remained in his vision. He had forgotten that phenomenon. Damned unnerving.

'Excuse me,' the Explainer called out. 'It's been three minutes, thirty-two seconds.'

'You're very specific,' Larksdale said, his eyes still on the keep's window.

'I've my reasons,' he said. He sighed. 'Anyway, you'll be pleased to know the chances are good Ean won't die.'

Carmotta ran over to the stricken king.

Larksdale took one last look at the keep-within. He looked down at Sir Willem Cutbill, crooning to himself on the stones. Larksdale craned his neck and took in the darkness above, the unseen roof of the hollow. He thought of Becken Keep beyond, with all its ways and manners. He did not imagine they would change.

'I cannot do this any more,' he muttered to himself. 'It's simply all too utter.'

He made his way over to the others. Carmotta and the Explainer were sitting on the floor beside King Ean, the pair of them talking some nonsense about 'hands fading'. Some commrach allusion, Larksdale assumed. Ean's forehead had fresh stitches. The blood had scabbed up inhumanly quickly.

'Healstone,' the Explainer told Larksdale, seemingly aware of his thoughts. The commrach waved a small bar of what looked like the purest silver. 'Another invention of my isle.'

'I saw another invention of your isle this very night,' Larksdale told him.

A cold look crossed the Explainer's face. 'Did it prosper?' he asked.

'It perished,' Larksdale said.

The Explainer looked suddenly sad. He nodded. He turned to Carmotta. 'Your husband will need plenty of rest. He's young. Strong. His chances are…'

'Good?' Carmotta asked.

'Better than mine,' the Explainer replied.

'What?'

He tapped the iron disc with its clockwork parts around his neck. 'The key got annihilated along with old Jans there, bless him. I've but moments.'

'Oh,' Carmotta said. 'Surely there is something we can do to stop it?'

'Nothing that hasn't occurred to me before,' he said, 'and been discarded.'

Carmotta looked up at Larksdale, her face pleading.

'I'm sorry to hear that, old fellow,' Larksdale said to the Explainer. 'Truly.'

'Appreciated,' the Explainer said. 'What dreadful luck.'

Carmotta took his hands in hers. 'Let us pray, then. You to your gods and we to ours.'

The Explainer shrugged. 'We don't really go in for that sort of thing where I come from.'

'Oh,' Carmotta said. 'Well… you had a good life, yes?'

The Explainer smiled. 'Given the chance,' he said, 'I'd happily do it all over again, each and every moment. But I'd probably not bother again after that.'

His head came off.

MIDSUMMER'S EVE

59

Carmotta

The Tetch stank in summer. Perhaps it stank all year round. Carmotta had never sailed upon it before. The sun cooked through the awning above her head. She was thankful for the breeze dancing over the low deck of her keep-shuttle.

Carmotta had had five of these keep-shuttles constructed, swift riverboats designed to taxi agents of Becken Keep around the city. The keep and the city – the head and the body – needed greater cohesion.

She stretched out her arm and trailed her fingers in the water.

His Majesty the king would make his first public appearance soon, his first since his injury on Yulenight Eve. A simple carriage journey through the streets of Keepside in two days' time. The prospect did not fill Carmotta with confidence. But Ean's absence this last half year was the talk in streets and taverns. Rumour had to be popped before it festered.

Practice had gone better than expected yesterday. Ean could be led to a throne and made to sit down. He seemed to recall how to do that, a sort of muscle memory. *Sit, my love,* she had said and Ean had said, *Banquet,* and did as she had asked.

There had been no other guests in the tertiary throne room,

with its wooden chairs and drab ceiling, save for Second-Queen Violee and Lady Larksdale. The two of them had been holed up in the latter's chambers since yulenight and were only detected when Lady Larksdale had stepped into the keep's west library late one April night, milk jug in hand, and asked for a tome on the subject of mammal hibernation. Within the hour they had been brought before a rudely awakened Carmotta in nightgown and slippers and, when asked for an explanation for kidnapping the hedgehog queen, Lady Larksdale had held her head high and babbled something about how her plot had so nearly prospered and that, given the chance, she would happily do it again. When asked for the details of her conspiracy Lady Larksdale became vague, saying she was still ironing out the particulars and, anyway, conspiracies were more about a state of mind than a definite plan. Regardless, both she and Queen Violee had broken down in tears the moment Carmotta ordered they be separated.

They were soon put together again. Queen Violee had simply refused to eat her food. Now, crouching in the throne room, her head leaning against Lady Larksdale and receiving head-pats, the second-queen had never looked so happy. *Perhaps she never lost her mind in the first place,* Carmotta thought. *Perhaps she found a truth the rest of us dare not seek.*

Getting Violee to sit on the throne beside Ean proved more difficult. Even when that goal was achieved, she would slump forward and sniff her own knees.

'Perhaps we are pushing them too fast,' Carmotta said to Lady Larksdale.

'Majesty,' the old lady replied, though she looked younger these days, 'if we aren't ready to let those we love stumble, they'll never soar.'

'True.' Carmotta had decided she was not one for pageantry and pomp. A queen of the backroom deal, of minting new laws, that was Carmotta. Violee would sit closest to Ean now. Besides, the way Carmotta had cleared the court of undesirables these last months, it would be hypocritical to sit on a throne and demand love.

She stepped closer to the king's throne, a simple chair.

'Your Majesty,' she addressed him.

Ean's blank stare shifted into a self-assurance more fitting for gods than men. He sat upright, his shoulders back and his brow – its wound hidden by a golden crown – rising to face the candelabra above. Ean was her husband and, once, her lover. But he was a shell now, a man half-erased. But how magnificent a shell! How dazzling a nothing! He looked the man he once was. Better: the man he had spent his life pretending to be.

'Yes,' she said. 'Yes, my love.'

Lady Larksdale stepped closer to her own charge.

'Good girl,' she told Violee. 'Who's a good girl?'

Violee's tongue popped out a moment. She stopped sniffing her knees and sat upright. She grinned as if someone were stroking her beneath the chin.

'Who's a good girl?'

'Your Majesty.'

'Good girl, yes you are!'

'Your Majesty. For king and Brintland!'

'Good girl, yes you are. Yes you are!'

Ean and Violee looked like Neyes and his Ledia reborn. He majestic, she a shining flower.

'The royal couple,' Lady Larksdale said. 'Aren't they a picture?'

Carmotta nodded. 'Lady Larksdale, might I ask a sensitive question? Now that we are allies?'

'If it's about Harry—'

'No, no. About me. No harm shall befall you, so please be honest. Was it you who sent the one-eyed man to my chamber? I thought Emmabelle had sent him but now I am not so certain.

Only you, I believe, would have had the – what's your word? – the gumption.'

'Honestly?' Lady Larksdale said. 'No. My plan was to send Harry to seed your loam, so to speak.' She looked at Carmotta's swollen belly. 'But that's academic now, Your Majesty.'

'An ambitious plan,' Carmotta admitted. 'Well, I suppose I shall never know.'

'I suppose', Lady Larksdale said, 'it's the sort of mystery your vocation collects.'

A steward told Carmotta the keep-shuttle was ready to disembark. She nodded goodbye to Lady Larksdale and turned to leave the throne room. As she did so, she noticed a sleek grin appear on Violee's face. The second-queen gave Carmotta a knowing sort of look.

No, Carmotta thought, *impossible.*

She shivered and left.

Her shuttle reached the Hook. To her surprise it stank no worse than the boroughs they had already sailed by.

The real difference was that everyone was aflutter with work. Men were atop roofs replacing old slate and new thatch, painting walls in the gayest tones. Others were laying down the foundations of a large building, its dimensions circular. The New Wreath they were calling it, the largest playhouse ever built. Rumour had it they would perform not just common folk-plays but keep-plays too. A crime, if true. Carmotta suspected this would be the least of this borough's transgressions.

At the very end of the Hook sat a galleon with its sails furled. Behind its mast Carmotta could just discern the top of the black obelisk that sat on a reef at the far side of the bay. She would have to pay a visit to the commrach soon. Set her boundaries.

The shuttle sailed up to the wharf that ran along the Hook. People, mostly the idle, were approaching to look at this new ship. Not for the first time, Carmotta wondered whether her tactic of bringing just herself and her guards would be enough. Sheer surprise, she had figured, would prevent anyone from forming a cohesive plot. And she had other defences at hand.

The shuttle's pilot tied the boat to the wharf and the honour guard stepped off. Six men and women from the Spine Mountains, sent as gift to the queen-who-saved-the-world. In memory of poor Mother Fwych they had all removed their own tongues. A savage ritual but they made for incorruptible bodyguards.

A female guard offered an arm to her and Carmotta stepped on to the wharf. No graceful task in her present condition.

A dwarf in priestly robes stepped out and greeted her.

'My Lady.' He did not bow. She was dressed as a noblewoman. Even if he didn't know she was queen, he should have known to bow.

'I would speak with Sir Harrance Larksdale,' she told him. 'Where would I find him, Father, er...'

'Squints,' the dwarf replied. 'Father Squints.'

'Tell him a noblewoman of Manca would speak with him,' she said. 'Tell him it is a matter of no little importance.' She placed a hand on her belly.

People in the crowd looked at one another. Someone laughed. It struck Carmotta she had overdressed, even dressing down like this. There was no one in merchant's wife's dress. Nor, it suddenly struck her, was there anyone dressed in sacks or old trousers. Clothes here were of acceptable quality, creative in cut. It was unnerving.

'I see,' Father Squints said. 'I suppose you had better follow me.'

'You,' Marla, Larksdale's henchman, said, looking down at Carmotta from the ramp that led on to Larksdale's houseboat. Her blonde hair was longer, in a topknot. She carried her curved sword in a fine scabbard.

'You were expecting some other queen?' Carmotta joked.

'With respect,' Marla said, 'he don't need to see you.'

'I think he will,' Carmotta said and she let her smile rot into the sneer of power. 'We both want what's best for him, Marla. Yes?'

Marla studied Carmotta, then said, 'Wait there.'

On her return, Marla said nothing, merely looking in Carmotta's shoulder bag and telling the honour guard to wait. Carmotta was led up the ramp to the upper deck.

House of the mustard king, Carmotta thought. The richest man this side of the Brintchild. Larksdale had made a fortune on barrels of that condiment – the only mustard available on the mainland – and had grown that wealth fivefold in the space of half a year. Carmotta had made it her business to know who had the gold in her city and what others with gold said of them. They all said the mustard king was mad.

Marla opened the door and ushered Carmotta through.

The room – though perhaps cabin was a better term – was all of varnished wood. Portraits hung upon the walls. No one Carmotta recognised. They looked like farmhands, prostitutes. Potters. In one corner sat a great vase full of dried flowers and peacock feathers. Behind that stood something under a blanket. It was the size and shape of a man, likely some suit of armour. A desk sat on the opposite side of the room to her. Beyond the desk was a window, its two doors wide open to the summer air. The window had a stupendous view of the New Wreath's foundations.

Larksdale was sitting before the desk, his back to his visitor, his hair a black mop. He wore some simple shirt.

Carmotta had expected this. Pure theatre.

'Your mother asks why you never visit,' Carmotta said.

She could see his shoulders relax.

'She's welcome to visit here,' he replied. 'I've a room for her.'

A silence followed. He did not turn to face her.

Carmotta adjusted her shoulder bag. She stepped forward into the centre of the cabin.

'It will be an awe-inspiring theatre,' she tried.

'And parliament,' he said. 'For all who live and work in the Hook.'

The talk of secession was true, then.

'Every man with a say?' she asked him. 'Really, now. Look what happened when the ancients tried it.'

'They denied their womenfolk a say,' he replied. 'A mistake we shan't make.'

Madness.

'Fine,' Carmotta said. 'You have my attention. I, a queen, have sailed across Becken to parley with you.' She laughed. 'What is this insanity? What do you want from me?'

He stood up and faced his queen.

Larksdale had lost his old chin beard and found four days' stubble. With his short hair and shirt and trousers cut like the citizens outside, Carmotta would not have guessed his standing if she had not known him. Indeed, he seemed a man from some other time. Yet he looked healthy. She had worried he might have caught the sickness they said stalked the Hook.

'You've taken a great risk,' he said, 'in coming here.'

'A threat?' Carmotta asked.

'An observation,' he replied.

The truth was she had a hundred city guard in a warehouse just fifty yards from the Hook, their new captain general waiting for Carmotta not to leave after too long a time. He was loyal, this new captain. After all, his predecessor had retired to a country villa the king had gifted him. The Crown rewarded well.

'I suppose I must trust you, Sir Harry,' she said. 'I am as shocked as you are.'

'To answer your earlier question,' Larksdale said, 'I want nothing from you, Your Majesty. Nothing. The Hook has no use for the keep.'

'You are part of the city,' she said. 'The city is overseen by the keep.'

'The Hook is no part of your city. It is not even part of the Brintland. It never was.'

Carmotta put her hands on her hips and laughed.

'We've seceded,' he insisted. 'Do not think we cannot feed ourselves. We've the bay for both fishing and imports. We're doing more than adequately at both and that's before the New Wreath opens.' He sniffed. 'Of course there is the question of import and export tax between our states, but we're both reasonable people who—'

'Tax?' Carmotta snapped, cutting him off. 'You'll pay your tax like everyone else, you absurd little man. The sheer nerve!'

'You never came to the Hook demanding tax before,' he said. 'No one ever did while it rotted. Becken Keep has not paid one penny on this place's welfare, has not lifted a single hand nor signed a single parchment. Now *that's* nerve, woman, coming here looking for free scraps. Listen to me: there is a sewer pipe runs through here. It carries the shit of the keep – and worse – to the sea. It was leaking, Your Majesty. Leaking for centuries and hundreds sickened and died. I spent half my first fortune fixing that pipe. I did all the initial work myself: it was far too dangerous to risk my friends. Unbelievable, isn't it? Fortune made me a genuine labourer. My proudest work.'

'If it were so lethal,' Carmotta said, though only half-sarcastically, 'how is it you are perfectly well?'

'I've a suit,' Larksdale said. 'A modified thing. I beat its sickles into trowels.' He smiled at Carmotta. 'Wish to see it?'

'I have no time for your nonsense,' Carmotta told him. 'Wipe that smile away. Becken Keep rules this place. You have no power.'

'And you'll never know how joyful that is,' he said.

'You're babbling.'

He took a step closer, his stomach inches from her bump.

'No good shall ever come from your keep,' he told her, 'because no change is possible there, not while a single stone of that obscenity stands atop another. Even a good monarch such as yourself is… a mere respite. I realised as much on Yulenight Eve.' He meant at midnight, when they had stood before the hidden thing that could never be alluded to, even now the hands had vanished. 'I will never return to your keep. I try my utmost never to look at it. For no new thing can prosper there. Not one thing.'

'Your new world,' Carmotta said mockingly. She looked to the unborn theatre outside. Musicians were setting up at its centre, readying to play for the carpenters and masons. She shook her head. 'You've always been pathetic.'

'I suppose you'd better break us, then,' Larksdale said. 'Be a good little keep's hound and send in your goons.'

She could. She should. She would sail out of here, back to her husband and her sister wife and she would plan the destruction of this treasonous borough and the arrest of Sir Harrance Larksdale. Such wild absurdity should not be seen to prosper.

Oh, but it could not prosper.

'No,' she told him. 'You would become a martyr for the groat-sheet wits. You have a year, Larksdale. A year of no taxation and no watch. No help. You will fail and you will come to me and beg. Or a follower will depose you, or criminals will muscle you straight out of the Hook. You build a dream on nothing and soon all Becken will see that truth. Everyone will see that only the keep – despite its ugliness, despite its cruelty – can ensure men are safe and civilised. Indeed, with a capable Crown, it may even help them.'

Larksdale chuckled. 'We shall see,' he said.

'Goodbye, Harry Larksdale.'

Carmotta reached the doorway. She stopped. She turned back around to see Larksdale still looking at her.

She walked back to him, opened her shoulder bag and passed him its contents.

He took it. His eyes widened. His mouth fell slack.

The thing was a wonky bowl fashioned by an amateur, its decoration similarly as laughable: a brushwork image of a bird. A lark.

Carmotta, first-queen of the Brintland, turned and left her sweet lunatic to his new realm.

ACKNOWLEDGEMENTS

It is a crime only one name gets to be on a book's cover. So many made *The Keep Within* happen. I feel a fraud.

Thanks to Max Edwards, archangel of agents. He keeps me from straying off a path with infamously too few streetlights.

Thanks to the legends George Sandison and Michael Beale, the Lennon and McCartney of editing and, whenever the moment required, the Morecambe and Wise too. Thanks to the ever wonderful Sam Matthews for her copyediting and suggestions. To Sarah Mather, Katherine Carroll and Kabriya Coghlan, the mightiest triumvirate of publicity anyone could hope for. To all of Titan Books' staff, in fact. Their kindness is only ever exceeded by their capability.

Did you see that cover by the way? Oh my! Julia Lloyd has worked her magic once more. She always does.

Thanks to Matthew Tope, the greatest sounding board known to humanity. However the reader may rate my novels they would be less than half of that but for Matt.

Thanks to the Speculators, Leicester's fantasy and sci-fi writing group, for reading the initial chapters and spurring me on. To Dennis Foxon, Phillip Irving, Jay Eales, Selina Lock,

Daniel Ribot (not least for the use of his surname), Susan O'Brien, Simon Fung, Foteini Oikonomitsiou, Stephen Payne, Will Ellwood, Jenny Walklate, Lucy Wade, Richard Unwin, Jeremy Thackray, Adele Smith, Samuel Parr, Holly Webster, Alexandra Popescu, Mike Jennings, Siobahn Logan, Daniel Walsh.

There's countless more. I'll list the ones I remember here and profusely apologise to those who I do not: Daniel Gilbert, Heather Wilson, Catherine Digman, Farah Mendlesohn, Edward James, R.J. Barker, Helen Cooper, Tiffani Angus, Tim Susman, Chris Stabback, the Chand brothers, Super Relaxed Fantasy Club, Meg MacDonald, Ian Whates and Helen Sansum, Tom Pepperdine, Tasha Qureshi, Leicester Quakers' Hall, Rhys Davies, Vijay Vega, Russell Smith, Stenni, Stephen Holloway, Emma Matthews, Jennie Lavelle, Alex Cotterill, Chris Callow-Evans, Josh Holtom, Ross Jones, Chris Potter, Chelsea Raine, Les and Fenris and Kirby and Racco and simply every regular at The Loaded Dog, Alex Davies, Audrey Taylor, Ginger Lee, Simon Gumley, Mark Brandon, Ivan Richardson, Pete Sheppard, John Shipp, Craig Walker, Anthony Ryan and Anna Smith Spark.

A humungous thank-you to my family: Carol, Patrick, Joel, Tom, Nicki, and Lucy and to the (this time around reverse alphabetical) neefs: Ruben, Kitty, Jake and Florence. You've all indulged my nonsense far longer than anyone should reasonably be asked to.

Finally, thank you for reading this book. Without you this world and its people are just ink.

ABOUT THE AUTHOR

J. L. Worrad lives in Leicester, England, and has for almost all his life. He has a degree in Classical Studies from Lampeter University, Wales. He has found this invaluable to his growth as a science-fiction and fantasy writer in that he soon discovered how varied and peculiar human cultures can be. In 2011 Worrad attended Clarion, the six-week SF workshop held at the University of California, San Diego. There, he studied under some of the genre's leading professionals and also got to see a lot of wild hummingbirds. 2018 saw the publication of his first and second novel, the space opera duology 'Feral Space'. He's had short stories published by *Daily Science Fiction, Flurb, NewCon Press* and *Obverse Books*. He also writes screenplays for short films, one of which, *Flawless,* was selected for both the Cannes and NYC independent film festivals.

ALSO AVAILABLE FROM TITAN BOOKS

PENNYBLADE

J. L. WORRAD

Exile. Mercenary. Lover. Monster. Pennyblade.

Kyra Cal'Adra has spent the last four years on the Main, living in exile from her people, her power and her past. A commrach, she's welcome among the humans only for her rapierwork. They don't care about her highblood, which of the gleaming towers she came from, nor that her family aspires to rule the Isle.

On the Main, superstitions and monsters are in every shadow, but Kyra is haunted by the ghost of Shen, the love of her life and lowblood servant she left behind. She survives by wit and blade alone in a land that would see her dead for who she is, for who she loves.

When her fellow pennyblades betray her, Kyra is forced to track the demon preying on the souls of the commoners. She must tear the masks off to see the true face of things, as the age-old conflict between the Main and the Isle threatens to erupt once more.

'*Pennyblade* doesn't so much reinvent well-worn fantasy tropes as stab them to death in a dark alley. Kyra Cal'Adra is a lethally alluring protagonist weaving an intricate tale rich in ferocious action and multifaceted intrigue, all topped off by a deliciously vicious twist.'
– Anthony Ryan, author of *Blood Song, The Wolf's Call* and more

'A violent, and wildly imaginative, riot of a book.'
– R. J. Barker, author of *Age of Assassins* and *The Bone Ships*

'Filthy, furious, wonderful.'
– Anna Smith Spark, author of *The Court of Broken Knives*

ALSO AVAILABLE FROM TITAN BOOKS

BARROW OF WINTER

H. M. LONG

Thray is the Last Daughter of Winter, haunted by the legacy of her blood. When offered a chance to visit the northern land of Duamel, where her father once ruled, she can't refuse – even if it means lying to the priesthood she serves and the man she loves.

In Duamel, Thray's demi-god siblings rule under the northern lights, worshipped by an arcane cult. An endless winter night cloaks the land, giving rise to strange beasts and terrible storms. The people of Duamel teeter on the edge of violence, and Thray's siblings, powerful and deathless, stand with them on the brink.

To earn her siblings' trust and find the answers she seeks, Thray will have to weather assassination attempts, conspiracies and icy wastelands. And as her siblings turn their gaze towards the warmer, brighter land she calls home, she must harness her own feral power and decide where her loyalties lie.

Because when the spring winds blow and the ice breaks up, the sons and daughters of Winter will bring her homeland to its knees.

'An epic fantasy set in a rich and wintry world of warriors, gods and monsters, with epic battles, dangerous magic, and complex family bonds.'
– Sue Lynn Tan, bestselling author of *Daughter of the Moon Goddess*

'Brimming with magic and intrigue, *Barrow of Winter* is a spellbinding read… A vivid story that lingers long after the last word.'
– Rebecca Ross, bestselling author of *A River Enchanted*